THE DRAGON KING

BOOK 2

BIANCA K. GRAY

To Shawntel
The first stranger to take a chance on me,
Thank you.

CONTENTS

1

Apsara watched, choking on the air as everyone around her was brutally slaughtered. She coughed up the blood-tainted water she had swallowed as her body forcefully turned her black-golden tail into two human legs. Biting back the scream that threatened to grace her lips, she ripped her two legs apart from one another as she rolled away from an elf's sword. It was an ambush.

She scrambled to her feet, wobbling ever so slightly, as she rushed towards King Maleko. He held a trident in his hands, but at his feet lay the unchanged body of Princess Luni. Her eyes stared out into nothing, and her lips were blue.

"She didn't make it," Maleko spoke, his voice breaking, as Apsara reached them. He placed two fingers onto Princess Luni's forehead, in respect. His brown eyes steeled as he suddenly lunged forward, piercing an elf's head with his trident. Blood splattered onto Apsara's face, but she didn't wince, didn't dare to in front of her king.

"We need to get you to safety," Apsara spoke, whispering quickly towards Maleko. Maleko's eyes roamed around him as he took in the situation. His eyes met Apsara's.

"Lead the way," he said, his voice without strength. Apsara quickly helped Maleko to his newfound feet. He had never left the Argenti Sea, had never traveled—nor ever wanted to—to the surface. The king walked as if he were a baby human, and leaned all of his weight onto Apsara. She grunted as she helped him along the shore of the Argenti Sea towards one of the many forests of Sylva. Maleko's guards surrounded them as she barked out orders to keep the elves away. They had no armor. No way of protecting themselves except with the tridents they had brought to the surface. Apsara searched desperately as guard after guard was killed.

"Come, my king," she whispered as she led him deeper into the forest. There was only one creature she could count on in Sylva.

She led Maleko to a large oak tree, the ground around it opening up to reveal a cage of roots. She gestured for him to crawl down there, and he wrinkled his nose at the suggestion.

"You want me to willingly put myself underground?" he asked, skeptical. Apsara raised her eyebrows.

"Do you have a better suggestion?" He stared at her, doubt still clouding his face. His own eyebrows raised at her tone.

"He's a dryad I would trust with my life," Apsara doubled down. She knew Maleko would know what those words meant to her. They weren't words she said easily. Eventually, he nodded and started to crawl into the hole in the ground. Apsara followed swiftly after him.

Once they were both in the crawl space, the ground closed above them as the roots moved back into their previous positions. Apsara grabbed the crudely made Sylva clothing from behind a large root and handed a pair to Maleko. He wrinkled his nose at the sight.

"It is what surface creatures wear," she explained. His eyebrows knitted together.

"They hide their bodies?" he asked. She nodded, pulling a green shirt over her head.

"I think it's to protect it from stuff on the surface," she explained. "And, maybe, to keep their bodies clean." He held the clothing between two fingers as his eyes roved over them.

"Is it not suffocating?" he asked, glancing over at Apsara. Sadness lay in those light brown eyes of his. She swallowed the lump forming in the back of her throat.

"It can be," she said, softly. He grunted as he pulled the shirt over his head. Apsara helped him put the pants over the two legs that he was still getting used to.

"Once the elves have retreated, we can leave, and I'll find out more information about where would be safe for us and our people," she said, staring at the wall of dirt in front of her.

"Nowhere is safe for Argentiundans anymore," Maleko breathed. Apsara knew he was right. The prophecy An—the God of All—had provided to them before he and the other Gods disappeared turned out to be correct. Maleko was a fool to not heed the warning, to not prepare for the plague that infected the seas. But, Apsara would never willingly tell him that.

"I guess I'm not the true King of the Seas," Maleko barely spoke, thinking about the same prophecy on Apsara's mind.

"An knew," was all she said.

"The God of All has always known," he whispered. She didn't dare look at him. Maleko was always an arrogant prince. Ever since they were young, he always thought *he* was right and no one knew better than him. *Now look at where that's gotten us*, she wanted to scream.

"I know you, Apsara," Maleko spoke. "And I know that face." She still refused to look at him. Instead, she laid down on the dirt floor and turned onto her side, away from her king.

"Tell me what you want to say," he almost pleaded.

"You wouldn't want to hear it," Apsara almost spat. She felt him stiffen next to her.

"You think I've killed our people," he breathed. She stilled.

The plague hit the city of Amnis Lux only a couple of days ago. She had heard of other merpeople suddenly dying of drowning. A merperson. Drowning. It sounded absolutely ludicrous. But, when she went to examine the body from a neighboring village, she saw that the rumors were true. Merpeople *were* drowning somehow. Their upper bodies were being forcefully transformed into their surface forms while still underwater. Their gills were always gone. When she had warned Maleko of the plague, he just ordered for no one to be able to enter or leave Amnis Lux. But, the plague still found its way in. *He* was the reason why they were unprepared for the ambush on the shores of the Argenti Sea.

"I didn't say that," Apsara muttered.

"You didn't have to," he said, just as quietly. "I've known you since we were fingerlings. I know every expression on that now hardened face." Apsara gritted her teeth before turning around to face her king.

"If you must know what I think, *your highness*, I think you're an arrogant, *selfish* king who put the lives of every merperson in danger. I think you should've heeded An's words more than you did, instead of believing *yourself* to be the uniter of ocean floors." Maleko's eyes flashed at her words, but she didn't cower.

"The King of the Seas, the uniter of ocean floors. He will cure the disease that plagues creatures beyond shores. He will lead the creatures of water back to the seas of Asynithis and help stop the slaughter of creature blood since," Maleko recited part of the prophecy. He cleared his throat. "I memorized it."

"If you memorized it," Apsara said, leaning in closer, "why wouldn't you have *heeded* it? *Prepared* for the danger? If you did, Luni would still be—" Her voice hitched in her throat as she turned away, remembering her fallen friend.

"I know," Maleko whispered. "Like you said, I was arrogant." He put his head into his hands as Apsara glanced over at him.

"We will be *slaughtered*, for who knows how many years before the Saviors come to Asynithis," she snapped. He didn't meet her gaze. Instead, he let out a dry laugh.

"And it's all *my* fault that this happened," he said.

"Yes, yes, it is. It *is* your fault, Maleko," Apsara retorted. His eyes darted up towards her, a curious glint in his eyes.

"It's been forever since you called me by my name,

Apsara," his voice was low. She looked at him, incredulously. He let himself stare at her for a moment longer before lowering his gaze.

"Apsara, did you ever think that maybe, no matter what I would've done, the prophecy would've come true anyways? Didn't you think that, maybe, there's no stopping a prophecy that's already been written into the stars?" he asked. Apsara scoffed.

"No future is set in stone," she retorted. Maleko's brown eyes met Apsara's dark ones.

"The Gods' were," was all he said.

2

*R*hea's thumb stroked the claw mark of scales that were on part of his cheek, as she wouldn't meet his eyes.

"My family is gone," she choked. "But, I'll make sure that you and your family are okay."

"What are you—"

"I love you, Khalon Draconia," Rhea whispered. Khalon frowned. Why was she saying this? "Me, Rhea. I love you."

"Rhea, why are you talking like you're about to die?" he asked. She looked down and then bit her lip. He had never seen her look more scared.

"I'll always love you," she whispered, stepping up on her tiptoes. She kissed him quickly on the lips and before Khalon could do anything, she turned away and her body disappeared into the shadows.

———

Khalon woke up with a gasp, his head nearly hitting Esi's as he sat up. He was startled by how close her white eyes were to him while he clutched his chest, trying to even his breathing.

"I heard something," she said, tucking a black ringlet behind her ear.

"You can't stand that close to me while I sleep, Esi," Khalon mumbled. Her eyes softened as she stared, unfocused.

"You dreamt of her again," she whispered. She was all Khalon *could* dream of since the day Rhea sacrificed herself for him. *"I love you, Khalon Draconia... I'll always love you."* He closed his eyes, tightly, as her voice echoed around in his head. The alcohol from earlier that evening threatened to crawl back up his throat. He swallowed.

It had been six months since the first battle between Aureum and Draconia. Since then, the beastoids allied themselves with Aureum, and it wasn't long after that Draconia had fallen. Anyone who was still alive at the end retreated into Ustrina, opened by their new queen, Kamaria.

"You heard something?" Khalon asked, changing the subject as he opened his eyes once more. Esi nodded her head. She jumped at every noise now.

She never talked about the Gods dying, or how they died, but he knew she saw everything in her head, felt what they felt in their last moments. Khalon never knew how to comfort her, but, in this moment, he decided to put a steadying hand on her forearm. Her red veins seemed to glow even brighter underneath her brown skin.

"I'll check it out," he said, getting up from the bed. Kamaria was generous enough to give him his own room in the newly rebuilt palace in the capital of Ustrina, the city of Invenire. Without the Mortiferis, the Ustrinian forces were able to keep the elven army back, for now.

"It sounded like something had fallen," Esi said once Khalon was on his feet. He pulled over a white flowing t-shirt over his bare chest and walked towards the door, Esi in tow. He grabbed her wrist as he pulled her along, careful to not walk too fast. Esi's legs were a lot shorter than Khalon's, and he noticed, sometimes, she had to lightly jog to keep up with him. Under her breath, she whispered the amount of steps they had taken before whipping her head towards another hallway. She pointed down it.

"I heard it come from that direction," she said. He released Esi's grip and turned towards her.

"Stay here," he warned. He slowly walked down the hallway, not hearing a single noise coming from the only room in it. Feeling himself transform into a dragon, he stalked into the room, his hands raised, as he looked upon his half brother Khai and the new Queen of Ustrina, Kamaria, who were both signing angrily at each other. Neither of them seemed to notice Khalon was standing there.

He felt himself slowly shrink as he tried to understand what was happening. His dark eyes darted towards the ground near Khai's feet. A giant glass bottle had shattered, dark crimson liquid pooling around the pieces. Khalon's nose flared.

"What's going on?" he asked. Khai turned towards the sound, and his eyes widened at the sight of Khalon in the doorway. Kamaria turned her head after seeing Khai notice someone, raising a single eyebrow. Her hair was in long twists down her back, and she was wearing a flowing night-gown, similar to the one Esi always wore.

"Why are *you* up?" Khai asked, crossing his arms. "Shouldn't you be drunk and dreaming about Rhea? Like always?" Khalon's lips thinned into a line as his eyes darted towards Kamaria. She simply rolled her own after reading his half-brother's lips.

"For your information, *Khai*," Khalon spat, "Esi woke me up because she heard something that frightened her." Kamaria's eyebrows furrowed downwards at the mention of Esi. She started signing angrily towards Khai again. Khalon could only pick up a few things, as he still wasn't fully fluent in sign language. Especially when Kamaria was signing that fast.

I told you the vibration was going to wake her up, was along the lines of what Kamaria said. Khai glowered at her.

"I'm not the one who hid my drink from me," he said, signing as he spoke aloud, if only for his brother's sake. "Also, no one feels vibrations from feet away. That's only you." Khalon sighed as his hands went to massage his temple. It felt like he was babysitting the most annoying royals he had ever met. Granted, they were the *only* royals he ever met. Besides that one elf guy before... And that mermaid...

I hid it from you because... and Khalon couldn't catch that last part except Kamaria did call Khai a self-entitled ankle biter for some reason which made his scowl become deeper.

"I grew two inches, for your information," Khai retorted.

Still short, Kamaria signed.

"I'm literally taller than you, so—"

Khalon is way *taller than you*, she signed.

"Khalon is also a freak who has the spirit of the dragon within him so not *everyone* can be like Khalon."

Khalon also has muscles like a—

"Okay," Khalon said, interrupting what Kamaria was about to sign. The tips of his ears reddened as Khai just stared at her in shock. She flashed him a smug smile in return.

"What's in the bottle, Khai?" Khalon probed. His half brother shifted uncomfortably.

What do you think it is? Kamaria signed. Khai glared at her before turning his attention back towards his brother.

"I don't answer to you. *I'm* king, remember? Not you," he retorted. Khalon clenched his jaw as he stared down his half brother, swallowing the words he wanted to say: King of what? Draconia is gone.

"It ruined our father. It ruined our grandfather before him. So many draconians *died* because of the delusions that this brings," Khalon said, instead. "I thought you were better than that." The image of King Vien on the ground in front of the pooled dragon's blood flickered through Khalon's mind. It was the last time he saw his father, and now that pathetic image of him was burned into his mind forever. His anger flared at the memory as Khai gritted his teeth and turned away, unable to look him in the eyes once more.

"Go to bed," Khalon ordered after the silence stretched. He turned towards Kamaria. "I apologize for my brother's behavior, your highness." After reading his lips, Kamaria smirked at Khai as she walked by him.

"I hate her," Khai muttered as she slipped out of the room. Khalon still didn't know how the two of them knew each other from before. *"A meeting,"* Kamaria had said when Khalon asked. *"Hell,"* was Khai's answer.

"I thought you weren't addicted to dragon's blood anymore," Khalon muttered. Khai shrugged.

"I didn't know you really *were* just a meathead," Khai retorted. Khalon's lips thinned.

"Is it because—"

"It's not because of our father, okay? It's not because of our—*my* mother. It's merely..." his words drifted off. Khai shook his head before glowering up at him. "You wouldn't understand." He shrugged past Khalon, exiting the room. Khalon took a deep breath as he stared at the empty space in front of him.

He never really spent a lot of time with his half brother. Not as much time as he had these past six months. And part of him wished he was back in the Ring of Fire than in this mess. This mess being the end of the world as he knew it. The Ring of Fire was simpler. All he had to do was fight for his life in front of a screaming, blood-thirsty audience. Managing people, making sure everyone was okay besides himself, that was harder than anything Khalon ever had to do before. Thoughts racing through his head, he rubbed his face with his hands before exiting the room.

Esi wasn't where Khalon had left her, Kamaria most likely taking her back to her room instead. He walked slowly down the newly built palace. The walls were painted a dark green, and the moldings depicting mythical phoenixes and Inkanyambas—a nod to Kamaria's background—were made of solid gold. It had taken a few months for the palace to be rebuilt based on Kamaria's demands, and some wings of the palace were still going through construction. Khalon wondered if this was what being a prince was like. Merely wandering through a large, empty palace. Causing arguments about any random thing due to boredom. Because that's all there was. Boredom.

Khalon would rather be in the thick of battle than sitting here in the palace. Or, if not in battle, then at least out there looking for Rhea. She was still alive, somewhere. He could feel her presence. The rest of the Gods—it was as if they had vanished into thin air. Their magnetism that was always felt at all times was now gone. But, when he called to Rhea, he could still feel it go somewhere. Like his prayer was being listened to by somebody. Although, he was never sure if it was *her* that it was going to, or to the God of Death himself.

Khalon froze as he heard the familiar clicking of heels down the hall, his hand seemingly soldered onto the knob of his bedroom door. The shuffling behind the sound told Khalon that the woman coming towards him wasn't alone. He looked over his shoulder to peer into the face of the Queen Mother Aoife.

Even though Khalon was older now, taller than she was, her presence still made him feel small. She stopped, a couple of feet away from him. She waited, those light brown eyes seemed to look down her nose at him despite having to look up. Those light brown eyes that Khai inherited. Khalon bristled, but lowered his head in response.

"Your highness," he said, through gritted teeth. She seemed to stand up a little straighter as she pulled the silken red robe tighter around her body. Her attendants kept their bodies bowed behind her, respecting Khalon's position even if Queen Aoife never did.

"I heard some voices," she responded. "Khai seemed upset." Her eyes glanced at Khalon, gauging his reaction.

"Princess Esi heard something, and I went to investigate," Khalon responded, his lips barely moving. His back was straight, tensed at how close the queen was to him.

"Ah," Queen Aoife said. "The Seer." She took a step closer as her eyes roved over Khalon. He fought the urge to take a step back at the movement. "So, you went from the God of Death's slave to the Queen of Witches' bodyguard. What a demotion." Her lips curled back into a smile as his jaw clenched.

"Queen Kamaria caught Khai with a bottle of dragon's blood. I don't suppose you know where he got it from?" Khalon's voice lilted slightly as he glowered at the Draconian Queen. Her smile didn't waver as she picked at her nails. A golden ring of a dragon's head was around her middle finger, displayed as if to remind Khalon of her status. Even if Draconia *was* taken over by maddened elves, she was still the queen, and the mother to the King of Draconia.

"Interesting that you respect Queen Kamaria's new title, but not Khai's," Aoife said, her eyes meeting Khalon's. He blinked. "I wonder how the king would take that." Khalon felt himself involuntarily swallow, and her piercing eyes caught the motion. She smirked.

"Well, good to know a bastard is protecting us from any evil that may lurk in the shadows," Aoife said, turning around. Her draconian attendants rushed to be behind her once more. She raised a hand as a departing and walked back to where she came from, the clicking of her heels echoing around him. He lowered his head as he stared at the knob in his hands, trying to ease the beating of his heart.

She still frightened him, after all these years. Perhaps, it was really her he was afraid of this whole time, not his father.

He turned the golden knob and entered his bedroom, looking at his face in the mirror. He looked tired. Bags were under his eyes from lack of sleep, the last memory of Rhea having played on repeat in his head for the last six months every time he tried to close his eyes.

"The only evil that lurks in the shadows of this palace is you, Aoife," Khalon whispered to himself, the retort he wished he told to her. He sighed as he pulled the flowing t-shirt off over his head, twisting himself to look at his back. The scales that formed the image of a dragon were still there, down his spine. But on top, like a reddened brand, were the letterings from the Celestial language. The letterings that he had seen on Rhea's spine. It had been there since the day she sacrificed herself. The mark of the Death God. The mark that claimed Khalon as *his*.

3

Queen Aoife quietly closed the door on her bowed attendants. She took off her heels and walked towards the mattress on the floor. When she had seen the raised bed in her room for the first time, all those months ago, she had thrown a fit.

"Draconians don't sleep on raised beds," she had squealed. *"We sleep on the floor."* At the thought of the recent memory, Aoife cursed the Ustrinians as she slowly took the golden ring off of her middle finger, resting it on her dresser. The air moved behind her, and a smile spread across her full lips.

"Back again so soon?" she asked, her voice nonchalant, as she turned around to look into the older face Khalon had inherited. The face of King Vien. He scowled at her. His ghostly self struggled to grab her, but his hand went through her due to the spell she had put on him.

"Why must you torture my son?" Vien finally asked, putting his hands down at his side. Aoife gave out a dry laugh.

"Your *son*? Need I remind you that you imprisoned *'your son'* in the Ring of Fire for over ten years?" Aoife said, removing her heavy earrings. She wrapped the silken robe around her body tighter as she went to sit on the mattress in her room, covered in golden silk blankets. Vien glowered as he took a step closer to her.

"You tricked me into putting him in there. I know all about your lies and secrets now. I know who you are. Death hides nothing," he hissed. Aoife laughed. Her voice twinkled as she glared at the former king. *How hideous he was*, she thought. *How arrogant.*

"You wouldn't have gotten anywhere without me. The spirit of the dragon lies within Khalon. You would've been beheaded by the people if it weren't for me," she retorted. His lips twisted in disgust.

"You're a *Crispus*," he hissed. Aoife repressed a wince as she was reminded of her tainted bloodline.

"And if I weren't one, you wouldn't have been as successful as you were, would you? If you knew, would it have changed anything? Would you have *really* cast me aside?" Aoife said, her voice even. He glowered at her with revulsion before closing his eyes, knowing the truth of her words. Slowly, he relaxed, hanging his head, his shoulders hunched.

"Why couldn't you let me die peacefully, Aoife? Let me move on into the afterlife?" Vien barely whispered. She couldn't help the quickening of her heart as she heard him utter her name. He rarely ever called her by her name, even when he was alive.

"Are you forgetful or have you always been this dense?"

she muttered, more to herself than to him, but his thick eyebrows raised at her tone.

"You cannot speak to me like that," he demanded. She smirked as her eyes met his. The ones that Khalon had inherited. She stifled the urge to scowl at the thought of the bastard prince.

"You are not king anymore, my dear. *My* son is. So, I can speak to you however I wish," she purred. "Plus, darling. You're dead." His jaw clenched. She pulled the golden blanket up to her chin as she laid down, staring up at the domed ceiling.

"You will take the spirit of the dragon from Khalon and place it into the rightful King of Draconia," Aoife ordered. "That is why you're still here. *That* is why I've kept you."

"You can't take the spirit of the dragon from a living being. Even as a ghost, I cannot do that," Vien argued. Aoife's head turned so she could look Vien in the eye.

"Who said you're taking it from a living being?" Vien's half-moon shaped eyes widened.

"You wouldn't," he whispered. She smiled to herself as she stared up at the ceiling once more.

"My son would do anything to please me. I raised him well," she breathed. Vien shuffled closer to Aoife.

"Dal won't let you do it," he said, his voice having some strength in it. The strength of a former king. Aoife barked out a laugh, but her blood ran cold at the mention of his first love's name.

"Dal?" she said, sitting up straight as she met Vien's fiery gaze. "What is *Dal* going to do from beyond the grave?" Vien simply looked at Aoife. A look that made her feel like she was missing something.

"Don't underestimate a mother's protection," was all Vien said as his form started to dissipate. Aoife gnashed her teeth together.

"The afterlife is gone so she is, too. The Gods have died, haven't you heard?" she screamed out as Vien's last remaining parts disappeared into the wind. She scowled at the empty space before her. Grabbing a cup of water next to her bed, she threw it at the space King Vien used to take up. The glass shattered when it hit the ground, Aoife glowering at the broken pieces.

Her bedroom doors opened promptly, her army of attendants rushing in to clean up the mess. Aoife rubbed her face as she sat on the edge of her mattress, the golden blankets a tangled mess in her lap.

Dal, that harlot, Aoife thought. Her anger slowly melted as the thought hit her like a bolt of lightning. She sat as still as possible, not even acknowledging the attendants leaving her room. *No, it couldn't be,* she thought. But, it was the only explanation that made sense.

Was it Dal who had protected Khalon from death all this time?

4

Maleko leaned against Apsara's strong figure as she walked towards a town in Sylva. She grunted while she carried him through the forest in the cover of night, the dryad following close behind them.

"Must he come with?" Maleko whined towards Apsara. She rolled her dark eyes as she blew a black lock of hair out of them. He always thought she was beautiful, but just as the thought came to the forefront of his mind, he repressed it.

"Val is a *friend,* and he'll help us find a safe place," she insisted. Val was her nickname for the creature who was called Valerian. Maleko stole a glance at the golden-haired dryad. He raised an eyebrow in response.

"Isn't he a dryad?" Maleko whispered. "Can't he not go far from his tree?" He watched as Apsara's lips twisted into an almost smile. He couldn't help but smile back as he watched her try to suppress her own.

"Valerian's tree is bewitched. He did a good thing for a witch, long ago, and was granted the freedom to go wherever he chooses. His tree will follow," Apsara explained.

"How do you even know this creature?" he practically demanded. Apsara gave him a sidelong glance.

"That's a long story," she answered. *Can't be* that *long of a story,* Maleko couldn't help but think.

"Where are we going?" Maleko asked. "And why is it taking so long to get there? We shouldn't be out of hiding for this long." Apsara's amused smile slowly morphed into a scowl as she looked straight ahead. She tugged on him, hard, and Maleko bit back his instinct to yelp.

"We're going to a safe house, *your highness*. And perhaps, if *your highness* would learn to walk with his two legs, we would be able to get there faster," she said, her voice as sweet as a catfish's flesh, but there was a bite behind every word. He cowered from her obvious frustration.

"Is anywhere *really* safe in Sylva?" Maleko's words spilled out of his mouth, though barely above the sound of a breath. Apsara just gritted her teeth in response, pulling him through the forest faster.

"There are those who aren't fond of the elven conquest," Valerian spoke up from behind, his voice eerily close. Maleko whirled around to find the dryad right next to him. Valerian flashed him a cherubic smile. The Argentiundan King grimaced in response.

"The Sylvans have always thought themselves to be an extension of Aureum. I find your comment hard to believe," Maleko responded, dryly. Valerian's smile dimmed as he nodded.

"I can't tell you you're wrong, as it *is* true. Many Sylvans wish themselves to be elves, believe that we were better off under the elven empire," Valerian lamented. "However, the elves are still under the rule of a God. Though they claim to have killed off all the Gods, they only did so under this God's bidding. Some Sylvans are against this." Apsara stiffened next to Maleko, and he glanced at her but her face gave away nothing.

"Which God are they being ruled by?" Valerian flashed another smile.

"The Death God," he answered. Maleko felt a cold chill run down his spine. He had met the Death God the night Aureum had started to make their move. She had seemed sweet, almost meek in a way, in the presence of the God of All. *What was it she called herself again?*

"Rhea?" Maleko asked, his eyes meeting the golden eyes of the dryad. The dryad's eyes widened.

"You know the Celestial's name?" he asked. He glanced up towards Apsara, searching for an explanation.

"The Death God showed up in Amnis Lux the night the Mortiferis attacked your surface world," Maleko explained. "She seemed... not like a creature who would plan to kill her siblings."

"The Celestial and the Death God are not always one and the same," Valerian muttered, his eyes on the horizon. "We are almost there." Maleko's gaze flickered over to the cabin up ahead. The lights were on, but no noise was made from inside the log cabin.

Valerian took the lead as he sauntered up to the front door. He gave a rhythmic knock and flashed Apsara a comforting smile as she came to a stop. She shifted Maleko's weight, a small grunt escaping her lips. A pang of guilt ran through his chest.

After a second of silence, the cabin door opened widely, revealing a man with long white hair and bright green eyes. An elf. Maleko and Apsara let out a synonymous hiss as their eyes darted towards Valerian. Valerian's hands were up as he tried to give a comforting smile.

"No, don't worry. He's an elf, but he's not on their side," Valerian explained. The elf's hardened face turned towards Maleko and Apsara. Nothing in his face showed that he had any kind of kindness within him. Maleko steeled his gaze as he met the elf's.

"Come in," the elf said, waving a hand towards the middle of the cabin as he took a step aside. Apsara didn't move an inch. The elf gave a small smile, the wrinkles around his eyes becoming more pronounced, though the smile was even less comforting than his straight face.

"Will it help if I say that more of you are here as well?" the elf said, his voice like gravel. Maleko frowned as he peeked into the main room of the cabin. Huddled in the corner were a few more creatures. Creatures with scared wide eyes, and Maleko could recognize them in an instant. They were merpeople. Merpeople who had escaped the clutches of the elves. His eyes roved over the elf once more before he cleared his throat.

"Enter the cabin," he ordered Apsara. Her dark eyes widened as she looked over at him.

"But, your highness, we don't know if we can trust—"

"There's other Argentiundans in there, Apsara," Maleko hissed. She glanced into the lit up room of the cabin. Her eyes met the frightened merpeoples' and she took in a sharp inhale.

"Your highness, we don't know if they are there by their own volition or if they're prisoners," she whispered. The elf's eyes turned amused.

"It doesn't matter," Maleko said, waving her words away. "We cannot leave them here to die." The elf glanced over at Valerian causing the dryad to sigh.

"They can leave when they want to. I helped bring them here," Valerian explained.

"You really *trust* this elf?" Apsara asked, her voice monotonous. Valerian shrugged.

"This elf is not like the others," he responded. "He has an agenda, but it isn't the same as Aureum's."

"Come in," the elf repeated, dramatically waving an arm once more. Maleko looked meaningfully at Apsara who scowled and started to pull him through the doorway. The elf whispered something to Valerian that Maleko couldn't catch before he closed the door with a resounding thud.

"Here, sit," the elf said, pulling up a chair. Apsara dropped Maleko into it, showing her disagreement with his decision to come inside of the room. *It's not like we really had a choice,* he wanted to say to her. *Plus, you were the one who brought us here,* but he kept his mouth shut. One of the girls who was huddled in the corner met Maleko's eyes. Her mouth opened and then promptly closed.

"Go ahead," he said, sighing as he ran a hand through his wavy, brown hair.

"She called you 'your highness,'" the girl spoke, her voice hoarse. *Oh right,* Maleko thought. Many Argentiundans never had the pleasure of seeing his face before.

"This is King Maleko of Argentiunda, uniter of ocean floors," Apsara said the last phrase sarcastically. The merpeople took a collective gasp before dropping to the floor in respect. He waved his hand, his cheeks reddening as he motioned for them to get up.

"Please, please. We're not in Argentiunda anymore. These manners are not needed, though they *are* appreciated," he said, smiling a little. He caught Apsara rolling her eyes in his peripheral vision. His gaze caught the elf who was leaning against the wall, his shrewd green eyes watching everything.

"Why are you not on the side of the elves?" Maleko asked. The elf's eyes met Maleko's brown ones.

"The elves are being ruled by the Death God, and I don't want any part of that," he responded. Maleko eyed him carefully.

"You're part of the organization Valerian was talking about. The Sylvans who don't want the elven conquest to continue," Maleko probed. He smiled slightly.

"Perhaps," he said.

"Why help the merpeople though? What do *you* get out of it?" Apsara demanded, taking a step forward towards the elf. The elf's eyes slithered towards her.

"We need creatures," he smiled.

"Creatures for what?" Apsara asked.

"We need desperate creatures who will do our bidding," he said. Apsara froze. Her eyes briefly met Maleko's, a look that told him she knew they shouldn't have entered this cabin.

"Who says we're desperate?" she said, through gritted

teeth. The elf's smile grew wider as he pushed off of the wall.

"You have no home to go to," he said. "The water that used to give you life is now killing you all. And, anywhere you go, you'll be turned over to the elves. Slaughtered where you stand. I would say you are pretty desperate, as a people." Apsara glowered at him. Maleko held up a hand, sighing as he closed his eyes. At this motion, she took a step back towards him.

"What is it that you would have us do?" Maleko asked, the words burning his tongue as he spoke. *Apsara was a fool to trust that dryad.* The elf's eyes darted towards him.

"Let's get familiar with one another first," the elf responded, his lips upturned in amusement. "I'm Ralnor Norovir." Maleko squinted as the name echoed around in his head. Where had he heard that name before?

"King Maleko," Maleko responded, putting a hand to his chest. "This is my faithful guard, Apsara." Apsara just continued to glare at the elf in response, her eyebrows furrowed as if she were thinking deeply about something. Maleko turned his attention back towards the elf.

"Your task?" he asked, an eyebrow raised. The elf met Maleko's gaze.

"I want you to kill my daughter," he responded. Both eyebrows jumped at the remark.

"Your daughter?" Maleko repeated, leaning forward a little. Killing a child didn't seem to be too hard of a task, though a terribly immoral one. Maleko didn't see why the elf needed a lot of merpeople to do it. He would gladly take the burden for himself, if only to save his people from the guilt.

"Yes, my daughter," the elf said, scowling at the thought. "She stubbornly goes by the name Rhea." *Oh.* Maleko froze as Apsara stiffened upon hearing the name.

"You want us to kill..." his words drifted as the elf clenched his jaw.

"The God of Death," he responded.

5

Poseidon breathed in a giant breath of air as he sat up straight, his wrists clanging against the wall they were tied to. The last thing he remembered was watching the Mortiferis rip Freya apart—before doing the same to him—turning the rest of her body into dust. He desperately glanced down at the body he was in now. This body was significantly shorter than his last. But, it was alive. *He* was alive. *Oh thank An,* he thought desperately, breathing out a sigh of relief.

Although, he might've given thanks a little too quickly. He looked around his surroundings. Poseidon was in a darkened room, bars in front of him. He pulled on his arms, but they wouldn't lower because metal manacles were around his new body's wrists.

He sighed, impatiently, willing himself into water droplets. But, that didn't work either. He only had part of his soul in this body. The rest of his soul was destroyed with his previous reincarnation, which meant his power had greatly decreased and some of his memories were gone as well. He sighed, loudly.

"Felicity," he whispered, hoping the Fate would hear his voice. There wasn't any response. He wondered if the God of Death destroyed the underworld as well.

"*Felicity*," he urged a little louder, his voice desperate. A clanging came from down the hall. He twisted his head to look through the bars of the cell, but couldn't see anything. His body's heart instinctively thundered in his chest.

Poseidon? Felicity's prayer echoed around in his head. Inwardly, he swore he would kiss the brunette's face the next time he saw her.

"Yes, yes, it's me," he whispered.

How are you alive? Your string... your string is white. Isn't it? Isn't it, Francine? He heard Felicity ask the other Fate.

"It's a long story," Poseidon hissed. The sound was coming closer. "Listen, Felicity, where am I?"

What?

"Where am I? The body I'm in, it's being restrained for some reason. I need to know where I am," Poseidon insisted.

Can't you just turn into water?

"Well," Poseidon sighed as he nodded, "That's part of the long story."

How is your string gold once more? Francine's voice cut into his brain loudly, and he winced at the sudden sound.

"Could someone please just tell me where I am?" Poseidon sighed.

Caedoxia, he heard the third Fate, Farrah, whisper into his mind. *You're in Caedoxia.* Well, that was just fantastic.

Poseidon looked down at his shrunken body as he tried to feel around for whatever magically inclined gifts this creature had. His soul rummaged around in the creature's soul but could find no magic at all. This creature was human. Another goddamn human. *Fuck.*

You're not still in a human's body, are you? Felicity's voice asked.

"Sweet Felicity, alas I am," Poseidon responded. The clanging stopped, and he looked up at the creature who stood in front of the bars. The creature was long and skinny, its face gaunt. Its eyes glowed in the dark as it took in Poseidon. A vampire. The creature that stood in front of him was unmistakably a vampire. Poseidon couldn't help the human instinct to gulp.

We won't tell him you're still alive, Felicity whispered into Poseidon's brain.

If you even survive tonight, Farrah muttered.

We shouldn't let him think he'll die again, Francine chastised. Ah, how he missed the Fates, the sworn servants of his brother. The brother who had him killed.

"Perhaps the Seer will find me," Poseidon said aloud. The vampire in front of him frowned as he tried to find the key that would open the door to Poseidon's cell.

Are you still going to go by Poseidon in this body? Felicity asked.

The Seer? Even if the Seer finds you, she's not going to be able to save you from your fate tonight, Farrah let out a laugh.

We'll try to alert her, if not, Francine reassured.

"I should go by Poseidon again. My last life was too short, don't you think?" Poseidon mused.

"Who are you talking to?" the vampire asked, his brows knitted together as he finally yanked the door open.

"Besides, it looks like I've been here for a while,"

Poseidon muttered. "Perhaps, I won't die tonight." The vampire smirked as he squatted down so he was eye level with Poseidon.

"No worries, little one, we like to keep our food living. It's harder to find ones like you nowadays," the vampire responded. Poseidon cursed his new body for being called little. Why did this human have to be so short?

Here's to hoping you live, Francine said. Her voice echoed around in his head until the presence of the Fates were gone.

"Poseidon," the vampire rocked his head side to side as he thought. A sharpened nail ran down the side of Poseidon's neck. "Why are you calling yourself the name of a God?"

"Because I am one," the Sea God responded, curtly. The vampire smirked.

"The Gods are dead." Poseidon flashed a smile at the vampire.

"Not all," he said.

"Guess I'll get to be tasting Celestial blood tonight then," the vampire mused before sinking his teeth into the side of Poseidon's throat. He resisted the urge to scream.

———

Esi almost collapsed onto the ground, her hand to her head. Strong hands held her up, and from the smell of soap and evergreen she knew it was Khalon who held her.

"What happened? What did you see?" Khalon's voice desperately asked. She waited until she could steady herself before turning towards the direction of his voice.

"I feel... I feel a presence," she muttered. She narrowed

her eyes as she tried to make sense of what she saw. Poseidon, *alive*? But, how? She felt his death. Felt his screams as he was torn apart by the Mortiferis. How in the world was he still alive?

"What presence?" Khai asked. She didn't feel him enter the room. He must've come in while she was still having her vision.

"Like a... ghost's?" Khalon's voice warily said. She heard a slap against flesh. Khai must've hit his arm.

"No, you idiot. She felt a presence in the *world*," Khai responded. "Is it the Saviors? Have they finally come?"

"The Saviors might not come for hundreds of years," Esi said, shaking her head. "No, it was the presence of a God. A Celestial. Partly." She wrinkled her nose.

"Who?" Khalon asked, his hand suddenly gripping her arm. She spoke too cryptically. She knew it now, by the pain that was erupting up her arm.

"It wasn't Rhea," she managed to squeak out. He released her, and she could practically feel his disappointment.

"The God of the Seas," she clarified. "I felt his presence." *And saw where he was*, she almost said. But, she didn't want to give that away quite yet. For Khalon to know the Fates were still living, that they gave her this vision, he would immediately try and go find Rhea. He hadn't been able to find her yet, and she doubted he would ever find Rhea unless she wanted him to. Besides, he was fated to meet her eventually. With those letterings down his back. But, she wanted to prolong that meeting for him. For she had seen how it was supposed to end.

"Didn't he die?" Khai asked.

"Didn't you *see* him die?" Khalon asked in the same breath. Esi's hands went to her head as she tried to think. She *did* see Poseidon lose his life. She heard An say that once he perished, they would all perish. Except, the God of Death didn't because his soul was in another's. Was Poseidon's soul...?

"He did die, but he's in a different body," Esi responded, her voice monotone. She felt Kamaria enter the room.

"How is the battle going?" Khai asked, changing the subject. Esi used her sight to see Kamaria's hands sign her words.

What are you guys talking about? she had asked.

"Nothing," Khai muttered. "The battle?" Kamaria was silent for a moment. Esi imagined she must've been glaring at Khai.

We've managed to hold them off, Kamaria signed. *For now. So, what were you guys talking about?*

"Poseidon's alive," Khalon said. Esi felt him shift his weight next to her. "Did you see where he was?" Esi weighed whether she should tell them everything or not. She didn't want them to know the Fates were still alive, but she wondered if Poseidon would tell Khalon when they saw each other. However, Poseidon needed help. And as a servant to the Gods, the daughter of An, she wasn't exactly in a position not to. She'll just tell him need-to-know information. And yet, the omission caused the taste of lies to fill her mouth.

"He's in Caedoxia," Esi whispered. "In a human's body."

"What?" Khalon thundered.

"He's locked up somewhere. I couldn't see exactly where. But, it's a feeding prison of some kind, for vampires."

"A *God* is getting fed on by vampires?" Khalon's voice reached a decibel Esi didn't know it could. Khai chuckled.

"Serves them right."

"Khai," Khalon warned.

"What? The Gods abandoned us. An apparently knew all along what was going to happen, right Esi? And he left us with no way to defend ourselves against these monstrous elves. And he didn't kill his brother the God of Death when he had the chance," Khai ranted.

"I'd be careful if I were you," Khalon's voice lowered, and she felt him take a step forward. She placed a hand on his forearm, hoping he wouldn't take another step. His body was pulsating with anger.

"Just because you feel guilty about what happened to Rhea, doesn't mean it excuses her from what she's done to us," Khai said, almost arrogantly.

"Rhea saved you. She saved all of us," Khalon growled.

"What? From the monsters *she* created? From the monsters *she* brought to Asynithis? Yeah, she definitely saved us," Khai said, sarcastically.

"It wasn't her. It was the Death God who did those things," Khalon snapped.

"What? Without her body?" Khai pressed. "When are you going to realize that they're both one and the same?" Esi felt Kamaria move towards them.

Chill out, she signed, her hands having a lot of force behind it. The brothers were silent as they stared each other down.

This is my *palace, and I* suggest *you stand down,* Kamaria signed, looking pointedly at Khai. There was a moment of tense silence, and then Esi heard Khai's footsteps exit the room.

"We need to save Poseidon," Khalon muttered.

"How? We can't leave this palace. And to Caedoxia?" Esi said. "We'd get killed in Caedoxia." The other two were silent. Esi sighed. "Okay, *I* would get killed in Caedoxia."

"They don't kill humans just on the streets of Caedoxia," Khalon pointed out. Then, he paused, remembering how he really had never been to Caedoxia before. At least, not to any of their cities. "Do they?"

No, Kamaria simply signed. With Khai out of the room, Kamaria didn't have a translator anymore. And they all knew how limited Khalon's signing was so she could only say that. Though, Esi had a feeling Kamaria wanted to say more. She heard Kamaria rub her head as she thought.

"You can't leave the palace," Esi whispered towards Kamaria. Kamaria's rubbing stopped, and Esi could feel her gaze.

"I could do it on my own," Khalon offered.

"You've never been there," Esi said as Kamaria signed, *You* are *an idiot, aren't you?* Esi felt Khalon throw up his hands as he took a couple of steps away from her.

"Well, I'm not only going to go with Khai," Khalon stubbornly said. "And I doubt he'd want to go with me anyways."

We'll all go together, Kamaria finally signed, sighing as she did.

"Jabu will take care of things in my place," Esi translated the rest of Kamaria's sentence for Khalon. Jabulani was Kamaria's right hand man and her most trusted advisor. He had just entered the palace, a representative for the Inkanyambas, and a treasured prince in his own right.

"You trust Jabulani that much?" Khalon asked, his voice lilting warily.

With my life, Kamaria signed. She had known Jabu since she was just a baby. He was her first friend and the first Inkanyamba that her mother had introduced her to. He was also the only one in the world who was like her. Half phoenix half Inkanyamba. If Kamaria trusted anyone more than Esi, it would be Jabulani.

"Fine," Khalon said, sighing as he did. "Let's get going tomorrow." There was silence and Esi assumed Kamaria made some kind of motion of agreement as Khalon started to walk away. He paused for a second, and Esi could feel his gaze on her. She tucked a ringlet behind her ear.

"Try to see exactly where he is, if you could," he beseeched. Esi nodded her head once and then heard his heavy footsteps exit the room before letting out her breath, slowly. Kamaria put a hand on Esi's shoulder and started to sign towards her.

He's taken, Kamaria's hands signed. *He has the mark of the Death God on him.*

"I never said anything," Esi muttered. Kamaria was silent for a moment before continuing to sign.

He can never be yours, Esi, she signed. *He's his.*

6

As Elion's brothers went over their plans for world domination, he sat back in his seat. He locked eyes with his third oldest brother, Prince Ardryll, who just gave a lazy, bored look back.

"The Inkanyambas are formidable warriors, almost as good as the draconians, but if we positioned the beastoids troop to the south of the wall, surrounding Invenire, we might be able to get through them," Elion's second oldest brother Prince Edwyrd said. His stout fingers traced a line on the map as Elion's oldest brother, the King of Aureum, stood over it with a furrowed brow.

"The beastoids were able to defeat the Draconian forces," Adamar, the King of Aureum, said. "I have no doubt they'll be able to do the same here." Elion curled his fingers into his palm underneath the ivory table.

"Are we going to call for breakfast, or will we be droning on about this forever?" Ardryll spoke up, slowly flipping a page from a book in his hands. His eyes glanced up over the spine, meeting Adamar's.

"Yes, yes," Adamar said, wiping his hands as he sat at the head of the table. "Let's move all of this and call for breakfast." Edwyrd looked between Ardryll and Adamar before sighing loudly. He gestured for one of the servants to whisk the map away.

"Pushing off talking about this is why the battle for Invenire is taking longer," Edwyrd mumbled.

"Food is good for the brain," Ardryll lazily spoke. His blue eyes darted towards Elion and roved over him. Elion sat as still and straight as possible.

"I see you've adopted Edwyrd's look," Ardryll pointed out with a nod of his head. Edwyrd ran a hand through his own short, white hair as he glanced over at Elion's.

Elion had cut his hair by hand the other morning. It was the only thing he could think of to protest his existence as an elf. Most elves wore their hair long, like how Adamar and Ardryll wore theirs, although Ardryll's wavy white hair was always cut at his chin. The stark whiteness of their hair is what elves admired the most, what elves valued. The purity of the elven race. It all made Elion sick.

"Is everything okay?" Edwyrd asked, his voice low as he leaned towards his little brother. Elion clenched his jaw in response.

"He's fine," Adamar interjected, waving a hand as the human servants came out of the woodworks to serve the brothers breakfast. "Just being a bit rebellious." Elion didn't dare utter a word. Edwyrd's gaze burned holes through him for a moment longer, before devouring the breakfast in front of him.

"I would like this battle to be over as soon as possible," Adamar said, gingerly placing a piece of egg into his mouth. Edwyrd chewed loudly as he stared at Adamar. He swallowed.

"You think I don't?" he asked, a tad bitter. "Batula is scheduled to give birth any day now." Lady Batula was Edwyrd's beloved wife. A year ago, she miscarried her baby. She was devastated. Luckily, she was with child once more.

"I have yet to see *your* child, Adamar," Ardryll muttered, turning another page before biting off a piece of buttered toast. Adamar bristled in his seat. He had told everyone his child had died during birth, but his brothers were told the truth, eventually. It wasn't likely that Adamar would be able to hide the Death God's spawn from them for long, so he had no choice but to tell them. He gestured for the servants to leave the room.

"Than is constantly asleep. I don't think he has ever awoken," he murmured. Ardryll's face didn't change at the news.

"Perhaps, it is because he isn't *really* alive," he said, flipping through another page.

"I would really appreciate *not* discussing this," Edwyrd hissed in a hushed breath. Elion gritted his teeth. He knew why Edwyrd didn't want to talk about Adamar's cursed child, Than. It was because the Death God lurked the hallways of the palace of Aureum. And the God of Death was here because *Adamar* brought him.

"He needs to grow," a high pitched voice said from across the room. Elion's head lifted at the sound, his eyes meeting the copper eyes of Rhea. But, it wasn't Rhea who controlled her body anymore, Elion knew this. Still, it was a weird sense of relief seeing her.

The last time Elion saw the Celestial, he was underwater in the city of Amnis Lux. She had left before the others, presumably to be by the draconian's side. However, something had happened during the battle because she appeared in the Aureum palace soon after, almost as if she were dead. Her eyes were open, a gray film covering them, and her chest wasn't rising or falling. However, one day, a few months ago, she took in a deep breath and was walking around again. Only, it wasn't her controlling the body anymore. It was *him*.

The same day Rhea had gone to be by Khalon's side, Elion had left to go help create the Saviors of Asynithis with An and the other Gods. He tried to save Freya. But, the Mortiferis just flung him aside, like he was nothing more than a decorated doll. Perhaps, he *was* just a decorated doll. Freya practically said so on more than one occasion. The thought of her brought an ache to Elion's chest. He subconsciously started to rub it.

"Grow?" Ardryll arched an eyebrow, but his eyes didn't leave the page he was reading. It was as though the Death God wasn't walking up to the breakfast table.

"I need a brain that can function properly," the God of Death said, a thousand voices, the voices of the dead, echoing after Rhea's. "That is why Than is growing rapidly."

"While we're on the subject of Than, when will you release Essarae from this spell that binds her to him?" Adamar said, through clenched teeth. Elion sat as still as possible as Rhea took the seat next to him. She started to grab a hard-boiled egg.

"Oh, that? She'll never not adore her son," Rhea responded, whispers surrounding her, as she peeled the egg. Adamar stayed silent.

"The war? How goes it?" she asked, casually, hellfire flickering behind her eyes. Edwyrd cleared his throat as he went over the plans for the next attack. Rhea nodded along, quietly eating the egg and breaking it into smaller pieces so she didn't eat the yolk inside.

"Sounds doable," Rhea said once Edwyrd finished his speech. Edwyrd nodded once, curtly, before returning to his breakfast. Elion knew he wanted nothing to do with this, but it had already been done. What could Edwyrd do against his blood-thirsty brother and the God of Death?

"I will be going to sleep for a while," Rhea muttered. Adamar's head popped up at this.

"Asleep?" Adamar asked. Rhea nodded her head once, the movement causing the hood of her cloak to fall around her shoulders.

"I need to gather my strength to pull the rest of my soul into Than's body," Rhea answered. "So the Mortiferis may rise once more."

"The Mortiferis destroy everything they touch," Elion couldn't help but say. Rhea's eyes flickered over to him, and Elion felt his blood run cold.

"Why would we awaken them?" he squeaked. Rhea looked back at the last piece of egg in her hands. She popped it into her mouth.

"We only have Sylva, Argentiunda, and Draconia under our control. I thought Adamar wanted to be the ruler of all of Asynithis?" Rhea said, raising an eyebrow. "Perhaps, someday, the King of all the Realms?" Adamar straightened in his seat. This was why he had gotten rid of all the Gods. World domination. *What a terribly egotistical venture*, Elion couldn't help but think.

"Our forces are doing just fi—"

"But, not fast enough," Rhea interrupted Edwyrd, her eyes flashing. The room started to become colder, as if she were sucking all the heat out of it. "The Mortiferis, my creatures, will do a better job."

"Of course," Edwyrd yielded, not voicing the obvious: The Mortiferis couldn't be controlled.

Rhea stood from the table, her hand running along the side of it as she walked back to where she came from. She paused, an unfamiliar smile gracing her face.

"Don't dare disappoint me, An's creatures," she warned before leaving the room. The heat returned as she exited. A breath involuntarily left Elion's lungs as he breathed in more deeply.

"Right," Edwyrd said, curtly.

"Just do as the God says," Adamar ordered. "Soon, we'll have our oasis." Once enough time had passed since Rhea had left the room, Edwyrd's head whipped towards him.

"I didn't sign up to help you conquer all the realms," he hissed. Adamar didn't look shaken at their giant brother who was radiating anger, instead opting to ignore Edwyrd, turning towards Ardryll instead.

"Speaking of realms, have you found the elf called Arveldir yet?" he asked. Ardryll shook his head, a resounding 'no.'

"But, we're looking for him," Ardryll responded.

"We cannot alert the witches that we're seeking him out. Make sure Lord Crispin is searching discreetly,"

Adamar warned. Ardryll nodded his head once in obedience. Lord Crispin was Ardryll's husband and was one of the best at getting information. Like Ardryll, Crispin didn't have any qualms about upholding morals. Elion wasn't sure Ardryll or Crispin had any. Crispin would do whatever it took to receive the information Adamar so desperately wanted.

Edwyrd, on the other hand, was seething next to Elion as he watched this back and forth between their two brothers.

"Did. You. Hear. Me?" he snapped, his voice low. He said the words so slowly that one could hear each consonant clearly.

"I heard you, Brother," Adamar spoke, picking up his fork.

"I refuse to help you conquer more than just this realm," Edwyrd hissed. Adamar's eyes flashed, and Elion looked away as he flipped the fork in his hand and stabbed Edwyrd's palm with it. Edwyrd screamed as Adamar stood up to further push the fork deeper into his hand.

"*What is wrong with you?*" Edwyrd protested, blue blood slowly pooling into his palm. Adamar ripped the fork out, causing the blood to gush as Edwyrd grabbed a napkin and pressed it against the wound. It was becoming quickly stained with blue.

Adamar wiped a stray white hair off of his forehead and sat back down, his face the epitome of composure. It was like he had never stabbed his brother with a fork.

"I am your *king*, Edwyrd," Adamar said, any hint of anger, gone. "It would be wise to remember that." Edwyrd's face was as red as the tomato that Ardryll was currently putting on his toast. He took an innocent bite as Edwyrd suddenly stood up.

"I want the beastoids troop to attack the capital tonight," Adamar said, his eyes on his own breakfast. Edwyrd stood still, but didn't acknowledge the command. Elion watched as his second oldest brother left the room in a fury, taking it as his own cue to leave.

"Elion," Adamar said as Elion stood up from the table. Elion paused as he looked at his brother. Adamar met his gaze, his blue eyes icier than ever. "Make sure not to cut your hair again." Elion involuntarily swallowed and nodded once. Satisfied with his answer, Adamar looked back at his breakfast. Ardryll gave him a dry smile over his book before Elion exited the room. He couldn't leave the dining area fast enough.

As he closed the door behind him, he watched in horror as a girl with curly, brown hair walked by him, holding linens in her hands. A girl who looked eerily like...

"Pilar?" The name slipped out of his mouth. The girl froze. *It couldn't be.* Elion's mind raced. *No, she was... Pilar was...* He saw her with his own two eyes. Slaughtered by his older brother, and yet... Elion took a small step towards her as the girl turned around. Hazel eyes were where dark eyes should've been. A puckered red scar ran diagonally across her face. It wasn't Pilar. But from the side... from her features... Elion took another step closer, as if entranced.

"Yes, your highness?" she asked, bowing deeply so that Elion couldn't get another good look at her face. Elion straightened before clearing his throat.

"Is your name Pilar?" he asked, hesitantly. The girl kept her head down. She was a servant—it was obvious by the way she was dressed in all white. Adamar preferred every-thing to be white. And she was human. All the servants in the Aureum palace were human. *Like Pilar*, Elion couldn't help but think.

"No, sire. My name is Lorena," she answered. Her voice wasn't like Pilar's. Hers was rough, as if she had some kind of vengeance she wanted to erupt onto the world.

"Why did you answer to the name Pilar?" he asked, an eyebrow raised. She lifted her head so he could feel the full glare of the human.

"Did you know someone named Pilar?" she answered with a question of her own, her voice low. Elion blinked.

"Um," he said. She straightened from her bow as she looked him over. A quiet anger was present behind Lorena's hazel eyes. Anger that Elion didn't want to bring to the forefront.

"There used to be a servant here by that name," he answered, honestly. Her glare didn't dissipate as she held up the linens in her hands.

"Are you in the habit of delaying servants?" she more said than asked. Elion shook his head quickly.

"No, I'm sorry. I just thought... I thought you looked like her."

"The servant." Her eyes scrutinized him. Elion nodded, sheepishly.

"Yeah," he responded.

"All us Hispanic humans look the same to you, huh?" she said before turning away. Heat quickly rose to the tops of Elion's cheeks.

"No, I'm sorry. No, I really thought... I thought you were... Never mind. It was impossible anyways," he stumbled through his words. Her head turned back towards him slightly.

"Impossible how?" she asked. There was something in her voice that made Elion not want to answer.

"It doesn't matter," he said, shaking his head. "I shouldn't delay you any longer." She paused for a moment, one eye on Elion as she thought. Elion could swear she heard his heartbeat quicken with his omission, and he tried to slow his breathing.

"Your highness," she finally said, giving a quick bow before darting down the hallway. Elion watched as her figure grew smaller. He shook his head, trying to rid himself of the memory of Pilar from his mind.

7

Maleko stared at the skin-like contraption being put over his fingers. He tried to exchange a look with Apsara as she glared past the elf—who was putting the contraptions onto her—at the dryad who she said she'd trust with her life. *Bet she's regretting that little comment*, Maleko thought, laughing in his mind. As though she could read his thoughts, her glare came to him. He tried to remove any amusement from his face.

"You think this was the safest option for us, *Val?*" she asked, spitting the nickname out.

"You'll be in disguise. I feel like that's a pretty safe option," Valerian said, leaning against the wall. His gold hair was pulled into a low ponytail.

"We'll be in Aureum," Apsara hissed.

"Hidden in plain sight," Valerian responded. She stared at him in disbelief. Maleko knew that look on her face, however. If she had a trident in her hands, that dryad would be dead twice over by now. He chuckled to himself. Her head whipped over to him.

"You think this is funny, *your highness*?" she snapped.

"Need I remind you, Apsara, that *you're* the one who brought us here." She just turned her head to look forward instead of continuing with the conversation. *Not even an apology*, Maleko thought, amused. *Such an Apsara thing to do.* He wiggled his fingers at the elf.

"What are these contraptions for again?" Maleko asked. Ralnor's green eyes glanced up from one of the other merpeople's hands.

"When pricked, human blood will seep out of it, instead of your own," Ralnor responded. Maleko's eyes widened as he stared at the invisible contraptions. They had blended seamlessly into his own skin.

"Is human blood really that different from ours?" he asked, fascinated. Ralnor grunted in response.

"Fascinating," Maleko said, wiggling his fingers in his face. Apsara grabbed his hand and pulled it down.

"Stop it," she ordered. He rolled his eyes.

"Human blood is red," Valerian clarified. "Merpeople's blood is black, I believe." Maleko nodded his head.

"Yes. Our blood is the color of the deepest waters," he responded. Valerian snorted.

"Right. And also the color of vampires' and werewolves' blood." Maleko simply glowered at the dryad.

"Dragon blood is also red," Apsara retorted. "They might think we're draconians with these on."

"Do you *think* you look like draconians?" Valerian asked, his golden eyes squinting. "I don't see any scales on you." Apsara's gaze was like a blade's.

"We can't go without water for too long," Maleko said. "Or we'll be stuck in these forms forever."

"Then, I suggest you get the job done as quickly as possible," Ralnor retorted. Maleko twisted his lips at the tone.

"How, pray tell, do you suggest we go about killing the God of Death?" he asked.

"By stabbing the girl in the chest, I assume."

"But, the God of Death will just reincarnate," Apsara pointed out.

"I don't really *care* to kill the God of Death, unlike the rest of the group," Ralnor sighed. Valerian raised an eyebrow. "I just want her dead. That's all."

"Why?" Apsara more demanded than asked. He ran a hand through his long, white hair.

"We will leave for Aureum tomorrow," he said, ignoring Apsara's question. "I suggest you all rest up before then."

"You said we can leave on our own volition," Maleko piped up. Ralnor turned around to look at him. His smile didn't reach his eyes.

"You can leave... for a price," he said. Maleko didn't even want to know what that price was.

"Let these other good merpeople go. Apsara and I will carry the task out on our own," Maleko said.

"You can't even walk," Apsara hissed.

"After I learn how to walk," Maleko corrected. Ralnor's hard green eyes turned amused.

"You and the girl can take on the job then," Ralnor said. "But, the rest of these merpeople are still going to go to Aureum. Collateral, in case you back out of it."

"And if we succeed?" Ralnor smiled.

"Then, we will make sure you all get safe passage out of Aureum," Ralnor said.

"To where?" Maleko pressed.

"To the only country Aureum isn't too excited to take over," Ralnor responded. "Caedoxia." Maleko froze. Death was better than trying to survive in Caedoxia.

———

The hover van paused in front of the gates of Regium, the capital city of Aureum. Maleko heard Ralnor roll down the window.

"What's in the van?" the—what Maleko assumed—elf asked him.

"Some humans that were requested by his majesty," Ralnor said, his tone changing to one of an arrogant elf. All elves had this way of speaking, as though they were predestined to be better than everyone else. Despite the fact that elves were probably the most useless creatures in all of Asynithis. At least, in Maleko's eyes.

"Open the back up," the elf ordered. Ralnor pressed a button in the front of the hover van, and the back lifted as Maleko blinked the sunlight out of his eyes. The elf stared them down, decked in white elven armor. His long, white hair was down around his shoulders and his light green eyes studied the merpeople in the back of the van. He gestured towards another elf with his dark hand as he looked away from them.

"It's okay," Maleko whispered to the boy trembling next to him. His dark brown eyes glanced up at the Argentiundan King.

"It'll be all right," Maleko reassured, putting a comforting arm around the shoulders of the boy. Another elf walked up, this time a woman. She held a tube-like metal container in her hand, a sharp point at the end of it. Maleko furrowed his eyebrows.

On the way to Aureum, Apsara made sure that all the merpeople knew that humans were not overly fascinated by surface creature inventions, mostly because it was humans who invented them in the first place.

"Don't ogle their machines, don't look too close, and for the love of Poseidon, don't have your mouth open in surprise," she had directed that last bit towards Maleko. So, at upon seeing this human contraption in the elf's hands, he took extra care not to have his jaw drop.

The elven woman went around to each of the merpeople, pricking their fingers with the contraption.

"Is this really necessary?" Ralnor drawled from the front of the van.

"It's procedure. Merpeople by the thousands have been coming up from the waters since last week. And they look eerily like humans without their unnatural fish tails," the elf responded. Her voice was too light for the topic she discussed. Maleko felt himself stiffen. Thousands of his people were having to climb onto the shores of the surface, where they were being slaughtered or—like him—were being enslaved in the name of safety. He gritted his teeth together.

"Where are you all from?" the woman asked as she pricked his finger. He didn't feel a thing, but red blood oozed out from the wound. He tried not to widen his eyes in fascination. He had told Apsara how he wished they could bring the human contraptions with them under the seas, but she unfortunately broke the news to him that the contraptions couldn't survive in water.

"We're originally from Draconia," Apsara responded without missing a beat. "But had moved to Sylva during the war." The woman didn't bat an eye as she finished checking the rest of the merpeople, though her eyes did rove over the open skin on each of them, checking for scales. Apparently, the humans that lived in Draconia looked somewhat similar to how merpeople looked when they were in their human forms. Similar enough that the elves didn't really see too much of a difference.

"Okay, they're good," the woman said. The other elf gestured for Ralnor to put down the back of the van. The door slowly slid down over their heads.

"So interesting," Maleko whispered as Ralnor started the hover van back up. He drove into the city, and Maleko crawled over to the small window in the back of the van. He held his breath as he took in the famed city of Regium. Though, it was a tad disappointing.

"*This* is Regium? The greatest city of all Asynithis?" Maleko spoke as he looked at it. The city was a mixture of old architecture and new. Sprawling buildings that were halfway between gothic and new-age. To Maleko, it kind of looked like a mess.

"It's no Amnis Lux," Apsara responded. The merpeople around them nodded their heads as they looked out the small window with Maleko. He shook his head as he crawled back to his seat.

"Where are you dropping us off?" he asked Ralnor through a small opening. Ralnor's eyes met his in the rear view mirror of the hover van. It was speeding through the airspace of Regium.

"I'm dropping you two off at the palace," Ralnor responded. "The rest, I'll put them around the city in some of the wealthier houses."

"You've made us slaves, you know that, right?" Maleko said, his voice low. Ralnor didn't respond for a while. He landed the hover van in front of the large gates of the palace of Aureum.

"If you're successful," Ralnor said as Maleko and Apsara came out of the van, "I'll take the rest of them to Caedoxia."

"And if we're not?" Apsara asked, a hand on her hip as Maleko leaned against her. He still hadn't figured out how to walk yet.

"Then, they'll stay in those houses," Ralnor said with a shrug. He rolled his window up and then flew back into the airspace, the hover van looking like a small, floating pill as it got further and further away. Apsara scowled at the disappearing van.

"You don't think they'll question why I can't walk, do you?" Maleko asked. Her glare turned to him.

"I'll think of an excuse," she muttered, flipping her long, black hair over one shoulder. She walked up to the gates, with Maleko in tow. A human with a scar over her face met them there. She regarded them with shrewd hazel eyes.

"Maleko," he introduced himself, putting a hand on his chest. He smiled warmly at the human as Apsara threw him a glare. *Shit*, he thought to himself, though a bit too late. He was supposed to use a fake name. The human raised an eyebrow.

"Is that not your name?" she asked. She had obviously

noticed the way Apsara had looked over at him when he revealed his real name.

"No, no it is," Apsara said, her smile brighter than he had ever seen it before. He shook his head at the sheer falsity of it. The human's eyes wandered towards Maleko's legs.

"Can your brother not walk?" she asked.

"Brother?" he couldn't help but burst out. *Brother?* Where in the world did he look like he was related to Apsara? Husband, he could understand. Anyone could make that mistake. But... *brother?*

"I'm so sorry for my brother," Apsara said, jabbing her thumb into the side of his waist. He tried hard not to show how much it hurt. "He has just woken up from the long, long trip. And unfortunately, he's a bit of a diva and his legs have fallen asleep. So, I'm helping him up to the palace, for now." *My legs have fallen asleep?* Maleko thought. It had to be the worst excuse in all of Asynithis.

"Mhmm," the human said, her arms crossed. He wasn't sure she was buying any of it. She rolled her eyes before walking up the hill towards the palace.

"I don't care where you're from or what's going on with you two. But, he needs to be able to walk in order to work in the palace. His majesty doesn't like anything less than perfection," she said.

"You have a scar on your face," Maleko pointed out. Apsara threw him a desperate and angry glare. He shrugged. The human chuckled as her fingers gingerly traced it.

"I do. And trust me, I don't see him often. If he were to see me, and was in a bad mood, I'd probably be killed right then and there," she said the last bit a touch bitterly. She looked over her shoulder as she gestured for Apsara to hurry.

"Matilda doesn't like to wait long," she said. Apsara shifted her weight as she glared down at Maleko. The guilt built up more in his chest as he looked back at the city of Regium. He was a failed king. A king who couldn't protect his people. A king who allowed his people to be enslaved and killed by these surface creatures. He would be remembered as a coward. And not only that, he had to rely on Apsara to carry him around because he couldn't manage to walk. He was more than a failure. He was a burden.

He swallowed as he looked back at the palace looming above them. Once he finally figured out how to walk, he was going to save his people.

8

The image of Rhea's unmoving body flickered behind his closed eyelids, her eyes staring up into nothing, a gray film overtaking them. Khalon squeezed his eyes harder, trying to will the memory out of his mind.

"Khalon, if you had to give your life up for me, would you?" she had asked him the first day they met. After Poseidon warned her to be careful, it was one of the first things out of her mouth. Like she knew her impending doom was coming. And Khalon had said he would. He was flippant about it, and he didn't know if he really meant it or not. But, he told her he would, gave her his word. And instead, she sacrificed herself without a second thought.

Khalon swallowed the lump in his throat, licking his lips as his mouth dried. He didn't cry often. The master of arms from the Ring of Fire used to call Khalon "pathetic" any time the budding tears began after a beating. He never wanted to be called pathetic again. By anybody. But, in the quiet of his room, alone, he couldn't help the tears that pricked at his eyes as the guilt bubbled up in his chest. He rubbed at them furiously.

Esi burst into Khalon's room. Her white eyes were always constantly shaking a little, due to her being unable to see, but her eyes were quivering frantically as she peered into the room.

"What is it?" he asked, standing up from his bed as he strode over to her. He was careful not to reveal the tears in his voice. She was panting, like she had just run a long distance. A bruise was starting to form on her forearm, meaning she definitely fell at least once on her way over to his room. A sigh escaped his lips. Khalon wished she would just send someone else if it was urgent instead of always insisting on doing everything herself.

"The wall," she panted. His eyebrows furrowed together. "The wall's been breached." Khalon stared at her for a moment, before cursing under his breath. He grabbed his draconian armor and the sword made of dragon stone, given to him by his father.

"Where's Kamaria?" he asked, as he grabbed Esi's forearm gingerly.

"She just told me to get you," she muttered, shaking her head. Khalon stopped, staring at Esi. Her black ringlets were pulled back from her heart-shaped face. Her white eyes trembled a little as she blinked, waiting for Khalon to say something.

"Stay here," he whispered. She looked up in his direction, her dark eyebrows furrowing together.

"I can't just—"

"Esi, you'll be a liability," he said, bluntly. She blinked

again, before nodding once. He dropped her forearm and turned away, but he glanced back at her, once, before turning the corner. She stood there, guilt filling her face. His eyebrows knitted together at seeing her expression and then shook his head. He couldn't think about what was plaguing her right now. The elves were in Invenire.

———

When Khalon entered the throne room, he noticed that Kamaria was completely decked out in her phoenix armor. It was what she had worn the first time he had met her. The armor was completely black, with spikes on the shoulders. Her hair was in twists, pulled into a ponytail at the top of her head.

"Of course they attack when we're planning on saving the Sea God from himself," Khai muttered as he passed Khalon. Queen Aoife was sitting nearby, watching them all with a dead expression on her face.

"They sent the beastoids troops to attack the walls," Aponi said, from behind Khalon. Khalon whipped around as he glowered at the lightning bird. Her straight black hair flowed out from behind her as she passed him.

"Where have you been?" he snapped. Her eyebrows jumped slightly at his tone. He was also surprised at how upset he was that Aponi had been missing for quite some time. He had gotten used to her presence, and she had disappeared without a goodbye months ago.

"I've been looking for *your* girlfriend, draconian," she spat back. Khalon stared at her, his heart pounding in his ears as he processed her words.

"From whose orders?" he asked, quietly. She snorted.

"Whose do you think?" she said, gesturing towards Kamaria. "I only serve one royal. And that's Queen Kamaria." Khai rolled his eyes at her words.

"Did you find her?" Khalon asked, hesitantly, his voice barely above a whisper. He didn't know whether he wanted to truly know the answer or not. At least, not if the answer was that she couldn't find Rhea.

"Let's save this for afterwards," Aponi said, her face relaxed as she translated for Kamaria. Khalon turned towards the Ustrinian Queen.

"I need to know."

"You don't, really," Khai said for Kamaria before she could even sign anything. She stared at him, annoyed. "Not when you're about to go into battle."

"It might motivate me," Khalon muttered.

"And it might crush you," Kamaria signed[1]. Aponi shrugged. Kamaria's large, round eyes glanced over at her action.

"Is it good news or bad news?" Kamaria asked. Aponi smirked as she signed back.

"I found her."

"You found her?" Khalon said, hope coating his voice.

"Yeah, she's popped up in Aureum. In the palace." He felt every part of him relax at the news. *She's alive*, his limbs seemed to sigh. *Rhea's okay.* Kamaria narrowed her eyes as she signed towards Aponi.

"But, there's bad news." Khai gritted his teeth.

"Of course there is," he said. Khalon turned towards Aponi, his eyes wide as he waited for the possible bad news. He tried to brace himself for it.

"It's not Rhea," Aponi murmured. Nothing could've prepared Khalon to hear those words. He just stared at Aponi, waiting. Waiting for some kind of further explanation. But, there wasn't. Her dark eyes avoided his.

"It's him, isn't it?" he asked, his voice hoarse.

"From what I've been told, she's not inside of her body at all," Aponi muttered. Her eyes darted up to look at him. "But, we don't know for sure. She might still be hidden there. If the soul of the body dies, the body is dead, isn't it?" Kamaria's jaw clenched. She looked like she was about to sign something else, probably to reprimand Aponi for her misleading information. But, her eyes focused on someone who was behind Khalon. Khalon turned around to look into the face of Jabulani.

Jabulani was decked out in the phoenix armor. If Khalon didn't know any better, he would've thought Jabulani was just an Inkanyamba, instead of a phoenix-Inkanyamba mix like Kamaria. His eyes were large and round, the pupils taking up most of the iris, a characteristic of Inkanyambas, and his teeth were pointed. But, he didn't have glowing red veins. Only royal phoenixes had that trait.

His large eyes glanced over at Khalon. Khalon was almost the same height as Jabulani, except Jabulani was, perhaps, an inch taller. Khalon straightened up as Jabulani walked past him towards Kamaria. He signed a single word.

Now. Kamaria nodded, grabbing her sword from one of her servants. She rested it on her shoulder as she walked past Khalon.

"Let's go," Jabulani said, his voice deep. It held the command of one who always knew they would grow up to be a leader. She walked out of the throne room, with Jabu-lani in tow.

"I don't like him," Khai muttered.

"You only don't like him because he's stronger than you and a better warrior than you'll ever be," Aponi pointed out.

"In love much?" She snorted at his words.

"I'm just stating the truth."

Khai sighed. "He's been alive for, like, sixty years. Of course he's stronger and a better warrior than me," he retorted. "I'm only 15."

"Phoenixes grow very slowly," Aponi said, crossing her arms. "So, he hasn't had *that* much time to train."

"Kamaria is younger than him," Khai said. "And she's a better warrior than I would ever be. So, obviously, they've had *a lot* of time training." Aponi smirked.

"You think Kamaria's a better warrior? I didn't think I'd live to see the day."

"Neither did I," Khalon admitted. Khai became flustered.

"If you ever tell her I admitted to that, thunderbird, I'll kill you," Khai threatened. Aponi snorted.

"Yeah, I'm sure."

"Are you children going to be joining them, or is Invenire going to be destroyed?" Queen Aoife said, sitting in her seat as she steeled her gaze at the three of them. Khalon had half a mind to tell her off. To tell her *she* could be in the front lines fighting if she cared so much. But, something in Khai's face told him not to. It wasn't him that would be punished for the embarrassment. She had no hold over him. But, for Khai... Khalon gritted his teeth.

"Let's go," he said, flicking the blade out of the hilt of his sword.

"If it's the beastoids troop, this will be a difficult battle," Aponi muttered. Khai grabbed his own sword by the door of the throne room.

"Still can't believe they joined the elves," he said as they exited the room. Khalon merely stared at him incredulously.

"What?" Khai said, responding to Khalon's expression.

"They offered the beastoids their own land," Khalon pointed out. "I wonder who thought *that* might've been a good idea."

"Stupid of those beasts to believe them," Khai shrugged. He might've been right, Khalon figured, but he could've made the choice in the beginning to have the beastoids on their side, instead of letting the elves lie to the creatures.

"Don't push yourself," Khalon muttered to Khai. Khai's jaw worked as he stared straight ahead. Khalon closed his eyes as he realized his mistake.

"I just mean—"

"I know what you meant, Khalon." Khai walked ahead of his older brother. Khalon just let out a breath as he caught up to Aponi and Khai.

———

Khai knew Khalon only wanted his younger brother to be safe. But, watching him fight like the legendary warrior he was, made Khai want to smash his head in. It wasn't his fault that he never got the chance to have real battle experience. *He* wasn't a Champion. His brother was. And, even though the comment was meant to express some kind of affection, or worry for him, it made Khai feel inferior.

His sword with the dragon glass blade hit the beastoid's.

Khai ran his tongue along his teeth as he pushed against the beastoid's sword before jumping back. Without dragon's blood, he was as weak as a child. He didn't have the strength of a king.

As his mind wandered, the beastoid jolted forward, giving Khai barely enough time to react. The blade hit his draconian armor, luckily, as Khai avoided it.

Twists hit the side of his face, as Khai spit them out of his mouth. Kamaria sliced the beastoid in half, as fast as lightning, and blood sprayed into Khai's open mouth. The metallic taste made his stomach churn, and he spit it out as much as possible as he glowered up at her.

I had it, he signed[2].

He almost killed you, she signed back. Khai clenched his jaw as he glared at her. Her round eyes narrowed back at him.

"I'm not a child," he said as he signed the words. "I know how to use a sword." She rolled her dark eyes, her lips parting slightly to reveal the sharpened teeth of an Inkanyamba.

Could've fooled me, she signed before darting away to attack another beastoid. Khai's eyes wandered, following after her figure as she cut down another one with ease. She was an infamous warrior. One of the best. And now she was a queen.

The one thing that helped against battling the beastoids, now that they were in Ustrina, was that Kamaria knew their sign language. She could see when they would give each other a command, and she understood what the command meant. It made her invaluable. But, Khai always knew she was invaluable. There wasn't anyone in all of Asynithis like Kamaria. Possibly in the whole universe.

"Pay attention, Khai," Khalon shouted as he ran past him, cutting down another beastoid that was about to attack him. "Keep your head on straight." Khalon was in his dragon form, giving him an extra foot of height. And also, an extra help in keeping himself alive. His black-red scales glinted in the moonlight. Khai clenched his jaw as he fought another oncoming attack.

Fighting the elves was one thing. Fighting the beastoids was an entirely different venture. They fought with the expertise of a warrior who had been in battle all their lives. It was as if they were forged from the blood of past soldiers, as if they ate and breathed fighting every second of every day. Khai found them impossible to overwhelm, and he had been taught by the general of the Draconian Army. The general who died when Draconia's capital, Furvus, fell.

Khai felt the muscles in his jaw tense as his sword hit another beastoid's. He knew he was a liability in a battle against them. He knew he should've stayed in the palace with Esi. But, what kind of a king would that make him?

He wiped the sweat off of his brow as he pressed forward. The beastoid now in front of him was a wolf. Khai lowered into a fighting stance as his heart hammered in his chest. This was it. He was going to die. Wolf beastoids were similar to the werewolves of Caedoxia, except they didn't have a human form. But, they loved to use their teeth as a weapon. The wolf beastoid stalked forward, snarling as he signed something towards another wolf nearby. Khai tried to slow his breathing, knowing they could smell the fear off of him from a mile away.

"King Khai," one of the wolves said, his voice garbled as he stalked towards him. Khai held his chin up high, his bloodied sword in front of his face. He didn't dare say a word. He swore the wolf sneered at him.

"You killed so many of us," the wolf said. "You will feel their wrath." Before he could say he wasn't even the one who started the war between the beastoids, Kamaria dashed in between them. She cut the head clean off of the wolf who was speaking without a second to spare. Her dark eyes glowered at the other wolves. They snarled at her, snapping their teeth in her direction.

Khai shook the fear off of him, like an over-worn blanket, and attacked the nearest wolf. The wolf turned around, grabbing Khai's blade with his hand-like paws. Crimson blood dripped from the paws, but the wolf didn't seem to mind as he stared straight into Khai's soul. Red blood. Like a human's. Like a draconian's. Like a dragon's. They were all the same, technically. Related in some sick way. Creatures of the earth.

Khai desperately tried to pull the sword out from the wolf's grip, but his strength was flimsy. After having relied on dragon's blood for the past six months, Khai didn't have his own natural strength anymore. The wolf pulled him closer and closer, as Khai's feet dragged against the ground. *Just let go of the sword,* Khai desperately thought to himself. But, he couldn't. It was a gift from his father. He couldn't let it go.

The wolf pulled him in until Khai was in close distance of his sharp canines. He opened his mouth, his jaw seemingly unhinging, as he came towards Khai's head. Khai stared, hopelessly, into the abyss that was the wolf's mouth.

But, then, the wolf stilled, before becoming limp. Hot blood sprayed onto Khai's face and the wolf fell on top of him, bringing him to the ground. He stared up into the night sky as the heavy wolf's carcass sucked the life out of him.

Kamaria gave Khai a look as she kicked the wolf's corpse off of his body. She blinked. Khai's eyes wandered towards her mouth, stained red from blood, as she wiped the remnants off of it. His stomach turned.

Must I always save you? She wiped the sweat off of her brow after she signed those words, her red veins glowing underneath her dark skin as Khai gazed upon her. He simply stared at her, wordlessly. Her eyebrows knitted together as she shook her head, moving on to her next victim. Khai's eyes followed her as he slowly got up from the ground. He smeared the blood across his face as his gaze lingered on her figure. Only one thought was on his mind: Kamaria was the coolest creature Khai ever had the pleasure of meeting. Though, he would have to be on his deathbed to ever tell her that.

9

Poseidon's head rocked back and forth from the sleep that still covered him. The lack of blood from his human body was making his vision blurry as he looked up at the vampire who had just entered his cell. The second vampire to enter it that night.

"Felicity," he called. He could feel the presence of the Fate in his mind, her green eyes peering out through his hazy sight.

He doesn't know yet, she whispered into his mind. *But, he felt a shift in the universe.*

"Not him," Poseidon panted as the vampire placed a cup of water near the entrance of the cell. Poseidon's sepia eyes focused on the liquid, his sight clearing for a moment.

The Seer received the message. However, Invenire has been attacked, Felicity said, her sweet voice breaking slightly. Poseidon's gaze steeled. Yeah, *sure* his brother didn't know.

"Ready for round two, God of the Sea?" the vampire asked, his fangs catching the moonlight. He sucked his teeth as he took a step forward. Poseidon continued to stare at the glass of water.

"Though, your blood still tasted like a human's," the vampire sneered, "Not like a Celestial's at all."

"Really?" Poseidon whispered, his voice hoarse from lack of use. The feeling of power slowly expanded out from him, like a third arm reaching out for the glass of water. The water trembled ever so slightly.

The vampire opened his jaw, readying to sink his fangs into Poseidon's neck. Clarity filled Poseidon as the water whipped up from the cup and as fast as light cut through the vampire's neck. The vampire's eyes widened in shock and pain, before falling towards the ground with a satisfying thud.

Poseidon's smug expression lasted for a second, as a tapping on the metal of one of the bars of his cell echoed around him. His eyes met golden ones. Poseidon immediately recognized the creature as a dryad, and he was possibly the most beautiful dryad he had ever seen. Like an angel saving him from the grips of darkness.

"You're the new God of the Sea, huh?" the dryad asked, his voice lazily drifting towards Poseidon's ears. Poseidon studied the dryad.

"How'd you find me?" he said, his voice without strength. The dryad smirked.

"Us trees speak to one another," he said, cocking the cell door open. "And the whole world shifts when a God finds their Celestial body once more. Although, this body is older than a babe."

"I split my soul a long time ago," Poseidon coughed. His eyes roved over the dryad's body. "Are you going to stand there or are you planning on releasing me?" The dryad gave a wolfish grin. He stalked forward, his long golden hair flowing behind him.

"Valerian," the dryad said as he released the manacles around Poseidon's wrists. Poseidon immediately rubbed them as his eyebrows knitted together.

"What?" he asked.

"My name is Valerian," the dryad said. "What's the name for this reincarnation?"

"The same as the last," Poseidon said, dryly.

"You're not as lively as the tales say," Valerian noted. Poseidon raised his eyebrows as he gestured to where they were.

"Would you?" he asked. The dryad smirked once more, the expression making his elegant features seem almost impish. Poseidon couldn't help the smirk that he gave back.

"So," Poseidon said, weakly getting to his feet. This body was way shorter than his last one, and he almost fell over from the difference in height messing with his balance. Valerian's arm steadied him. Poseidon gave a grateful smile his way.

"So, Valerian," he spoke once more, "What's the price for this release?"

"Who says there's a price?" Valerian's golden eyes sparkled.

"There always is one." The dryad regarded him, looking over the human features that Poseidon possessed. The human imperfections that were sure to be on his face. But, he knew his eyes held the waters of the seas. The proof that he was who he said was.

"Do you know how to kill the God of Death?" Valerian

asked. Poseidon's jaw clenched at the mention of his brother.

"The world is at odds with one another when there's only you two living," Valerian explained. "The rest of the Gods are dead and Asynithis is losing its magic. We need all the Gods or none at all. With two living, death and the sea, you're selfishly keeping your lives while draining the magic from the world you helped create."

"What do you mean we're draining the magic?" Poseidon asked, carefully.

"An is gone. In order for you two to stay alive, you take the magic that he has left behind. And the magic that An has left is in every living creature in Asynithis, in every breath they take. It's unnatural for the God of All's younger brothers to still live while he is gone," Valerian whispered. Poseidon's blood stilled. Was it selfish of him? He knew the end was coming. He tasted it in every new breath he took in a new Celestial body. It was why a century ago he had split his soul. In case something happened to one, he would still live through another. As long as a God's soul was in another, a God couldn't die. Even if the one who created them did. The vampire on the ground next to them twitched, coming back to life after being in death's grasp momentarily.

"You want to kill the God of Death," Poseidon said, slowly. "And then after?" Valerian glanced at him. A cold, sinister feeling slithered over his spine as those golden eyes appraised him.

"Either all the Gods live, or none at all," Valerian declared.

———

"You're absolutely useless in battle, did you know that?" Aponi translated for Kamaria, if only for the sake of Khalon. He really needed to learn sign language more so that he didn't need to rely on Aponi's or Khai's presence in order to understand Kamaria.

"Useless?" Khai scoffed as he signed the word. "I killed a couple of those beasts."

"Killed? More like ran away and hid underneath a corpse for twenty minutes," Kamaria signed. Khai reeled as he glared at her. His hands flew angrily as he signed back at her.

"I didn't—You literally killed a wolf and it fell on top of me. What was I supposed to do?" Aponi translated for Khai.

"I already kicked the corpse off of you," Kamaria signed.

"Yeah, but not *all* the way," Aponi said for Khai. Khai focused his glare onto the lightning bird.

"I don't need for you to announce what Kamaria and I are talking about," Khai snapped. Aponi blinked her eyes innocently.

"Oh, I thought you wanted Khalon to know what was being said," she purred. Khai's jaw clenched as Khalon rolled his eyes at their antics.

The beastoids were pushed back past the wall and retreated, for the time being. Though, Khalon knew it would be a matter of days before Aureum moved their forces against Invenire once more. And if Invenire fell, all of Ustrina would be lost.

Esi was waiting at the entrance of the palace. She was wringing her dark hands as she gazed into nothingness, her white eyes still glowing like two lightning bugs. Kamaria rushed over to her, holding her hands that were flushed red from the constant pressure.

"What's wrong?" Khalon asked as he looked down at the Seer.

"He's going to try and find the Saviors," Esi whispered, her eyes flashing white light as she glanced up at Khalon.

"Who?" he asked.

"The Death God," she breathed. "They're looking for Arveldir."

"Who's Arveldir?" Khai asked.

"Obviously an elf with that name," Aponi muttered.

"They'll find him. And they'll find a way to open the portals back up between our two worlds," she hissed. She closed her eyes, the light making the back of her eyelids glow red.

"The Saviors will be in danger," she finished, the light from her eyes slowly fading. She opened them, as she glanced around. The veins that glowed red underneath her skin seemed to glow brighter, darting throughout her body, as her face contorted into panic.

"Let's get inside of the palace," Kamaria signed, looking around outside to see if any of the guards overheard their conversation. Khalon reached towards Esi's arm, in order to lead her back into the palace, but Kamaria placed a hand on her wrist instead, shooting Khalon a glare before walking ahead. The sun was starting to rise.

"Why would this elf be able to open the portals?" Khai asked once the palace doors closed. Aponi translated for Kamaria, and Kamaria's head whipped around to glower at him as she signed: *Not here*. Khai rolled his eyes in response.

"How did you learn sign language, by the way?" Khalon

asked, once he was in step with his little brother. Khai glanced up at him, a flicker of insecurity flashed in his light brown eyes before they hardened once more.

"I've met Kamaria before all of this," Khai muttered. He threw a glare at Aponi that said she shouldn't translate any of this to Kamaria who was walking ahead of them. Aponi put her hands up in defense.

"Right. In hell," Khalon said, repeating Khai's response from a while ago. Khai nodded his head, smiling.

"You said you never met her before, when we were in Draconia," Khalon pointed out. Although, it was pretty obvious that they did despite his words. A smirk spread on Khai's lips.

"She's just easy to rile up," he chuckled. Khalon glanced down at the facial expression on his half brother's face. An expression that was unfamiliar on those features he inherited from Aoife. His eyebrows scrunched together as he surveyed Khai's expression.

"So, why learn to communicate with her if you only met her occasionally?" Khalon asked. Khai's small smile wiped from his face as he stared at the back of Kamaria's head. Her armor was covered in dried blood, and some of her twists were soaked in it as if she had bathed in the beastoids' corpses.

"For a long time, Kamaria was going to become Queen of Ustrina," Khai explained. He clasped his hands together as his gaze lowered from her figure. "Even after Esi was born, she was still first in line. That was, until Sipho was born." Khalon nodded. This was how it normally went with royal families. The first legitimate son was normally the heir to the throne. A woman was hardly ever accepted as ruler, unless absolutely necessary. Sipho was born to a phoenix woman, a true phoenix through and through, unlike his sisters who were either half human or half Inkanyamba.

"You guys were betrothed after," Khalon guessed. Khai's eyes darted over to Khalon's face before nodding once, his lips tightening into a thin line.

"Father thought it would strengthen the bond between Draconia and Ustrina. We have always been close neighbors," Khai muttered.

"And you... learned it for her," Khalon mused, his eyes widening as he looked at his little brother. Granted, Khalon didn't know Khai very well. They were separated when Khai was only three years old. But, he didn't seem the type of person to do anything for anyone.

"I needed to be able to communicate with my future queen, don't you agree?" Khai said, his voice almost arrogant. He shrugged his shoulders. "So, I learned it. It's not that hard. You've just been hit in the head a thousand times." Khalon suppressed the urge to roll his eyes. Khai's face softened as he glanced up at Kamaria once more.

"We probably won't marry now," he muttered. "It would've been weird anyways. Her body grows so slowly and she lives for so long. I would die before she would look like she's in her forties, probably." Khalon guessed she would stop aging by the time her body looked like she was in her thirties, considering how the former king looked.

"Yeah, she'll probably marry Jabulani now to strengthen the ties with the Inkanyambas," Aponi pointed out. Khai's expression hardened. *Yeah*, Khalon thought to himself as he appraised Khai's face. This expression, though unfamiliar in Khai's features, *was* familiar. Khalon knew he shouldn't ask the question that was rising up in his throat, but he couldn't stop himself.

"Khai, do you—" Kamaria turned around abruptly, interrupting Khalon's badly timed question, and put her hands on her hips. She gazed around the area as she nodded her head towards Esi.

"This is a good spot to speak," she signed. Khalon's eyes wandered around the room as Aponi closed the doors behind them. It was a room in the palace that was still being worked on. Long white sheets hung over the open holes in the room, wind billowing them towards the inside.

"Should we have Jabulani here or...?" Aponi asked, pointing her thumb over her shoulder as she glanced at Khai's face. Khai's ears reddened as he glared at Aponi who gave him a smug smile back. Kamaria's eyes squinted until Aponi translated what she said for her. She shrugged in response.

"Jabulani being here is unnecessary," she signed. "He should focus on rallying the troops and drawing up a battle plan."

"Who's Arveldir and why would he be able to open up the portals?" Khai asked again, getting straight to the point.

"I don't know exactly what his role is. But, he was given some kind of magic from the God of All. His family, actually, was given it. Poseidon would probably know more," Esi responded.

"The God of All's plan was to get rid of all the portals, wasn't it? So that no one would be able to follow the Saviors into... the other world," Khalon said.

"Terra is what An referred to it as. It's a newer world, but they call their planet Earth instead of Asynithis."

"Right," Khalon said, the memories flooding back to him. "And Earth isn't in our universe but in a different universe."

"A parallel one."

"And the portals can connect us to Earth," Khalon said slowly.

"Reflections, if used correctly, can take you into a parallel universe, yes," Esi responded.

"But, An closed them all," Aponi pointed out. Esi's head moved towards her, her white eyes devoid of any color staring in her direction.

"With the last of his energy, he did."

"Okay, so how would this elf be able to open the portals?" Khai asked, crossing his arms. Esi shrugged her shoulders as she looked down at the ground.

"I have no idea," she whispered. "Somehow, he has some kind of magic that is able to do so. And if he opens one portal, any portal could be opened."

"What happens when he opens the portal?" Khalon said, taking a step forward towards Esi. Her eyes darted up to him as she heard his voice.

"Witches and other creatures will start to infiltrate Terra, in order to get away from Aureum's clutches," Esi said.

"It will be a mass exodus," Aponi breathed.

"Earth is meant to be a world without magic. With mortals. It's a world for humans and is run by humans. A lot of our history is the same, but there are slight differences because of this. If magical creatures crawl into Earth, we don't know what will become of that world," Esi sighed. She shook her head as she tried to redirect her thoughts. "But, most importantly, if the portals open, the Saviors could be killed."

"And Asynithis won't be saved," Kamaria signed. Esi nodded.

"If we could just go into a different world to escape Aureum and the Mortiferis, why shouldn't we?" Khai asked, leaning against the wall behind him. Kamaria rolled her eyes.

"Because the elves will just follow us into that world," Esi pointed out. "And the Mortiferis will follow as well. The only ones who can successfully get rid of the threat of the Mortiferis is the Saviors."

"What is it that those Savior heads say all the time in the streets?" Khai mused as he looked up at the ceiling. "Oh right. Seven lives they will live before they come back. I think killing them once isn't going to be a big deal."

"But killing them seven times?" Kamaria signed. "I feel like Adamar would do anything to get rid of them."

"Not just Adamar, but..." Aponi's words drifted off as she stole a glance at Khalon. Khalon's jaw hardened.

"How do we stop them?" Khalon asked, his voice rough. Esi shook her head.

"We can't stop them from opening the portals," she muttered. "But, we will need to close them again."

"How are we supposed to do that?" Aponi asked, incredulously. Esi's dark eyebrows knitted together as she looked back down at the ground.

"I don't know."

10

Apsara watched, drying her hair from her bath, as Maleko stumbled past her bed for the thousandth time. He grumbled something under his breath as he held the end of the bed frame, panting as though he had swam through a whole ocean in one day.

"Your highness," Apsara drawled, "it isn't really this difficult. Walking."

"It's the most difficult thing I've ever done, and I have to be done with it in a few hours or our people will be tortured." Apsara rolled her eyes. He had always been a tad *too* dramatic.

"The elf never said anything about torture," she pointed out.

"It might as well be the same thing," his eyes flashed at her. She raised her hands up in defense as he turned around to start walking once more.

"Just put one foot in front of the other. Your human legs are strong so they should be able to keep you standing," she said, trying to give helpful advice. Maleko looked through his wavy brown hair to glare at her.

"It is not the *act* of walking that is so difficult, Apsara. It is the *balancing* part that is proving impossible." She pursed her lips.

"Matilda will be here in two hours, your highness," she said, pointedly. "You must master it by then."

"I'm aware," he said, coldly. Matilda was the head of the house staff in the palace of Aureum. The human, Lorena, had brought Apsara and Maleko to Matilda, another human. Matilda had her short blonde hair pulled away from her face as her gray eyes shrewdly roved over them. Apsara had never felt more bare in front of another being, despite being fully clothed.

"I don't particularly want to see her angry," Apsara mused. The human was weirdly frightening. She watched as Maleko shuddered at the thought. He must've thought the same.

He picked himself up and started walking once more. Apsara must admit he was doing a lot better than he was earlier in the night. Bruises were starting to bloom all over his arms and probably underneath the shirt he was wearing from how often he had fallen. But, he hadn't fallen once this morning. Her eyes lingered on his loose shirt as he tried to walk past her once more.

"Do you have a plan, your highness?" she asked, dragging her gaze up to his face. He frowned.

"Call me Maleko while we're here, Apsara," he muttered. He collapsed onto the ground, opting to take a break instead, as he chugged back the glass of water Apsara left for him.

"Do you have a plan, *Maleko*?" Apsara corrected. His name wasn't unfamiliar on her tongue. They had known each other forever. And before he had become King of Argentiunda, she called him by his name constantly. But, her being in the king's guard meant that she wasn't to call him by his first name anymore. Only by his title. Saying his name, after all these years, made her feel... weird.

"A plan for what, Apsara?" He blinked his eyes up at her, innocently. She suppressed the urge to roll her own.

"For killing the God of Death," she hissed. He lowered his gaze after a moment, focusing on the marbled floor. The elves seemed to really love marble. The whole palace was made out of it. It was an ugly stone, in Apsara's humble opinion. Coral was much more attractive.

"Ah, well, I figured we would stake her out first," Maleko mused. "And then strike while she's asleep."

"Does the God of Death sleep?"

"Her vessel is a creature, is it not? Creatures must sleep," he pointed out. "We don't need to kill the soul of the Death God. Just her vessel. That enough will satisfy Ralnor."

"And killing the God of Death's vessel is easy enough, you assume," Apsara frowned. Maleko shrugged a shoulder.

"It will be easier than trying to figure out how to kill the soul that is inside," he said.

"So your winning plan is that you will come up with one after working here." Apsara crossed her arms over her chest. He cocked an eyebrow.

"You disapprove?" he asked, a ghost of a smile on his face. She resisted the urge to smile back, keeping her face completely still.

"I just thought the great King of Argentiunda would

have a more sound plan than that," she muttered. Any trace of a smile was wiped from his face.

"Apsara..." his voice drifted off as the door to her bedroom suddenly opened. Standing in the entrance, earlier than she said she would, was Matilda. Her light blonde hair was pushed off of her face with a headband as her gray eyes surveyed the room. Maleko stared at her, slack-jawed.

"Are you ready?" the human asked them. Apsara blinked as Maleko tried to rise to his feet. To her surprise, he kept upright.

"As ready as we'll ever be," he quipped. Matilda's stone eyes rolled towards him.

"Good," she said.

———

"You'll clean this hallway," Matilda said, her hands behind her back as she walked the length of the gold detailed hallway. It was wide and large, full of painted portraits of elves. Apsara scrunched her nose up as she turned away from the white faces and white-haired royal elves of Aureum.

"Lorena will show you the ropes," she continued, her arm gesturing towards the human who was on her hands and knees, vigorously wiping at the marbled floor with a white rag. Lorena's hazel eyes glowered up at them.

"Matilda, you know I prefer to work—"

"You brought them to me, you teach them," Matilda snapped. Lorena's mouth tightened into a line. Matilda's gray eyes met Apsara's.

"Watch out for your brother," she warned before turning on her heel and walking back down the length of the hallway. The clicking of her heels echoed all around them. Lorena started to viciously scrub at the floor.

"Well?" she said, not taking her eyes off of her task. "Grab a rag and start scrubbing." Maleko, who had been wobbly but managed not to fall the whole way here, got down on all fours and grabbed a white rag from the bag near Lorena's knees. He dipped it into the soapy water in the bucket next to her, and slowly started to wash the floor.

Apsara stared in horror at the sight of her king cleaning the elven palace's floors. His light brown eyes wandered up towards her and then darted towards the rag in his hands.

"Are you too big and mighty to clean the floors of a hall-way?" Lorena drawled. Her hazel eyes were glowering up at Apsara. Apsara cleared her throat before getting on her hands and knees. She snatched a rag from the bag and started to make powerful swipes at the floor.

"I'm just not used to seeing my brother wash floors, is all," Apsara muttered as she crawled away from them, scrubbing the floors as she went. Maleko gave her a desperate glance that read: *Are we really sticking to that narrative?*

"Why would you decide to come work in the palace then?" Lorena asked, pointedly. Her curly brown hair was pulled back into a low ponytail, and the hairstyle made her face look sharper, the scar across it more noticeable.

"Money," Apsara remarked. Lorena's eyes narrowed.

"You two aren't human, are you?" she muttered, her voice lower than a whisper. Maleko's eyes widened.

"Was money the wrong answer?" Apsara mused, her lips twitching as she met Lorena's gaze. Lorena shrugged.

"Money doesn't really help a human in Aureum," she

answered. "If a human works at the palace, it's because they either want to live a semi-comfortable life, or because they have a death wish. Not for money."

"What's *your* reason for working in the palace?" Lorena smiled slightly.

"I have a death wish." Maleko and Apsara exchanged looks that didn't go unnoticed by the human. Her smile widened as she returned to scrubbing the floors.

"Do you two have a death wish? I mean, you must if you're posing as humans," she whispered.

"You could say that," Maleko responded, slowly. Apsara reached into her pockets and clutched the broken shard of glass she had hidden there.

"Will you tell anyone?" Maleko asked, leaning towards the human. Apsara watched the exchange intensely as her grip tightened.

"It's none of my business," Lorena said, shrugging. "I don't care if you're human or not. And I don't care why you decided to come here." Apsara involuntarily let out a sigh of relief as she loosened her grip. Maleko grinned at her.

"What do you know about the Death God?" he asked. Apsara swore if he wasn't her king, she would wring his neck out. Lorena's eyebrows scrunched together as she glanced over at the Argentiundan King.

"The Death God?" she said. "I don't know much. I've only seen her in passing, and she's not as frightening as they make her out to be."

"She isn't," Apsara retorted. "But *he* is." Lorena's face was like stone as she went back to scrubbing the floors.

"So that's why you're here," she mused. "You want the God of Death."

"Maybe," Maleko said. He stared at the human for a bit longer. "You're pretty observant, for a human." Lorena snorted.

"We're made to be," she said. "At least, in this world." Maleko didn't say anything else in response.

11

"My cousin, who's enslaved by a witch in Caedoxia, might be able to help," Aponi said, walking up to the breakfast table as Kamaria froze, mid-bite. Jabulani was joining them this morning as Kamaria was discussing plans with him. She was planning to leave him behind in charge of protecting the city during this war between Aureum and Ustrina, and he translated Aponi's words for her as her large, round, black eyes roved over to him. The same black eyes on Jabulani's face roved over to Aponi, distrust glazing them.

"If they're enslaved, how are they going to be able to help?" Khai droned, letting the soup drip out of his spoon as he watched with sleep-coated eyes.

"Esi said that this elf—Arveldir—had a special kind of magic granted to his family. If anyone's an expert on magic, especially any special magic, it would be this witch," Aponi explained.

"Still doesn't answer my question," Khai said, his bored eyes glancing up at the lightning bird. She rolled her own.

"I thought about it, and my cousin is enslaved to a witch from a very old family. A witch who would know of special kinds of magic, considering her morals," Aponi explained. She narrowed her dark eyes at Khai. "Besides, do you have closer access to a witch that I'm unaware of?" Khai opened his mouth as if he had a retort, but then closed it quickly. He *did* know of a witch, but he wasn't about to disclose his mother's family history.

"Is that how you got your magic?" Khai asked, chewing slowly as he gazed at Aponi. It was clear she had magic, she had used it a fair amount of times during battle. There was only one way a lightning bird could do magic like a witch. Aponi stared at Khai, her gaze unchanging.

"I killed her," she answered, simply. Khai's facial expression didn't move an inch. It was what he expected. But, he was surprised there was a lightning bird who was able to kill their owner without ramifications. No wonder why she liked to be called a thunderbird.

"You weren't executed for it?" Khai asked, an eyebrow cocked. Aponi's chin raised.

"It was in self defense," she declared. Her eyes darted towards Kamaria. "And the queen vouched for me." Khai's gaze drifted over to the Ustrinian Queen. She raised her eyebrows in response, as if to ask what he was looking at. He looked back at his food.

"Sounds like an interesting story," he muttered.

"It's not something she likes to talk about," Khai heard Aponi's voice say with enough attitude coating it that he knew she was translating for Kamaria. He looked up at the

Ustrinian Queen through his lashes. She gave her usual glare back at him. Khai opened his mouth to respond to her, but he was interrupted by the entrance of his half brother with Esi in tow.

"Esi filled me in," he said.

Kamaria's eyebrows rose as she signed: *That was quick.*

"We're heading to Caedoxia, right? To find out information about this Arveldir character?" Khalon asked, stopping right behind Khai's seat. "Esi says it's the right move to take." He felt his older brother lean against the back of his chair, to Khai's annoyance. For whatever reason, Khalon seemed to feel comfortable with Khai, despite hardly knowing him. Khai could never seem to feel that same familial bond.

"Yes, my cousin is enslaved by a witch there. She might know some information. Though, she probably won't speak to me about it," Aponi said, mumbling the last sentence under her breath.

"If she won't speak to you about it, then why are we going?" Khai asked. He turned towards Kamaria as he signed at her, not translating for the rest of the table on purpose.

If we leave, Invenire might fall, he signed. Kamaria scoffed as she signed back.

Jabu can take care of it. Jabulani's eyes darted towards Khai after reading Kamaria's signs. Khai's lips twisted in response. He couldn't freely sign to her, not when Jabulani was fluent in the language as well. Kamaria's black eyes studied Khai's expression for a moment before smirking.

Jabu is a great warrior. He won't let Invenire fall, she signed, guessing at his thoughts.

Good thing I'm not leaving the country to you and your mother, she added. He rolled his eyes.

"Everything good?" Khalon asked, his half-moon shaped eyes glancing at the queen. Kamaria nodded her head once.

"You really should learn sign language," Khai drawled. Khalon's face hardened but his gaze didn't leave Kamaria's face.

"If we're going to be in Caedoxia anyways, we should also find Poseidon," Khalon ordered. "Esi saw a dryad take him."

"A dryad?" Aponi's eyebrow raised as she looked over at Esi. Esi nodded once, the same expression on her face as her sister's. Khai often wondered if Khalon and him ever made the same facial expressions. If they were somehow connected in that way.

"His name is Valerian. He's a very old dryad. I couldn't see exactly what he wants with Poseidon, but he knows Poseidon is truly the God of the Seas. Trees are very talkative," Esi shrugged.

"We could kill two stones with one bird," Khalon pointed out.

"You mean kill two birds with one stone," Khai said, looking up at his brother. Khalon's eyebrows scrunched together.

"That's what I said." Khai opened his mouth to argue with him but then thought better of it, slumping in his seat instead. Kamaria pursed her lips as she thought after Aponi translated for her. Her eyes darted over towards Esi's, as if trying to read some kind of expression on her face, before she glanced over at Jabulani.

It means we'll be gone for longer, she signed towards him.

Jabulani shrugged before standing up straight. He stared straight at Khai.

"I'll take care of everything," he said as he signed. His eyes flitted back towards Kamaria. "Your people will be in good hands, my queen." Kamaria gave Jabulani a small smile as she clapped a hand onto his shoulder. Khai looked away.

"So, we've agreed? We'll save Poseidon from this dryad and get some information about the portals and that elf," Khalon said, straightening up. The pressure on Khai's seat lessened as he did.

"I still don't think this is a good idea," Khai mumbled under his breath, glancing over at Jabulani. Jabulani met his gaze.

"You're the only one who thinks so, buddy," Aponi said, squeezing Khai's shoulder as she walked past. She followed Khalon out of the room. Khai and Kamaria stared at each other as Khai tried to convey to her that he needed to talk to her. Esi stood there for a moment longer before clearing her throat.

"Should I leave? I'm sensing some tension."

"I just want to talk to Kamaria," Khai said, glancing at Jabulani before adding, "Alone."

"Anything you want to say to my queen, you can say in front of me," Jabulani spoke, his deep voice rumbling through the earth. The "my" felt possessive, and it made the scales on Khai's exposed skin bristle.

"Jabu," Esi said quietly, "Kamaria can handle Khai on her own." Jabulani's black, round eyes looked over at the Seer. They then glanced over at Kamaria who sighed and waved him away. He gave one last glare to Khai before getting up and leaving the room with Esi gripping his arm.

What is it? Kamaria signed, her gaze stabbing daggers into him.

A queen shouldn't leave her people in the middle of a war, Khai signed back. She scoffed.

Is that not what you did? You fled Draconia, she pointed out.

I fled *because it was either stay and be killed or leave and, perhaps, take back Draconia someday.* Her gaze softened as she lowered her head, her dark eyes looking through her lashes.

But, you have no plans to take back Draconia, do you? Khai stayed quiet for a moment, just staring at her hands. They weren't the hands of a princess. They were a warrior's hands. Calloused and cracked. Strong.

He looked down at his own before signing: *I'm no warrior, Kamaria. What would I be able to do on my own?* And his hands reflected that. They were soft, unmarred by any kind of trauma. He knew how to hold a sword. He knew how to fight, in theory. But on a battlefield, as he had come to find out, all rules of etiquette went out the window.

Kamaria's eyes seemed to melt in pity as she stared at him. Her lips parted ever-so-slightly to the point where Khai could see the points of her sharpened teeth.

You're a king, Khai. Khai's jaw worked as he looked away from her gaze, concentrating only on her hands.

"I'm not a true Draconian King," he muttered out loud as he quickly signed the words. Kamaria's lips pursed.

You're no warrior. Not like Khalon, she signed. The words almost made Khai wince. *But, you have the other aspects of a king. Arrogance being one of them.* Khai repressed the urge to roll his eyes at her. She smirked.

"You still shouldn't leave," Khai said, under his breath. Kamaria narrowed her eyes as she read Khai's lips.

Asynithis is more important than a single country. What is the point of saving Ustrina if the rest of Asynithis is destroyed?

Saving all of Asynithis isn't your responsibility, he signed back. She stared at him for a long moment. Her eyebrows furrowed together as she looked away, as though looking at him for too long was overwhelming her.

Khai, she signed the sign that she had given him a year ago, the sign that represented his name. A sign that only she knew. *We're not betrothed anymore.* Khai stiffened.

I know, he signed quickly. A little too quickly. She studied his expression.

You're a king. I'm a queen, she signed. *There's no need for us to be married. Our marriage wouldn't even make sense. Would we rule two different countries? Be apart yet still be married?* Khai could feel the heat rise up into his cheeks.

I didn't say any of that. I know we're not betrothed. I know we can't marry, he signed, but she didn't seem to really pay attention. She tightened her lips into a line.

Besides, you would never give up your title just for me, she pointed out. Khai's heart stilled.

She got up from her seat before signing: *You don't need to care so much about my well-being anymore. I've always been able to take care of myself.*

As she walked out of the room, Khai could almost hear the unspoken words that surrounded him. *And you wouldn't be able to.*

He stared at the empty seat for what felt like an eternity

before getting up. She had a point. But, then again, Kamaria always had a point.

———

His mother grabbed his arm before he entered his chambers. She was alone, meaning her attendants didn't know she had gone to see him. Khai shrugged his mother's grip off of him as she glowered. Her light brown eyes darkened.

"I heard you're heading to Caedoxia," she whispered as she followed him into his room. He closed the door behind them so no one would hear Queen Aoife's voice.

"Yeah? What about it?" he said. Queen Aoife's gaze hardened as she stared at her son.

"Do not speak to me in that tone," she ordered. Khai almost cowered at the sound of his mother's voice.

"Sorry," he mumbled.

"Caedoxia would be the perfect time to do what we have planned," she said. Khai's blood chilled as he walked away from his mother, sitting down in one of the couches in his room.

"I don't know, Mother," he muttered. "I just don't think it's the right time and—"

"Of course it's the right time. Caedoxia is known for its darkness. For mysterious and unexplained deaths," Aoife said, taking a step towards Khai. He tried to hide his trembling hands, placing them underneath him as he rocked forward.

"I-I don't know if—"

"You're not having second thoughts, are you?" Aoife

said, her voice eerily low. Her head cocked to the side as she studied him. Khai's breath hitched in his throat.

"N-No, it's just that I'm not... I'm not as strong as he is, Mother. He is... You haven't seen him in true battle. He truly is a *warrior*. It's as if death is resting on his shoulder, helping him every step of the way," Khai quickly explained, his voice shaking. Aoife's gaze hardened before softening.

"If it is about strength, my dear son, I can help you with that," she said, her voice sweet. His heart quickened as he stared at the bottle his mother took out from underneath her silk robe. Her gaze examined him, coldly, as she took another step forward. Careful, as if he were a cornered animal and she were a predator.

"You want to be king, don't you? Have your rule unquestioned, correct? You know that as long as Khalon is alive, your reign will be threatened. You told me so yourself." How Khai wished he could take back those words.

"Draconia has fallen. And, you never know, Khalon might help us get it back. Khalon might help save Asynithis, for Alator's sake. I can't just *kill* him. Not when he might be destined for greater—" For a moment, Khai saw stars. The slap across his face stung, bringing immediate tears to his eyes. Queen Aoife's own eyes were wide as she glared at her son. All she could see was red.

"Did I make a mistake in raising you?" she said, her voice low and threatening. "Did I raise a coward? Did I raise a *failure*?" He didn't move, his face still turned to the side from his mother's attack.

"Khalon is destined for *nothing*. Khalon is destined for *death*. For a worthless life," Aoife hissed. Khai said nothing.

"Answer me. Did. I. Raise. A. Coward? Did I make a

mistake in ever having you?" she snapped, her face close to his. He could feel her breath on him. Khai shook his head, scared to open his mouth and reveal the knot of tears in the back of his throat.

"Then, you will kill him," she ordered after taking his silence as an answer, straightening back up. He nodded his head. She grabbed his face with one hand, turning him to look at her.

"Say it to me," she hissed.

"I'll kill him," Khai whispered, his voice breaking. He could see the disappointment in his mother's eyes. She clenched her jaw and released his face. He looked down at her feet and watched as she opened the bottle that was in her hands.

"Look at me," she said, grabbing his face once more. She gripped the sides of his jaw hard enough that he was worried bruises might form in its place. Unwillingly, even though his whole body wanted the liquid, he opened his mouth. She poured the dragon's blood into it, his body involuntarily sputtering at the speed in which the liquid went down his throat, causing him to erupt in a coughing fit.

"Drink it all," she ordered. "It will last you for a while." Khai didn't argue. The taste of the dragon's blood lit up every nerve in his brain. And he *wanted* more. Despite the little voice in his head telling him he shouldn't, he wanted every last drop.

After downing it, Khai could feel the liquid churning through him, strengthening every part of him. His mother left, a satisfied look on her face, and as she opened his bedroom door, down the hall he could see glowing red veins and inky black eyes. If Queen Aoife noticed the Ustrinian Queen, she didn't say anything.

Kamaria stared at him, her face giving nothing away. But, her eyes darted down towards his mouth, where the blood stained it, and flickered towards his cheek, where he was sure the red hand print of his mother was still present. Khai's heart stilled at the sight of her, unable to move. Aoife slowly closed the door as she left, and Khai watched as Kamaria turned on her heel before the door clicked in place.

He stared at the closed door, thoughts racing, before he just hung his head, staring at his long fingers, the only trait Khalon and him seemed to share.

Kamaria wouldn't understand. He repeated the thought in his head over and over again until the words had started to lose its meaning.

12

As Elion moved throughout the palace, he had the feeling someone was watching him. But, whenever he looked over his shoulder, he never saw anyone.

"Are you listening?" Edwyrd asked, his voice uncharacteristically annoyed. Elion turned back towards him, his eyes darting once more to look at the empty space behind him before sighing and running a hand through his short, white hair. Now that his hair was shorter, it would rest on his forehead a lot more and get into his eyes, a feeling he didn't particularly appreciate.

"I'm listening," Elion absentmindedly said. Edwyrd's blue eyes roved over his face as he stopped walking. He turned to face him more directly.

"Elion, has something been bothering you lately?" Edwyrd's voice was low. Lower than a whisper. Elion stared at his older brother, confusion marring his brow. Edwyrd looked around the hallway before taking a step closer to his youngest brother.

"If you feel unsafe in this palace, I'm sure I can think of some excuse as to why you'd be staying with me," Edwyrd clarified. Elion let out a breath.

"No, it's not that I feel unsafe," Elion muttered. "I just feel... Never mind. Go ahead with what you were saying." Edwyrd studied Elion for a moment longer before resuming his walking that seemed to shake the whole palace with every step. Elion tried to keep up with him.

"With Batula about to give birth any day now, I won't be able to lead the war for much longer. Adamar..." his voice drifted off as he tried to think of the best way to phrase his thoughts, "he's not... really... the best in combat and war strategy. You know what I mean." Elion nodded.

It was something their father used to say as well. Adamar and Ardryll were more adept for the life of politics, while Elion and his brother Edwyrd seemed to love the game of war a little more. However, even though Elion never corrected their father when he would say this, Elion was only mildly good at it, and he didn't particularly enjoy it.

"You're going to have to be in charge of the armies while I'm gone," Edwyrd finished. Elion gritted his teeth as he tried to keep his expression still.

"Are you sure *I'm* the best replacement you could come up with?" Elion said, his voice monotonous. Edwyrd raised an eyebrow as he threw Elion a sidelong glance.

"One of my soldiers would be a better fit, for sure. But, Adamar won't let a commoner be in charge of his armies," he explained. "And Ardryll would just let the world burn if he had the chance." He chuckled under his breath at the thought of Ardryll, their brother who loved to just lay about, leading Aureum's armies.

"Why me?" Elion asked, his voice small.

"Well, you'd at least listen to the advice of the more experienced elves, unlike..." he let his voice drift off once again, his arms stretched behind his head. But, Elion knew he was talking about their oldest brother, the King of Aureum.

He turned towards Edwyrd, his heart hammering in his chest. He took a deep breath, letting it out shakily as Edwyrd gave him a curious look.

"Edwyrd, to be honest," Elion whispered, his voice trembling, "I don't... really agree... with..."

"The war?" a voice spoke, interrupting the brothers. A thousand whispers encased the words. Elion could feel the hairs on every part of his body stand straight up. Edwyrd stiffened.

"Your holiness," Edwyrd spoke, his voice like ice as he bowed. "If we disturbed you, we're incredibly—" Rhea held up a hand, her hellfire eyes on the youngest prince.

"You don't agree with the war?" Rhea asked, her voice as high and twinkling as Elion remembered it. But, the whispers following it showed that it wasn't truly her anymore. The Death God had taken over.

"He never said that he doesn't agree with the war. Right, Elion?" Edwyrd said, his blue eyes wide. Elion closed his mouth and nodded once, his face tight.

"I know sweet Elion doesn't agree," Rhea said, her eyes not leaving his face.

"If you're speaking about how he was found with the other Gods, he was bewitched by the Love God's spell in order to protect herself. It wasn't of his own accord," Edwyrd defended, his voice almost growling. Rhea smirked, but her eyes finally left Elion's as they flickered towards Edwyrd.

"My sister never worked like that. She always could protect herself fairly well. Until, well, the end of course," Rhea said. Her eyes found Elion's once more as she took a step forward, her head cocking to the side. "Speaking of my siblings, have you felt a shift in the world?" He blinked.

"What?" he asked. Rhea's smile grew.

"So he does speak," she joked, her eyes glancing over at Edwyrd. Edwyrd said nothing in response.

"What do you mean by a shift in the world?" Elion repeated. Rhea turned back towards him.

"I thought... since you had spent a lot of time with them, you might've felt it. But, perhaps not," she mused. She took a step back as she looked over Elion.

"For the record, I don't care if Aureum conquers all of Asynithis or not. I don't care for Adamar's agenda. I'm using him for a different cause. So, if you want to derail the war when you lead it for a while, I don't mind," she said, her voice almost nonchalant. Her gaze hardened as she turned her body slightly. "But, do not go against me, little elf. For your sake." She started to walk away, but then paused, her back towards the brothers.

"Things are about to get interesting," she said, before disappearing into the shadows. Elion looked over at Edwyrd to gauge his reaction. A muscle feathered in his jaw as he stared at the empty space the Death God used to take up.

"Perhaps, you shouldn't be in charge of the armies,"

Edwyrd finally spoke. His blue eyes met Elion's, softening as they did.

"I'm sorry," Elion whispered, his voice breaking. The unspoken words filled the air: *Please don't tell Adamar.*

"It's for the best," Edwyrd said, his voice low. "I would prefer if you weren't mixed up in this anyhow." He started down the hallway. At the corner, he stopped, his hand on the wall as he looked over at his little brother.

"Besides, I wouldn't want you to feel as I do," he said, his voice echoing down the hall. Before Elion could say another word, he disappeared around the corner, his footsteps thundering throughout the palace.

———

Elion watched as Freya bent over, covering her ears as the Mortiferis let out a thousand screams from the pain of Freya's sword. Without hesitation, Elion ran up to the Mortiferis, brandishing his sword in front of its face as he lunged forward. Before his sword could meet the monster's flesh, its arm hit Elion's side, flinging him across the field. He felt the bones in his body snap, but his gaze wouldn't leave Freya's figure, the snow clouding his vision. She dodged the Mortiferis' mouth, and all Elion could feel was pain as his vision faded to black.

Elion kept his eyes closed even as his body awoke. His body still felt like it was mangled as guilt radiated through every part of him. If he wasn't so weak, maybe he could've spared Freya's life. He thought he had become stronger since Pilar's death. Instead, he was just as fragile as he was then.

He heard the sheets next to him rustle, and abruptly, he

opened his eyes, his arm reaching out towards the metal that was rushing towards him. Elion gripped the wrist, hard, as he pulled the knife away from the hollow of his throat. He wrestled with the assailant before straddling them to his bed. Then did he recognize the face glowering up at him. Pilar's face.

"Lorena," he said, her name flickering through his mind. Then, a little louder, "Lorena?" She spat in his face. Elion banged Lorena's arm down, hard, until her grip loosened from the knife. With his knee, he moved the knife away from Lorena's hands.

"Why?" he asked, as he looked down at her. Her face twisted into disgust as she struggled more against his weight, to no avail.

"You're just going to hurt yourself," Elion muttered.

"Go to hell," she hissed.

"Why are you trying to kill a prince of Aureum?" he asked, his voice slightly amused. It had been a while since someone was trying to actively kill him. It was a nice reprieve from the political dangers he had been dealing with for the past six months.

"You killed Pilar, *didn't* you?" she snapped. Elion froze at the mention of Pilar.

"What?" he said, his voice quiet.

"You killed her." She held her chin up as her eyes glared at him down her nose. Elion's grip on her wrists tightened.

"How do you figure that?" he said, his voice cold.

"You knew her. You recognized her in me," she pointed out, arrogantly. In the moonlight, the scar across Lorena's face looked darker.

"How do you know she was killed?" Elion whispered.

She frowned as she struggled more against him. Her scowl deepened.

"How do you think I got this scar?" she snarled.

"You're related to her."

"I'm her cousin," Lorena confirmed.

"You look... how do you look so much like her?" Elion asked, his voice just above a whisper.

"Our mothers were identical twins," she answered, hastily. "Stop asking personal questions. Admit that you killed her."

"I didn't kill her," he stated. Lorena's hazel eyes blinked.

"You did."

"I didn't."

"If you *didn't*, then how did you know what she looked like? She was a servant," she pointed out.

"Me and her were... friends," Elion said, his voice breaking a little at the word. Her body became less tense as she stared up at him, her brows knitting together.

"Friends? What the fuck does that mean?"

"We were friends," Elion said, more definitively. "If I let you go, will you try to stab me again?" Lorena's eyes didn't leave his face as she her lips twitched.

"Maybe." He stared at her for a moment more, before letting go of her wrists and immediately grabbing the knife next to her. He quickly rolled off of her and got off of the bed, knife in hand.

"I'll answer any of your questions about Pilar," he said, holding the knife up. "Just, don't try this again. It'll get you into a lot of trouble." Lorena slowly sat up in Elion's bed, her upper body turning towards him.

"How can a servant and a prince be friends?" she asked, her voice like stone.

"Princes are lonely. And Pilar was the same age as me. She was… kind," Elion mumbled, leaning against the wall behind him. Lorena didn't look at him as she stared at her hands.

"She was killed because you two were friends, right?" she asked, her hateful eyes meeting his. Elion's breath quickened as the familiar guilt started to seep into his bones.

"Yes," was all he said. She crawled towards him on the bed before getting off of it, walking slowly up to him, like a panther stalking their prey.

"So you *did* kill her," she hissed.

"I didn't—"

"But, because of *you*, she died. Our whole *family* died." Lorena's face contorted into a vicious expression as she looked up at him, so close that he could feel her chest move with breath. It wasn't just Pilar that Lorena was avenging. It was her whole family. It was herself, who managed to escape with just a nasty scar.

"A-Adamar killed her," Elion stammered, his instincts not allowing him to admit any guilt in Pilar's death. He had spent the years since Pilar's death trying to re-train his brain into realizing that it wasn't his fault he had feelings for the human. That *he* wasn't the reason why she had died. But, Lorena was undoing all of that work for him.

"How?" she demanded.

"He sliced her throat open," Elion whispered, his voice haunted. Lorena smirked as she took the knife from his hands, Elion letting her.

"A fitting end for you then," she remarked. He closed his eyes, waiting for the cold metal to run across his throat. But, instead, he heard the door squeak. Lorena froze as Elion's eyes flickered open. Standing in the doorway was a man with wavy brown hair and a strong square jaw. Elion narrowed his eyes as he stared at the man whose mouth dropped open. A woman's head popped out next to him as she peered into the room, her long black hair shrouding half of her face, though her dark eyes were familiar. Elion knew both of them.

"Guessing you're still not done yet," the woman said.

"You guys are... you guys are *merpeople*, aren't you? And you're... the *King* of Argentiunda, right?" Elion's voice went up as he stared at the two creatures. The woman's face put on the same facial expression of surprise as the man who was still just standing there. Lorena lowered her knife.

"You two know each other?" she asked, gesturing towards Elion. The king cleared his throat.

"Ah, yes. Um, before everything happened, this elf was with us in Amnis Lux when An told us of his plan," the king said. He turned towards Elion. "You cut your hair." Lorena slowly processed what was being said and then her eyes widened as she looked at the king.

"You're a *king*?" she asked, her voice almost shrill. "You said your name was Maleko and that you were a king's guard." Maleko ducked his head as he shyly looked over at the woman.

"Apsara is actually a king's guard. Well, *my* guard," Maleko said. Lorena stared at the two of them, slack-jawed.

"And you, a king, were going to help me kill a prince of Aureum? Isn't that, like, an international nightmare?"

"You were *helping* her kill me?" Elion asked, incredulously. Apsara took a step forward, closing the door behind her.

"If she was going to help us, yes," she retorted. Maleko put his hands up.

"Well, we didn't know it was *you*, of course," he clarified. Apsara waited a beat.

"Of course," she echoed.

"Sorry, wait a minute," Lorena said, taking a step back. "You're the King of the Seas, basically. A merperson. But, *you* are trying to kill the God of Death?"

"I never said I was going to *kill* the God of—"

"No, but it was *heavily* implied," Lorena pointed out.

"You're trying to kill the God of Death?" Elion asked in disbelief. Apsara took a step forward, her hands gripping a shard of glass.

"I'll help you kill him, since you can't seem to do it properly," she spoke, her voice without feeling. Elion took a step back, until his spine was pressed up against the wall behind him.

"Wait," Maleko said, putting up a hand. Apsara paused, her eyes still on Elion. "It might be good to keep this elf alive. He's obviously on our side."

"I don't see how it's obvious," Apsara stated.

"I have to agree with her," Lorena said. Maleko waved their words away.

"Elion will be able to know exactly where the God of Death is at all times. He'd be a perfect help. And if you want to kill him afterwards, you have the right to do so," Maleko said to Lorena. Elion could see the wheels turning in her head.

"You do know that I could just get you all locked up instead of helping you, right?" Elion said. "Maybe, let's not kill me at the end of this?"

"We could either kill you now or kill you later," Lorena declared. Elion looked at each of their eyes before nodding, dejectedly. He would rather postpone his demise and think of a plan to get out of it in the meantime.

"Fine, sure," he said.

"So, we're not killing him," Apsara said, her eyes still not leaving Elion's. Her hands were gripping the shard of glass so hard, Elion didn't know how she wasn't bleeding. Maleko shook his head.

"No, we're not," he stated. She put the shard of glass in her pockets so quickly Elion barely had time to register it.

"He'll help us," Maleko said, smiling. Elion tried to smile back.

13

"Find the witch, find the portals, protect the Saviors," Rhea said, as she turned towards Khalon. It was the same scene on the battlefield. The same memory Khalon kept playing over and over in his head. But, this time, she was saying something different.

"Rhea? Rhea, are you okay?" Khalon asked, his voice desperate. He reached for her, but she took a step back. Her copper eyes were glazed over as she stared at him.

"Find the witch, find the portals, protect the Saviors," Rhea repeated. "They're in terrible danger."

"Rhea, where are you? I'll come find you," Khalon promised, his heart pounding in his chest.

"Don't," her voice was harsh. He took a step back as he took her in. Her face looked more gaunt than usual, but still had round features. Her hair was a little longer, almost fiery in the light. Hellfire flickered deep in her eyes, like she was trying to keep the flames from coming to the surface.

"Why?" Khalon's voice broke.

"There's more important duties that you need to attend to. You're the only person I can trust, Khalon. I'm risking everything just by talking to you," Rhea whispered. Guilt bubbled up in his throat as he reached out for her again. She seemed to glide backwards.

"I promised you I would've sacrificed myself to save you," he said, roughly. Rhea's eyes bore into his.

"Khalon, I'm a Celestial. My fate was always to die, eventually. You and I could never be."

"But, you said—"

"I know what I said," her voice was dismissive. "Listen to my words now. Find the Saviors. Then, come find me. You have a score to settle."

"A score?"

"That brand on your back. The Death God has claimed you," she said, pointing towards her own back. He knew ink went down the length of her spine, a tattoo that had Celestial letterings on it marking her as the God of Death. The same letterings burned into his own skin.

"What does it mean?" he asked, his voice quiet. Her eyes looked down before glancing back up at him.

"Death is coming for you."

———

Khalon's eyes snapped open, the domed ceiling the only thing above him. He wiped the sheen of sweat off of his forehead as he rolled onto his side. It was Rhea. It was *really* her, not just a memory. And she wanted him to do something.

"Death is coming for you," her voice repeated the phrase in his head. He reached back to touch his spine, feeling the

puckered Celestial lettering that was identical to Rhea's. Death was coming for him. But, to be honest, that wasn't anything new.

"Are you up?" Aponi asked, sticking her head into Khalon's room. Khalon pulled the blanket up to his chin.

"I'm not," he muttered. "Also, do you ever knock?"

"I forget that you're a dude, honestly," Aponi mused. She closed the door, and then opened it a sliver.

"But, seriously, we have to go," she said. "So, get a move on."

Before she could shut the door, Khalon asked, "You're sure Rhea's gone?" Aponi paused.

"As far as I know, Rhea hasn't appeared in the body. It's just been him," she said. "But, she might still be in there. I doubt it's a very big part, though."

"What do you mean by that?" Khalon asked, forgetting about holding the blanket to his chest. Aponi wasn't fazed. She opened the door wider as she stepped in, closing it behind her.

"Her soul is what put the Mortiferis to sleep. You realize that, right? She exploded, essentially. The imprint of the Death God's soul on her is what caused the Mortiferis to obey," Aponi explained. She grabbed a random shirt from Khalon's dresser and threw it to him. He caught it. "But, if she's still in there, it's just the bits of her soul that the God of Death was holding on to. It's not enough for her to be... living. Not like how she was before."

"She sacrificed herself. Split herself," Khalon muttered.

"Right," Aponi said. "It's complicated, but I don't think that when you find her, you're going to like what you find."

"She spoke to me, in a dream," he said, his voice faraway. Aponi squinted her eyes.

"You've dreamt of her before, in the past," she pointed out. "You're connected to the Death God in some way. Perhaps, even Rhea herself. What did she say?"

"She told me not to try and find her right now. She said find the witch, find the portals, protect the Saviors," Khalon repeated. "She told me to come find her after that. But, only because Death has a score to settle with me."

"You've been claimed by the Death God," Aponi nodded.

"She doesn't want me to save her," he whispered, dumb-founded. He looked down at his scarred hands.

"She can't be saved, Khalon," Aponi mumbled. "But, you better not let yourself get down about it. I don't think Khai will be very helpful in protecting the lot of us as we go through Caedoxia." Khalon flashed a small smile at the lightning bird.

"Kamaria is plenty of protection," he pointed out. Aponi smirked.

"Even the Goddess of War praised her," she said.

"The highest honor," Khalon smiled. She grabbed his armor and his dragon stone sword, handing it to him.

"Let's go," she said. "There's no time to waste. Especially if Rhea herself is warning us." Khalon took the armor and the weapon from Aponi's small hands.

"All right, all right," he muttered, slipping his clothes on. "I'm coming."

———

Kamaria was tapping a booted foot as Khalon walked up. She threw him a silent glare as the sound from the giant hover car gave him a headache. The hover car was in the shape of a sleek, silver pill. Nothing like the car that Rhea pointed out to him all those months ago that humans used to drive in the past.

"What?" he mouthed. She signed something Khalon couldn't catch and then walked towards the opened door of the hover car. Jabulani graciously helped her into the car as Khai rolled his eyes next to Khalon.

"She hates when people are late." His voice drifted towards Khalon's ears. *So, that must've been what she was signing*, Khalon thought.

"Where's Esi?" Khalon asked, looking around.

"Esi's not coming," Aponi said as she sauntered past him.

"Why?" he inquired. He felt weird that the one person who could predict how this would turn out would not be coming with them.

"She's a liability. Especially in Caedoxia," Khai pointed out.

"But, she can literally tell us the future," Khalon retorted. His eyes darted down towards the small bruises on the sides of Khai's face. As his jaw clenched, Khai turned away.

"Yeah, but she could possibly die if we take her with us," Aponi threw over her shoulder. Khalon's lips tightened. He didn't know if leaving Esi in Invenire was really a great idea. But, before he could open his mouth to say so, Jabulani clapped his shoulder.

"Esi will be protected. I won't let her leave my sight," he

said, his voice comforting. Khai rolled his eyes again, and even though Jabulani caught the action, he didn't say anything.

"Thanks Jabu," Khalon said, mirroring Jabulani. He patted his shoulder and walked towards the hover car. Kamaria was sitting in the front seat, her arms crossed. She gave Khalon a bored look.

"Get in," she signed. Khalon knew better than to disobey the Ustrinian Queen. He quickly got into the back seat of the hover car. Khai sat in the front seat next to Kamaria, for whatever reason, and Aponi took the seat next to Khalon.

Once the last door closed, Kamaria flew out of the castle at an alarming speed, Jabulani becoming a speck of dust in a second.

"Wait, what are you doing? Where are you going?" Aponi asked, grabbing Khai's headrest as she pulled herself forward. Khai signed the words to Kamaria who glanced at him. Khalon was sure she only saw half of the signs.

"Can't land in Caedoxia," she signed, haltingly. Khalon's eyebrows furrowed as Khai translated, annoyance dripping in every word.

"Why?" Aponi asked, her voice going up an octave.

"Because she's Kamaria and she doesn't know what she's doing most of the time," Khai muttered. Kamaria jerked the hover car, Khai hitting the side of his head on the window next to him. He quickly threw a glare in her direction. She beamed back, her sharpened teeth on full display.

"Seriously, why are we not going all the way to Caedoxia?" Aponi asked. Khai quickly translated to Kamaria who rolled her eyes at his obvious attempt to get her to miss most of the words.

"Throw them off," she signed, haltingly again. Khalon looked out the window at the trees underneath them. He recognized this forest. No Man's Land.

"The God of Death's temple?" he asked, his eyebrows raised.

"Throw *who* off?" Aponi asked as Khai loosely translated. Kamaria let out a huff as she signed, demandingly: *Quiet.* Aponi gave Khalon a look as she slowly turned to look out the window.

"Why would we go to the God of Death's temple?" Khalon asked her. Aponi shrugged, annoyed.

"Who knows."

Kamaria landed the hover car at the base of the temple. It was just as Khalon remembered it. Unlike the other temples around Asynithis, this temple was still standing. It wasn't in ruins.

The black ebony steps leading up to the black temple shone in the setting sunlight as Khalon walked out of the hover car. The pond of tears was still there by the side of the temple. The only thing different was that it was colder than it was before. The trees around them had lost their leaves, and it looked like no one had cleaned the steps in a while.

Khalon kept imagining Rhea would be sitting on the giant seat in the middle of the temple. And even though he could hardly see it, he knew it was empty.

"Why are we here?" Khalon asked, his voice gruff. Kamaria was signing at Khai as Khai just stared at her hands, his light brown eyes almost glazed over.

"What is she saying?" asked Khalon. Khai's unfocused eyes focused on him. He shrugged.

"I don't know. I'm not listening," he muttered. Kamaria's jaw dropped.

"I only caught a little of it," Aponi said. "Something about his mother and—" She stopped talking as Khai gave her a cold stare.

"It doesn't pertain to what's going on right now," he said, his cold gaze on Khalon. He had seen that gaze on Queen Aoife's face before.

"Okay," Khalon said, dismissing the matter. "I just want to know why we're here." Aponi translated for Kamaria who looked at the untouched temple in disgust.

"Taking an official Ustrinian hover car into Caedoxia air space would alert our enemies that I'm out of the country. And we don't really want Aureum to know we're headed to Caedoxia," Kamaria signed as Aponi translated.

"Wouldn't the troops have seen the hover car leave?" Khalon pointed out. She flashed a pointed smile.

"In the direction towards Aureum," she signed. "They might think we have a lead on their magic elf, considering who my sister is. They'll be too busy searching Aureum, rather than attacking Invenire."

"You really think they won't attack Invenire knowing that their queen is gone?" Khai asked, his arms crossed over his chest.

"I didn't really have much of a choice. This was the next best plan," she signed, a scowl on her face.

"How did you not have a choice?" he retorted, his face twisted in confusion.

"Jabulani, probably," Aponi muttered. Kamaria nodded her head.

"What? You can't say no to him or something?" Khai asked, taking a step forward as he signed.

"He's just concerned about my safety," Kamaria signed back, her head held up high.

"Concerned? If he was concerned about your safety, would he have you leave in an official Ustrinian hover car?" Khai pointed out.

"No matter what, what's done is done," Khalon said, stepping in between the two.

"So, how do we get to Caedoxia?" Aponi asked, looking at the three of them. She frowned as Kamaria smiled at her.

"I better not be a part of this plan," Aponi muttered.

"Oh, but you are," Kamaria signed. As she told Aponi what she wanted her to do, Khalon looked back towards Ustrina. There was a growing, gnawing feeling in the back of his neck as he stared at the horizon. Despite what Kamaria wanted to believe, Invenire was going to fall. He could feel it.

14

Valerian helped Poseidon out of the dungeons of the ruined building. Caedoxia, somehow, still stood. The bright lights illuminated the stark darkness of night.

"The oligarchy wasn't destroyed?" Poseidon asked, an eyebrow raised as he stood on the edge of the cliff that looked down at the city of Byrrus, the capital of Caedoxia. It almost looked untouched, like a battle never occurred there. Perhaps it never did.

"The Court is made of mostly the undead. Not easy to kill. But also, easy to replace," Valerian spoke. He walked down the length of the cliff, a path leading towards Byrrus. Valerian looked over his shoulder, his golden hair swishing along his back as he did. His golden eyes seemed to glow in the darkness.

"Are you coming?" Poseidon resisted the urge to say, *"I'd follow you anywhere"* hypnotized by the dryad's beauty. Instead, he cleared his throat and nodded. They walked side by side for a little while, the cover of trees slightly obscuring the light from the city below.

"So, you want me to kill my brother," Poseidon stated, filling the silence. Valerian nodded.

"We have two operatives in the palace now, but I have a feeling they will only be able to destroy the Celestial vessel rather than the soul of Death."

"This is a group of people?" Poseidon's eyebrows jumped. Valerian smirked as he looked away.

"You thought I was acting alone?" he quipped.

"Would be easier if you were acting alone," Poseidon murmured. Valerian's eyebrow cocked as he glanced at the Sea God.

"You were planning on killing me," he mused. Poseidon flashed him a brilliant smile.

"Better than the other way around."

"You're afraid of dying," Valerian said, almost matter-of-factly. The arrogance in the dryad's voice made Poseidon bristle. He stood up straighter.

"Afraid is a big word."

"You're not fearful of what lies beyond?" Poseidon shrugged at the question.

"If the underworld is no more, there isn't anything else after life ends," he said.

"How are you so sure?"

"I came from nothing. I will return to nothing," was all he said. Valerian turned slightly, his full lips pursed as he regarded the Sea God. Poseidon shook his head, determined to change the subject.

"So, you're a dryad. A male one at that," Poseidon said. Valerian smirked.

"What about it? In all your years, you've never seen a male dryad?"

"I've seen one. But, only once," Poseidon remembered. "Freya had one as a temple servant. Although, she went by Jacheongbi then. One of the most beautiful creatures I'd ever seen. Dryads are gorgeous. But, a rare male dryad. Well..."

"Do you miss her?" the dryad asked, suddenly.

"Of course," Poseidon said, his voice barely above a whisper. Freya's last reincarnation's face flashed through his mind. The memory was enough to cause a pang in his chest. The city of Byrrus was closer now, the mouth of the forest opening towards an alleyway.

"Killing my brother won't be easy," Poseidon said, as his feet touched the asphalt road.

"Adamar was able to kill all of you. Surely, there is *some* way," Valerian spoke, leading the way into the heart of Byrrus. Poseidon had seen the capital city of Caedoxia multiple times in his long life. But, every time, it amazed him. It was so different to the rest of Asynithis, much like how the world was when humans ran it, so long ago. Some of the buildings were made of glass, full of windows. And they seemed to touch the sky.

Byrrus was most busy at night, since most of the creatures who lived in Caedoxia were nocturnal. And with the moon high in the sky, the streets were filled with creatures going about their night. Rushing to work or fulfilling errands. Poseidon looked at the creatures as he considered Valerian's request.

"There is one way to kill the Gods," he said, his voice low so no one would overhear them. He turned towards Valerian. "The problem would be getting it."

———

Elion turned the corner quickly as he walked down the length of the palace. There was only one section of the Aureum castle that no one usually ventured down, and that was the late queen's greenhouse. The marble floors that led up to the arched green doors were covered in dust. The door was slightly ajar as Elion pushed against it, the wooden door creaking as he did. Maleko, Apsara, and Lorena turned their heads to look at him as he pushed the green doors shut. A resounding thud filled the room.

"*This* was the best meeting place you could come up with?" Lorena asked, her arms across her chest.

"You don't think Matilda would come looking for us, do you?" Maleko asked, his brown eyes worried. Lorena snorted.

"Oh, she'll definitely be looking for us in about..." she looked out the large glass windows that overlooked the gardens as she squinted at the sun, "an hour, probably."

"What do you know, Elion?" Apsara said, getting right to the point.

The other night, the three of them pretty much threatened Elion into helping them kill the God of Death. However, even if Elion wouldn't fully admit it to himself, he was glad to be doing something other than sitting in this palace, listening to his brothers talk about taking over the world.

"The God of Death tends to visit Than frequently, when Essarae isn't staring at him listlessly," Elion informed. Lorena wrinkled her nose.

"Who's Than?" He turned towards her, but couldn't

meet her eyes. The look of hatred on her face, the face so similar to Pilar's, was burned into the back of his eyelids.

"He's the son of Adamar," Elion said. Her mouth dropped.

"You mean the *dead* son of the king? The reason why so many servants were slaughtered that night?"

"Adamar had a son?" Maleko asked, rubbing his chin as he thought.

"Why would he hide the fact that he has an heir?" Apsara said, her dark eyes boring holes into Elion's skin.

"It's not really Adamar's. I mean, I guess it is. But, he's supposed to be the son of Death, as well," Elion explained, shrugging. Maleko's eyes widened.

"Is that even possible?" he asked, turning towards Apsara, as though she would have the answer. She didn't move.

"Celestials are infertile. They can't have children," Apsara said, repeating a common morsel of knowledge that all creatures of Asynithis knew.

"I don't know how," Elion shrugged. "I just know the Death God created Than and put him into Essarae. Than isn't a normal looking elf either. Freya—the God of Love— could see it right away when the baby was still in Essarae."

"So, he has a spawn," Maleko said, his jaw clenching.

"The God of Death plans to put the rest of his soul into Than's, eventually. I think the Death God will be using him as his vessel, but the child is different from normal Celestials," Elion said.

"Different how?" Apsara asked, her eyes flashing.

"He grows really fast. He's never awake. I don't really think he's alive. Not yet, anyways."

"How is she going to put the rest of her soul into Than's?" Maleko asked, taking a wobbly step forward. *"I will be going to sleep for a while,"* Rhea had said.

"She said she needs to sleep," Elion repeated. "I think that would probably be the perfect time to strike." Maleko cracked his neck before nodding his head.

"Sounds good to me," he said, looking over at Apsara, as if for validation. She nodded her head, her eyes not leaving Elion's. He could remember what she looked like as a mermaid. How beautiful, but how lethal she looked in the water. In her human form, she still looked like she could snap his spine in half. Elion shook his head.

"I think this is bigger than killing the Celestial body. We might need to destroy Than as well," Elion whispered.

"That sounds like too much work," Lorena said, picking at her nails. "The merpeople just want their people to be safe. For them to be taken to a safe place, they need to kill Rhea's body. Am I right?" She turned to look at the King of Argentiunda. Maleko nodded his head, curtly.

"I hope I'm not overstepping, your highness," Elion started. Maleko shook his head as Apsara narrowed her eyes. "To be frank, wouldn't you be able to save the merpeople by destroying the soul of the God of Death?"

"That sounds more difficult, as Lorena pointed out," Maleko mused.

"Yes, but... My brother plans on, not just conquering this world, but all the worlds. The worlds in different realms. And if he succeeds in that, your people will never be able to go back to the water. Ever." Maleko's eyes mirrored Apsara's.

"How do you figure that?"

"Because he will kill the Saviors. The Death God plans

on killing them. And if they never step foot into Asynithis, the plague the merpeople are inflicted with will never be cured," Elion stated. Maleko stared at him for a long while, processing Elion's words.

"The King of the Seas, the uniter of ocean floors. He will cure the disease that plagues creatures beyond shores..." Maleko said, under his breath.

"It's written into the stars," Apsara said, pointedly looking at Maleko. He rolled his eyes at her words.

"You're talking about what those Savior heads say out in the streets?" Lorena asked, a hand on her hip.

"Savior heads?" Elion asked, his head cocking to the side.

"Tell us more about these... Savior heads. What is it that they say?" Maleko said, gesturing for Lorena to continue. She blew a curl off of her face.

"Basically, they just repeat some prophecy. They believe that the world can only be saved by the Saviors. And if the Saviors don't come, our world will be destroyed by the Mortiferis," Lorena droned. She rolled her eyes. "No one is going to come save us though. Saviors or no Saviors."

"The Saviors are real," Elion insisted. "I watched An create them." Lorena's eyebrows furrowed as he finally met her eyes.

"Then, you really think we'll all be asleep at some point. Only to awaken once the Saviors come to Asynithis." She seemed to be asking a question, but her voice stayed flat.

"Why do you think we'd stay asleep?"

"It's what they say in the streets. 'Asynithis will awaken once the Mother takes a step. The world will be retaken once the Mother has wept. For she has all life coursing through her veins. And the world will grow despite the ash that remains.' It's saying that we'll all be asleep and our world would be made of ash by the time the Mother comes, isn't it?" Lorena said.

"You memorized it?" Elion asked.

"It's basically like a song at this point," she said, crossing her arms once again.

"I don't like that fate," Maleko muttered.

"Maybe killing the God of Death will change Asynithis' fate," Elion pointed out. "*Really* killing him."

"Perhaps killing Adamar would change the course of destiny," Apsara pointed out. "Rather than just the God of Death." Elion froze. He hated his brother. A part of him really despised him. But, he was still his brother. And that instinctual part of him wanted to protect Adamar.

Even though these thoughts were going through his head, he merely said, "Perhaps."

"We can kill both," Lorena said, steel in her eyes. She looked over at Elion. "You said he killed my cousin?"

"He did."

"Then, I'll kill him," she resolved. The look on her face told him that she was serious about it as well.

"Adamar was manipulated by the God of—"

"Don't pull that," Lorena interrupted. His eyes widened as her hazel eyes met his. "You know who he is." And Elion couldn't argue with that. Instead, he closed his mouth.

"So, we try to change the fate of Asynithis," Maleko said, turning towards Apsara. A smirk twitched at the corners of her mouth as she met Maleko's gaze.

"I thought you said you can't change one's fate."

"I never said I wouldn't try to," he said back. He turned towards Elion, a determined look on his brown face.

"Do you know how to kill the God of Death?" he asked. Elion nodded his head, almost sheepishly.

"The only way to kill a God's soul is by using a Mortiferis."

15

If Adamar could kill every single person who spoke to him right now, he would. After a dismal meeting with his brother Edwyrd where he said:

"Batula is giving birth! I have to go." In which he promptly left the room without even *waiting* for Adamar's permission. And with Ardryll not listening to a single word Adamar was saying as well as Elion being nowhere to be found, he was in a positively murderous mood. He contemplated stabbing Ardryll in the eye as his brother flipped through a holographic newspaper.

"Ardryll," he said, his voice the epitome of patience. Ardryll raised his eyebrows but didn't look up.

"Did Edwyrd mention who was going to replace him?" he asked. Ardryll dragged his finger across the hologram, moving the page. Adamar didn't know when Ardryll even got a holographic machine. He normally preferred to read the old fashioned way.

"No, not to me at least. Perhaps Elion is replacing him,"

Ardryll drawled, his voice in the same bored tone it always was. Adamar clenched his jaw.

"Speaking of Elion, I suppose you haven't seen him?" He shook his head, his wavy white hair slightly obscuring his face.

"No, but you know Elion. Still a child," Ardryll said.

"He needs to stop acting like one," Adamar spoke through gritted teeth. Ardryll's eyes glanced up upon recognizing his tone. *Finally*, Adamar thought bitterly.

"Why? So you can conquer all the realms?" The sarcastic tone Ardryll was using made Adamar want to rip his throat out. He slowly closed his palm as he leaned forward, the table pushing against his chest.

"You're lucky that you're my brother," he threatened, his voice low. Ardryll just looked away.

"Has Lord Crispin heard any news about the elf?" Adamar said, after a moment. He leaned back in his chair. Ardryll dragged his finger across the hologram, his posture still lazy and bored, but his finger trembled ever so slightly.

"I haven't heard from him yet, no," he said, his voice quiet. Adamar stared at his brother for a long while, Ardryll not meeting his gaze.

"You can go," he ordered. Ardryll didn't waste a moment's notice, gathering his things as quick as lightning as he nearly fled out of the room. Adamar put his head into his hands.

His brothers were all idiots. They couldn't see the world that he was trying to create, the vision that he had. Edwyrd was more obsessed with Batula than anything, Ardryll was the laziest person Adamar had ever met, and Elion... Well, Elion just seemed like a child. A child who still had an ideal vision of the world and who refused to see reality. Not everything was as black and white as Elion thought it was.

Adamar nearly growled as he pushed out of his seat. It felt as if he were trying to babysit more than one person, and he needed his brothers to be ready to help him rule all the realms. He would be the greatest Aureum King to ever wear the crown, if he were to pull it off. And, unfortunately, he needed the God of Death to do it.

The Mortiferis were asleep, hidden in the abandoned dungeons of the Aureum palace. They were the ultimate army. Anything they touched was consequently immediately destroyed. And without the God of Death, Adamar didn't have the Mortiferis. But, to possess his son...

He clenched his fist as he pushed through the doors of his son's quarters. Essarae was asleep, half her body lying on the child's bed. Her body was sprawled across Than's as his little chest rose and fell. He tried to keep the shock from spreading onto his face as he looked at the child.

Than only looked around two years old the last time Adamar had checked in on him, despite being around six months old. Now, he looked like he was around four or five. Adamar ground his teeth together as he made his way towards his wife.

"Essarae, my darling," he whispered, trying to make his voice as gentle as possible. She looked up at him. Her cheeks were sunken in and her eyes were glazed over. It was as if the child was, somehow, taking her life force away.

It was only for a second. Only a second could Adamar look into the eyes of his beloved before she turned away, as though he weren't there, as if he were simply just air. His fist clenched as he stared at the back of her head. Her white hair was done up in complicated braids. It wasn't something she did herself. The woman who used to love doing her hair was now letting her handmaidens do it.

If Than wasn't the property of the God of Death, Adamar would've killed him. He would've slit his throat like he did to every admirer that caught Essarae's attention.

"He's grown," her voice pierced through Adamar's murderous thoughts. Quickly, he kneeled down to be beside her, her light gray eyes still on the face of Than, the child she carried.

"Yes, by a lot it seems," Adamar confirmed, not knowing what else to say. Essarae suddenly grabbed his hand, her grip like iron and her fingers were as cold as ice.

"What if he doesn't stop growing? What if he goes through his whole life in a mere year?" she asked, her eyes searching Than's face, like the answer was written some-where in his porcelain skin.

"He will stop growing. I guarantee it," Adamar promised. Essarae's eyes finally roved over to him.

"How?" she asked. Her voice was without feeling, without strength.

"He just will."

"He is always asleep, Adamar. He hasn't opened his eyes since that first day," Essarae spoke, her hand releasing his. The loss of touch made the emptiness in Adamar grow.

Before he could tell her anything to comfort her, the doors to Than's room opened. Adamar whipped around to start telling off whoever it was that was disturbing his time with his wife, but the words got stuck in his throat.

Rhea glided into the room with ease, her feet hardly touching the ground as she moved towards the sleeping child. Essarae suddenly stood up, her gray eyes flashing angrily as she looked at the Death God.

"You poisoned him," she hissed. "You should leave. I demand for you to leave." Rhea ignored Essarae's outburst, not even deigning to give the queen a glance. Her hand pushed back the growing black hair of Than, off of his forehead.

"You should have your wife leave the room as we talk," Rhea said, a thousand whispers following after. Her copper eyes glanced up, meeting Adamar's.

"I'm not leaving. This is my son. And I'm Queen of Aur—"

"If you don't get your wife out of here, Adamar," Rhea interrupted, her gaze unmoving, "Then I'll be forced to get rid of her myself. And I'm sure you wouldn't like that." His blood ran cold.

"Essarae, please." Essarae shook her head at Adamar's pleading. He tried to pull her hands into his own, but she tore them out of his grip.

"My darling, you need to leave the room," he whispered. She refused, refused to even take her eyes off of the Death God.

"As your king," Adamar said, his voice lowering, "I order you to leave the room." His wife shuddered at the tone of his voice, but she didn't dare disobey him. Mechanically, Essarae slowly left the room. The handmaidens outside of the door rushed to her side as the door was gently closed shut.

"What is it?" Adamar asked, his tone annoyed. Rhea cut him a look that almost made him cower. He lowered his gaze.

"It's almost time," she said, staring back at Than. She tucked his shaggy black hair behind an elven ear.

"What is it exactly that you will be doing?" Adamar asked, daring to take a step closer to the Death God.

"I am moving the rest of my soul into Than's body," Rhea explained. "He already has part of my soul. But, it isn't enough for him to be walking around and living. He is a shell. Much like the Mortiferis. I can't create living souls, unfortunately."

"So, he's not a Celestial," Adamar said. He already knew this. When Than was a baby, he had checked his back for the Celestial marking. The one that would proclaim him to be the God of Death's vessel. But, nothing was there.

"No," Rhea shook her head. "He's not a Celestial. He's something different. Much like how the Saviors will be something different. A being but without a creature soul."

"The Saviors are not human?" Adamar asked. He had heard the prophecy and knew the Saviors were sent to a realm that only had humans.

"Their bodies are. Their souls are not," Rhea shrugged. "The last of the Celestials. But, not. Not really, anyways." Adamar's eyebrows furrowed together as Rhea looked up at him.

"Than doesn't have his own soul. He will just have mine. And hopefully, without any of this girl's soul mixed into it," Rhea said, waving her arms as she looked upon them in disgust.

"Annoying child," she whispered under her breath.

"What do you need me to do?" Adamar asked. Rhea glanced up at him, the hellfire in her eyes seemed to blaze brighter.

"You have to protect this body as I transfer over to the other one. And while I transfer over, if you do find Arveldir, I urge you to rush the process in finding the Saviors. I won't be able to reincarnate in this body," the God of Death said. She looked down at herself. "It might take a long while as I try to detangle myself from this wretched creature."

"It is done," Adamar said, bowing his head slightly. Her lips formed into a smirk.

"I expect nothing less from you, Adamar. Future King of All the Realms." He couldn't help the twitch at the corners of his mouth.

Before he could reply, a knock on the door reverberated throughout the room.

"Yes?" Adamar spoke, lifting his head as the door was opened. A human with short blonde hair stuck her head through the door.

"Lord Crispin is here, your highness," she said, keeping her eyes on the ground. "He has a guest with him." *Right*, Adamar thought. That was why he liked this servant more than the others. A human who knew her place. It was why she was head of the household.

"I must leave, your holiness. I hope you understand," Adamar said, turning towards the God of Death. Rhea didn't look up at him, her fiery gaze still on the sleeping child. Adamar's teeth almost ground together.

"It's probably about Arveldir. Remember what I told you. Find the Saviors, before the others do," Rhea said, turning her gaze onto the Aureum King. His forehead wrinkled.

"Before the others?"

"Yes, those children," she scoffed. She waved the words

away from her as she gestured for Adamar to get a move on. The human servant still stayed bowed, her eyes unblinkingly boring holes into the ground. He nodded once, confusion still marring his brow.

"Yes, of course," he muttered, almost under his breath. The human stood upright at Adamar's words and led him out of the room. The doors closed behind him as he stared at the long hallway before him.

"Children," Adamar said to himself. The human beside him didn't so much as flinch at his words. "What *children* could she be talking about?"

16

Khai stared at Kamaria, flabbergasted.

"You want her to do *what*?" he said, forgetting to sign as he spoke. Kamaria watched his lips before flipping her newly tied braids over her shoulder. He bit the inside of his cheek. *Fuck*, he thought. A lump in his throat grew as he looked away from her. Forgetting to sign to her as he spoke was one of the things he vowed he'd never do to her. Although, she didn't know about this vow.

"Aponi is going to teleport us from here to Byrrus, the capital of Caedoxia," Aponi said for Kamaria as she signed. Aponi sighed and then spoke for herself, "But, I've never worked with that kind of magic before. Not for that long of a distance."

"But you've teleported before?" Khalon assumed. Her shoulders raised to her ears before she dropped them.

"Kamaria had me do it one time a couple of years ago. She thought it would be a good battle strategy, someday," she explained.

Well, we can't just fly there, Kamaria signed, a scowl on her face. *You can at least try.*

"Trying could get someone torn into pieces," Aponi barely mumbled. Khai's eyebrows raised. The dagger in his pocket felt like hot iron as the wheels inside his head turned. It wouldn't be a bad idea. It could save him from what he had to do if Aponi accidentally killed Khalon while transporting him to Caedoxia. He closed his eyes, the guilt bubbling up into his throat, but he swallowed it down.

"Kamaria's right," Khai said. The words felt like poison in his mouth. Not just because of what he was about to suggest, but *also* because he had to say Kamaria was right. The words didn't kill him like he expected them to, but they still hurt like hell.

Kamaria cocked an eyebrow as she leaned back a little, her arms crossing over her chest.

I'm right? she signed quickly, a smirk playing on her lips. Khai tried to ignore her.

"We don't really have a choice," he said, shrugging. "We can't walk to Caedoxia in one night. And we don't know when Adamar is going to find this Arveldir person, so Kamaria... has a point." He wished he could rinse the words out of his mouth with soap.

I truly never thought I'd see the day, Kamaria signed, almost beaming at him. But, her eyes roved over him suspiciously.

"So, you want me to accidentally tear someone up into pieces," Aponi nodded. Khai could feel the tips of his ears redden.

"That's not what I was saying," he said, lifting his chin.

"I'll do it," Khalon said. They were the words Khai was

hoping he would utter. The words that he knew Khalon would say. A martyr to the bitter end.

"I really don't think this is a good—"

"Like Khai said, we don't really have a choice. And I trust you," Khalon interrupted. Aponi stared at him, desperation and pity clouding her eyes.

"I truly think you're putting your trust in the wrong person," she said under her breath.

"Let's just hope your hair doesn't turn as white as an elf's again," Khalon smiled. Aponi shook her head, fear glowing deep in her dark eyes.

"Are you sure you want me to do this?" she asked, signing as she spoke to Kamaria. Kamaria nodded her head once, her arms still crossed. Aponi pursed her lips as she looked up at Khalon. He gave her a disarming smile.

"I'll be okay," he said. "I've been through worse."

"That doesn't make me feel better, Khalon," Aponi pointed out. He put his hand into hers as she closed her eyes. Her lashes fluttered as the eyes beneath her lids moved rapidly.

"Byrrus," she whispered. And then, in a blink, the two of them were gone.

Kamaria slowly turned her body towards Khai and raised an eyebrow.

What? he signed.

You want Khalon dead or something?

What makes you think that? She touched her index finger to her nose as she lowered her chin, her gaze still on Khai, before pointing at him.

I know you. Khai turned away from her.

"Barely," he whispered, signing the words. Kamaria

tapped his shoulder so that he would look at her. Her expression was unreadable.

Is it what Queen Aoife wants... or is it what you want? Her ebony eyes held Khai as prisoner.

"I..." Khai opened his mouth, but his eyes caught sight of Aponi materializing behind Kamaria. Kamaria followed his gaze and looked over her shoulder at Aponi, whose black hair was streaked with white. She was bent over, breathing heavily. But, her dark eyes were resolute.

"Who's next?"

———

Teleporting was a magic Khai had never experienced before. In a blink, he was in the city of Byrrus. It wasn't the first time he had been in Caedoxia's capital, but the sheer difference of the country compared to the rest of Asynithis was always jarring. The cities were built like how humans once built them. Lights were everywhere, and the buildings seemed to touch the sky.

Other countries in Asynithis reverted back to how buildings looked in the olden days, when magical creatures ruled the world. Most magical creatures hated the way the humans decorated Asynithis, with their concrete and steel buildings. But, not the creatures of the night.

Khai turned his head to look at his older brother, knowing he had never stepped foot in Byrrus before. And, just as Khai expected, Khalon's mouth hung open and his eyes looked like they were about to pop out of his head as he stared at the bustling night city.

"You're going to catch a bug in your mouth at this rate,"

Khai muttered. Khalon closed it, swallowing as he did. His eyes roved, taking in the last human made city.

They were dropped at the opening of an alleyway, the concrete sidewalk dipping into the asphalt road. Sleek hover cars were zipping past, almost stacked upon each other. The cars nearly went as high as the buildings.

"I've never seen a city like this before," Khalon said.

"I figured." He turned towards Khai, his eyes lit up like a child's. It made the knife in Khai's stomach twist at the thought of what he had to do to him. His brother's face was normally like stone, unreadable. The vulnerability in Khalon's expression almost made him want to throw up. He trusted Khai enough to show that part of him. To put some walls down. *His trust is misplaced*, Khai couldn't help but bitterly think.

"I thought you said the cities of the humans were all destroyed," Khalon said, referring to the lessons Khai used to share with him when he was locked up in the Ring of Fire. Khai's mouth went dry at the memory. *He remembers them?*

"Uh," he cleared his throat. "They were. But the creatures of the night were never really in hiding. They grew to like the metallic jungle." Khalon nodded as he craned his head to look up at the building next to them.

"Do you think it really reaches the sky?" he asked, his voice low. Khai blinked. He knew Khalon never had any teachings, nothing besides what Khai had taught him. But, it was almost insulting how little he knew about the world. The fact that a member of the Draconian Royal Family was never taught any lessons was degrading, to say the least.

"No, it... it doesn't," Khai whispered. Kamaria appeared next to them, with Aponi gripping her arm tightly. Sweat covered Aponi's tan skin and her dark hair had turned completely white. As white as an elf's. She gritted her teeth.

"I *never* want to teleport again," Aponi hissed. Khai made sure to sign her words to Kamaria, which earned him a shocked glare from the lightning bird.

"Don't tell her!" she insisted. He simply shrugged, smiling widely. Kamaria rolled her eyes before taking in the city before them. It was alive, despite it being the middle of the night, with many creatures—terrifying creatures—walking through the streets.

"Where does the witch live?" Kamaria signed to Aponi. Aponi squinted her eyes after translating, trying to see the name of the road they were standing on.

"She lives on 81st street," Aponi said.

———

Khai and Kamaria stared up at the brick front townhouse in awe. The silver nameplate on the side of the house read "Crispus" in fancy lettering. Khalon still looked absolutely starstruck about the whole city. Contrary to their fears, the creatures of Caedoxia barely looked twice at them, consumed by their own schedule to notice two draconians, a phoenix-Inkanyamba, and a lightning bird. Khai slowly turned his head to look at Aponi who was glaring at the townhouse.

"Your cousin is owned by a Crispus?" His voice almost went up an octave. Aponi shrugged as Kamaria gave him a wary glance.

The Crispus witches were some of the most powerful—and morally questionable—witches in all of Asynithis. They were also, unfortunately, a distant relative of Khai's mother. Khai just crossed his fingers that this particular witch wouldn't recognize him.

"Which Crispus is it?" Kamaria signed and Aponi narrowed her eyes as she pressed a small circular button next to the black iron gate.

"Hyacinth Crispus," Aponi said. Khai sucked in a breath.

"Who's that?" Khalon asked, looking between Khai and Kamaria, who had froze. "Who are the Crispus?"

"The Crispus family is the most powerful and oldest family of witches in Asynithis," Khai whispered, his voice barely audible.

"Well, that's what they say anyways," Aponi said, rolling her eyes. Khai darted his eyes towards her, shaking his head slightly.

"No, they are. Even their distant relatives are powerful." Khai looked at the brick townhouse in front of him as he thought about his mother. She only had a fraction of the Crispus power, and yet she was incredibly powerful on her own. He couldn't imagine what a true member of the Crispus family might be like.

"And Hyacinth? Should we be worried about her?" Khalon asked, crossing his lean, muscular arms.

Very, Kamaria signed.

"Great," he said under his breath.

"*Who is it?*" a disembodied voice said over a speaker.

"It's Aponi," Aponi said, her voice sickeningly sweet. The voice paused for a long moment.

"*Who?*" Aponi scowled before plastering on a fake smile.

"Sinopa's cousin?"

"*Who's Sinopa?*" the voice asked. Her jaw clenched as she glared at the speaker.

"The lightning bird in your possession," Aponi hissed.

"*Ohhh,* that *Sinopa,*" the voice said, almost smugly. "*Come in. Though, you're not normally allowed guests.*"

"It's important," Aponi snapped. The gate popped open as the light outside of the townhouse clicked on. Aponi took a deep breath before stepping through the gates. Khai and Kamaria exchanged a look before following after her. Khalon's eyes narrowed as he surveyed the area, his head on a constant pivot.

Before Aponi could touch the knob, the door opened. A woman in her thirties with dark hair and silver eyes stood in the foyer. She smiled, her teeth impeccably white.

"Hyacinth," Aponi said, her voice mechanical.

"Lightning bird," she said, her voice like butter. Her glowing silvery eyes slithered over each and every one of them. Khai held his breath as her eyes met his. She smirked.

"What is the Queen of Ustrina and the false King of Draconia doing on my doorstep?" she asked, her voice piercing the night. His jaw tensed at her words. Is this what the rest of Asynithis thought of him? It wasn't a secret, now, that Khalon had the spirit of the dragon within him. But, Khai stupidly thought maybe people would think he had it too... somehow.

"Could you let us inside first? You know, away from prying eyes?" Aponi said, her voice a tad harsh. Khai looked at her in surprise. *She couldn't possibly be stupid enough to provoke a Crispus witch, could she? What am I thinking, of course she is.*

Hyacinth's gaze turned amused as her eyes stopped on

Khalon's figure. He just held her silvery gaze with not a morsel of emotion flickering across his face. She finally broke eye contact, looking back at Aponi.

"Come in," she said, smiling wider. She waited until they were all inside before flicking her wrist, the door closing behind them as she did.

"Where's Sinopa?" Aponi asked, crossing her arms. Her eyes studied the foyer. Hyacinth shrugged as she beckoned for them to come deeper into her home.

The townhouse was covered in dark wood decorations. The walls were a deep mahogany with moldings of different depictions of the war between the magical creatures and humans. Khai stared at the gruesome scenes as he walked by them, Hyacinth leading them to her sitting room. Khalon leaned down towards Khai's ear, causing him to flinch.

"Sorry," Khalon muttered. "But, why are her eyes silver? She smells like a human." If Hyacinth heard Khalon's question, she didn't show it. Khai glared up at his older half-brother as he shook his head.

"The Crispus witches *are* human, technically. Physically speaking. However, they have so much magic in their bodies, that it changed the color of their eyes," he hissed. "Some Crispus witches' bodies can't handle the magic, so much so that they combust at some point."

"What do you mean?" Khalon asked, his eyebrows furrowed.

"I mean, their body melts to nothing. The silver in their eyes seems to encase their whole body. It's why they stopped intermarrying because the magic was too much for their physical selves," Khai whispered.

"Intermarrying?" Khalon said, his voice louder than it

should've been. Hyacinth's head turned as she looked at the two brothers, her arm extended towards the sitting room.

"We haven't done that for years," she said, smoothly. Her gaze focused onto Khai. "You should know that better than anyone else." Khai felt the heat fill his face.

"I don't know what you mean," he muttered. She smirked. Circling around the room, her heels clicking along the floor, she grabbed a glass of amber liquid before settling down in one of her dark green couches. She gestured for them to do the same.

Khai sat across from her, Kamaria taking the seat next to him. Khalon and Aponi hung back, clearly showing the difference between the ranks. Khai rubbed his hands on his dragon-scaled pants.

"This must be serious if the lightning bird's hair is white," Hyacinth said, sipping on her drink. "She must've used a bit too much of her stolen magic."

"Where is Sinopa, Hyacinth?" Aponi said, enunciating every word. Hyacinth smirked.

"First, ask what it is you came here for," she said, meeting Aponi's fiery gaze. "Then, I'll lead you to dear Sinopa."

"If you hurt her—"

"What? You'll kill me like you did with your witch?" Hyacinth said, her gaze hardening. "I'd love for you to try."

"What do you know about the other realms?" Kamaria spoke. Khai's eyes widened at hearing her voice. She had a slight lisp, but other than that, she sounded like she spoke all the time.

Since when could you talk? Khai signed to her. Kamaria glared at him.

I'm deaf, not mute. Khai's jaw remained open. She tapped it with her pointer finger before he closed it.

"The other realms? You mean the alternate universes that An created?" Hyacinth clarified, her finger circling the top of her glass. Aponi signed for Kamaria and then Kamaria nodded.

"Correct," she said. Khai was still reeling from hearing her voice for the first time.

"I know enough about it," Hyacinth replied, her voice slow and drawn out.

"Do you know how one would travel to a different realm?" Kamaria asked after Aponi translated for her. Hyacinth's eyes narrowed.

"The portals have been closed," she said.

"But, could they be opened?" Khai asked. Hyacinth stared at him for a long while, her silver eyes burning holes into his face.

"You seem to already know the answer, draconian," she said, her voice harsh.

"Arveldir," Kamaria spoke, pronouncing his name slowly. "What do you know about him and his family?" The witch was quiet for a moment as she sipped on her drink.

"Hmm," Hyacinth said, as she thought. Her silver eyes looked up at the ceiling before returning to Kamaria.

"It's old magic. And it's only magic given to the protectors of the world," she finally said. Khai leaned forward.

"What do you mean by protectors of the world?" She took another small sip.

"An gave each world a protector. There's a Protector of Asynithis, a Protector of Earth, and so on. It's passed down to the oldest child. They can control the portals, to an extent," Hyacinth said.

"And Arveldir is…?" Khalon said, speaking out of turn. Khai looked up at him, a reprimand burning his tongue. Hyacinth smiled as she met Khalon's gaze.

"The Protector of Asynithis, yes."

"So, he can open the portals of Asynithis," Khalon muttered.

"Yes," she confirmed. "And when he does, we are leaving this world."

"What do you mean by 'we?'" Khai asked, his eyes narrowing.

"The witches. Maybe some other creatures of Caedoxia. But, we're leaving and going to Earth," she said, shrugging. "No one wants to be ruled by the elves. And no one can go up against those monsters they're using."

"Is this just among witches or is this the plan for all of Caedoxia?" Kamaria asked. Hyacinth's gaze slithered over to her.

"The Court decided it," she said. Khai and Kamaria exchanged a glance. The Court was the group of creatures who ruled over Caedoxia, as they didn't have a royal family. This meant that Caedoxia knew Aureum's plan before Esi had come to see it. So much in advance that they had already begun to plan for the portals to be opened.

"So all of Caedoxia will be infiltrating Earth?" Khalon more said than asked. Hyacinth blinked as she cocked her head to the side.

"I don't like that word. 'Infiltrating.'"

"But that's what you'll be doing. Earth is a planet filled

with humans," Khalon pointed out. "There aren't magical creatures there."

"My body is human," she retorted. "And we'll be saving that planet from them, I'm sure. Considering what the humans did to Asynithis, we'd be doing them a favor by migrating to their world."

"Or you'll destroy it," Aponi said. Hyacinth's gaze turned icy as she looked upon Aponi.

"The portals will open whether you want them to or not. And Caedoxia won't be the only country to find refuge in the new world," Hyacinth said. "The merpeople are dying. I'm sure they will find their way to Earth quickly."

"The merpeople?" Khalon said, his eyes wide with surprise.

"The plague has hit them. The one spoken about in the prophecy," Hyacinth clarified. "They're being killed or enslaved by the thousands. You're saying they shouldn't find refuge on Earth? The magic is being drained from this world. We would all soon cease to exist if we stay here."

"Who's to say the humans won't kill us magical creatures there too?"

"We beat them once. We could beat them again," she said, leaning back in her seat. She shook her head.

"I'm tiring of this conversation. And the sun will be up soon," she said, waving her hand. "You should all go."

"Arveldir," Kamaria spoke as Khai stood up from the couch. "Have they found him?" Kamaria didn't need Aponi to translate the words Hyacinth uttered, her gaze meeting the Ustrinian Queen's.

"Yes."

17

The doors opened to reveal the decadent throne room, Ardryll on one side of the throne. Elion ducked his head as he hurried across the giant space, decorated in white and gold moldings, towards the other side of Adamar who was sitting atop the golden throne shaped like the sun.

"Where were you?" Adamar snapped. He stared straight ahead as Elion hid his hands behind his back.

"Sorry, Brother, I was in a different part of the palace," he whispered. Adamar put up his hand and gestured for the guards to let in their guest.

"This is important," Adamar said under his breath. "Don't make me regret letting you live." Elion stiffened as he focused his attention on the elf walking through the larger-than-life doors. The elf bowed deeply, his long white hair like curtains over his face.

"Please," Adamar said, his voice the epitome of kindness. He gestured for the elf to stand and as he did, his lavender eyes met Elion's. Elion's eyebrows knitted together as he narrowed his gaze. *Lavender eyes?* He had never seen an elf with eyes that color before. Most elves' eyes were gray, green, blue, or some variation of all three. Not purple.

"Arveldir, I presume," Adamar said as the elf's gaze focused on the Aureum King.

"Yes, your highness. I've been told you've been looking for me for some time," Arveldir said. His voice was slow, and he seemed to enunciate every consonant and syllable. Instead of making Elion feel at ease, fear seeped into every one of his bones. There was a distinct metallic smell in the air. The smell of magic. There weren't many elves that had the ability to wield magic. But, this creature seemed to be *made* of it.

"Yes, we have been looking for you for a long while. If you knew about it, may I ask why it took you so long to come to your king?" Adamar said, his pointer finger lightly tapping the armrest of the throne. His voice was innocent enough, but Elion could see the muscle in Adamar's jaw feather. Arveldir smiled.

"Well, I do have a duty, your highness, besides being a citizen of Aureum." It was the wrong answer. Adamar's long fingers gripped the sides of his armrest.

"Is that so?" He cocked his head to the side as he appraised the elf before him.

"However, I have decided this cause is a good one," Arveldir continued, his lavender eyes not darting down in the face of the king's anger. Adamar forced a smile onto his face. *Even* he *could feel the magic pouring out of this elf, surely,* Elion thought. *He wouldn't do something stupid, would he?*

"We're so glad, Arveldir," the name in Adamar's voice sounded like a curse. "So, you will do as we have asked."

"No one says no to the God of Death," Arveldir replied. Elion winced as Adamar stood up slowly, walking towards Arveldir like he was his prey. *What was I thinking? Adamar believes himself to be a god.*

"Let me correct you, dear elf," the king said, twirling a small dagger in his fingers before pressing it against Arveldir's jugular. Arveldir didn't flinch in the slightest. Instead, he looked down at Adamar as though he were a petulant child.

Elion glanced over at Ardryll, hoping he would do something to stop their brother, but his older brother just had a small smirk playing on his lips. Elion held his breath as he looked back at his eldest brother.

"You do not say no *to me*," Adamar hissed. Arveldir's face remained stoic, his lavender eyes meeting Adamar's blue ones.

"You *do* need me, don't you?" he asked, his voice quiet but matter-of-fact. Adamar pressed the dagger harder, blue blood starting to appear on Arveldir's pale skin. He didn't drop his gaze, however.

"Where do you get the confidence to disrespect your king?" Ardryll finally spoke up. The elf glanced up at the third oldest brother. His eyebrow just raised.

"My family were the first creatures to ever breathe the air of Asynithis. We protect this world. We have no king," Arveldir said, his voice without emotion. Elion blinked. His family protects Asynithis?

Ardryll cracked a lazy smile before saying, "Your family is still mortal." Arveldir's lavender eyes hardened. Adamar took the dagger away from the elf's neck before placing it back in his robes.

"What would happen if Asynithis' protectors all died?" Ardryll finished, as he picked his nails. His light blue eyes looked up to meet Arveldir's gaze.

"What is it that you would have me do?" Arveldir said, his voice mechanical. Ardryll just smirked, looking towards Adamar. Adamar, on the other hand, looked like he was about to go on a rampage, and Elion felt bad for the servant who walked in his path after this.

The elven king slowly walked back to his throne, sitting upon it as he ran a hand through his long, white hair.

"You'll open the portals," he ordered. Arveldir looked at the king curiously.

"The ones that the God of All closed?"

"Those very same ones," Adamar said, flashing a forced smile. Arveldir mirrored the smile on his own face.

"How are you so sure I can open them?"

"The Death God informed me," Adamar stated, dryly. Arveldir lowered his head a bit, his lavender eyes still on the Aureum King.

"And you want me to open all of them? To all the worlds?" Arveldir clarified.

"Yes," Adamar ordered, his lips hardly moving. Elion looked at his brother in horror. *All of them?* He wanted *all* of them to be opened?

"To open all the portals to all of An's worlds, it will take a long while," Arveldir said, nodding his head. His lavender gaze turned towards Ardryll. "Might be good to keep me alive."

"Of course," Adamar said, leaning back into his throne. "We want you to open the portals to only Earth now."

"Now?" he asked, his lavender eyes widening. The king leaned forward.

"Now." Elion stared at his brother.

"Why now, Adamar? Surely we should wait until Edwyrd comes back," Elion said, interrupting. His brother's cold gaze turned towards him.

"I mean, your highness," Elion corrected, his voice quiet.

"We can't wait. We need to get rid of any opposition as soon as possible," Adamar said, his voice as cold as his gaze.

"But, don't we need to send our armies? And Edwyrd is —" Adamar cracked a small smile.

"We don't need an army to kill the Saviors, Brother," he said, turning his head away. "Ardryll and Lord Crispin's assassins will suffice." He gestured towards Arveldir.

"But, Ada—your highness—" Elion's voice was desperate.

"Open the portals," Adamar said, his voice reverberating throughout the throne room. Arveldir bowed deeply, before standing upright. The room started to shake and the metallic smell became stronger as Arveldir's lavender eyes began to glow.

"This is madness, Adamar," Elion said, his voice still being heard over the wind that had started to pick up around Arveldir. Adamar turned his head to look at Elion, his gaze unfeeling.

"If you're not with me, my dear brother, you're against me," he stated. Elion shook his head, backing away from his oldest brother. Ardryll looked at Elion from beside Adamar, both of their blue eyes staring daggers into him.

"I can't condone this, Adamar. I can't do it." Elion paused before continuing, "I'm not fourteen anymore." Adamar's face contorted as his fingers gripped the sides of his throne.

"Is this about Pilar?" Elion didn't know if he heard the words right, but Adamar's sapphire eyes looked murderous.

"It's about more than her," Elion muttered before turning away. He ran down the length of the throne room, the objects in the room swirling around the mini tornado that was now around Arveldir. His lavender eyes seemed to follow Elion out of the room.

Everywhere he went, the metallic smell of magic followed him. It was seeping out of the earth, at this point. He frantically ran down the hallways, turning any dark-haired servant around as he desperately tried to look for Lorena and the others.

"What's going on little elf?" a deep, rich voice said. Elion turned around. Maleko and Apsara stood in front of him.

"You need to go. You need to get out of here now," he said, pushing them towards the front of the palace. Maleko's brow creased as he stood his ground, turning himself into an immovable rock.

"What is this about?" Apsara said, pushing Elion off of Maleko.

"Do you not smell that?" he asked, his voice trembling. Apsara gently sniffed the air, her dark eyes widening.

"There's... too much magic in the air," Apsara stated, turning towards Maleko. "More than I've felt in months."

"What do you mean by that?" Elion asked. She put her unflinching gaze onto the elf.

"The magic of the world has been lessening. Anyone

who uses magic can feel it," Apsara said, her voice without emotion.

"Merpeople use magic?" Maleko nodded.

"It is how we can transform when we are out of water. It is a… form of magic," he explained. Elion shook his head, waving the words away from his face.

"It doesn't matter. It all doesn't matter now. You need to go. You're not going to be safe here and with him here, you'll be found out immediately. I have a feeling he can see everything that goes on in this world," Elion said, moving to push Apsara's arm but then thought against it after looking at her face. He put his hand down to his side.

"Him? Who's here?" Maleko asked. Apsara gingerly sniffed the air again.

"Probably the creature producing this much magic in the air. Magic strong enough to go against the God of All himself, I'm sure," she guessed. Elion nodded his head ferociously.

"Yes, he said something about being the first creatures to breathe the air of Asynithis or something. He has magic I've never seen before in my life. Magic I've never heard talked about or written about in any of the books," Elion said, waving his hands around as he spoke. He ran a hand through his short, white hair as he took in a shaky breath. Maleko frowned as he stared at the elf.

"Okay, let's take a deep breath, little elf," Maleko said. He motioned for Elion to follow him as he took in a deep breath, puffing out his cheeks. Elion just stared at him before realizing that the Argentiundan King was serious. Maleko gestured more desperately, his face turning a light shade of red. *He can't be serious*, Elion thought, but he quickly took a half-hearted breath in. Maleko blew out the breath he was holding and Elion followed afterwards.

"Doesn't that feel better?" he asked, beaming at Elion.

"Yeah, I guess. A little," Elion said, rubbing the back of his head.

"Good, good. So, you were saying that this creature is the Protector of Asynithis?" Maleko asked. Elion froze. *How did he know about that?*

As if he could see the thought on Elion's face, Maleko said, "Ah, there are legends of one in Argentiunda. I guess not up on the surface though, huh?" He turned towards Apsara. She shrugged, her eyes still on Elion.

"He's opening up the portals," Apsara guessed. Elion nodded.

"He'll do anything the God of Death asks of him," he said. "I have no idea why."

"And if your brother sweetens the deal, I'm sure he'll do anything Adamar asks of him to do as well," Maleko said, his tone sour. He didn't think Adamar would give the elf anything. But, then again, his brother was manipulative in more ways than one.

"You need to go. It's not safe, I'm telling you," Elion insisted.

"Where would we go?" Maleko pushed. "What about my people?"

"You won't be able to save them," Elion said. Apsara glared at him as she took a step forward.

"Do you want to consider changing that sentence?" Apsara said, her voice eerily calm. Elion swallowed as he shook his head.

"Killing the God of Death is going to do nothing now.

Don't you two *see* that? Killing the Death God's body or soul or whatever isn't going to close the portals. Once they're opened, they're opened," Elion explained. "There won't be a refuge for any of you to hide in. My brother plans on taking over all the realms. There won't be anywhere for your people." Maleko and Apsara exchanged a look.

"What do you suggest, exactly?" Apsara finally said after finding an answer in Maleko's expression, crossing her arms.

"Go to Caedoxia. Maybe try to find as many merpeople in Aureum as you can and take them with you."

"We can't just *go* to Caedoxia," she insisted. "We don't have any means to do so." Elion searched his robes and grabbed the keys to the only hover car that he had access to. He put them in Apsara's hands as she stared at them, quizzically.

"Take this hover car," he said, pushing her hands back towards her body. "You need to go. Quickly." Maleko's face was like stone as he looked at Apsara. She pulled a face and then nodded once.

"Let's go," she said, putting a hand on Maleko's shoulder. He kept her gaze before closing his eyes and nodding. Prior to them heading down the hallway that had started to tremble from the sheer magnitude of magic pouring out of Arveldir, Elion grabbed Maleko's arm.

"Where's Lorena?" he asked, his voice distressed.

"Lorena?" Maleko repeated, his eyes widening from the sudden outburst. He looked up at the ceiling as he thought. "She's cleaning one of the bathrooms." Elion's grip tightened as he searched Maleko's face.

"Which one?"

18

Aponi took a step forward, blocking Hyacinth's way out. The witch towered over her, but there was a determination in Aponi's eyes that sent chills down Khalon's spine.

"Step out of my way, lightning bird," Hyacinth said, her face tense. Aponi stood up straighter, as if she were trying to reach the same height that Hyacinth was.

"Where is Sinopa? We're not leaving until I see her," she ordered, her chin held up high. Hyacinth flashed a feral smile as she looked down at the lightning bird.

"Have it your way," she said, waving her hand. The doors to the sitting room opened and the air in front of them seemed to sparkle and glint. A line of sparkles led towards a door down the darkened hallway.

"After you," she said, gesturing towards Aponi. Aponi blinked before walking out of the room, following the sparkled air. Kamaria and Khai seemed to exchange a wary glance before they followed her out. Khalon walked up to

Hyacinth and stood beside her. She was the tallest woman he had ever come across, that wasn't a vampire.

"Yes, Dragon King?" she said, her silver eyes studying the scales on the side of Khalon's face before meeting his eyes. Khalon wrinkled his nose at the remark. She smirked.

"You don't like the title?" she asked, turning her body to face him.

"It's not mine," he responded. Her smirk grew into a grin.

"By the laws of Draconia, you are their rightful king," she said. "You reject your own rules?"

"It's Khai's. I want nothing to do with it," Khalon emphasized, his face unreadable. She searched his eyes before shrugging.

"With Khai as king, you'll never get Draconia back," she said. He could feel that she wanted him to ask. To press for more information. But, Khalon didn't want to know. Whatever it was, if it had to do with Khai, he didn't—couldn't—know.

"Ask the Seer," Hyacinth shrugged. His eyebrows pulled downwards as he glanced at the witch. Esi knew. Whatever it was, Esi knew and didn't tell him. Khalon shook his head. That's not what he needed to know, what he wanted to ask.

"What did you mean when you said the magic is draining from this world?" Hyacinth's dark eyebrows raised.

"Aponi, I'm sure, has felt it, even if her magic was stolen. She hasn't disclosed anything?" Khalon just gave her a blank look. She let out a chuckle.

"She holds things close to her chest, that one. Even though every witch despises her and wants her dead, I do admire her, in a way," Hyacinth said, looking out the doorway that Aponi had walked through. Her silver eyes made its way back to Khalon. "The magic in this world is diminishing. I feel it every day. And with the magic disappearing, so will us magical creatures."

"We'll disappear?" She nodded.

"Anyone who's not human will. Turn into dust as the world drains the magic from us," she said. "Asynithis was made with magic. It needs magic to continue to survive. If the magic is disappearing from its core, it'll take from us."

"You talk as if Asynithis is a creature of its own," Khalon pointed out. She gave him a stern look.

"It is," she said, simply. "The world feeds off of us, and we feed off of it. And if we don't want to die, we must go through the portals once they open."

"The magic will return when the Saviors come?" Khalon asked. A small smile appeared on Hyacinth's lips.

"No, dear draconian," she said, putting a hand on Khalon's cheek. The cheek that had the claw mark of black-red scales. "The magic returns once all the Gods are gone." Khalon's heart fell as he stared at the witch.

"You mean..."

"Yes. Your beloved must die," she whispered. Her silver eyes turned amused. Rhea's face came to the forefront of Khalon's mind. The image of her smiled, her copper eyes turning into two crescent moons as she did.

"How do you—" Before Khalon could finish his sentence, Aponi screamed. Hyacinth's smile grew wider as she turned towards the sound, her face positively gleeful.

"Shall we?" He hurried down the hallway towards the door that was now open at the end of the hall. Khai looked shell shocked as he backed out of the room. Khalon quickly entered it.

Aponi was on her knees, a small white bird in the palm of her hands. Kamaria stood above her, patting her back as Aponi stared at the white bird in horror. It looked like its wings were broken, wrapped in a yellow cast.

"What happened? What is it?" Khalon asked as he got down on his knees to help her. Aponi looked at him and showed him the white bird. The bird's black eyes studied him as she shook her hands.

"Look! Look what she did to my cousin!" she exclaimed. Hyacinth leaned against the door frame as Aponi glowered up at her.

"Although it'll hurt my reputation if you tell anyone, contrary to what you might believe, I didn't hurt a feather on her," Hyacinth said.

"The fuck you mean you didn't hurt a feather on her?" Aponi almost screeched. She lifted her hands so Hyacinth could see the white bird clearly. "Both of her wings are broken!"

"True, but it wasn't *I* who broke her wings," Hyacinth plainly said.

"And she's been turned into this tiny, weak bird!" Aponi cried as she ignored Hyacinth's words.

"I can't very well have a human-sized white bird walk around with me when I go shopping and what not," she said, picking at her nails. Aponi gingerly put her cousin on a perch before stalking up to the Crispus witch.

"You can fix her easily. With a snap of your fingers. And yet, you're letting her walk around as a little paperweight with broken wings," she snapped. "You say you didn't break her wings? No one else should've been able to if my cousin is *your* property. I know how witches treat their thunderbirds." Her white hair seemed to quiver, as if electricity was running down each strand. Hyacinth raised an eyebrow.

"Believe what you want about me, child. But, I don't harm her. I think she's confirmed that for you multiple times," Hyacinth said, her voice quiet.

"How did her wings get broken?" Aponi said through gritted teeth.

"Well, I was having a little soirée," the witch said, running a hand through her dark hair, "and Sinopa had an attitude towards one of the witches. The witch broke both of her arms as punishment."

"And what did you do to the witch?" Aponi said, her voice like ice.

"Nothing," Hyacinth said, frowning at her tone. "What am I supposed to do to a witch who's in her right to punish my lightning bird as she sees fit?"

"Stop it?" Aponi retorted. "You're a Crispus. If you said jump, those witches would ask how high?"

"I *am* a Crispus, Aponi," Hyacinth said, pushing off of the door frame and reaching her full height. Aponi continued to glower at her, the smell of sulfur filling the air. Khalon rubbed his arms as a tingling sensation filled the room. He glanced warily at the lightning bird.

"I'm a Crispus and so I have rules to uphold," Hyacinth said, looking down her nose at Aponi. "I can't very well let my lightning bird go or let her go unpunished for things she should be punished for. But, you should rejoice. On Earth, we won't be able to keep our lightning birds. They'd have to be let go. So, it's better for all of us to just find refuge in that world." Aponi scoffed as she turned towards her cousin.

"Don't act like you're a good person just because you don't purposefully hurt Sinopa or treat her like other witches treat the rest of us. You don't use her because you don't need her to amplify your magic. But, you still own her. You still treat and talk about her as if she's your property," Aponi said, looking at Hyacinth over one shoulder. It was the first time in this whole interaction that Khalon saw a flicker of emotion on the witch's pale face. Aponi's words hit their mark.

"Turn her back," she demanded. Hyacinth didn't say another word and snapped her fingers. The small white bird slowly transformed into a larger one and then into a human. She was slightly taller than Aponi, but her hair was as dark as night just like hers. Her hair had little braids throughout it and her nose had a bump on it that Aponi did not have, like a bird's beak. Her black eyes were slightly upturned and her cheekbones were high on her face. She looked as strong and determined as Aponi always looked. A sort of harshness in her face that they both seemed to inherit.

Aponi immediately threw her arms around her cousin. Sinopa closed her eyes as she settled her head onto Aponi's shoulder.

"How much is the lightning bird?" Khai spoke up, from behind Hyacinth. Her eyebrows rose as she looked at Khalon's half brother.

"Sorry? You want to buy her?" Khai nodded. The sun started to illuminate the small room.

"Lightning birds can't be bought. They're only gifted.

And only to other witches," Hyacinth said. She looked at Khai meaningfully. He didn't let his gaze waver.

"Right. So, gift her to me," he ordered. Khalon watched as Hyacinth smiled.

"Khai, she said that they can only be gifted to other witches," Khalon explained, taking a small step forward. Khai's light brown eyes met Khalon's dark ones.

"I know what she said."

"You *are* a Crispus witch, aren't you?" Hyacinth smiled. Khalon froze. *What did she mean* he *was a Crispus witch?* Khalon knew that Rhea had called Aoife a power hungry witch. But, he didn't think anything of it at the time. And he certainly didn't think she hailed from the most powerful witch families of Asynithis. Khai nodded his head, almost somberly.

"Fine," Hyacinth said, snapping her fingers. "She's yours." A wind seemed to blow his hair back as his eyes widened. He looked down at his hands and then back up at Sinopa who glared.

"You're free," he muttered. "I don't want to own you, and no one else will be able to own you either." The words seemed to have some weight behind them, as though it were a prophecy Esi was speaking out into the universe. Sinopa's black eyes widened as she looked over at Aponi. Aponi just nodded once and then snapped her own fingers. A cracking sound was heard and Sinopa winced at the pain. Afterwards, she took off her casts and stretched out her arms. She smiled.

"Finally," she said. "I thought I was going to have to kill her, eventually." Hyacinth's eyebrows jumped.

"You could always try," Hyacinth smirked.

"Could you imagine the power I'd have?" Sinopa smiled at Aponi. Aponi rolled her eyes.

"Crispus magic would destroy you," she retorted. Khai walked up to Sinopa and pulled a dagger out from his pants pocket. He placed the dagger into her brown hands and stared deep into her eyes.

"Free the others," he said, his voice low. "Don't let anyone keep your people as prisoner." Sinopa stared at him for a moment before curling her fingers around the dagger.

"You're supposed to be a king," she said. "Don't let anyone keep *you* prisoner." Khai didn't say anything and backed away from her. Khalon followed his younger brother's figure with his eyes as he walked out of the room. His shoulders were tense as his head hung. Khalon's eyes darted down to the small bruises on Khai's jaw. Shaped as if someone was holding his head very tightly.

"By the way, if you were looking for the newly reincarnated Sea God," Hyacinth said, "Might be a good time to find him. He's here, in Byrrus." She cocked an eyebrow as she looked up at the ceiling. Before Khalon could respond to the witch, a strong metallic smell filled the room, and the room started to shake slightly. Her silver eyes met Khalon's.

"The portals are opening."

———

Poseidon followed Valerian into the bar attached to a glass skyscraper. The neon lights hung over the entrance read: "Vampire's Lair."

"You took me out of a vampire's lair just to bring me to

another one?" Poseidon asked, an eyebrow cocked. Valerian rolled his golden eyes.

"You first," he said, opening the door as a bell twinkled. Poseidon smirked at the dryad as he walked into the room. The bar was filled with the terrifying creatures of Caedoxia. Werewolves, vampires, manananggals, some witches, banshees, along with others. Poseidon stared at the group that was in front of him.

"Is that Steve?" a vampire behind the bar said with a large smile. "It's been a while since I've seen you here." Poseidon's eyes widened.

"This body's name is Steve? Everything about this human just makes me want to keel over and die from absolute embarrassment," Poseidon muttered. Valerian tried to hide his laughter.

"Sorry about putting you in that vampire dungeon," the bartender continued. He shrugged. "You didn't pay your fee when you said you would." Poseidon just grimaced at the man.

"Hell of a group you have here," he said under his breath. A small smile spread on Valerian's lips as he placed his hand on Poseidon's lower back, leading him further into the bar.

"We are among those that want the God of Death to be removed, Steve," Valerian said. Poseidon rolled his eyes.

"My brother can only be killed in one way," Poseidon explained. At those words, the conversation in the bar died down as they all stared at him.

"We trust that you understand what's at stake," someone said in the crowd. The creatures parted to reveal a man with dark hair and silver eyes. Poseidon knew the moment he looked at him.

"Ambrose Crispus," he said, his eyes twinkling as he looked at the young man. One of the new members of the Court of Caedoxia, he assumed. "How's your father?" Ambrose lifted his eyebrows as he swirled his golden drink. He took a sip.

"The old man croaked," Ambrose simply stated. "Thought your brother would've told you, considering he was the cause." Poseidon couldn't help the smirk that appeared on his lips.

"My brother doesn't share stuff like that with me," he said. "And, as you can see, we're not exactly on speaking terms."

"But, you care for him, don't you?" Ambrose said, pointing a finger in Poseidon's direction. "That's why you don't want to kill him."

"I haven't given my answer yet," he said, his voice dropping. He narrowed his eyes at the witch. "Killing the God of Death doesn't rid yourself of your elf problem. Or does the Court not understand that?" Ambrose chuckled.

"The Court understands the situation we're in. That's why, when the portals open, we're taking refuge on Earth," he said, leaning against the bar table. Poseidon tried to hide the expression on his face, but he couldn't help his eyes widening for a moment.

"How do you know about Terra?" Poseidon said, his voice barely above a whisper. His eyes darted at the other creatures who were paying extra attention to this conversation. Ambrose leered.

"It's not hard to decipher the prophecy that the God of All left us," Ambrose simply said, shrugging. "Plus, when you have as much magic in your system as a Crispus witch, it's easy to feel the presence of other worlds. Other magics."

"You can't just invade Earth," Poseidon argued. "It's a place specifically without magic." Ambrose leaned forward.

"Then we'll be able to keep the magic in our bones," he hissed. "The magic that you and the Death God are draining from us. The magic that our own world is stealing back. If we just stand around and wait, we would cease to exist." Poseidon's eyelids fluttered as he took in the other creatures' expressions. They looked angry at the thought of them disappearing.

"When the Saviors come to Asynithis—"

"We don't know how long that will take. And I don't want to be a pile of dust when they finally decide to come and save us," Ambrose drawled. Creatures behind him mumbled their agreements.

"To kill my brother, you need a Mortiferis. And they don't obey just anyone," Poseidon pointed out. Ambrose smirked as he exchanged a look with Valerian. Poseidon's dark eyes narrowed.

"I heard an interesting rumor," the witch said, sitting down as he gestured for Poseidon to do the same. He hesitantly sat down in the bar stool next to him.

"What rumor?"

"You know the bastard prince of Draconia, don't you? I heard he was close to the God of Death."

"What are you getting at, Ambrose?" Poseidon said, sighing impatiently. A twinkle appeared in Ambrose's silvery eyes.

"Some draconians, who managed to escape the war, claim that he has the mark of the Death God on his spine," he explained. Poseidon froze as his eyebrows furrowed together. He stared at the witch, intensely, before gesturing to go on.

"It means the Death God has claimed him, right? That Death is coming for him," the witch said, his confidence unwavering.

"Yes, so what?" Poseidon said, his voice uncharacteristically annoyed. Ambrose smiled.

"Some of the ghosts have told me a story about the Death Mark," Ambrose said, swirling the liquid in his glass before taking another small sip, his gaze not leaving Poseidon's. "Sure, it means Death is coming for him. But, it also means that the bastard can kill Death as well, doesn't it?"

"Why are you asking me? It seems like you know all the answers," Poseidon said, through gritted teeth. Ambrose shrugged, nonchalantly.

"Just wanted to confirm," he said. "And by your reaction, I must be right." Poseidon stared at the witch for a long time before closing his eyes. Betraying his brother went against the deepest parts of his soul, but there was no other way to stop him. Even though his brother tried to kill him, and killed the rest of their family, there was still a strong instinct in Poseidon to protect his little brother. But, no more. He opened his eyes, his mind made up.

"The mark signifies a duel. No one can touch Khalon—which is his name, by the way—without dying themselves. Only *he* can kill Khalon, and unfortunately, the mark has a weakness. If you are going to claim a creature for yourself, it means you belong to the creature as well. Balance. An was big on balance," he said, wrinkling his nose at the thought. He thought it was ridiculous. But, to give a creature a God's mark made them almost as equal to the Gods themselves. He would be remiss if he didn't admit that he had done it once or twice to lovers, just to show how much they meant to him. He loved them so much he wanted them to know that they weren't any average creature, but a creature equal to him.

Poseidon didn't know if Rhea gave Khalon the mark because she wanted to kill him, or if she just wanted to show him that she loved him. To protect him. Or if it was really his brother who did it, as some sort of revenge against Rhea for stopping him.

"So, Khalon can kill the Death God," Ambrose said, leaning back as he looked up at Valerian. Valerian raised his glass to Ambrose, and they cheered against the possible demise of Poseidon's brother. Poseidon grimaced.

"You have a problem there, though," he uttered. Ambrose raised an eyebrow.

"Oh?"

"I don't know if those draconians told you, but that boy is in love with the Celestial," Poseidon said meeting Ambrose's silvery gaze. The witch's expression turned dark. The smell of metal started to fill the air, causing Poseidon to wrinkle his nose.

"The true King of Draconia is in love with the Death God?"

"Yup," Poseidon said, downing a glass that was in front of him. The liquid burned his throat. "Good luck getting him to kill her."

19

Elion ran down the palace hallways as fast as possible. He nearly slid as he turned the corner into Essarae's quarters. His brother's wife was nowhere to be seen as he rushed through the Queen of Aureum's chambers. He hurried into the bathroom, seeing Lorena staring up at him in horror as he closed the door behind him.

"You need to go, hide, *something*," Elion said, gathering her cleaning supplies and putting them back in the cart that she brought. She frowned as Elion snatched the rag from her hands.

"What are you going on about?"

"The portals have opened. And you're not safe here. I don't think any of the servants are," Elion explained quickly. He put his hands underneath Lorena's arms and lifted her up from the ground as she swatted him away.

"Don't touch me," she warned. He let go of her immediately, putting his hands up in defense. She hugged herself as she looked around the room, her eyes narrowing at the elf.

"What about Apsara and Maleko? I told them I'd help them kill the God of Death," she whispered.

"They're gone," Elion said. She blinked.

"What do you *mean* they're gone?"

"I mean, I gave them a hover car and they're leaving. I told them to go," he explained. "Like I'm trying to do for you."

"They're gone?" she repeated, staring at the ground, her hand in her pocket.

"Yes, and you need to go, too," Elion said, taking a step towards her. She glowered up at him as she pulled her hand out, a dagger in her grip.

"Are you serious?" he said, exasperatedly. She pointed the dagger towards Elion.

"They said if I helped them, I would get to kill you." Her hazel eyes were dark.

"Do you not hear what I'm telling you?" Elion asked, as he dodged her attack. She whirled around to look at him.

"What I'm hearing is that my life is doomed anyways. I might as well take you with me," she shrugged. She glowered at him as she rushed towards him again. Elion grabbed her as he was pushed into the sink. Lorena brought the dagger closer to Elion's face, causing him to push backwards on his hands against the sink as he tried to get away from her murderous weapon of choice.

"Lorena," he started to say, but he felt the back of his head hit something cold. He turned slightly and saw the reflection ripple.

"Lorena!" His voice was desperate, but she still charged

forward, which caused him to fall backwards. Fall backwards into his reflection. His hands reached out, trying to grab something, anything, but all he had was Lorena. Her clothes were in his fists as he pulled her into the reflection with him. She screamed as they seemed to fall into nothingness.

Elion's whole body hurt as he fell onto something hard, Lorena falling on top of him, causing the wind to be knocked out of his body. She rolled off as he stared up at the ceiling, his eyes starting to focus again. It was a low ceiling and white, covered in little three dimensional dots. He lifted himself up as he stared at the ceiling curiously. He had never seen a design like this.

"Where are we?" Lorena asked, coughing as she took in their surroundings. Elion lifted his upper body, staring into his own reflection from a full length mirror. He turned from the mirror to see the rest of the room. It was small and had a weird musty smell to it. There was one queen-sized bed, a night stand, a lamp, and a door to a bathroom. He rubbed his head as he stood from the ground, his vision becoming blurry from standing up too quickly. He hadn't been in a room like this before.

"Elion?" Lorena called, her voice low as she pulled back the curtains. Lights flickered across her face and through the room. Elion stood next to her, pulling the curtain back further. He couldn't believe what he was seeing.

In front of them was some kind of archaic parking lot. And beyond the parking lot was a black road, cars speeding down them. But, not hover cars. Cars. The vehicles humans used before the magical creatures took back Asynithis during the War.

"Where are we?" Lorena whispered, her voice becoming shrill as she stared in horror at the moving vehicles. He swallowed as he looked at her, his gaze resting on her scar for a moment before meeting her hazel eyes.

"I think... I think we're on Earth."

20

Khai leaned against the brick walls of the townhouse as he stared at the rising sun. The streets of Byrrus were abandoned, as the sun grew brighter. But, it wasn't as bright as it used to be. The consequences of the Gods being murdered. Everything was just a smidge duller in life.

Khalon bounded down the steps, whirling around to look for Khai. He pushed off of the brick and took a step forward as Khalon met his gaze.

"We're going to find Poseidon," Khalon said. He furrowed his eyebrows, like he wanted to ask Khai a question. Khai silently begged him to ask. To ask why he had that dagger hidden. To ask about what the lightning bird had said. But, instead, Khalon asked a question Khai didn't want to answer.

"*Are* you a Crispus witch?" His question hung in the air as Khai simply stared at his older brother. For a draconian to claim a heritage other than draconian was considered disgraceful. It was the reason why Khai's mother hid her heritage, having never claimed it until she felt King Vien forced her hand. He licked his lips.

"On my mother's side," he admitted, quietly. Khalon narrowed his half-moon shaped eyes.

"Does Aoife know she's a Crispus witch?" Khai lowered his gaze, staring past him at the Ustrinian Queen who walked behind Khalon.

"I don't know," he lied. He didn't check to see if his brother believed him. Khalon stood in front of Khai for a long while before walking towards the street. Aponi gave a quizzical look as she walked past Khai. He just shook his head.

Before he could start following them, a hand gripped his arm. He looked down at the sinewy hand—its long nails a deep crimson red—before looking up at its owner. Hyacinth's silver eyes seemed to keep him from moving.

"Does Aoife know that you know?" Hyacinth asked, a glint in her eyes. Khai pulled his arm away from the witch.

"How do you think I know about it?" he snapped. She leaned back as she looked over the Draconian King.

"My cousin never knew what was best for her. She always thinks so small," she said, staring down at him.

"My mother has grand plans for herself, don't worry," Khai scoffed. Hyacinth smiled and then leaned forward, her eyes staring past him.

"Does he know?" she asked, her eyes meeting Khai's. "Does he know what you've been ordered to do? And the consequences if you don't?" He held his breath as she pulled away. He could hear the warning in her words. She gave a smirk as she leaned against the front door.

"He has the mark of Death on him," she whispered. "I wouldn't touch him unless you were on a suicide mission, if I were you."

"I wasn't going to—"

"Good luck with your mother's wrath," Hyacinth said, wiggling her fingers in farewell as she opened the front door of her house, walking backwards into it.

"Good luck with avoiding Sinopa's," Khai bit back. Hyacinth let out a laugh as she turned around.

"Sinopa will be going after the witch who broke her arms first," she said, looking at Khai over her shoulder. "When she comes for me, I'll be ready for it. Will you be ready for Aoife's?" She winked before closing the door fully. Khai fought the urge to shudder as he walked back to the group.

"What was that about?" Aponi asked, glaring at the door Hyacinth just closed.

"A needless warning, that's all," he mumbled. He looked up at Khalon. "What's this about Poseidon?"

"She said he'd be in a place called 'Vampire's Lair,'" Khalon said, looking down at the words scrawled over his palm. He squinted as he looked around the empty street. "Would it even be open during daylight?"

"Is it an actual vampire's lair or is it a place called 'Vampire's Lair?'" Khai asked.

Are you an idiot? Did you not see what he said? Kamaria signed, annoyed.

*I heard *what he said*, Khai signed back. Kamaria rolled her eyes at him emphasizing the word "heard."

He said a place called *Vampire's Lair*, Kamaria signed. Khalon looked back and forth between Khai and Kamaria before clearing his throat.

"It's a bar, apparently," he said, interrupting. She gestured towards Khalon with her hand as if she were proven right.

"You really need to clarify when you speak," Khai said, walking past Khalon.

"It's this way," Khalon said, quietly. Khai turned on his heel, walking in the correct direction this time.

"Yeah, I knew that," he muttered. Khalon tried to hide his smile.

———

Kamaria looked up at the sign that read "Vampire's Lair" and peered into the frosted windows of the establishment. She bit back the urge to rub her arms due to the cold. It was the coldest weather Kamaria had ever experienced, due to Ustrina being a fairly hot country to live in. She preferred the dry heat over seeing her breath any day.

I don't see him, she signed. She watched as Aponi translated what she said and then looked carefully at Khalon's lips as he said something.

He won't be in the same body, Aponi signed afterwards. Kamaria shrugged as she looked into the bar for longer. The figures were blurry, but she recognized Ambrose Crispus. She'd recognize that scoundrel anywhere.

Crispus is here, she signed. Khalon's face turned to ice as he pulled the bar door open. She followed after him, staring down anyone who looked her way. The bar was filled, even though the sun was high in the sky now.

Kamaria, Ambrose signed towards her as he tipped his head down a little. She lifted her chin.

Queen Kamaria, to you, she signed. He smirked.

"Of course," she watched his lips say. She looked at the man who was sitting next to Ambrose. She didn't recognize the human, but she could see waves crashing in his sepia eyes.

You're shorter this time, Kamaria signed. Poseidon sighed deeply.

Thanks for reminding me, he signed back. *Can you believe that this body is named Steve? Why does this universe hate me so?* She hid her smile at Poseidon's theatrics.

The rest of them said their pleasantries before they all migrated to a large table in the back of the bar. Kamaria looked over at Khai, whose eyebrows were scrunched together as he seemed to be tuning out everything everyone was saying.

What's going on? She signed after tapping his shoulder. He didn't meet her eyes. Kamaria's own eyes flickered to the small bruises sprinkled over his jaw. When her gaze finally rested back onto his, they were staring deeply into her soul. She felt the heat rise to her cheeks as she realized that he saw her looking at his bruises.

I'm fine, he finally signed.

You know, if you were *having trouble, I can—*

I'm fine. Kamaria stared at him for a moment longer. His brown hair fell into his light brown eyes as he looked away, trying to pay attention to the conversation at hand.

If your mom is a Crispus, she signed, *then you're in more danger than you realize.* Khai threw her a glare.

Not here, is all he signed back.

"You want me to do what?" Khalon said. Kamaria watched his lips as he pursed them, glowering at the Sea God and the two creatures by his side.

"I told you he wouldn't be up to it," Poseidon said, leaning back in his seat as he crossed his dark arms. The creature with golden eyes stole a glance at Ambrose who seemed to be studying Khalon.

"Are you *not* the true King of Draconia?" Ambrose asked. Kamaria felt Khai stiffen beside her.

"I am not," Khalon spit. "And you would have to kill me before I'd let you touch a single hair on her head."

"I admire your loyalty to the Celestial, but she's not *really* the God of Death. And, from what I've heard, she's not even really there anymore," Ambrose pointed out. She watched as Khalon's stony face tightened.

"I'm not killing her. I'll follow *her* directions. Not yours," he spat, standing up from the table.

"If you don't kill her, Khalon, we'll all die," Poseidon said, his eyes holding him there.

"What were the Celestial's directions?" Ambrose said, leaning in. "I'm curious." He gave Khalon a lazy but arrogant look.

"Her *name* is Rhea," Khalon hissed. "And she told me to find the witch, find the portals, and protect the Saviors. Then I can make my way back to her." He barely moved his lips when speaking his last sentence making Kamaria turn to Aponi for a translation.

"When you make your way back to her," Ambrose seemed to be mocking Khalon, "kill her then."

"What part of *I'm not killing her* do you not understand?" Fury was written all over Khalon's usually unreadable face.

"Your duty is to Asynithis, not a Celestial," Poseidon pointed out. Kamaria could feel the energy pulsating from Poseidon. His words were the words of a God.

"My duty isn't to anyone," Khalon said, sitting back down, glowering at all of them.

"You are the rightful King of Draconia, Khalon. You have the spirit of the dragon within you. Rhea told you that," Poseidon said, leaning forward. Kamaria stole a glance at Khai whose face was suddenly expressionless. Even though he tried to mimic the facial expression that his brother always put on, he wasn't quite as good at it. The cracks of his mask were seeped in anger and... hurt.

"Just because I have the spirit of the dragon in me doesn't mean that I have to—"

"Actually, it does. You have a duty to Asynithis. The spirit of the dragon chose you. It *chose* you. And Rhea understands that," Poseidon said.

"Don't talk to me like you know what Rhea wants," Khalon snapped, his mouth contorted.

"This world will cease to exist, Khalon, if he and I are allowed to live," the Sea God said, sighing as though he was talking to a stubborn child. Khalon let out a dry laugh.

"*She's* more important," he said. "She'll always be."

If the God of Death needs to die, doesn't that mean you have to, too? Kamaria signed. Poseidon twisted his lips before nodding his head slowly.

"Yes, I need to cease to exist as well," he said, signing as he spoke.

"Pardon me, if I'm overstepping," Ambrose started.

"I can tell you, you are," Aponi interrupted. Ambrose pretended the lightning bird wasn't there.

"You were stuck in the Ring of Fire all this time. Not many female Champions come out of the Ring of Fire…"

"What are you getting at?" Khai finally spoke up. Ambrose's silver eyes turned towards him.

"I'm just saying, Khalon spent a lot of time with a female creature, the Celestial, and he never had before." Before Khai could retort with a response, Khalon started to laugh maniacally. Kamaria and Khai shared a look.

I think he's going crazy, Khai signed.

You're going to have to stop him when he tries to murder Ambrose Crispus, Kamaria signed back. His lips spread into a smirk as he regarded the witch.

Let him.

At least pretend to stop him, Kamaria signed.

"You think I'm attached to Rhea because she's the first girl to give me attention?" Khalon asked, his lips barely moving. Ambrose gave him a lazy look.

"Is she not?" Khalon leaned forward, his obsidian eyes murderous.

"She sacrificed her life for mine. I would sacrifice the whole universe for hers." Ambrose's eyebrows jumped a little.

"Good to know," he said. Kamaria glanced at Khalon's fingers gripping the sides of the table. His knuckles were white and she wouldn't be surprised if the table was left with finger imprints. Khalon stood up from the table for a second time. He leaned down towards Ambrose, unflinching from those silver eyes.

"If I hear that this plan is still in motion, I'll kill you," he whispered. "And I don't hesitate." He patted Ambrose's shoulder before walking past him. Ambrose's smile slowly faded as he watched the draconian walk away.

"We always could get a Mortiferis. Though, they *are* difficult to order around," Poseidon shrugged, leaning into his chair.

"Where would we get a Mortiferis?" Ambrose asked, his face dark. He shook his head before leaving the table, going to talk to a vampire who had an inquisitive look on his face. Kamaria didn't recognize the vampire, but she guessed he was a part of the Court as well.

The portals are open, she signed towards Poseidon. *Find one in a different world.*

"Only one portal is open," he said, putting a chin to his hand. "And the Mortiferis aren't on Earth." He was quiet for a moment, his eyes looking up towards the ceiling before he started signing at Kamaria once more. "Though, I doubt that Rhea doesn't know what Khalon has to do."

You mean she wants Khalon to kill her?

"She told him to find a witch, find the portals, and then protect the Saviors, did she not? Afterwards, she told him to find her," Poseidon said. "Death is coming for him, she knows that. I believe that she fully expects him to kill her. Or he'll die himself, and that's a fate she would never want for him."

"He wouldn't. You heard him," Aponi responded. He turned towards her.

"Consult with the Fates," he said. "They would know what's going on in her mind more than we would."

"Summon the Fates?" Khai asked. "Can we do that?" Poseidon's eyes roved over him.

"I don't know. You tell me," he said, a knowing look in his eyes.

21

"Earth? You're telling me we're on *Earth*?" Lorena exclaimed, letting go of the white, almost translucent curtain. Elion nodded, still staring out the window at the strange world.

"We can't be," she breathed, her gaze on herself in the full length mirror.

"It looks like we are," he said, finally removing himself from the window. It was nighttime wherever they were on Earth.

"How did we get here?" Lorena asked, narrowing her eyes at Elion. He held up his hands, a gesture he seemed to do a lot around her.

"*I'm* not the one who brought us here," he said, guessing at what she was thinking. Her face contorted into a scowl as she stared more carefully at the mirror.

"You fell... through the mirror," Lorena pointed out. She gingerly touched the reflective glass in front of her with her pointer finger. If only they could go back... She turned to look at the prince who was standing in front of her. If she didn't know he was a prince, she probably would have been able to guess it, simply from how he always held himself. Like the whole universe revolved around him.

"You pulled me through... with you," Lorena said, turning to look at him. The accusation met its mark as Elion's pointed ears flushed red.

"I-I didn't *mean* to," he stammered. "You pushed me and I was just trying to grab anything to stop my fall."

"Sure," she rolled her eyes, turning back towards the mirror. She could still see the prince in the reflection, standing a bit behind her. Lorena would never admit it to herself, but he was beautiful. For an elf.

"Take us back," she demanded, taking a step away from the mirror. Elion's eyebrows furrowed as he looked at it in front of her. He cautiously walked up to the mirror and pressed his index finger against the reflective material. It didn't give in the slightest. His shoulders fell as he straightened back up to look at Lorena.

"I have no idea how to get back," Elion said.

"*You're* the one who brought us here. You surely must know how to get us back to Asynithis!"

"I just know that the portals are reflections. How to fall into a reflection to go into another world? Yeah, I have no idea about that one," he said, crossing his arms.

"You've gotta be joking," Lorena muttered under her breath. She took another glance at those pointed ears, the pointed ears that marked him as better than her.

"What creatures are on Earth?" she asked, her voice contorting as she said the word. Elion sheepishly smiled as he ducked his head.

"Humans. Earth only has humans, apparently," Elion mumbled. Lorena didn't even try to hide the smile that spread on her face.

"Guess you better hide those ears, princeling," she said, opening the closet in the room. There was a lone hat in the small storage space. She grabbed it and threw it in Elion's direction. He stared at the hat, his eyebrows knitting together, as she gestured for him to put it on.

"Over your ears," she demanded. He did as he was told, the hat concealing the tips of his ears. She grabbed the knife that had fallen to the ground when they fell into this world and stuffed it into her pocket.

"Let's go see what this world is like," she said, opening the door to the room. It led to a balcony which had identical doors down the length of it. Elion followed after her, wordlessly, as she walked down the balcony towards the metal stairway.

"We should find a way back," he finally said, once they reached the first floor of the building.

"Are you sure there aren't any magical creatures in this realm?" Lorena hissed. Elion shrugged.

"The portals just opened, but there's no telling what year you'd fall into. So, there might've been magical creatures that came years ago and have descendants living here," Elion mused.

"That's not super helpful," she muttered. There was a light on in the front room of the building.

"Well, we can't stay here," Lorena said. "We might as well ask this lady how to get to a place with more people. If there's magical creatures in this realm, they'll be out at night." Elion raised his eyebrows as he looked down at her, stunned.

"What? You thought I was an idiot?" He quickly shook his head.

"No, I just... I thought you would've killed me by now," he teased, lowering his head slightly so he could get a better look at her. But, there was a twinge of truth in his words. Lorena blinked.

"It's not off the table," she mumbled under her breath as she pushed the glass door open. The lady at the front desk barely even lifted her head as she flipped through a magazine of some kind. The letters were, luckily, familiar to Lorena. *English*. This world still spoke English.

"Excuse me," Lorena said, walking up to the front desk.

"For an hour, it'll be twenty dollars," the lady said, flipping a page.

"Uh... No," Lorena said with disgust as she tucked a curl behind her ear. "We're wondering how to get to a place with more people around." The lady's eyebrows pulled downwards as she glanced up over the edge of her magazine.

"A place with more people around?" she asked, her eyes narrowing. "It's the middle of the night."

"It is. That's true," Lorena said. "But, we just need to get to a... city? Of some sorts?"

"A city? The closest city is New York City. Is that the *city* you're trying to get to?" the lady asked, a healthy dose of snark coating her words. Lorena bit back what she wanted to say to her, instead opting to put on a disarming smile.

"Right. New York City," Lorena smiled. "How do we get there?" The lady seemed to finally register Lorena's features, her eyes roving over the scar that ran across her face. Even in a different world, people were disgusted by it.

"How do you get to New York City? You can call a cab. Or an Uber. How exactly did you get here?"

"We walked," Lorena stated. The lady's eyebrows furrowed once more.

"Can *you* call us a cab or an Uber?" Elion asked, finally speaking up. The lady seemed to melt at the sight of him. *I mean, he's handsome but he's not* that *handsome,* Lorena couldn't help but think.

"Do you two not have cell phones?" the lady finally said, composing herself after seeing Elion. Her voice seemed to have gone up a little, to sound more girly and sweet. Lorena resisted the urge to roll her eyes.

"Unfortunately, we lost them," he said, the lie flicking off of his tongue with ease.

"I guess I can call one for you. Shouldn't be too much money as New York is pretty close by," she mused.

"We would greatly appreciate it," Elion said, flashing her a smile. Lorena just stared at him like he was a completely different person.

"Are you serious right now?" she couldn't help but say. The lady threw a glare Lorena's way before smiling back at Elion.

"Yeah, sure. I don't mind," she said, tucking a stray hair behind her ear. She pulled out a thin, glass rectangle from underneath the desk and started to type onto it. Lorena stared at it, wide-eyed.

"The Uber should be here in ten minutes, sweetheart," the lady said, smiling once more at Elion.

"Thank you so much," he said, his voice sincere as he

opened the front door. Lorena grumbled under her breath as she walked underneath Elion's arm to the outdoors. They stood in the dark parking lot, waiting for this... Uber.

"What the hell is an Uber?" Lorena finally asked as she stood beside Elion. He shrugged.

"I thought you would know," he said.

"Why would *I* know?"

"Aren't you human?"

"Just because I'm human doesn't mean I know what's going on in *this* world," Lorena huffed.

"Our worlds are the same, except for the lack of magic being here and our world is obviously in the future while this one is in the past. Don't you know your human history?" Elion teased. Lorena rolled her eyes as she hugged her arms around herself. He stared at the passing cars on the street.

"Can you feel it? The lack of magic. The emptiness in this world," Elion whispered. She didn't feel whatever it was that he felt. She felt the same as she did in Asynithis. Flexing her hands, she put them down at her side.

"I don't feel anything," she begrudgingly responded. She wasn't sure if he heard her or not as a car pulled into the parking lot. The window rolled down and the man in the front seat looked at his phone.

"For Trudy?" the man asked.

"Yup," Elion said, opening the car door for Lorena. She grimaced as she scooted into the small car. The inside was somewhat similar to a hover car, not that she'd been in many. Humans had cars on Asynithis, in the past. The hover car was an improvement on the human car, but the outside looked nothing like the old cars. Hover cars were shaped like ovals, a sleek vehicle with no lines or crevices. Cars... looked like weird boxes. Humans created both, though, not that the elves would ever admit it.

"You two are heading to New York? First time?" the man asked, trying to make conversation.

"Yeah, it's our first time," Elion answered. "Do you have tips on where to visit?"

"Oh man, do I? There's a lot of great places you gotta see when you're in New York. For one, definitely visit the Empire State Building. I mean, it's just a building, but it's a land-mark, you know?" Elion nodded along as Lorena looked out the window, the world speeding past them.

Slowly, the road started to change and there was a huge line of cars, even in the dead of night, as tall buildings loomed over them. Elion looked out the window for a moment, taking a break from the talkative driver.

"Looks like Caedoxia," Elion muttered under his breath, so low that only Lorena could hear it. Lorena had never been to Caedoxia, but nodded in agreement anyhow.

"Well, this is your stop," the driver said. He looked out the window at the establishment they were being dropped off at. It was a bookstore with a sign that read "24 Hours."

"I've never been to this bookstore," the driver commented.

"Thanks for the ride," Elion said before he closed the door behind him, ignoring the driver's comment.

"Sure thing," the driver said before speeding off.

"She sent us to a bookstore?" Lorena asked, raising an eyebrow.

"We're lucky it's open. Unlike Caedoxia, this world seems to sleep at night," Elion mused as he pushed open the door. Lorena looked down the empty streets. There were still cars, but not a lot of people were on the sidewalks.

A jingle went off as Elion opened the door, and a boy who couldn't be older than fourteen lifted his head. He had snow white hair, like an elf's, but it wasn't that which unnerved Lorena. It was his eyes. They seemed to constantly change color.

Lorena blinked and rubbed her eyes before she looked back at the boy. He just stared quizzically back at them.

"Uh, I know it says we're open twenty-four hours but... what are you guys doing here at three in the morning?" the boy asked. There was weight to his words, like they were words she was supposed to listen to, had no choice *but* to listen to. Elion frowned as he stared at the boy, probably feeling the same as Lorena.

"We're just looking for some historical information," Elion said, finally composing himself.

"Oh sure," the boy said, walking out from behind the desk. The badge on his shirt read "Cyril." He beckoned for them to follow him. It was as though Lorena didn't have a choice. Her legs started to move like they had a mind of their own. She stared in horror at Elion who also was unwillingly following this boy. If the boy knew he was controlling the legs of Lorena and Elion, he didn't show it.

"This is the history section," Cyril said, his eyes still constantly changing color until he locked eyes with Lorena. Then, they were stuck on hazel. The color of her eyes.

"Right, thanks," she said quietly, her voice haunted. He blinked and then his eye color changed from hazel to blue as he looked at Elion.

"No problem," the boy said before walking away. Lorena widened her eyes as she looked at Elion.

"You felt weird too, didn't you?" she hissed. Elion just watched the figure of the boy disappearing down the many shelves.

"He's not human," he muttered. "But, he's not a normal magical creature either."

"I don't know of any magical creature that can order me to do things, can you?" Lorena pointed out. Elion pursed his lips, his eyebrows knitting together as he watched the boy sit back down on the chair in front of the cash register. He was writing something on a piece of parchment.

"I've met only one person who has weight to their words like that," Elion whispered.

"Who?" Lorena prodded. His gaze looked mildly frightened as he looked at her.

"The God of All," Elion whispered. "Only the God of All has been known to do that."

22

Esi sifted through the white powder as she squinted into the sun. Everything was covered in gray-white ash. She leaned down to touch it, letting it run through her fingers.

"Can you see him too?" a dulcet voice said. Esi looked up to see a girl with long, wavy, golden blonde hair and deep golden-brown eyes. The girl furrowed her ash brown eyebrows together as she pointed at the boy who suddenly stood before them.

"I see him every night," the girl softly said. Esi turned to look at the boy whose back was facing them. He had night black hair that was cut at his ears and didn't look older than twelve or thirteen. She walked slowly towards him, her feet shuffling through the ash.

She reached out towards the boy, but he turned before Esi could reach him. His black eyes seemed to almost stare through her.

"This is the future, Daughter of An," the boy whispered. "This is the future for all the realms."

"Who are you?" Esi felt herself ask. The boy shook his head, a sad smile on his face.

"I don't know anymore." Esi opened her mouth to inquire further but the world started to shake.

"Esi? Esi!" a voice from above started to say.

"Don't go," she heard the girl cry out. "Don't leave me!" She turned towards the girl and before the vision faded in front of her, she watched as the girl started to glow as she wordlessly screamed.

Esi's lids fluttered open as she felt her body be shaken. She felt large hands on her shoulders, and she wordlessly pushed them off.

"Jabulani," she uttered his name, guessing at who was waking her. The person above her gave a sigh of relief.

"Your eyes were glowing and this is really the worst time to be having a vision right now, unless it's a vision on how to defeat these godsdamn elves," Jabulani ranted.

"What's happening?" she asked. She could see a flicker of white light coming from what she believed to be the window. It was daytime, that much she knew. It was jarring to go from being able to see everything in her visions, to once again being blind in her waking life.

"We're being invaded again," Jabulani said. "I need you to hide yourself somewhere."

"Where's Kamaria?" she asked, her voice piercing.

"She's not back yet."

"The others?" Jabulani was silent.

"They're not back either. But, don't worry. I can handle

it," he said, confidently. But, Esi could still hear the subtle quiver in his voice. Her eyebrows knitted together.

"I'll hide where I get my visitors," she told him.

"Are you sure that's a good idea?" Jabulani asked. *It doesn't matter*, Esi wanted to say. *The world is going to be destroyed no matter what.*

"Jabu," she said. She felt Jabulani pause.

"Yeah?"

"Be careful." He grabbed her hand and kissed the top of it before patting it with his other hand, a gesture he always did with her and Kamaria.

"Always," he said. He let go of her and placed a dagger in Esi's dress before rushing down the hallway. She slowly felt her way down to her old quarters, counting the steps as one hand traced the wall. Kamaria didn't bother to renovate her old rooms, but they, luckily, weren't destroyed from the Mortiferis attack almost seven months ago.

She sat down in front of her crystal ball, waiting. Esi didn't know what to make of her vision from before. There was a girl she had never seen, and Esi could feel that she was a girl that was alive, not *really* a part of the vision.

"I see him every night," the girl had said. *Another Seer?* Esi shook her head. There was only one Seer and that was her. An chooses a child after the previous Seer dies. And, if An is gone, would there be a seer after Esi? Perhaps, the girl was a past Seer? Time *was* a weird concept...

One thing Esi was sure of. The world full of ash and nothing else was *their* world, Asynithis. It was their future. A future set in stone.

Esi jumped as she heard commotion coming from above her. Just as there was a sound of ruckus, she heard the doors to her rooms burst open. She gripped the dagger in her pocket, holding it out in front of her. She wasn't a fighter and she could feel her outstretched hand tremble.

Esi winced as she heard the door in front of her begin to break down. Taking a deep breath, she tried to steady her hand with the dagger and stood up straighter.

"Found her," an unfamiliar voice said.

"Take another step forward, and I won't hesitate to stab you," Esi said, her voice even. The unfamiliar voice laughed.

"Isn't she blind?" the voice asked someone.

"Yeah, I'm pretty sure she is. Every Seer is blind," another voice that Esi couldn't place laughed.

"My sister is Queen Kamaria of Ustrina. I'm sure you've heard of her accomplishments in battle. She wouldn't leave her little sister defenseless with no skills in battle," Esi fibbed, lifting her chin higher. Her words gave the strangers some pause.

"Queen Kamaria isn't here though, is she?" the voice sneered.

"Plus, isn't your lifespan a human's? So, if you *have* been getting lessons from her, you wouldn't be better than us," the other voice retorted.

"Go ahead and try," she said, trying to call their bluff. The room was silent momentarily. Soon, Esi heard their feet shuffle and inwardly cursed herself for never taking her lessons seriously. She waved her arm around, doing her best to strike one of them. One of the attackers yelped.

"Ow! She cut me!"

"Okay, that's it. Let's just use that stuff the guy gave us," the other voice said. Esi could feel the rest of her body start to tremble.

"Jabu!" she started to scream at the top of her lungs. "Jabulani!"

"Use it now!" the voice said. Esi felt air rush towards her face and little specks—what felt like sand—hit her cheeks and nose. She breathed in some of the specks before realizing she should've held her breath. Almost immediately, she couldn't tell what was up and what was down.

"Thank An," the voice muttered under his breath as Esi lost consciousness.

———

"Is she up yet?" a vitriolic voice said. Esi held her head as she was pushed into a sitting position.

"She is, your highness," another voice said. The unfamiliarity of voices was giving her a giant headache. Or maybe that was the sand she had breathed in. At the thought of the sand-like specks she inhaled, Esi started to cough ferociously.

"Get her some water," the voice who was referred to as *"your highness"* ordered. Suddenly, glass was being pushed against her lips and she hesitantly swallowed the tasteless liquid.

"What do you want from me?" her voice didn't sound like her own. It sounded weaker, almost tired.

"Do you know where you are, Daughter of An?" the royal creature said, ignoring her question. She swallowed as she tried to sit up straighter.

"I have no idea," she lied. She could feel the presence of the earth at all times. She always knew where she was.

"You're in Aureum. Regium, to be exact. In my palace," the voice said.

"You must be King Adamar, then," Esi's voice was monotone.

"Correct. Do you know what that means?"

"I have a feeling you'll tell me," she bit. Adamar chuckled.

"I've heard the Ustrinian royals had more courage than they should," he said, almost under his breath. A little louder, he said, "It means that Invenire has fallen. Ustrina has been taken. By me."

"Well, with help from the beastoids," she clarified. "Without them, the elves wouldn't have managed it." He paused and she could almost feel the anger radiating off of him.

"Why did you take me?" she asked, not giving him time to throw poisonous words at her.

"You are the Seer, aren't you? Isn't it obvious?" Esi could feel Adamar circle around her.

"What do you want to know?" she asked. Her voice sounded strangled. It was her role as the Seer to give whoever asked their future. But, to give Adamar his made her want to gouge her eyes out.

"What is my future? What do you see?" Adamar said, his voice halting. Esi frowned. It wasn't that she didn't expect him to ask about his future. However, she thought maybe he would ask about the future of Aureum. His conquests. Not about *his* future, specifically.

"What happened to Jabulani?" Esi asked, her voice small.

"Jabulani? Who is that?" he said. She swallowed and then shook her head.

"What about the Queen Mother Aoife?" Esi asked.

"The draconian Queen is fine," Adamar answered, his voice impatient. "Now, what about my future can you see?"

"If you go down on the same path, your future is grim. Are you sure you still want to know?" she said, her voice faraway. She could feel her eyes start to glow.

"Tell me," he whispered. She heard Adamar sit across from her as the vision started to come. She reached out her hands to Adamar, who placed his in hers, and she gripped them, hard, as his future came to her forefront.

They came in fragmented images. She could see Adamar slowly turn into ash. A wordless scream on his white, pale face, his blue eyes almost bulging out.

"What if we kill the Saviors?" Adamar's voice pierced the vision. The image re-emerged and was the same. Adamar screaming as he was slowly turned to ash, the rest of the world with him.

"What if we don't kill the Saviors?" he asked, impatient. The image changed. Adamar stood on a battlefield of sorts. A boy with everchanging eyes ran towards him, cutting his head clean off. Adamar's last vision being the boy with snow white hair staring down at him, blood from his sword dripping onto Adamar's face.

Adamar ripped his hands away from her. She heard him stand up and start to pace. Part of her feared that he would kill her for giving him such an unfavorable future.

"You're telling me that no matter what I do, I'll die?" he thundered.

"You didn't ask what would happen if you didn't try to conquer all the realms," Esi pointed out.

"I *will* conquer all the realms," Adamar hissed. Esi merely shrugged.

"Then you'll die," she said. "Gruesomely."

"Who is that boy? The boy in that vision who cut my head off?" She shook her head.

"I don't know."

"What *do* you know? Your visions are merely lies. You're trying to manipulate me right now, aren't you?" Adamar sneered.

"I can't change my visions," Esi murmured.

"The future can change," he mused. "I can change my future. Even if we go ahead with killing the Saviors on Earth, I can survive."

"It's true that the future can change. But it only changes based on the choices you make," Esi retorted.

"I'll make sure I survive," he growled. "Don't you worry, Queen of the Witches." She stayed quiet as she heard him walk further away from her. The King of Aureum paused at the door, turning towards Esi.

"What about the God of Death?" he asked, his voice barely above a whisper.

"Sorry?"

"The God of Death. What's *his* future?" Adamar pressed, louder than before. Esi sat still, feeling the manacles around her legs that were keeping her in place. She felt her eyes glow and a series of images came rushing towards her.

Rhea's face came to the forefront. Her copper eyes were full of fear as she mouthed the words *"I love you."* Blood gushed out of her pale, corpse-like throat as a blade was pressed against it. Suddenly, black eyes opened and the boy that Esi saw in a vision earlier was standing there. Somberly looking at the world made of ash. Esi held her head as the vision started to fade away.

"He lives," Esi muttered. "The God of Death will always live. No matter what he does, he'll always live." Adamar stood still briefly. Then, the door slammed as Esi jumped. She could feel the tears start to prick at her eyes.

"*I love you,*" Rhea had mouthed before the life drained from her own eyes. It was too much like how she sacrificed herself before. Esi couldn't see the person who held the knife against Rhea's throat, but she knew what the Death Mark meant on Khalon's back. What Khalon had to do.

And Esi knew it would kill him.

23

All Rhea could see was darkness. A sea of darkness, her body covered in shadows.

"Khalon," she called out, reached out. She stretched her mind, trying to find the soul that she so desperately wanted—no, *needed*.

"Did you think I'd be asleep in here?" a thousand whispers echoed around her. Rhea turned within her mind, trying to find the source.

"Why are you doing this?"

"To save all the realms," he said. Shadows swirled in front of her to make a figure.

"You're going to destroy all the realms to... save it?" Rhea asked the shadowy figure.

"I don't plan on destroying anything," the Death God said, almost annoyed.

"The Mortiferis will—"

"The Mortiferis will *cleanse* the realms," the Death God interrupted. He sighed. "They won't destroy anything."

"Cleanse it?" Rhea whispered. "What do you mean?"

"You creatures are violent, left to your own devices. You have no morality, no compassion for one another. I need to cleanse the world of creatures like you."

"Why kill all the Gods then, if it's us that you wanted to get rid of?"

"Do you really think the God of All would've let that happen? Would let me cleanse the realms of his creations? Besides, my family needed to go. They were the problem. The reason why the realms are the way they are."

"I don't understand," Rhea said, hugging herself. The dark shadow took a small step forward, causing her to take a shaky step back.

"Gods are supposed to protect their creations. To lead them in the right direction. That's what Gods should do. But, An—as you called him—he didn't do that. He let his creations suffer. Sometimes, in the most horrible ways," the voices sounded mournful, almost. Rhea's eyebrows scrunched together.

"So, what? You think by 'cleansing' the realms, you're *freeing* us?" Rhea asked, taking a step forward. "You're not freeing us. You're destroying everything. That elf—"

"Adamar is not a threat."

"To you, maybe. But to the rest of Asynithis, he might as well be the most frightening creature to ever exist. He's taking their freedoms away. You took away all the Gods but yourself for what? Because you think you're more... *compassionate* than the others?"

"I don't understand your anger with me, child," he said, taking a menacing step forward as the shadowy figure grew taller.

"You want to control us," Rhea murmured. "Creatures go through tough times. We are individuals. We think differently from one another. Not all creatures are immoral. And just because some are, doesn't mean that the Gods should interfere. We deserve to have the freedom of choice. To live our lives the way that we want to."

"What about your beloved then?" Rhea glanced up at the mention of Khalon.

"What about him?" she asked, her voice small.

"He's gone through so much. Death walking beside him every day. Since he was five. And those weren't choices made by him, but rather by other creatures around him. Don't you think he deserved to live a happy life with a family that adored him?"

"Of course I think—"

"Don't you think the God of All should've intervened? Should've saved him? Instead, *I* saved him, day after day."

"You didn't save him. You're the one who *condemned* him," Rhea spat. The figure paused.

"Condemned?"

"If you didn't take me as your Celestial body, his mom would still be alive. And maybe, maybe he would've had a better life. You took that choice from her by deciding to be reincarnated," Rhea hissed, staring him square in his face made of shadows.

"Ah, Dal," Death sighed. "If Dal didn't die, Khalon wouldn't be alive today."

"He wouldn't have been put into the Ring of Fire if his mom was still—" Death laughed in Rhea's face.

"You really think his self-loving father wouldn't have put him in there? He's still a bastard child, dear Rhea. A bastard child who is a pure royal draconian. He was always going to be in the Ring of Fire. The only difference would've been he'd have died in his first battle."

"He has the spirit of the dragon within him. He wouldn't have died," Rhea said, holding her head up. Death gave a dry chuckle.

"Who do you think gave him the spirit of the dragon?" Rhea froze as she stared into the ebony abyss in front of her.

"Dal..." she whispered.

"His mother had it before him. When she died, she transferred it over to her one and only son. The only heir to both the Black and Red dragon families," Death stated. The shadows paused, studying Rhea.

"Dal didn't die from that storm in Aureum the night you were born," he said, the whispers repeating the words. Rhea froze.

"What?"

"She died from Khalon's father's fiery breath. Like I said, I need to cleanse the realms of you violent creatures. Without me, I'm sure Vien would've killed his beloved son then and there as well." Rhea searched the shadows swirling in front of her.

"You talk about how you saved him, but *you're* going to kill him," she said, her words almost twisted into some kind of plea. *Don't kill him*, her words seemed to say.

"The Death Mark? He's interfered... far too much," the voices echoed his words around her. "It's time for him to go."

"Please," Rhea said, bowing her head. "*Please.*"

"Your affections are misplaced. A Celestial should never

feel anything for a creature," Death said, almost arrogantly. She looked up at him, her eyes steeled.

"Is this all because of Tallulah? Because of what happened to her?" Tallulah's face flashed through both their minds.

"*Do not speak her name*," Death hissed. The shadows grew closer to Rhea, who tried to keep herself from shaking. She took a deep breath.

"The Gods didn't intervene when she was tortured," she whispered, the memory flooding back to her.

"He could've waved his hands and saved her. Instead, he let her suffer. Just like thousands—*millions*—of others," he growled. "And yet *he* was worshipped by all."

"Is that why you've helped Khalon all this time? Because he reminded you of her. Because you knew how important he was going to be to us, someday," she whispered, realization flooding her. The shadowy figure stood still, silence enveloping them.

"Please," Rhea got down on her knees. "Let him live. I won't warn him anymore of your plans. Please just—let him live."

"You fool," Death snapped. "Khalon will die, sooner than the others. Death has been waiting for him for a long time. I cannot delay it any longer." Rhea thought she heard a twinge of sadness within his voice.

"Then, let me go!" she cried, throwing her head back to look up at the shadowy figure. "Take my life for his. Leave my body and go into Than's and just let me *go*."

"Poor child. You sealed your own fate that day," the shadowy figure said as he started to dissipate.

"You want to save everyone but me? Don't you feel bad

for *my* life? The life *you* stole?" Rhea thundered as she stood up. She reached towards the shadows but they evaded her touch as they disappeared. "Don't you pity *me*? The life you clung onto? The life you *destroyed*?" Silence answered her as tears started to roll down her cheeks.

"Let me go, you monster," she whispered. "Let me live my life. Let me try and save him." The tears started to run more freely as she dropped to her knees.

"Khalon," she whispered, trying to search for him. But all she felt were walls being put up all around her. "Khalon..."

"You're seriously not going to kill the God of Death?" Khai asked once he had caught up to Khalon. Khalon's mouth twisted as he faced his half-brother. Outside of the Vampire's Lair, Khalon's hands balled up into fists as he stared down Khai.

"You want me to kill Rhea," he said, his voice barely above a whisper.

"I don't—You don't gotta phrase it like that, Khalon. I don't want you to *kill* Rhea. Of course not. But, we don't really have much of a choice. The God of Death is draining the magic from the world, you heard what they said and I've..."

"What? You've felt it? Because you're a witch now, right? After all these years, you think you're a witch? Just because your mom is one doesn't mean you are." Khai held his chin up as he looked up at his brother.

"I am one, Khalon. I might not practice it, but I can feel it inside of me. And the world *has* been feeling different. And ridding the world of Rhea will save the Saviors. That's the important part, isn't it? That's what we're supposed to do. That's what *you're* supposed to do since you can—"

"Duty? That's your argument?" Khalon asked, taking a step forward. Khai stood his ground.

"She told you herself, right? Find the witch, find the portals, and protect the Saviors. Then you can come to her. She must *know* she's going to die," he pointed out.

"She thinks *I'm* going to die," Khalon corrected.

"And you're okay with that? Dying for her? Even though the rest of us would—"

"Did I not make myself clear?" Khalon snarled, getting close to his face. "I don't care if the *world* burns if Rhea isn't in it."

"Khalon, she's barely in there," Aponi said, interrupting the two brothers. Khai's nostrils flared as he stared up at his older brother. They didn't look away from each other.

"You *know* she's barely in there. If the Death God leaves her body, she's going to die," Aponi implored.

"You don't know that," Khalon snapped, turning his head towards her. She raised her hands as she took a step back.

"You're going to throw everything away for a girl you've barely known for a month?" Khai exclaimed, throwing his hands up. Khalon felt something in his chest break. *"Khalon,"* Rhea's voice seemed to echo around his head. He winced.

"Yes," he said through the pain, "I would."

"We'll just get a Mortiferis then," Aponi said, turning towards Khai. "You can summon—"

"You're not touching her," Khalon growled as he felt his body change. The world seemed to get slightly smaller as he felt himself grow a foot taller. His skin turned into black scales that flashed red. He bared his teeth at Khai.

"Fine," Khai said, his gaze hardening. "I guess I will obey my mother one last time." Khalon paused at his words. Khai's body slowly turned into a dragon humanoid. His body lengthened a foot and his skin flipped into red scales. His eyes morphed from light brown to red—just like their father's dragon form.

"You drank the blood," Khalon hissed.

"To kill you, yeah," Khai glowered. "And I'll kill you if I have to." And then they were at each other's throats.

"Khai!" Khalon heard Aponi shout, but it wasn't enough to deter the two of them. They snapped at each other's faces, before Khalon threw Khai onto the ground. Khalon was about to jump onto him but paused once he saw the pained expression on Khai's face.

Slowly, his scales were turning back to skin, and his red eyes were morphing back into his light brown ones. Khai let out a wordless scream as he closed his eyes, curling up into the fetal position on the ground.

"Khai?" Khalon said, feeling himself turn back to normal as he rushed towards his younger brother. "Khai? What's wrong?" Kamaria flew out of the bar towards the Draconian King and kneeled down next to him. Her eyes roved over his body, looking for any sign of injury.

Khai was in so much pain that he couldn't talk. Instead, he signed something to Kamaria. She held still for a moment, before glancing towards Khalon.

"What is it? What's wrong?" he asked. Kamaria shook her head as she started to pull off Khai's clothes.

"He said he feels like he's burning," Aponi murmured, from next to Khalon. He turned towards her, his eyebrows furrowing.

"Burning?" he repeated. Kamaria finished pulling off Khai's shirt and turned him over. Khalon's eyes widened as he looked at the branding that was starting to show up along Khai's spine, right over top of the red scales shaped like a dragon, the sign of a royal draconian.

"The mark of the Death God," Khalon heard a voice say above him. Poseidon was standing over them. Khai let out a whimper as another Celestial letter was branded onto his skin.

"How?" Khalon asked, turning his attention back towards his little brother.

"He tried to kill you," Poseidon said. "Now, he has to face my brother's wrath."

24

Feeling a presence in the back of his head, Maleko paused. He turned towards Apsara who was trying to figure out how to drive the hover car.

King Maleko, a faraway voice whispered into his ear. He looked around the hover car, trying to find the source of the whispering.

King of the Seas, another voice whispered. Maleko frowned as he turned towards Apsara. She didn't seem to be hearing anything.

Save the Seer, a different voice echoed around his head.

"You're hearing this, too, right?" he asked Apsara. She brushed her long, black hair off of her face as she gave him an incredulous look.

"Hear what?"

"Those voices," he insisted.

"I hear nothing, Maleko," she grumbled as she turned back to the console of the hover car. It was just sleek white steel. No buttons, no steering wheel, nothing. Her hardly there eyebrows were furrowed as she stared at the technology.

Save the Seer, the voice repeated.

The Daughter of An, the Queen of Witches, the other voice said.

Stuck in a room of gold and white, the last voice whispered.

Only you can save her, the three voices said simultaneously. And then the presence was gone. Maleko rubbed the back of his neck as he felt the presence start to dissipate.

"Is there some kind of entity that is able to speak to you in your head?" he asked. Apsara wrinkled her nose as she glanced over at him. She ran her hand along the smooth console, her finger finally catching onto something. She pressed down, and a steering wheel popped out of the console, the hover car finally roaring to life.

"The Fates," Apsara finally said after letting out a gleeful noise from her success. She turned towards Maleko as the hover car started to lift into the air.

"Valerian should know *exactly* where the other merpeople are," she said, a determined look on her face. *Great, the dryad*, he thought. Maleko twisted his mouth as he stared at the shrinking ground.

"Apsara, I think the Fates were speaking to me," he said. Apsara snorted.

"Why would the Fates be speaking to *you*?"

"I'm the King of Argentiunda. Why wouldn't they speak to me?"

"Argentiunda is no more. There's no point in speaking to you unless they tell us how to save our people," she said matter-of-factly. Maleko leaned back into his chair as she pushed the steering wheel to get the hover car to move forward.

"You really trust Valerian still?" he asked. Her face hardened as she concentrated on keeping the hover car in the air, almost hitting another elven hover car in the process.

"I don't know," she muttered. "But, I *do* know he'll know where they are and how to save them."

"You *really* think the Fates weren't speaking to me?" he asked after a moment of silence. Apsara's beautiful face contorted into confusion as she stared straight ahead.

"The Fates aren't known for meddling with the living. They would only say something if you summoned them or if it were something extremely important. It could be a witch who was talking to you instead," she suggested. His eyebrows knitted together as he gazed at the passing scenery.

"How do you know where Valerian is?" Apsara gritted her teeth at his question as she looked down at the passing buildings below.

"I'm connected to his tree," she said, flipping her hand over to show the inside of her ring finger. There, a small image of a tree was imprinted onto her skin. He stared at the image for the longest time.

"You... You *married* him?" Maleko said, his voice shrill. Apsara clicked her tongue in distaste as she took away her hand.

"Married is a strong word," she muttered.

"A strong word? Apsara," Maleko's mind was racing. "You can't marry without my permission as a guard of the king." She rolled her perfect brown eyes.

"It's not like that," she said. "We married so that way I can find his tree if I ever need protection. That's all."

"That's *all?*" his voice was strident.

"Your highness," she said the words sarcastically, "the dryad doesn't find me appealing. Don't worry."

"What do you mean he doesn't find you *appealing?*" he said, distraught. "He has *eyes*, Apsara. And he's a man. Just because he's a dryad, and female dryads are known for their otherworldly beauty, doesn't mean that he doesn't find you the most beautiful creature to have ever lived!" Apsara's eyebrows raised as she glanced over at him.

"He prefers males, Maleko," she said, her voice quiet, her eyes back on the air space in front of her. Maleko stilled as he slowly sat back in his seat.

"Right," he mumbled. "I mean, that's the only explanation that makes sense." Apsara was quiet for a little while.

"That's the only explanation that makes sense?" she asked, repeating his words back to him. He looked over at her, his eyes taking in her profile. His eyes followed the soft edges of her wide nose, the angles in her cheeks, before resting on her full lips. He shook his head.

"Yes," he answered, his voice low. "Any creature would be lucky to have you." He felt her gaze on him, but he couldn't bring himself to look at her.

"Thank you for the kind words, your highness," her voice said, barely above a whisper. Maleko didn't allow the words he wanted to say slip through his lips: They weren't just words.

————

"You don't think he's the God of All of this world, do you?" Lorena whispered as she glanced at the boy with stark white hair. He continued to scribble on some sheet of white parchment. Elion frowned as he shook his head. He focused on the shelves in front of them.

"The God of All is the God of all realms, not just ours. He's not him. But, he *is* something special," Elion muttered, his blue eyes glancing at the boy.

"His name is Cyril," Lorena said. She couldn't keep her eyes off of him, like she wanted to kill him for making her body move without permission. Elion had to refrain from letting out a chuckle. She looked up at him, her hazel eyes meeting his. "Does that name mean anything to you?"

"No," he mused. "I've never heard the name before." She grumbled under her breath as she walked down the length of the bookshelves.

"So, we're looking for some kind of evidence that something magical occurred here in this world," Lorena whispered. Elion nodded as he looked at the sea of history books in front of him.

"Yeah," he mumbled. "Might be harder than we thought."

"Maybe," she said, striding up to him as she spoke quietly, "You should ask the kid with the weird eyes."

"He looks like he's only a couple of years younger than you," Elion pointed out.

"Exactly," she said, not lowering her gaze, "A child." Elion couldn't help the small smile that appeared on his face.

"Sure," he whispered, leaning his face down closer to Lorena's. She fluttered her lashes in confusion. "I'll ask him." He straightened up as he heard her let out a breath and walked over to the boy.

"Cyril, is it?" Elion asked. The boy lifted his head. He looked exhausted as he rubbed his face before nodding.

"Did you find what you were looking for?" the boy asked, a yellow writing utensil still in his hand.

"Uh, actually, we're having some trouble. We're looking for stuff in history about... things that are... unnaturally occurring?" Elion struggled to say. Cyril's white eyebrows knitted together as he stared at the elf.

"Unnaturally occurring? Like... weird landmarks or something?"

"No," Elion shook his head. "Things like... in myths. Mythology!" Elion nodded his head ferociously. "Things like in mythology. But with... magical creatures... perhaps?" Cyril's ever-changing eyes stopped on the color blue once Elion said the words "magical creatures." Elion studied the boy as he looked up, thinking. Once he looked back at Elion, his eyes started changing color constantly again.

"Oh, like the Salem witch trials? Stuff like that?" Cyril asked.

"Witch trials?" Elion said, his eyebrows raised. Then, he shook his head before nodding. "Yeah, exactly. Stuff like that." Cyril slowly got up before leading Elion back to the history section of the store. He pulled out a book titled appropriately: *The Salem Witch Trials*.

"This is about the witch trials in Massachusetts," Cyril said, handing it over to Elion as Lorena hovered around the book, trying to see the title of it.

"What's Massachusetts?" she asked, her eyes narrowing. Cyril frowned as he looked at her.

"The... state?" he said slowly. He shook his head before heading back to his post at the front of the store.

"What's a state?" she asked Elion. Elion shrugged as he started to flip through the book.

"I have no idea, but I'm guessing it's some kind of place," he said. He sat down on the ground, Lorena following his actions.

"So, there were witches here," she whispered. Elion nodded as he tried to skim through the book.

"It looks like it. And it looks like they faced some of the most horrible persecution," he whispered back as he read the words that detailed how the witches were hung and executed. Some died in harsh prison conditions and others were buried alive underneath stones. Elion couldn't help the shudder that ran down his spine.

"The humans here hate magical creatures," Lorena muttered as she read the same words over his shoulder. He closed the book, squeezing his eyes shut in the process.

"All those women," he muttered. Lorena scoffed.

"Don't act like you feel bad for them. Your brother slaughters humans like we're some kind pastime exercise, and you've never done anything about it," she hissed. Elion looked away from her, his jaw clenching.

"I know," he whispered. She was right. She was always right about him.

"Creatures everywhere are just violent and selfish," she murmured. "It's like all we know how to do is kill."

"Do you think they murdered *all* the witches who escaped into this world?" Elion asked, changing the subject. Lorena shrugged.

"There's no way they got all of them. But, I doubt there's

a lot still practicing. I wouldn't continue practicing witch-craft after an event like that," she pointed out. Elion winced as he looked at the boy's back.

"We need to find one, in order to get back to our world," he whispered. She looked around as she shrugged.

"I don't know," she muttered. "I think I like it here more." Elion frowned.

"You can't stay here," he argued. "This isn't our world."

"Well, here, I won't be murdered just for existing," she retorted.

"We can't just invade another world. It's wrong," he insisted.

"They're human and I'm human. It's only wrong for you magical creatures to invade a world without magic," she said, holding her head up high. "I want to stay."

"You can't."

"Is that an order, your majesty?" she asked, her eyes dripping with contempt. Elion studied her expression for a moment before looking away.

"Let's just find a witch before you decide," he murmured. He could still feel her hateful gaze on him as he heard the front door open. Elion looked up and he watched as elven assassins walked up to the boy at the front desk.

"Do you need help finding something?" Cyril asked the assassins. Elion glanced at Lorena whose eyes were wide. He motioned for her to stay put as he slowly walked towards the front of the store.

"You think he's one of them?" one of the assassins said. His long white hair barely covered his elven ears.

"What was the prophecy again? The one on who we're supposed to kill?" one of the other assassins uttered.

"Sorry, do you need help or not?" Cyril asked, his voice monotonous. But Elion could see his hand tremble ever so slightly.

"Six eggs were sent away, but six eggs will come to stay. For when the heir arrives, all will bow. For no one can resist the Gods' ancient vow. Ever-changing eyes, who see all, only he can stop the Mortiferis and reverse death's fall," another assassin said, reading from a hologram. "The Seer said he would be at this bookstore." Elion froze as he stared at the boy. *The Seer?* How was his brother in contact with the Seer?

"Ever-changing eyes, huh?" the first assassin said, looking at Cyril. "Looks like this kid is it."

"If you guys don't leave, I'm calling the cops," Cyril said, his voice quivering faintly.

"You're a Savior," Elion said, stepping out from behind a bookshelf. The assassins froze as they regarded him.

"Your highness," one of them whispered, recognizing Elion as one of the Princes of Aureum. Confusion etched across Cyril's brow as he turned towards Elion.

"We are just following King Adamar's orders. We've been ordered to find and eliminate—"

"Anything you say, they will have to listen to," Elion whispered to Cyril, whose ever-changing eyes were wide, ignoring the assassin's justification.

"What are you talking about?" Cyril said, his voice shaking.

"Tell them to implode," Elion ordered. "And they will."

"Tell them to... what?"

"Or tell them to stab each other," Lorena said, appearing next to Elion.

"If you don't, they'll kill you," he implored.

"And we don't have any weapons besides this dagger," she said, holding up her blade as she shrugged.

"We don't have time for this. Prince Elion is the lowest of all princes and we're following orders," one of the assassins said to the other.

"Do it now," Elion insisted. Cyril looked at him like he was crazy but turned towards the elves who were starting to come towards him.

"Stab each other to death," Cyril said to them. Even though the order wasn't directed towards Elion, he felt the subtlest urge to grab Lorena's dagger and impale her with it. He shook his head, trying to get the order out.

The elven assassins, on the other hand, stood still as they heard the order. And with the ferociousness of a well-trained swordsman, they unsheathed their weapons and cut off each other's heads. Cyril's jaw dropped as his ever-changing eyes stopped on the color dark blue, the color of the elves' blood.

"Oh my God," the boy muttered under his breath. His eyes were wide, the color still frozen as he stared at the pooling blood.

"They only have one God here?" Lorena asked, turning towards Elion.

"The humans believed in only one God during the dark ages," Elion whispered towards her. "You didn't know that?" She made a motion towards him like she was going to stab him herself.

"What is happening?" Cyril whispered to himself.

"That's what I should be asking," a woman said as she entered the store, a jingling echoing throughout it. Elion frowned as he looked at the woman. He had only seen the

Draconian Queen once during a meeting, but this woman looked exactly like her.

"Queen Aoife?" he whispered. She shook her head.

"My name's Kaydee, not Aoife," she muttered. She looked exactly like Aoife, except her hair was a wavy strawberry blonde, her eyes were gray, and she didn't have any scales on her body.

"Kaydee what?" Lorena asked, her eyes studying the new human.

"Kaydee Crispus," she said as she waved a hand. A metallic smell filled the room as the bodies trembled into nothing, the blue blood disappearing with them.

"A Crispus," Elion heard Lorena breathe next to him.

"What is going on?" Cyril asked, his eyes changing color quicker than before. He stared at all of them in horror. "Who are you all?"

"No one you need to know, for now," Kaydee said, waving a hand over his face. He stared at her, his eyes almost silver, before falling asleep onto the counter. Kaydee's face contorted into anger as she looked at Elion.

"You two are from Asynithis, right?" she asked, crossing her arms. Elion nodded his head slowly, still in shock from looking at a woman who was Queen Aoife but not.

"This is his seventh life. He's not supposed to know about any of this yet. Not until his powers come in fully," Kaydee explained.

"Come in fully?" Elion asked. He gestured to the empty spot that used to contain the slaughtered elves. "He clearly can use his powers."

"No," she shook her head. "He hasn't come into his own yet. It happens when they're all sixteen."

"This is his seventh life? Then, he should be in Asynithis soon," Lorena said, almost sighing in relief.

"For him, it'll be in a couple of years. For you, it could be hundreds of years," Kaydee said, her voice low. "But, until he turns sixteen, he cannot know about Asynithis."

"Why?" asked Elion. Kaydee shook her head, her wavy hair spilling over her shoulders.

"I just know it's bad, if they do," she said, looking at the boy who was fast asleep on the counter. "I erased his memory so he won't remember."

"How old are you?" Elion asked. Kaydee frowned.

"I'm 26, not that you need to know," she said. His eyebrows raised as he realized that she wasn't thousands of years old.

"And how do you know about Asynithis?" he said. She cocked an eyebrow.

"I know my family history pretty well," she said. "We are, apparently, pure magic. Though, it's been diluted through the years."

"You look exactly like..."

"A Queen Aoife? I know. I've been told by a different elf," she said.

"You've seen more elves," Lorena more said than asked. She nodded her head.

"They're always coming after the Saviors. And I usually have to kill them before they ruin everything," she grumbled.

"You're protecting them, the Saviors," Elion mused.

"It's our family duty, apparently. Help save Asynithis," Kaydee shrugged. Lorena scoffed.

"The Crispus witches are selfish, murderous, psychotic, little—" Elion put a hand over her mouth.

"We appreciate you helping the Saviors," he said, a smile on his face. Kaydee narrowed her gray eyes. Eyes that should've been pure silver.

"Are you here to kill them too?" she asked, pointing to her ears. Elion felt the heat rush towards his face as he pulled the hat he was wearing down lower over his pointed ones.

"No," he said. "We accidentally fell into a portal."

"You need help getting back?"

"Actually, yes we do," Elion said. She smiled at him as she opened the store door, the jingle echoing throughout the establishment once more.

"Follow me, then," she said.

25

"Is there a way to remove the Death Mark from Khai?" Khalon asked once they were settled in the lobby of a nearby hotel. Sweat drenched Khai's brow as he winced, leaning back into the chair he was sitting on.

"There's no way to get rid of it," Poseidon said. It was weird for Khalon to look at a completely different creature and realize it was the Sea God he traveled with months ago. Poseidon was shorter than he was before, a bit more stout, and he was darker in color. His hair was short and black, cut close to his head. His eyes were sepia colored instead of hazel. The only recognizable part of him were the waves crashing behind his irises.

"Do you know everything about a mark from the Gods?" Aponi asked, her face blank. Khalon glanced over at Kamaria who was patiently waiting for the answer, her large, black eyes wide.

"I don't know *everything* about every individual God's

mark, no," Poseidon said. "But, I do know enough that the Death Mark can only be removed by the God of Death."

"Why were you stupid enough to attack Khalon?" Kamaria signed at Khai. He rolled his eyes before squeezing them shut. Another Celestial letter was branded onto him.

"I wasn't in that much pain when I was branded," Khalon pointed out. "Why is it like this for him?"

"The Death Mark isn't for him. It's only being put onto Khai because he attacked you," Poseidon explained. "He's being punished." Kamaria glowered at Khalon's half brother as he took in another sharp inhale.

"This is worse than being stabbed with an elven sword," Khai muttered.

"As if you've ever felt that pain," Aponi translated Kamaria's signing. Kamaria scowled at him. He tried to give her a small smile that she refused to return.

"It scratched my arm once," he whispered as he signed to her. Khalon turned towards Poseidon, his voice low as he looked into the Sea God's eyes.

"How do we save Rhea and Khai from him?" Khalon barely whispered. Poseidon gave him a smirk.

"Summon the Fates," Poseidon whispered back, before winking.

"Can't you just talk to them?" Khalon asked. He shrugged.

"I can, but then I'm just talking to who they are now. Not the Fates, if that makes sense."

"It makes no sense," Khalon stated.

"The Fates, when summoned by creatures, can give you a glimpse into your future, can answer any question. Farrah, Felicity, and Francine won't be able to do that for you if I just call them here," Poseidon said. "Especially since they work for my brother."

"How do you summon the Fates?" Khalon asked after thinking for a long while. Poseidon nodded towards Aponi.

"The lightning bird could do it, with the magic she stole from her witch. Or the current King of Draconia," Poseidon said.

"She calls herself a thunderbird," Khalon clarified.

"Different cultures call her different things. I'm not surprised that she prefers to be called a thunderbird," Poseidon said, his eyebrows furrowing upwards. It was almost as if he pitied her. Khalon turned back towards Aponi who was clearly listening to the conversation. Her gaze was like ice. He cleared his throat.

"Right, so—"

"I'll summon the Fates," she said, her voice powerful as she stood up. Just as she declared this, Valerian sauntered back to the group.

"Here are some rooms for the day," Valerian said, handing out room keys. Kamaria and Aponi in one room. Khalon, Khai, and Poseidon in the other.

"What about you?" Poseidon asked the dryad.

"I have to stay in my tree," the dryad clarified. "I can't sleep if I'm not in my tree."

"Of course," Poseidon said, his face falling a bit. "We can summon the Fates in our room." Khalon nodded at his words.

"Do you think Khai will be okay?" Khalon asked. Kamaria motioned for Khai to get up, and he obeyed, begrudgingly. She gingerly lifted his billowing undershirt to look at the branding. Her gaze was unreadable as she put the shirt back down, Khai wincing as she did.

"It's done," she signed. Anger simmered in her gaze as she tore her eyes away from Khai's back.

"Let's go," Khalon whispered as Khai slowly stood up. The guilt ate him alive as he looked at his younger brother.

"I'm fine," Khai snapped, seeing the pity in Khalon's eyes.

"I know," Khalon said, his face once again like stone. "You'll be fine."

———

Aponi took the sand from Poseidon's hands once they got into the hotel room. There were two impeccably made queen-sized beds and the carpet felt like heaven underneath Khalon's bare feet. *Whoever that Valerian is, he must be loaded,* he couldn't help but think.

On the other hand, Khai's nose wrinkled as he entered the room. His narrowed eyes took in the small area—the heavy, blackout curtains keeping the sunlight from entering —before he sat down on one of the beds in disappointment.

"This room is way too small," he lamented. Khalon turned towards him in surprise.

"You think?"

"You think it's not?" Khai retorted, making a face of disgust as he turned away. Khalon shrugged as he sat down on the other bed, deciding against answering.

"Have you summoned anything before?" Khai asked Aponi.

"I've summoned stuff," she responded, quickly. A little

too quickly. Khai's eyebrow cocked as he lowered his head to look at her.

"Really?" Aponi grumbled under her breath in response as she continued finishing up the circle.

"I've summoned things for her majesty," she finally said as she stood up.

"Like what?" Khai said, looking over at Kamaria. Kamaria signed something really quick to him, which made him smile.

"An obsidian sword that she lost once," Aponi translated for Khalon under her breath. Khalon couldn't help the smile that spread across his own face.

"So, really, you haven't summoned anything before," Khai said, crossing his arms.

"I wouldn't look so smug if I were you. You're a... what? A Crispus witch? But have no idea how to use magic? Yeah, that's what I thought," Aponi retorted as she stood in the middle of the circle. Khai's smirk was wiped off of his face.

"Just like how you summoned that sword," Poseidon said, interrupting, "Try and summon the Fates. If it helps, since you've never summoned entities before, their current names are Farrah, Francine, and Felicity."

"And I'm guessing you like Felicity the most," Aponi said. A sly smile spread on Poseidon's face.

"You're good," he said, nodding his head. He, then, gestured for her to start. Aponi took a deep breath before closing her eyes. A metallic smell filled Khalon's nostrils as the floating lights in the room started to flicker.

Aponi's hair—that was just starting to turn back into its ebony color—turned pure white as lightning skittered across her body. Her eyes opened, lightning filling up her entire sclera. The floating lights hummed before exploding. Khalon covered his head as the shards of glass went around the room, the room covered in darkness.

Aponi fell to the ground, panting as three figures emerged from the ground. She took a step outside of the circle to give the figures room. They were women. One with blonde hair, one with wavy brown hair, and the other with curly dark brown hair. Their eyes glowed as they stared at the group.

"Welcome Moirai," Poseidon said. He turned towards Khalon. "Farrah is the blonde, Felicity is the brunette, and Francine is the one with her hair up." They all turned towards him simultaneously.

"Who called upon us?" their voices spoke in unison. "Who has a question?" Poseidon looked over at Khalon. Khalon swallowed before taking a step forward.

"The Dragon King," Farrah mused.

"The bastard child," Felicity whispered.

"The God of Death's," Francine said. They all watched him as he took a deep breath. He opened his mouth to ask his question, but was interrupted.

"Only one question," Felicity said.

"Per person," Farrah ordered, as she looked around the room.

"It's the rules," Francine explained. Khalon nodded his head as he glanced at Khai. Khai's eyes were wide as he took in the sight of the three Fates. There were so many questions Khalon had, but there was only one that he really wanted to ask.

"How do I save Rhea?" Felicity almost giggled as she looked at her sisters.

"What a question," Farrah said.

"Should've been more specific," Francine warned. Khalon opened his mouth.

"Can't change it now," Felicity interrupted.

"Only one way to save Rhea," they said simultaneously, their words reverberating throughout the room. "Sever the God from the soul."

"But it'll be hard," Farrah said.

"Nearly impossible," Felicity nodded.

"How do I sever the God of Death from her?" Khalon asked, taking another step forward. Francine held up a finger.

"Ah, ah, ah, one question only, *Dragon* King," Francine responded.

"You gave him too much of a hint, Sister," Farrah reprimanded. Francine smiled at Khalon and winked a glowing brown eye.

"Who's next?" they asked in unison, turning away from Khalon. He took a step back as he watched Khai walk in front of the Fates.

"Me, I have a question," Khai said. The Fates looked him up and down.

"The false king," Farrah said.

"The dragon slayer," Felicity whispered.

"The imprisoned prince," Francine muttered.

"We can guess your question, draconian," the Fates said. "The Death God claims you as punishment."

"How do I escape the fate the Death God has for me?" Khai asked. The Fates smiled simultaneously, causing shivers to go down Khalon's spine.

"You can't escape Death," the Fates said. "No one can."

"Only one way to escape it, for now," Felicity said, her green, glowing eyes on Khai.

"One must," Francine started.

"Give their life," Farrah finished.

"Not just any life," Felicity warned. "A life worth more."

"Or by killing him before he kills you," they said.

"A life worth more? What does that mean?" Khai pressed.

"One question," they hissed.

"We have a message. Find the witch, find the portals, protect the Saviors," the Fates whispered. Khalon's eyebrows furrowed as he took a step forward. They turned their heads towards him.

"You've already had your turn," they snapped. Aponi took a step forward and nodded towards Khalon.

"What witch? We've already found her," Aponi pointed out. The Fates clicked their tongue as they shook their heads.

"With hair like rose-gold," Francine whispered.

"Eyes like a storm," Farrah said.

"And the face of a scorned mother," Felicity finished.

"This is the Crispus witch you must find," they said in unison.

"You're out of questions," Farrah declared. And then suddenly, they disappeared, the room covered in complete darkness once more.

Kamaria pulled open the heavy curtains, letting in the sunlight. And as she did, her eyebrows knitted together.

"Where's Aponi?" she signed. Khalon looked back at the circle of sand that had been broken, like someone was dragged in.

"Well," Poseidon said, as he sat down on one of the beds, "They *did* say '*you* must find.'"

————

Aponi sat up from the dirt that she landed in as she took in her surroundings. She was in a forest of some kind and in the distance, she could hear some kind of squelching sound. Slowly, Aponi walked towards the sound, the brush hiding her figure. Hunched over a man's corpse was a woman with long, black hair tied into a single braid down her back. She wore a long, white skirt that made her look shapeless. The ends of her white, loose, long sleeves were stained red. Taking another step closer, a branch snapped underneath Aponi's foot. She froze.

The girl turned around, her heavy-lidded eyes an unnatural dark gray. Her pale face was covered in blood. Aponi took a hesitant step backwards as the girl slowly stood up. She didn't look like a vampire—not like the vampires that Aponi had ever seen—and yet, it was clear she was one. The girl, who couldn't have been older than sixteen, cocked her head as she took another step forward, like she was prowling.

The girl stood still for a moment longer. Aponi could hear her short breaths in the silence. And then, the girl raced towards her. Aponi turned swiftly as she started to run. But, once she did, the world around her blurred together until she fell face first.

She scurried onto her back as she felt the immense heat coming towards her. In front of her was a building that was in flames. A boy with red hair was jumping up and down in front of the building. Fire spewed out of his hands, causing another section of the building to be put aflame. Aponi's eyes slowly looked over at the sign in front of her. She could only make out the words "High School" on it. She glanced back at the boy who was wearing light gray jeans and a matching jean jacket. He was still laughing maniacally as he destroyed the building.

Aponi looked down as she tried to get herself up. *I need to get out of here*, she thought to herself.

"Who the hell are you?" she heard a voice way too close to her say. She glanced up at the boy who was suddenly standing in front of her. His hateful copper eyes reminded her of Rhea's.

"I—" but before Aponi could say anything, the world started spinning. Until she landed right in front of a woman with the face of the Draconian Queen Mother Aoife.

"Are you okay?" she asked as she leaned down, holding out a hand. Aponi looked up, into a familiar face who was next to the woman.

"You're that elf," she said, pointing at his face in astonishment.

"Elion," he said, putting a hand over his chest. "This is Lorena."

"How—Why are you here?" Aponi asked, shocked. She looked back at the woman with Aoife's face.

"And who are you?" she demanded.

"I'm Kaydee. Who are you?" the woman said, putting a hand on her hip.

"*The witch*," voices in Aponi's head said. "*You're welcome.*"

"Wait, you're the Crispus wi—" and then suddenly

Aponi was back in the hotel room with Khalon staring at her in disbelief.

"You were just gone," he said. "And then you reappeared out of thin air!"

"How long was I gone?" Aponi asked as she looked at their faces.

"Only a few minutes," Khai shrugged.

What happened? Kamaria signed.

"I saw these... people... evil people," Aponi muttered, signing for Kamaria as she spoke. "One was a vampire, but didn't look it. The other was burning down a building called a 'High School,' whatever that is. Then, I was transported in front of the witch the Fates were talking about."

"They showed you two kids?" Poseidon asked. Aponi cocked her head side to side.

"They looked like they were around my age," Aponi clarified.

"You saw the witch? How do we find her?" Khalon asked.

"I don't know. Her name is Kaydee and she looks exactly like Queen Aoife," Aponi shuddered as she spoke.

"She looks like my mom?" Khai's face dropped before repeating the words the Fates had said earlier, "The face of a scorned mother."

"That elf was with her," she said, turning towards Khalon.

"The one who was with Freya," Poseidon mused. He leaned back as he looked up at the ceiling. "Elion."

"Yeah, that was his name," Aponi said, pointing towards Poseidon.

"So, the witch is in Aureum," Khalon said, getting up.

"No," Poseidon shook his head. "The witch is on Earth. It sounds like our friend got stuck there."

"What?"

"And the two kids... I bet you they're a couple of the Saviors," Poseidon mused.

"You think that *those* two were the Saviors?" Aponi said, incredulously. "One of them was eating another human, and the other was burning down a building while laughing. I don't think that those two are part of the Saviors."

"The Fates wouldn't have shown you them otherwise," Poseidon pointed out. "Two of them battle with their dark natures."

"If they're evil, how are they going to be able to save Asynithis?" Khalon asked.

"They're not evil. They just have the same urges as a lot of creatures in Caedoxia do. Each of the Saviors represents something in Asynithis. Those two represent the creatures in Caedoxia," Poseidon pointed out. "Though, I wonder why the Fates showed you them. It's not them in their seventh life, is it?"

"I don't know," Aponi answered honestly. "It wasn't clear."

"So, we've found the witch. Now what?" Khai asked.

"We all go our separate ways," Poseidon said. "I need to take care of my brother. Perhaps, Khai, you could help me with that?"

"You don't touch Rhea. Not until I figure out how to sever her soul from the God of Death's," Khalon growled. Poseidon put his hands up as his mouth twisted into a smirk.

"The Fates gave you a hint. They rarely do that, draconian," he said.

"The only thing they did was call me the Dragon King," Khalon pointed out. Poseidon's smile spread.

"Exactly."

26

Apsara scoured the forest around the city of Byrrus for Valerian's tree. She felt a tugging deep inside her, pulling her in one direction, but she couldn't pinpoint where his tree was exactly.

"We need to land," Apsara said as she tried to find a good spot to park the hover car.

"Tell me, how do you know the dryad again? You must know him pretty well, since you guys got married and everything," Maleko said as the hover car shuttered against the ground. He looked at her through his lashes, brushing his tousled hair back.

"It's a long story," Apsara responded, getting out of the hover car. Hundreds of trees surrounded them, and she narrowed her eyes as she glowered at any within her sight. *Do not tell Valerian,* her gaze seemed to say.

"Why are you glaring at the trees?" Maleko asked, suddenly, snapping her out of her staring contest. She scowled as she started to walk forward, following the tugging within her.

"Trees are talkative," she whispered. "Incredibly gossipy." Maleko looked up at the naked branches in wonder.

"Really?" he breathed. "That's so interesting." He turned towards her, an eyebrow raised on his tanned face.

"So, Valerian?" he said. Apsara turned her scowl towards him, and he seemed to shrink a little in her gaze.

"What about him?"

"You married him... when?" Apsara rolled her eyes.

"You seem really interested in my private life, your highness," she said.

"I just want to know if when you met him is when you married him, is all," he explained, gesturing as he spoke. She stared at his hands before looking back at his face. Letting out a deep sigh, she closed her eyes.

"Fine, I'll tell you if you really want to know," she muttered. Maleko nodded his head anxiously, encouraging her to continue. She opened her eyes and gave him a side-long glance.

"I met Valerian in a bar in Sylva during one of my rounds. We had a really enlightening conversation about the world and history. I had never spoken with anyone on such a personal level before," she muttered, her eyes glazed over.

"You liked him, at first," Maleko pointed out. Apsara let out a dry laugh.

"Maybe," she said. "But, I did seek him out the next time and the next time and the time after that." She shrugged. "He's so old that it was interesting to talk to him. He made me feel... safe. Small, in a way." Her face softened as she spoke. Something twisted in Maleko's chest as he watched her recount her interaction with the dryad. She glanced over at him and then shook her head.

"I always have to protect, not be the protected. It was a different experience to feel like someone else had my back. That's all," she whispered. "When the prophecy was announced all those months ago, he suggested I use his tree as a place of safety, if need be."

"And so that's when you got married." Apsara nodded her head.

"Yes," she said. "It was also when he made his preferences clear to me, in case I got the wrong idea." Maleko nodded his head slowly as the crunching of dead leaves underneath their shoes filled the silence.

"It's cold in Caedoxia," he said, almost under his breath.

"It is." He stole a glance at her as she walked, her mind faraway. He peered at her for a moment longer before looking down at his own feet.

"I want you to feel safe around me, Apsara," he whispered. He could feel her gaze on him as they continued to walk in the direction that the tree pulled her in. For a minute, she was quiet. And then, Maleko heard her take a deep breath.

"I do, Maleko," she barely breathed. His head jolted up to look at her, but she refused to return his gaze. Instead, she stood still in front of a tree.

"This is it," she said. She knocked on the tree's trunk, hard. The brown leaves still on the branches rustled in the winter breeze.

"Maybe he's not in the tree..." Maleko whispered.

"No, he's in here," she said, her voice resolute. She took

the open palm of her hand and banged it against the side of the tree.

"If you don't come out here and face me, Val, I'll take a knife and cut up the trunk of this tree," Apsara threatened as she continued to bang against the tree trunk. "Do you hear me? I'll make sure you feel so much pain. I'll grab a saw and start to cut down your tree. How would you like that, *Val?*"

"All right, I hear you, Aps," an otherworldly voice spoke from inside the tree. *Aps?* Maleko's brow wrinkled in distaste. Apsara was such a beautiful name. Why would he ruin her name by demoting it to an ugly nickname like *Aps?* He looked over at Apsara with disapproval. Why would she *let* him?

Valerian stepped out of his tree, the bark stretching as he pulled himself out of it. His golden hair was tied up in a low ponytail. His equally golden eyes roved over his intruders.

"What are you doing here? Did you kill the God of Death?"

"Does it *look* like we've killed the God of Death?" Apsara thundered. Valerian put up his hands as he focused his attention on the mermaid in front of him.

"Apsara, I understand that you're angry—"

"I *trusted* you," she seethed.

"She doesn't trust many people," Maleko spoke up. Neither of them bothered to look at him.

"I put you in a safe place," Valerian argued, crossing his arms.

"A safe place? You think that's a safe place?" Her face contorted into pure rage as she took a prowling step forward.

"You wouldn't have been suspected," Valerian said, his head held up high.

"Except, we were suspected. And turns out, we know the prince of Aureum, so that wasn't great either," Maleko interrupted. Finally, Valerian's gold eyes glanced at him.

"You know the prince of Aureum?"

"Well, I am a king, aren't I?" Maleko bristled.

"I thought the Argentiundans didn't join any Asynithis world meetings," he mused. Maleko blinked.

"He doesn't," Apsara interjected. "But, I do." She whipped out her glass shard, quickly pressing it against Valerian's throat. He swallowed, his Adam's apple bobbing as Apsara pushed the glass against him harder.

"Aps, let's think about this," he whispered.

"Don't call her Aps," Maleko snapped. Apsara's expression softened as she glanced at him.

"Tell us where the other merpeople are," she hissed, recovering quickly as she glowered at the dryad.

"I don't know exactly..." Apsara pressed the glass further into his throat, breaking the skin. Amber liquid started to appear against his pale complexion.

"But, I do know who might," Valerian said quickly. "I know someone who will know where Ralnor will be." Apsara stared at him, hard, before finally removing her weapon. She gestured towards him.

"Show us the way." Valerian gave a frightened glance her way before starting to quickly walk through the forest.

"You need an actual weapon," Maleko whispered to Apsara. She gestured around herself.

"Do you see any tridents lying around?" she retorted. Maleko shrugged.

"If not a trident, something. Other than a piece of glass."

"It's the only thing I could find at short notice," she muttered. Then, she focused her glare on him. "Where's *your* weapon?"

"I left my trident," Maleko murmured, lowering his head. Apsara looked at the looming city in front of them.

"Perhaps Byrrus will have weapons we can get," she said, her expression settled.

They followed Valerian through the city of Byrrus, Maleko staring up at it all in wonder. The streets of Byrrus were empty, save for a few drunk creatures wandering around. Valerian led them to a tall, beige building with windows in rows down it.

"Why are we at a hotel?" Apsara asked. Maleko analyzed the building. *This* was a hotel?

"I have to stop here first," Valerian muttered. He went through the revolving doors. Apsara let out a loud sigh before following after him, dragging Maleko with her.

Valerian went up to the front desk as Maleko stared at the establishment they were standing in. He had to admit, the surface creatures were able to make their buildings a bit more diverse. It seemed like every interior he walked into was different than the last one.

A ding caught him by surprise as he looked over at the metal doors that slid open. Standing there was a short, dark man who seemed to light up at the sight of Valerian.

"Back so soon?" the human said as he walked up to the dryad. Following after him was someone Maleko recognized.

"Draconian?" he asked. The boy turned his head to look at the Argentiundan King. His gaze was intimidating, the scar on his left eye always catching anyone's attention. The mark of scales down his cheek and jaw looked as though someone clawed at him. And his short, buzzed hairstyle made the angles in his face seem sharper. He narrowed his black eyes as he took in the sight of Maleko.

"Do I know you?" he asked, his voice gruff. The dark man glanced over at Maleko and let out a chuckle.

"King Maleko, good to see you once more," the man said as he walked closer to him. Maleko frowned as he took in the human.

"It's Poseidon," Valerian clarified as he made his way back to Maleko and Apsara. His frown merely got deeper.

"Poseidon? Didn't he...?"

"Die? Yes, technically. But, I split my soul as one does," Poseidon said. Maleko's eyebrows raised as he exchanged a look with Apsara. They both bowed their heads in respect for their God. Before he could say a word, heavy steps rushed towards them.

"Khalon," the deep voice said, breathless. The draconian looked at the creature that stood in front of them.

"Jabulani? What are you doing here?" Khalon asked, bewildered. The creature with large black eyes and sharpened teeth looked around the lobby area.

"Where's Kamaria?" he asked.

"What's going on?" Khalon pressed, his face hardening as he crossed his arms. His dark eyes narrowed as he stared at the large creature standing before them. The creature named Jabulani took in a sharp inhale.

"Esi," he whispered. Khalon's stony mask fell as his eyebrows twitched.

"What. Happened?"

"Invenire fell, and she was taken... by Aureum, we think," Jabulani barely voiced. He hung his head, unable to meet Khalon's sharp gaze.

"Who's Esi?" Maleko piped up. Jabulani looked over at the Argentiundan King in surprise.

"She's the Seer," Poseidon explained. Maleko's eyebrows raised as he remembered the voices in his head.

"Is she considered the Daughter of An? The Queen of Witches?" he asked. Khalon took a step forward, towards him.

"Yes," he merely said. "Why? Do you know something?" Maleko cocked his head to the side as he tried to remember what the voice earlier had said.

"I heard three voices in my head on the way here," Maleko muttered. "Something about how only I can save the Seer."

"Only you?" Khalon looked at him in disbelief. Maleko nodded his head.

"Yes. And that she's..." he struggled to remember the exact words the voices used. "She's stuck in a room of gold and white, apparently."

"The Fates," Poseidon shook his head, chuckling. Khalon whipped his head over to him.

"We need to save her," he pressed.

"*We* don't need to do anything. It seems that's Maleko's journey."

"But, we can't just—"

"You and I have a different journey to go on, as it seems," Poseidon said. Khalon just stared at him.

"I'll go with the mermaid," a boy interjected. His light brown hair was pushed off of his face, and while he had the angular features that Khalon had, they were clearly different in how they held themselves. Khalon seemed to hold himself like a live wire, ready for anything that might be thrown at him. This boy, who was obviously related to him, held himself like he had all the time in the world.

"Kamaria and I will go," the boy corrected himself. A girl stood beside him, with red veins glowing sporadically underneath her dark skin. She gave Maleko an intimidating look.

"Khai—" Khalon started to say.

"I'll be fine. I learned how to be stealthy from the best," the boy named Khai shrugged. "Plus, we need to find a Mortiferis. Just in case." His eyes cut to Khalon whose face was like stone once more.

"Protect her with your life," Khalon said, meeting Maleko's eyes. Maleko nodded.

"I'll do my best," he said.

"We'll distract Aureum well enough," Poseidon smirked as he glanced at Valerian. Valerian nodded.

"They'll never see it coming," the dryad confirmed.

"So, it's settled then," Khalon said, leaning back. "We'll take back Draconia."

27

"Who in the world was that?" Kaydee exclaimed, her light gray eyes wide. Elion furrowed his eyebrows as he remembered the girl who had just disappeared into thin air.

"I've seen her with the Princess of Ustrina," he said.

"She's Queen now," Lorena corrected. "Princess Kamaria is Queen of Ustrina, now, for your information."

"Apologies," Elion said, bowing his head slightly.

"What the hell is Ustrina?" Kaydee asked, fully closing the door to the bookstore. The boy, Cyril, was still fast asleep. The sky had begun to burst into pastel colors as the sun was starting to rise.

"Ustrina is a country in Asynithis," Elion explained. "Filled with witches, phoenixes, Inkanyambas, humans, and other various creatures."

"Oh, I see," she said, confusion still creasing her brow.

"How did she get here?" Lorena asked, turning towards Elion. He shrugged as he looked back at the empty space that used to be filled with the girl with pure white hair and golden skin.

"She didn't use a portal," Elion muttered. Kaydee's lips were pursed as she continued to stare at the ground.

"She knew who I was," she said. "Like she was looking for me."

"Or someone was *having* her look for you," Lorena pointed out. Kaydee was silent for a brief moment before nodding her head.

"Come with me," she said. "I need to summon the Mother, the Crone, and the Maiden."

———

Kaydee's living quarters were incredibly small. There was a bed, a tiny kitchen, a little bit of storage space, and it was basically all a few steps away from one another. Elion viewed the room with dumbfounded eyes.

As if noticing his look, Kaydee blew a strawberry blonde lock out of her face. "Can you believe I pay two thousand dollars a month for this shit hole?" Elion didn't know what "dollars" were but he could infer that it was a type of currency. And by the way she was talking, it sounded like two thousand of it was a lot.

"I can't," he mumbled. She grabbed a bunch of items from her kitchen cabinets, holding them in her arms as she rushed towards the pink and purple rug that—kind of— separated the "bedroom" from the "kitchen."

"What is all of this for?" Elion asked as she started to draw a circle with sand.

"To summon the Mother, the Crone, and the Maiden," Kaydee said, making a face. "Obviously."

"You need all of this to summon an entity?" Elion asked. Kaydee shrugged.

"My ancestors *apparently* didn't need all of this. Magic just coursed through our blood and bodies like no other. But, it's been... diluted, I suppose, throughout the ages," Kaydee muttered. "Which is a good thing. No one needs that much magic."

"You still have more magic than most witches," Elion reassured. "I can smell it." Kaydee's eyes glazed over as she gave Elion a sad smile.

"I don't want more magic," she said, almost under her breath. She placed three crystal cups in the circle, filling each one up with different kinds of wine. One was red, the other was white, and the last cup was filled with a pink liquid.

"Rosé," she said. "The Maiden loves it." Lorena gave Elion a look that showed she felt like Kaydee might be off her rocker as she crossed the room towards him.

"They're... offerings," Elion more said than asked. Kaydee nodded her head as she closed her eyes.

"What entity needs offerings besides the Gods?" he whispered to Lorena. She shrugged in response.

"I thought all the Gods were dead," she whispered back.

"Shh!" Kaydee interjected. She closed her gray eyes once more as she seemed to tie an invisible string. The electrical lights in the apartment started to flicker, until they all went out, the only light coming from the small window behind her bed frame.

Elion watched with wide eyes as the wine started to

decrease in the cups, until all the liquid was gone. The cups suddenly were pushed outside the circle of sand as the three figures started to appear in its place.

"Ah, can always count on you to give exactly what is needed," one of the figures said as they started to come into focus.

"Of course," Kaydee said, bowing her head. Finally, the three figures stood in their entirety in front of them, eyes glowing. One had blonde hair and blue eyes, one had brown, wavy hair and green eyes, and the last one had curly, dark brown hair and brown eyes.

"The last Crispus witch," the blue-eyed figure said, her face slowly turning into an older woman's. The Crone.

"The teacher," the green-eyed figure said, her face aging only slightly. The Mother.

"The protector of the Saviors," the brown-eyed figure said, her face staying the same. The Maiden.

"We have a message for you," they said in unison.

"I figured," Kaydee responded. "But, I have a question."

"One question," the Crone said.

"Per person," the Mother ordered. Kaydee nodded her head.

"Of course," she whispered.

"What's your question, Crispus witch?" the Maiden asked, gesturing towards her with a brown hand.

"Who was the girl that appeared in front of us earlier today?" Kaydee asked, her eyes steeled.

"The lightning bird," the Mother responded.

"The witch killer," the Crone hissed.

"Aponi, servant to Queen Kamaria," the Maiden said. Kaydee's eyebrows rose.

"Witch killer?" she asked.

"One question," they hissed in unison.

"Right," Kaydee said under her breath. She looked over at Elion, gesturing towards him. Before Elion could take a step forward, all three of them raised their hands at the same time, stopping him from speaking.

"Now, our message," they said. "A danger is presented. In their seventh life, blood will run. Beware any reflection. Protect the Saviors."

"What does that even mean?" Lorena uttered. The three women turned towards her and Elion.

"Home will be out of reach until you eliminate the danger," they hissed. Kaydee opened her mouth to say something else, but the three women closed their eyes and disappeared into thin air.

All three of their mouths hung open as the lights flickered back on.

"A danger is presented. In their seventh life, blood will run. Beware any reflection. Protect the Saviors," Kaydee repeated under her breath. She turned towards Elion and Lorena. "As far as I know, this is the Saviors' seventh life. They're all in one place for the first time in history."

"They're all here, in this city?" Lorena asked. Kaydee nodded.

"They're not sixteen yet, so none of them know who they truly are," she explained. "It also means, they're not at full power either yet."

"The portals are open. And I know my brother is aiming for their seventh life," Elion pointed out. Kaydee raised an eyebrow.

"Your brother?"

"He's... He's the one who is helping the God of Death. He wants to conquer all the realms," he muttered. Kaydee stared at Elion for a moment more.

"Right," was all she said before turning away.

"Who's the witch killer?" she asked once she was in her kitchen. She grabbed a mug from a cabinet that read "Best Aunt Ever!"

The lightning bird's face flickered through Elion's mind. Her sharp gaze widened in recognition when she had saw him, an almost accusatory finger pointed.

"Oh, Aponi? The girl?" he said. He looked up at the ceiling. "If she's a lightning bird, she probably belonged to a witch at one point. Lightning birds are usually sold when they're young to other witches. They use them as familiars. The only way she could've left the possession of a witch is if she..." Elion let his words drift off as he remembered the white hair Aponi was sporting.

"If she killed a witch," Kaydee finished for him. She nodded her head. "Good for her." He turned towards Kaydee, an idea forming in his head.

"She must have magic. If a lightning bird kills a witch, they absorb their magic. Lightning birds are conductors, it's why witches use them. Perhaps, we're meant to use her in some way," he said.

"Use her how?" she asked.

"Maybe to jump through the portals. Use her as a conductor. You've had enough time to feel her essence, haven't you?"

"The weird women said to beware any reflections," Lorena pointed out. Elion looked at her, his eyes wide from excitement.

"They said to beware them, not to use them." He turned back towards Kaydee. "My brother can't control what time the portals spit out his assassins. Perhaps, the Saviors' blood will run if we don't protect them throughout time."

"So... what you're saying is that you want to use this lightning bird as a conductor to follow them?" Elion nodded his head.

"Yes," he confirmed. "She's still in Asynithis. Every magical being is connected to Asynithis in some way. She, even subconsciously, will be able to know where the portals are sending each group of soldiers."

"Because the portals are essentially connecting Earth and Asynithis together," Kaydee mused.

"Exactly," Elion said, beaming.

"I don't really get it," Lorena muttered.

"Using Aponi's magic that is connected to Asynithis, we'll be able to follow the assassins to whatever time they're sent to here on Earth," Elion explained, more concisely.

"I don't really feel comfortable using someone else's magic..." Kaydee murmured. His gaze softened as he thought about Aponi.

"We don't really have a choice," he whispered. Kaydee twisted her lips.

"No, I'll ask for her permission," she said, determined.

"How will you do that? We're in a completely different realm," Lorena pointed out.

"If what you say is true, and every magical creature of Asynithis is connected to it in some way, then I'm connected, too," Kaydee said. "With the portals open, I'm sure I can connect with her."

"You're just gonna summon her or something?" Lorena asked. Kaydee shook her head, a gleam in her light gray eyes.

"I'll step into her dreams," she smiled.

Khalon walked into the darkness, aimlessly. He couldn't see more than a foot in front of him, but there was something pulling him in one direction. No, not something. Someone.

He could feel her pain, her anguish as he walked through the darkness, pushing through the sleeping shadows. They seemed to have no idea he was even there.

Khalon's throat constricted as he heard the sound of soft sobbing. He picked up his pace, squinting his eyes into the darkness. Soon, he saw a hunched over figure. Her hair was copper brown and ran down the length of her back which was covered in a black cloak.

"Rhea," he whispered. The figure's head lifted as she heard his voice. Slowly, her head turned to face him.

"Khalon?" her twinkling voice said. Her copper eyes blinked before she rubbed them. She stared at him harder, but her face wasn't the look of relief like Khalon thought it would be. Instead, she looked... scared.

"What are you doing here?" she whispered.

"I don't know," Khalon said. "I was brought here."

"By who?"

"By you, I was assuming," he said. She got up, the cloak covering her whole body. She took a hesitant step forward, towards him. And it took everything in Khalon not to pull her into his arms.

"You can't be here," she said, softly, not meeting his eyes.

"Why?" he asked. "Why can't I be here?"

"This is my mind," she said. "You're in my mind. Which means, you're in…"

"His mind," Khalon finished. She nodded her head as she finally met his gaze once more. Her hand reached up, like she wanted to touch his face, but her fingers curled into her palm. As she started to put her arm back down, Khalon grabbed it. He pulled her slightly closer, her eyes widening as he did, and placed her fist onto his cheek. Rhea paused, her eyes staring into Khalon's soul, before opening up her fist and pressing her small hand against his cheek, her thumb stroking his scales.

"I've been looking for you," he whispered. She took a small breath as her eyebrows furrowed.

"What's wrong?" he asked.

"I have to ask you to do something for me," she muttered.

"What?"

"I need you to free me," she said. Khalon took a step forward, leaning into her palm.

"Of course. I talked to the Fates, and they gave me a hint on how to sever your soul from… his. Poseidon and I are on our way now to—" Rhea shook her head.

"No," she said. "No, that's not what I meant." Khalon stared at her for a long while, studying her face, trying to burn it into his memory.

"No," he whispered. "No, I'm not going to do that."

"Khalon…" He took a step back, her hand falling from his face.

"You can't ask me to do that to you, Rhea," he said, his voice hoarse.

"Look at this mind, Khalon. Look at it. How much of me are you seeing in here?" she asked, her face becoming like ice. Khalon knew she only did that when she was shutting down her emotions, when she didn't want to deal with the other person's grief. He took her small hands into his own.

"Rhea, it doesn't matter. It doesn't matter if he has taken over completely. You are still *here*. This is proof of that. There's still so much of you here that you were able to call me into your mind," he said, gripping her hands hard. She winced somewhat as she tried to pull her hands away from him.

"When I sacrificed myself, I thought I was sacrificing *all* of myself. And if all of myself disappeared, he would disappear, too. Would he have reincarnated? Yes, probably. If he wanted to. But, I had thought I was dying, when I did it, Khalon. I'm not scared of death," she muttered.

"I don't want to lose you," he whispered, meeting her eyes. Rhea's eyebrows pulled upwards as her lips tightened. She looked down.

"Khalon, I'm a Celestial. It's my duty," she said, barely above a whisper. "I'll buy you time—"

"I promised you," Khalon interrupted. "I vowed that I would sacrifice myself for you."

"Khalon, please," Rhea said, shaking her head angrily. "You can't. You're a living being. *This* was my destiny from the start. And I... I *need* you to do this for me." Khalon was quiet for a long while as he memorized the way her copper eyes gazed up at him.

"What do you want me to do?" he asked, his voice monotonous.

"I want you to free me," she said, almost sighing in relief at his obedience. "I want you to kill me. Kill me before he finishes moving his soul into the child." Khalon's lips thinned. Rhea looked at him with bated breath, but he didn't say a word. She took a step closer to Khalon, cupping his head into her hands as she pulled his head down so that they were eye-to-eye.

"I know it's not fair, Khalon. I know it's not fair to you. And I know you've had an unfair life thus far," Rhea whispered. "But, you'll love again. And it's the only way to save you. You *have* to kill him before he kills you."

"Don't talk to me, Rhea. I won't love anyone besides you. I hope you know that," Khalon responded, his voice rough. Rhea fluttered her lashes as she looked down.

"I know," she whispered, though Khalon could taste the falsity in her voice. "I know that. But, if you love me, you'll do this." She lifted her eyes. "For me." Khalon stared into the copper eyes of his beloved, the one person who ever cared about him in his entire life. And he lied to her face.

"I will," he lied. "I'll do anything you ask me to do." Khalon must've been a better liar than he thought because Rhea beamed up at him. She softly kissed him, her lips tasting of fire and smoke.

"Go," she said. "Before he awakes." And before Khalon could say another word, his eyes snapped open.

Above him was the dirt ground as he looked at his surroundings. Poseidon was fast asleep beside him, and Aponi was asleep next to Poseidon. They were underneath Valerian's tree, roots covering them like a cage, with Jabulani keeping watch outside. The five of them were on their way to Draconia, to find the dragon that hid underneath the city of Furvus. The dragon that Khalon believed was still alive, and the very same dragon that Khai kept drinking the blood of.

Khalon put his head into his hands as he rubbed his face, trying to swallow the lump in his throat. His fingers grazed over his lips, the imprint of hers still there. He knew what he had to do. And he just hoped Rhea would forgive him for it.

28

Ambrose's face was the epitome of shock at the sight of the four of them on his doorstep. The sun was just beginning to set, and he was wearing a black robe with the Crispus crest—a serpent resting in a spiral—embroidered in gold on the front of it.

"Your highnesses," he said, quickly composing himself. His silver eyes darted towards Maleko as his eyebrows furrowed upwards a smidge.

"King of Argentiunda. Don't think we've met before," Maleko introduced himself, putting a hand to his chest. Khai had also never met the Argentiundan King—no one from the surface had. He had met his charge, Apsara, though. She had come to nearly every world meeting, and Khai could never forget a face like hers. She was mesmerizing, but also danger lurked in every shadow of her face. She never spoke at these meetings. Just always quietly listening. It unnerved Khai. But, most importantly, it always unnerved his father.

"Who does that mermaid think she is?" King Vien had

always said under his breath as they would leave the meeting.

As if she could feel Khai staring at her, Apsara's eyes slithered towards him. Khai quickly looked away.

Ambrose's eyes widened. "No, I don't think I've had the pleasure." He moved to the side, opening the door a little wider.

"Come in," he said. Kamaria raised an eyebrow as Khai met her eyes before they walked in. It was unlike a Crispus to be so accommodating, but perhaps he knew what they were there for.

"So, what's the occasion?" Ambrose asked, leaning against a mural. *Or perhaps not*, Khai thought to himself.

Maleko cracked his neck. "We're taking your weapons." Ambrose's eyebrows raised.

"You're taking them? Just like that?" he said, a smirk spreading onto his face. He looked so much like Hyacinth, his sister.

"We've heard you have the finest weapons in Caedoxia, Cousin," Khai interjected. Ambrose's silver eyes slowly took in the Draconian King. Khai tried not to let the movement shake him. "We need them."

"Cousin? Your mother never acknowledged her witch side, from what I remember, was ashamed of it, and still is. Though, she came to my grandmother for help when she was only eighteen, *begging* to learn from her, the most powerful Crispus witch. Giving her lavish promises and vows. And then, she abandoned her. Wanted nothing to do with us. And now, when you need something, you call me 'Cousin?'" Ambrose cocked his head to the side. "Like mother like son, I suppose." Khai's fingers curled into his palm.

"You'll give us the weapons," Maleko said, taking a step forward. He was large, muscles flexing with every movement. Ambrose's silver eyes darted towards him. But, fear never flickered there.

"Hmm," he said, crossing his arms. "I will. But only for an alliance with Argentiunda, of course." No one had an alliance with Argentiunda, not ever in history. Maleko's face turned amused as he stared down the Crispus witch.

"You do realize my people are spread across the world, have been slaughtered by the elven army, enslaved by others, and cannot return to the seas, yes? But, you want an alliance with us?" Maleko asked, his voice low. Ambrose met his gaze and held it.

"When the Saviors come, the world will be in chaos. We will have to fight for our lands back. And the merpeople will be able to return to the seas. And when that happens, I want to make sure our two countries have an alliance and will look out for one another," Ambrose said. Maleko and Ambrose stared at each other for a moment more.

"Deal." Maleko held out his large hand. Ambrose's slimmer hand looked like a child's in his, but to Khai's surprise, they both shook on it. He and Kamaria exchanged a wary look.

Caedoxia having an alliance with anyone? They've never kept a long term alliance due to the negative reputation of the citizens living within Caedoxia. Mainly because a Caedoxian would almost always eat another citizen from another country, causing any alliance to be erased. Khai doubted this alliance would stick either.

"So, the weapons?" Maleko continued. Ambrose smiled as he gestured towards the closet door to his right.

"All yours," he said.

The closet held a bunch of rare swords, some were made from dragon stone—almost translucent glass from Draconia, some were made of obsidian like from Ustrina, and others were crystal blades from Aureum. Khai held a dagger in his hand, one that looked similar to Khalon's sword, and furrowed his eyebrows together as he looked up at Ambrose.

"How do you have a weapon like this? There aren't many of these left," Khai said. Ambrose looked at the weapon in his hand. He shrugged.

"I have no idea. This was passed down." The answer made him see red. In other words, these weapons were stolen. He secured the dagger to his belt after putting it in its sheath.

Apsara lifted the white shirt she was wearing, the clothes servants of Aureum wore, and revealed a holster around her body. She placed two daggers into it and then lifted her white pants to reveal thigh holsters that ran down the length of it. Again, noticing Khai's gaze, she gave him a look. Khai could feel the heat rise to his face.

"Apsara is always prepared for any battle," Maleko said, clapping a hand onto Khai's shoulder. "Although, she wasn't prepared when we left Argentiunda." Apsara threw a murderous glare in Maleko's direction.

"I didn't have these wonderful contraptions then, *your highness*," she hissed. The words had a tinge of sarcasm to them. Maleko seemed to laugh nervously.

"Where did you get them, then?" he asked. "The contraptions." She shrugged.

"Aureum has a lot of unguarded places." Maleko blinked.

Are you ready? Kamaria signed towards Khai after putting away a couple of obsidian blades. When she held them, they seemed like they were an extension of her body, like the blades were also limbs of her own, coming back home.

As ready as I'll ever be, Khai signed back. She gave him a knowing look.

Don't hurt yourself with that blade, she signed, a small smirk spreading on her lips. Khai couldn't help his eyes from rolling.

———

"I heard there was a camp of displaced draconians just over this cliff," Jabulani declared, leading the way. His eyes looked different than before. They were darker, and almost like fear lurked in every shadow of his iris. Something during the battle with Aureum had shaken him, Khalon just didn't know what.

"Let's hope they'll join arms with Khalon," Aponi said, holding her arms close to her body. It was cold in No Man's Land. The sky was an ash gray, and it looked like it was going to storm in a few hours.

"From the whisperings I've heard from the trees, they'd rather follow Khalon than the false king," Valerian said, his voice regal.

"Don't call him that." Khalon turned to look at the dryad, to meet his strange golden eyes. "Khai's the King of Draconia. Treat him as such." Valerian seemed to stare straight into the depths of Khalon's soul before lowering his head.

"I apologize," he said.

"Why do you accept Khai as king?" Poseidon piped up, staring up at him. Waves crashed in his sepia eyes.

"He's king. He's the rightful heir to the throne," Khalon muttered.

"You're the first born child. You have the spirit of the dragon within you. Isn't that how succession works in Draconia?" Poseidon pressed. Khalon's eyebrows twitched.

"I'm a bastard child," he retorted. Before he could continue the conversation, he watched Jabulani's face pale as he stopped at the top of the cliff. Khalon rushed towards him, only to see a spear pressed against the hollow of his neck. Holding the end of it was a panther. A beastoid.

"Hands up," her gargled voice said. "Drop any weapons." The thought that Khalon could easily overtake her started to drift into his mind before he saw other bear beastoids step out from behind the trees nearby. They had them surrounded.

"Okay," Khalon said, meeting Poseidon's and Aponi's eyes before placing his weapon on the ground.

"Hands on your head," she ordered. Khalon followed her directions without hesitation. The others followed his lead. The panther stalked around Khalon before pressing the tip of her spear into Khalon's back.

"Walk," she demanded. Khalon's legs felt like cement, and every instinct in his body was telling him not to, but he walked forwards anyway. She led them down the small cliff towards the shabby tents of the beastoid camp. As the realization sunk in, Khalon kicked himself within his mind. This was the same camp he had brought the small cub to months ago.

The other beastoids near them stopped whatever task they were doing. Their strangely human eyes seemed to register Khalon's scales, their gaze hardening with hate.

The panther and the other beastoids herded them into one tent, taking the time to tie each of them to various poles. The panther's yellow eyes were like ice as she stared down Khalon while she tightened the rope. Khalon winced as it pinched his skin.

"Wait here," she said.

"We ain't going anywhere, darling," Poseidon called out, an annoyed smile on his face. She mocked his smile as she pivoted on her paw, stalking out of the tent.

Poseidon turned his attention towards Jabulani. "I thought you said there was a draconian camp here." Jabulani shook his head, unable to meet anyone's eyes.

"I've failed again," he mumbled. "I'm sorry."

"It's fine, Jabu," Aponi said. He raised his head slightly at her words, but he still wouldn't look at her. "You were doing your best."

"If this is his best, no wonder why he's so down," Valerian piped up. Poseidon nodded his head in agreement. Khalon threw a glare in both their directions.

"Well, it would've been better if they were elves." Poseidon stretched his back as he started to settle into the pole behind him. "We might've been able to talk them out of killing us."

"You think they'll kill us?" Aponi asked, eyes panicked. Poseidon nodded his head towards Khalon. Khalon could feel the heat reach the tips of his ears as he looked away.

"We have a draconian with us. And not just any draconian, a royal draconian. Unfortunately for us, dear lightning bird, we're about to become dinner." Aponi scoffed.

"They don't know Khalon is a royal draconian," she pointed out.

"If they don't know from his scent alone, they'll figure it out soon enough," Poseidon said. Khalon frowned at his words. Did he *really* smell different from other draconians?

The sound of the front of the tent opening interrupted any more conversation. Walking in were three huge bears. All of them were black. Behind the giant three, a smaller brown bear walked in. The brown bear's eyes widened as it took in Khalon.

"Well, well, well," the first black bear said as it thundered forward. He leaned down so he could look at Khalon better. Khalon's face tightened as he met the bear's gaze.

"We have a royal draconian here with us," he said, turning back towards the other bears.

Told you so, Poseidon mouthed across the room.

"Aureum would forgive our transgressions if we handed him over to them," the second black bear voiced, his voice higher than the other. Khalon knew they were talking out loud for their sake, to scare them. Otherwise they would just use hand signals or their own bear language. But, there was a word that stuck out to Khalon. *Transgressions?*

The first black bear growled low as he stared at the other. The other bear cowered in response. He turned back towards Khalon, his dark eyes roving over him, lingering on his scales.

"Your scales are different from the others," he said, his paw gesturing towards Khalon's face.

"I'm descended from both of the last dragons." The bear snorted.

"The last dragons," he muttered. "All you royal draconians know that's not true." Khalon had to admit that the bear was right, but how did *he* know that?

"What should we do with you?" he seemed to say, almost under his breath as he sniffed Khalon's face.

"Michael," the smaller brown bear finally spoke up. The black bear named Michael growled towards the smaller one.

"What is it, Luke?" he snarled. Khalon's eyes widened as he looked at the brown bear. *Luke?* His mind raced as he took in the beastoid in front of him. It had only been around seven months since he had helped the cub called Luke. He was smaller then, almost like a child. But here, in front of Khalon's eyes, he was larger, practically full grown.

"How fast do you beastoids grow?" Khalon couldn't help the words spilling out of his mouth as he stared in shock at the—now—full grown beastoid in front of him.

"I know this draconian," Luke said, quietly, as he looked at Michael. Michael's bear face seemed to frown as he looked back at Khalon. He studied Khalon for a moment before his face slowly fell as he closed his dark eyes.

"Luke, you better not be about to tell me that *this* is the draconian that—"

"He's the one who saved me from those vampires." Khalon swore that Michael's groan rumbled through the earth. His eyes opened back up as they hardened, looking over Khalon.

"Guess you're living tonight, draconian."

29

Khai and Kamaria hid outside the Aureum palace as Maleko and Apsara snuck their way inside, still wearing their servant clothes.

Something is bothering you, Kamaria signed to Khai as they hid in the brush of the large gardens behind the palace. Khai pursed his lips as he tried not to look at Kamaria. She had been sporting those eyes of pity since they left Ustrina. Since she saw what happened that night with his mother.

Nothing's bothering me, Khai signed back, wanting the conversation to be over with. He saw her frown in his peripheral. He wished she wouldn't push the issue. But, this was Kamaria. She was going to talk about whatever was on her mind. No matter whether the other wanted to be an active participant in the conversation or not.

She tapped his shoulder so he would look at her. Khai froze for a moment. He didn't want to have this conversation, and it would be so *easy* to ignore her. It's not like he *had* to look at her hands. But, he couldn't do that to her. For whatever reason, he couldn't ignore her like that. Begrudgingly, Khai turned towards her, but refused to look at her face.

You can talk to me. I probably understand more than anyone else, she signed. The veins underneath her dark hands shone red in some parts as the blood moved through her system. How *would* she understand? By all accounts, her father was incredibly loving towards her, and her mother died when she was young.

There's nothing to talk about. She twisted her face in frustration and then grabbed Khai's face with her hand, turning it to the side so she could see the healing bruises on his face better. She gestured towards it as she let go of his face. Khai's jaw tightened.

There's that *to talk about,* she signed.

Just because you saw something, doesn't mean I have to talk about it, Khai signed back, putting more energy behind his hands. He met her dark eyes which flashed with anger.

I'm just trying to help *you.*

By badgering me?

By giving you space to talk about it.

I don't know how forcing me to talk about it is considered giving me space, Kamaria. They glowered at each other.

She forces you to take the dragon's blood, Kamaria signed. Khai stared at her for a moment longer before leaning back slightly.

Is this what you wanted? To appease your own curiosity? Kamaria's jaw dropped as she stared at him in half horror and half fury.

Is this what you *want, Khai? To become a blood raged monster? Like your father? Like your grandfather before you?*

And you wonder why Draconia fell. Khai clenched his jaw as Kamaria began to realize what she said.

Right. Because I'm the false king, Khai signed bitterly. Her eyes softened.

This isn't who you are, she signed slowly.

Because you of all people know who I am, Khai signed back. Her eyebrows knitted together as she looked at him.

I would like to think I do, she signed. Her eyes narrowed as she looked away from him. Khai's eyes followed the lines in her profile, cursing himself for always being in an argument with her. Why was he always so angry with her? Why did it matter if she asked questions about his life? Would it be so bad to open up to her? To finally have someone to talk to?

Khai lifted his hand to tap her shoulder, so that she would look at him, but a flash of light interrupted. He turned to look at the old greenhouse attached to the back of the palace. There was another flash of light.

"Let's go," Khai said, as he put his hands in front of Kamaria's face. He signed the words to her as she looked over at him, annoyed. He smirked.

I got it, ankle biter, she signed back as they gathered their wits. Khai lifted his hands to retort back to her, but she got up before he could. Grumbling to himself, he followed after her as they made their way over to the abandoned greenhouse.

———

Apsara pushed open one of the windows for Khai and Kamaria to crawl through. Khai pushed himself through it, nearly landing on his head. Looking around the greenhouse, it was clearly abandoned. It didn't look like anyone had even cleaned it, let alone been in there, for years. Khai's eyebrows furrowed. It was odd that a room in a palace wasn't cared for.

"Well?" he asked, turning towards the two mermaids.

"We found out where Esi is," Apsara responded, crossing her arms.

"How were you able to figure that information out?" he asked. Maleko gestured towards a corner of the greenhouse. There was a woman with short blonde hair, dressed in servant clothes, tied up in the corner. She had cloth covering her mouth as she struggled against her restraints. Khai's lips thinned.

"Great," he muttered.

"Her name is Matilda. Really a nice woman." Maleko gave the woman a pitying glance. She looked outraged, pushing against her restraints once more. Khai rubbed his face with his hands as he tried to catch Kamaria's gaze. She refused to look at him. Apsara raised an eyebrow as she watched the exchange between them.

"Did something happen between you two?" she asked.

No, Kamaria signed, quickly and definitively. Khai couldn't help the sigh that escaped his lips.

"Where is she? Esi?" he asked, changing the subject. Kamaria's gaze was determined as she stared down the two mermaids.

"Matilda said she's not being held in the dungeons. Adamar is keeping his prize in a nice room, in one of the guest quarters," Maleko said, crossing his own muscular arms. They rippled at the movement.

"His prize?" Khai narrowed his eyes.

"She is the Seer. Any king would want to keep the Seer captive so that she is forced to tell them their future," Maleko said, looking over at Apsara. "I know I would."

"So, you're not any better than Adamar," Khai concluded, his face tightening. Maleko gave him a nonchalant look.

"You wouldn't keep the Seer, if you could? You wouldn't want to know your future as a ruler?" Maleko asked. It was a heavy question, but it was asked as if it were the same as inquiring how someone's day was.

"I wouldn't keep her captive," Khai responded. Maleko gave him a small smile.

"You're young," was all he said.

If she's in one of the guest quarters, it should be easy getting her out, Kamaria signed.

"It's guarded," Apsara said, after Khai translated for Kamaria. "Heavily guarded."

"Well, the Fates told you you're the one who's supposed to save her, right? I'm sure you two will think of something," Khai said, looking out the window. Maleko's eyebrow raised.

"Where will *you* be going?"

"I have something else I need to find."

Your mother? Kamaria signed. Khai shrugged.

"Her and something else," he muttered. Kamaria's face scrunched together as she looked at Maleko and then back at Khai.

"You should go with Maleko," he said. "Find your sister." Her eyebrows pulled downwards as she looked at her own hands.

I have to. She's my little sister. The only family I have left, she signed.

I know. It's okay, Khai signed back.

"I can't leave the king's side," Apsara declared. "You're on your own, draconian."

"You *could* leave my side. I'm sure I'll be fine..." Apsara threw a glare in Maleko's direction which caused his voice to drift off.

"I'm not leaving you," she hissed. Maleko put up his hands.

"Okay, okay," he said.

Your king would be safe with me, Kamaria signed, her face obviously annoyed. It was true. Kamaria was probably the best warrior Khai had ever seen.

"I trust no one with my king." Apsara glowered at Kamaria for even suggesting that she could protect Maleko.

"You'll be fine, won't you?" Maleko asked Khai. He nodded his head in confirmation. He wasn't totally pitiful. He could at least keep himself from getting killed. Kamaria's eyes returned to their look of pity, and Khai's eyes darted away.

You know, contrary to your belief, I can protect myself, he signed to her.

Khai, I don't want to be mean, but you know that you can't really—

I can protect myself, Kamaria. And it's insulting that you don't think so, Khai signed back. They glared at each other for a moment longer before Kamaria ripped her gaze away.

Fine, die. I don't care, she signed before turning away. Maleko looked back and forth between them until Apsara grabbed his arm and dragged him in the direction Kamaria was going.

"Make sure Matilda's restraints are secure. We don't want her alerting the whole palace that we're here," Apsara said, nodding her head to the blonde woman in the corner. She responded by a series of grunts as she struggled more against the ropes around her.

"Sure," Khai muttered. Apsara narrowed her eyes before following after Kamaria.

"Meet in the gardens before sunrise," she said over her shoulder. Khai only had a night. One night to find his mother and a Mortiferis.

30

"What are you doing at our camp?" Luke asked Khalon as the other beastoids started to leave the tent to discuss what to do with their prisoners.

"We're trying to find a camp of draconian refugees," Khalon muttered. Luke's bear face scrunched together.

"What for?" he asked.

"We're going to take back Draconia, or try to take back Furvus at least," Khalon disclosed.

"Are you sure you should be telling the enemy what we're planning on doing?" Aponi spoke out. Luke's brown eyes finally took in the other prisoners. His eyes widened from seeing all the different creatures.

"We won't tell anyone," Luke reassured.

"Why is that, little beastoid?" Poseidon asked, somehow twisting so he was laying on his side. Luke turned towards the Sea God.

"We've..." his voice drifted off as he looked back towards

where the other beastoids were gathered. Their shadows could be seen on the fabric of the tent.

"It's okay. You can tell us, Luke," Khalon pressed. It was still insane for Khalon to look at this bear beastoid and realize that it was Luke. He had grown so fast in such a short amount of time. Luke's features used to make Khalon's stomach turn. But now, seeing him, Khalon could only feel relief. The kid was okay. He succeeded in saving at least one person.

Luke's face scrunched together again as he let out a large sigh. A sigh that made him sound even more adult.

"We've broken away from the other beastoids," he said under his breath. His eyes darted back to those silhouettes whose growls were getting louder as they were discussing what to do.

"You broke away?" Khalon whispered. Luke nodded.

"The elves don't treat us beastoids very well. Most beastoids were sticking it out so we would get our own land. Some have even said the King of Aureum would give us our own planet to rule over. But, my brother couldn't put up with it anymore. So, we broke away," Luke explained.

"Your brother?" Luke gestured towards the bears outside of the tent.

"Michael is my brother." Khalon's eyebrows raised as he exchanged looks with Poseidon.

"Michael is in charge of this company of beastoids," Poseidon more said than asked. Luke nodded his head.

"He's a great leader," Luke whispered. "I hope to be like him one day."

"Are the elves after your company?" Poseidon asked.

Luke frowned as he looked back at his brother who seemed to snarl at another bear.

"I... I don't know about all of that," he muttered. He moved away from Khalon as his brother re-entered the tent.

"Since you've saved my brother once, I'll let you all go this one time," Michael said as he entered, his dark eyes glowering at Khalon. "An eye for an eye."

"Thank you," Khalon said, trying to show as much gratitude as possible in his voice. But, for someone who wasn't very expressive, it was hard for him to do so. He winced at the odd tone.

"Actually, instead of just letting us go, maybe you could help us," Khalon muttered. He didn't know if this would actually work or not. Michael bared his teeth as he gestured for Khalon to go on. Khalon opened his mouth, but no words came out. He didn't know how to say it. He had never done anything diplomatic before. Michael's dark eyes narrowed.

"We heard about your predicament," Poseidon said, speaking up. Khalon let out a sigh of relief. "Perhaps we can help each other." Michael turned to glare in Luke's direction, causing the young bear to crouch down in fear.

"Oh, you heard, huh?" Michael said through gritted teeth as he turned back towards the Sea God. "Help in what way?"

"We are trying to take back the city of Furvus from the elves," Poseidon said, his posture incredibly relaxed. "You could help with that."

"How does that help us? It seems like we'd just be helping you draconians." Michael spat out the last word like it was poison in his mouth. Shame washed over Khalon as he tried to gather his bearings.

"The elves are going to punish your company for your leadership," Khalon said, meeting Michael's gaze. "The issue between the draconians and the beastoids was caused by my father. And my father is dead. Your kind made sure of that. It won't be the same as it was before." Michael's eyes narrowed once more as he took a threatening step forward.

"The new king isn't too fond of us either, Prince Khalon." Khalon's title was dripping in sarcasm.

"Khai... he's young. He still believes what our father did was right," Khalon muttered. "And is still upset about our father's death, but he will come around." Michael shrugged his large bear shoulders as he moved towards the exit. Another bear came to untie Khalon's arms. He rubbed his wrist where the rope was.

"You can't promise us anything," Michael said. "You don't have an army behind you. It sounds like to me, you'll just use my family to serve yours."

"What have you heard about the politics in Draconia, lately?" Poseidon asked. Michael paused before turning towards him.

"What specifically are you referring to?"

"Have you heard of the saying 'the one who holds the spirit of the dragon within them is the ruler of Draconia?'" Michael continued to stare at Poseidon. After a long while, he slowly nodded.

"I've heard of it," he said.

"Khalon has the spirit of the dragon within him, which, by Draconian law, makes him the ruler of Draconia," Poseidon merely said. Tossed the words out there into the universe as if they weren't the most life changing words in

Khalon's life. Khalon's jaw clenched as Michael looked curiously over at him.

"Is this true?" he asked.

"You can ask any draconian what they think of King Khai. They all refer to him as the false king," Poseidon said, not letting Khalon speak. "When we get to the draconian camp, they would pledge their allegiance to Khalon without question."

"Poseidon," Khalon said, his voice caked with warning. Michael seemed to smile a bit.

"So, *you're* the true leader of Draconia."

"Khai is king," Khalon said through his clenched jaw. Michael stared at him for a moment longer before shrugging once more. He walked towards the entrance of the tent.

"You can stay here for as long as you need to, for saving my brother's life. But, we're not helping you take back Furvus unless you're making a claim for the Draconian throne," Michael declared. He turned back slightly, Luke behind him.

"I'm not following someone who can only give false promises for my people. For my family." Then he left the tent. Khalon turned swiftly towards Poseidon.

"What was *that* all about?" he snapped. Poseidon shrugged as he rubbed his own released wrists.

"Francine gave you a hint. She called you the Dragon King. Do you want to save Rhea or don't you?" Poseidon snapped back. Khalon recoiled from his tone. He had never heard Poseidon speak in anything other than his lazy, laid-back voice.

"But, Khai—"

"This isn't about Khai, Khalon," Poseidon said, getting

up. Even though he was short, he carried himself as if he were seven feet tall. "This is about Asynithis. It's about, not just this world, but the realms. The realms my brothers and I have spent many millenniums creating. You won't kill Rhea. You refuse to, even though she's a Celestial housing the most dangerous God on this planet right now. You're *determined* to save her. Then, you need to listen to those who know the answers of this world."

"The Fates," Khalon muttered.

"Yes. The Fates. They know what they're talking about."

"I don't see how me being King of Draconia changes Rhea's fate," Khalon pointed out. Poseidon shrugged.

"Perhaps you being the King of Draconia will let you get to the dragon underneath the city of Furvus," Poseidon pointed out.

"How do you know that the dragon would help?" Khalon asked, suddenly exhausted. He sat down, leaning against the pole behind him. Poseidon looked down at him.

"Because she didn't say the Draconian King. She called you the Dragon King."

"A lot of people call the Draconian King a Dragon King," Khalon said.

"Francine doesn't say anything she doesn't mean. She would've called you the Draconian King if that's what she wanted to burn into your memory," Poseidon said, clearly over the conversation. He rubbed his temples as he threw a desperate glance in Valerian's direction.

"I can't deal with these angsty teenagers anymore," Poseidon muttered. "I'm too old."

"It sounds like not enough magic is coursing through

you already," Valerian pointed out. Poseidon gritted his teeth as he looked down at his Celestial body.

"Listen, Khalon, I want to save Rhea as much as you do."

"I doubt it," Khalon murmured. One eye twitched as Poseidon sighed.

"But, Khalon, lives come and go. What matters is the future. The good of everyone else. You can't save one person and risk the lives of millions."

Khalon turned sharply towards him. "I don't care if—"

"I know. You don't care if millions die if Rhea does. I got it," he rubbed his temples more as he walked away from Khalon. "But, if you are determined to save Rhea, then you need to be the Dragon King." Khalon felt the blood in his body freeze as he closed his eyes. Khai was king. And a large part of him didn't want to take that away from his little brother. But, he also couldn't let Rhea die. Not without trying everything he possibly could.

"What would it take?" Khalon slowly said, lifting his head to look at Poseidon. "For me to be the Dragon King, what would I need to do?" Poseidon turned towards him, a crooked smile spreading across his lips.

"You just need to be yourself, Khalon," he said. "You just need to declare yourself the Dragon King. And those who have followed you since the beginning will make your words a reality. It's how you creatures have always done it."

"What if no one wants me to be?" Khalon asked, insecurity finding its way into his words.

"You don't know, do you?" Aponi spoke up. He looked over at her, confusion wrinkling his brow.

"Know what?"

"There's always been people who declared you the

Dragon King. Since you were a baby. Since you were in the Ring of Fire. You've always been hailed as the King of Dragons," Aponi whispered.

"You're the only draconian who hails from both the Black Dragon and Red Dragon families. You're a dragon, through and through," Poseidon said. "Who else would the draconians want as king?"

"Khalon, King of Draconia," Jabulani said under his breath. Aponi smiled at Khalon as she took a step forward, bowing her head slightly, her eyes still meeting his.

"Khalon, the Dragon King."

31

Khai tightened the human's restraints as she scowled at him. He looked at the folded, white servant clothes Apsara or Maleko brought into the greenhouse and glanced back at the human.

"Close your eyes," he said, adding, "Please." The human called Matilda looked him up and down before obeying his request. He shrugged off the draconian vest he was wearing, similar to the one Khalon always wore, and removed the silk shirt underneath. He changed into the human clothes, flicking the collar up so that it would hide the cluster of scales on his neck. Fortunately, he didn't have scales on his face, unlike Khalon.

Khalon, Khai thought bitterly as he put the dagger that was a smaller version of Khalon's sword into a holster around his chest. He buttoned the white shirt over top of it as his half-brother's face came to the forefront of his mind. *What was he planning on doing in Draconia?* His jaw tightened as he finished hiding his belongings. *Khalon's a good guy,* Khai convinced himself. He wouldn't do anything that would go against his little brother... *Would he?*

The human mumbled something underneath the cloth gag. Khai paused before walking towards her.

"If I pull this off of you, will you scream?" he asked, meeting her shrewd, gray eyes. She simply stared back at him. He cringed slightly under her gaze and slowly took the gag off of her mouth.

"I could probably help you find what it is you're looking for," Matilda said, her voice clear. Khai cocked his head to the side as his eyes roved over her before meeting her eyes once more.

"What's the catch?" he asked.

"You let me go." Khai's light brown eyes narrowed.

"You wouldn't be able to tell me where it is," he murmured, moving to put the gag back over her lips. Her eyes widened for a split second.

"I'm the head of the household. I know where everything is in this palace," she hurriedly spoke out. He moved his head side to side as he thought.

"Do you know where I can find a Mortiferis?" Matilda's blonde eyebrows pulled downwards as her gray eyes searched for something in his face. Her lips thinned.

"Yeah, didn't think so," Khai muttered.

"I know where they are." She held her chin up high as she looked away from him. He moved closer towards her.

"Where?"

"What are *you* going to do with a Mortiferis?" she asked, her voice hushed as she closed her eyes. A shudder ran through her body, as though she were remembering something traumatic. Khai shrugged a shoulder.

"Kill a God with it," he said. "Maybe get rid of a few more people."

"Your mother?" the human asked, her eyes snapping open as she glanced at him. Khai's body froze as his face tightened.

"Maybe." Matilda smirked as she glared at the ground.

"Your mother lives up to her reputation," she muttered.

"I don't expect anything less from her," Khai replied. Matilda seemed to weigh her options before meeting his eyes once more.

"Fine, I'll tell you where the Mortiferis are if you let me go," she negotiated. Khai gave her a disarming smile.

"Sure," he said. The mask of stone on her face seemed to crack slightly as she took a deep breath.

"The Mortiferis are in the dungeon. They're locked up and asleep. Hopefully, they stay asleep for an eternity."

"Do you have a key to the dungeon?" She held her head up high once more.

"Who do you think cleans around them?" she asked.

"Where is it? The key?" Matilda glanced down at the belt around her waist. Khai's eyes followed the movement before giving her a smile.

"Thanks, Matilda," he said. He pulled the gag back around her mouth as Matilda's eyebrows knitted together. She started to thrash wildly against her restraints as more murmurings poured out from behind the cloth gag. Khai expertly snatched the key from around her waist and backed away from the wild human. He held his hands up in defense, the key in one of them.

"Listen, I would let you go. But, you would've just ran straight to King Adamar. And we can't have that happen,"

Khai pursed his lips as he threw her a pitying look. "Sorry." He pivoted on one foot and pushed open the door of the greenhouse, the desperate pleas of the human following after him.

———

"Do you know sign language?" Maleko whispered towards Apsara. Apsara threw him a dirty look.

"You don't?" she asked. "You're a king. A *diplomat.*" Maleko winced at her clipped words.

"I know," he muttered as he glanced over at the Ustrinian Queen who was strutting down the hallway as if she were begging for someone to attack her. "I just never learned."

Maleko looked back at Apsara, pleading with his eyes. She scrunched up her nose as she turned away.

"I never learned either," she mumbled under her breath. It was hard for Apsara to admit anything other than perfection. Maleko sighed loudly as he looked back at Kamaria.

"So, we have no way of communicating with her," he whispered.

"I don't know why you're whispering," Apsara said. "She can't hear you."

"Still. It's weird to talk out loud about someone who's right in front of you." At his words, Kamaria swiftly turned around to look at them. She put a hand on her hip.

"Were you guys talking about me?" she asked. She spoke aloud with a slight lisp. Maleko nearly jumped out of his skin. He looked over at Apsara as if to tell her: *See?*

"We just don't know how we can communicate with

you. Neither of us can use sign language," Apsara said slowly. Kamaria stared at her lips intensely, and at the end of Apsara's words, she scoffed.

"You never learned sign language?" she asked, her voice heavy with disgust. Maleko blinked.

"I'm sorry. I should've but we never—" Kamaria closed her eyes. Maleko stopped talking as he exchanged a look with Apsara.

"I don't want to see your excuses," she said as she turned back around. Maleko couldn't help his mouth from dropping.

"Did she just close her eyes so she wouldn't have to read my lips?" Maleko whispered towards Apsara. Before Apsara could say anything to him, Kamaria turned back around.

"You two should lead towards Esi's room," she said, crossing her arms. "I have no idea where I'm going."

"Of course, your majesty," Apsara muttered as she sidestepped around the Ustrinian Queen. Maleko avoided looking Kamaria in the eye as he walked around her. He and Apsara exchanged another look before silently leading the way to where Esi was being held captive.

———

Khai didn't necessarily know where the dungeons were in the Aureum palace, but something seemed to be drawing him towards it, like a moth to a flame. He kept his head down as he walked through the hallways in the palace. Everything was so white and adorned in gold. Everything elves seemed to love.

The stone door to the dungeons was hidden in the

corner of, what seemed to be, a deserted section of the palace. He fumbled with the bronze key as he tried to fit it into its lock.

"I don't recognize you," a lazy voice said. Khai froze as he looked out the side of his eye to see an elf with white, wavy hair cut to his chin. His eyes were so blue that they were the only noticeable feature on his face. Khai recognized him immediately. The third prince of Aureum, Ardryll.

"I'm new," Khai said, deepening his voice. He wasn't sure the prince would recognize him, but he didn't want to be too sure. His hands went to his neck to adjust the collar on his shirt so Ardryll wouldn't see his dragon scales clearly marking him as a draconian and not as a human.

Ardryll's blue eyes narrowed. "I thought only that haughty, blonde one goes into the dungeons." Khai's leg started to shake.

"She's sick. She gave me the key to go clean the dungeons in her place," he lied, holding up the key. He still refused to face the prince head-on. Ardryll's eyebrows knitted together as he took another step forward.

"Do I know you?" Khai turned his head back towards the stone door in front of him as he placed a hand on his dagger underneath his shirt.

"I *do* work here, your highness," he said. "You might've seen me in the halls." Ardryll shook his head as his eyes widened, as if trying to see Khai clearer. He cocked his head to the side.

"No, I'm sure I've seen you before. But, not in the palace. No, this palace doesn't fit you," he murmured, taking another step closer. Khai closed his eyes as he tightened his grip on his dagger.

"Prince Ardryll," a voice called from the end of the hallway. Ardryll snapped towards the sound.

"What is it?" he asked. Khai turned the key in its lock and pushed the door open while Ardryll was distracted.

"The king is calling for you," the voice said.

"All right. I'll be there in a minute," Ardryll said, turning back towards Khai. But, he was gone.

Khai pressed his back against the stone as he put a steadying hand over his heart. He looked down into the darkness of the dungeon, his pupils dilating. He had never experienced anything like that before. His whole life was sheltered, never able to take a step out of turn. And deceiving a prince of Aureum was... exhilarating.

The corners of his lips turned upwards as he bounded down the stone steps towards the bottom of the dungeon. The stairs opened up to reveal a room filled with sleeping, giant Mortiferis.

The blood in Khai's body went cold as his eyes took in the nightmare creatures. He couldn't tell if they were sleeping or not, but the steady rise and fall of—what Khai assumed to be—their chests indicated that they might be. He carefully walked around their shadowy bodies as he aimlessly looked around the room.

It wasn't as if he could lug around a whole Mortiferis. He needed whatever it was that made a God's soul disappear. Khai looked down at the ground of the dungeon, looking for something—anything—that he could use as an experiment. The only objects he could find were rocks or pebbles.

Khai twisted his lips as he grabbed a rock and, foolishly, threw it at one of the Mortiferis. The Mortiferis stopped breathing for a moment, and his body tensed. It was the longest second of Khai's life, but the Mortiferis continued to breathe heavily. He glanced down at the rock that was thrown, but it didn't turn into ash when it touched the the monster's skin.

Khai picked up another rock, throwing it up in the air and catching it as he thought. When the Mortiferis came to destroy Furvus, he was the only one who was able to keep it from completely destroying their city. And it seemed like everything it touched turned into ash. Khai closed his eyes as he felt for the last of the dragon's blood within him. His body slowly grew as red scales replaced skin, the memory playing in the back of his mind.

The Mortiferis was destroying everything in its path. Its jaw was unhinged as it seemed to consume everything in front of it.

Khai's eyes—now a blood red—snapped open. He looked down at the Mortiferis as he wandered around it, keeping his newly grown dragon's tail above the ground so it didn't touch any of the other monsters.

It used its mouth. It always used its mouth to destroy. Khai carefully placed the rock above the Mortiferis' seemingly-always-opened mouth. The rock dissipated once touching its teeth. Khai's eyebrows jumped.

The Mortiferis didn't move an inch, as if a rock wasn't just dropped into its mouth. Khai took a closer look as he stared into the depths of the nightmare's opening.

"It's their teeth. Their teeth are what makes someone disappear," he mumbled under his breath. But, was it the whole tooth? Was it just the tip of it?

Whatever the Mortiferis used, Khai didn't want to accidentally disappear while trying to get its tooth. He pulled out his dagger from underneath his shirt and started to slice into the Mortiferis' jaw. He glanced up at the its face... or what he thought was its face. It didn't even flinch. There wasn't any blood either, like it wasn't living at all. Khai finished cutting off part of the jaw, one tooth attached to the skin. He covered the tooth with the excess skin he cut off of the Mortiferis.

He stared down at the monster after placing the large tooth into his pocket, his skin crawling as he took in the sight. It was still sleeping peacefully, no sign of it ever feeling any pain. And it made Khai's stomach turn.

They really were monsters. But, they were monsters without thought. Without feeling. Without mercy. All destruction. And it frightened Khai. It frightened Khai to his very core.

32

Aponi watched in the back of the tent as Khalon made promises to the beastoids that she truly hoped he could keep. She knew what Khai's reaction would be, and she wondered if Khalon would fight him. Truly fight him, for himself. Not to protect anyone else.

As he shook Michael's bear paw, Aponi shook her head. Khalon would never do anything that selfish. If Khai wanted it, he would give in. As long as it was *after* Rhea was saved.

Aponi's eyebrows pulled downwards as she rubbed the back of her neck. She felt someone whispering something there, even though no one was behind her. Cracking her neck, she tried to ignore the feeling.

"Is everything okay?" Poseidon whispered from next to her. He pointed at her rubbing her neck. She slowly lowered her hand.

"It's fine," she muttered.

"The Fates took you," he said. "You might be connected

to that world now." Aponi frowned as she turned towards him.

"What do you mean?" she whispered.

"You might have a foot in this world and another in Terra," Poseidon shrugged. "Especially since you're a lightning bird." Aponi looked away from him as she watched Khalon chug a drink of alcohol, one of the bear beastoids clapping his back enthusiastically.

"What the witches do to us is wrong," she said. Poseidon turned towards her slightly.

"I never said it wasn't."

"They use us as conductors for their own magic. To make their magic stronger," she hissed. "I don't *want* to be connected to a world where witches went for refuge. If I'm connected, they could find my energy. They could *use* me." The whispering seemed to grow louder. Poseidon turned away from her as he appeared to be in deep thought.

"Perhaps my brother was always right then," he murmured.

"About what?"

"Perhaps we did just create worlds for creatures to simply suffer in," he said, his gaze faraway like he was recalling a past memory. He shook his head as he stepped towards Valerian whose golden eyes were eyeing him like a predator's.

"You should take a drink. Enjoy fighting back against the elves," Poseidon said, waving a hand absentmindedly as he went towards Valerian's side. Aponi watched as Valerian's eyes seemed to melt like honey as they whispered to one another.

The whispering feeling in the back of her neck continued

as she reached for a flute filled with golden liquid. She knocked it back, feeling the burning settle into the pit of her stomach before spreading through her. Her dark eyes met Jabulani's. He still had this permanent look of terror in his eyes, and he looked away from Aponi quickly. She licked her lips, tasting more of the bittersweet liquid, before walking towards him.

"Jabu," she said, raising her empty glass. He handed her a full one.

"Aponi." They stood in silence as they surveyed the beastoids clamoring to talk to Khalon.

"He's going to be King of Draconia, huh?" Jabulani said. Aponi nodded her head, watching as Khalon's mask of stone slowly melted away. He cracked a smile at one of the younger beastoids.

"He'll be a good king," she said, sipping on her drink.

"How do you know?" he asked, leaning down towards her a bit so she could hear him.

"Because he doesn't want to be one," she shrugged.

"How do you think Khai will respond?" He leaned against a pole behind him. Aponi smirked as she thought of the temper tantrum Khai would probably throw.

"He'll be upset." Jabulani's eyes softened as he shook his head.

"No, I don't think he will," he said. Aponi glanced up at him.

"Khai loves being king."

"But as King of Draconia, he can't marry Kamaria," Jabulani pointed out. *Why would Khai marry Kamaria?*

"What are you talking about?"

"Khai's in love with Kamaria," he simply said as he took a sip of his drink. Aponi's eyes almost fell out of her head.

"*What* are you *talking* about? Khai and Kamaria?" Aponi ferociously shook her head. "No, they would never work out. Kamaria hates him. And Khai is too selfish to care about anyone else but himself."

"Kamaria is always talking about him. Especially lately," Jabulani said, his eyes closing as his face tightened. He opened them. "I don't think Khai would contest Khalon, simply because of Kamaria."

"Kamaria *only* talks about how *annoying* Khai is and how much she dislikes him. How she wished she never opened Ustrina for him to take refuge in because she has to see him every day. That she sees him so much he now *plagues* her nightmares," Aponi retorted. Jabulani gave her a small smile.

"She also talks about how worried she is of him. He looks too skinny to be a warrior. How will he be able to protect himself in battle? Why does he always insist on going with us when he knows he can't fight properly? She complains about how she has to look out for him and worries about whether he's still drinking dragon's blood or not. That doesn't sound like she hates him to me," he said.

"You should hear how she talks about you," Aponi retorted, her voice small as realization was starting to settle in.

"It's not anything like how she talks about him," Jabulani responded. He looked up at the ceiling of the tent. "Besides, after losing Esi, she'll never speak to me again." Aponi couldn't say anything to reassure him because they both knew how Kamaria felt about her younger sister. She would kill anyone who touched a curl on her head.

"What happened?" Aponi whispered. She felt him freeze next to her.

"I... can't, Aponi," he responded, his voice almost disappearing. Aponi gritted her teeth but nodded her head.

"Of course," she said. She moved her head to the side as the whispering grew painful. Her hand went to rub the back of her neck as she grimaced. Jabulani's eyebrows pulled together before putting a comforting hand on her shoulder.

"Aponi? Are you okay?" She gritted her teeth as she continued to try and rub the pain away. She could feel the lightning within her flicker throughout her body, causing Jabulani to jerk his hand away.

"I—" Aponi took a deep breath. "It's too painful." She looked up at him with desperate eyes as she suddenly lost control of her body. She could feel the magic being forced awake within her as her vision disappeared.

Darkness consumed Aponi's sight as she heard her name be yelled out by Khalon. It was the last thing she heard from her own world.

"Witch killer," a voice whispered. The darkness rippled to reveal a pale, white face with gray eyes. Her strawberry blonde hair fell into them a little as Aponi pulled back.

"You're that witch from Earth," she gasped. It was hard for her to breathe, like she was being split in two.

"Yes, my name is Kaydee."

"*Get out of my head,*" Aponi hissed. Kaydee's face turned apologetic.

"I'm sorry, Aponi. I would talk to you in your dreams, but they're oddly very protected," she explained.

"They're protected against witches like you."

"Right. I heard how you got your magic. You're a lightning bird?"

"A thunderbird," Aponi snapped.

"What's the difference?" Aponi held her head as it started to pound.

"In human legends, I like how the thunderbird is presented. They protect from evil. They are powerful."

"What about a lightning bird?"

"A lightning bird, or an impundulu, is just used by witches," Aponi muttered. "Servants for witches."

"I see," Kaydee whispered. Aponi met her gaze.

"I don't have time for a history lesson. Let me go," she demanded. Kaydee bit the inside of her cheek as she seemed to look at something next to her, something Aponi couldn't see.

"We need your help, Aponi," she said.

"Who's we? You and that elf?" The witch nodded.

"We need you to let me use you as a conductor. So that we can hop through time," Kaydee explained. Aponi glowered at her.

"I vowed to never let another witch use me to amplify her powers ever again," she said, her voice low. Kaydee nodded her head.

"I understand that. Completely, I do. But—"

"*Do* you understand? How would you be able to understand, *witch*? Have you ever been at the mercy of any other being? Have you ever felt *utterly* powerless?" Kaydee's eyes widened as her image started to tremble.

"Aponi, we need to follow the assassins from Asynithis into the different times that they're landing in. To protect the Saviors. To protect Asynithis," Kaydee pleaded as her face became blurry.

"Get out of my head," Aponi hissed. The lightning within her skittered across her skin and coiled around her bones.

"Aponi," her voice was fainter, now.

"*Get out!*" Aponi was covered in darkness once more. And slowly, the darkness was peeled away to reveal her sight again. She stared at the ground of the tent that she was in. She was laying on her side, and she could hear someone sigh a breath of relief from above her. She looked up into Khalon's eyes.

"Your hair is white again," was the first thing he said. Aponi's hands went to her head as she pulled a strand of her hair in front of her face. She let go of the strand in disgust as Jabulani helped her to her feet.

"Great. I'll never escape it," she muttered.

"What happened? Your eyes went white, filled with lightning—kind of like Esi's actually—and you weren't responding to anyone," Khalon said. Aponi gritted her teeth as she met Poseidon's gaze.

"You were right. I have one foot in each world," she muttered. "A witch is trying to use me."

33

Kamaria stared at the two guards outside of Esi's room. The guards looked half asleep, which boded well for their attack. Her eyes moved to look at Maleko and Apsara who whispered heatedly to one another. Their lips moved lightning fast to the point where Kamaria couldn't follow their conversation.

"Attack," was all Kamaria could really make out. She tried to form the words in her throat, not sure how loud she should speak.

"Attack?" she asked, hoping the words were quiet enough. Maleko side-eyed her.

"Not yet," he seemed to say.

"There's only two," she said aloud.

"There's more inside," Apsara responded. Kamaria's ebony eyes fixed on the white, stone door that led to Esi's room. She furrowed her eyebrows as she looked at the two merpeople in distaste. Did they not know who she was? She could level a battlefield. A few guards was child's play.

She stood up, stretching out of her crouching position as she started towards the door, a hand on her obsidian blade. Maleko's large hand grabbed her wrist, stopping her from taking a step closer.

"We can't just storm the room. It'll alert Adamar," he said. She glowered at him.

"What does that have to do with me?"

"Don't you want to give Khai time?" he asked. Kamaria swallowed as she continued to glare at the Argentiundan King. Of course she wanted to give him time, but she was worried about giving him *too* much time. Khai only knew how to fight within the confines of his royal duties. He barely seemed to survive each time on the battlefield.

I'm fine, she could see him sign in her mind. It's something he definitely would say. Kamaria *wanted* to give Khai time. Time to get whatever it was he was looking for. Time to confront his mother. But... the image of the small bruises peppered across his jaw appeared in her mind. Kamaria's eyes steeled. It was too much time with his mother that she couldn't bear to give him.

Kamaria had only spoken to the Queen Mother of Draconia a handful of times. However, it was clear she was a selfish person. She wouldn't hesitate to—at least—severely hurt Khai if she thought he was against her. Killing him wasn't completely off the table either for Queen Aoife, that much Kamaria knew.

"We can't give him too much time," she decided. She took a step forward, cracking her neck as she revealed herself to the two guards. She didn't give them time to yell out for help as she swiftly threw her two blades into both of their necks, meeting their marks. Blue blood poured out as they stood for a moment more before falling to the ground, causing a vibration to be felt underneath her booted feet.

Kamaria glowered at the stone door as she pulled the blades out of each of the elves' necks. The sight of corpses had long stopped making her stomach turn.

She turned towards Maleko and Apsara. The Argentiundan King's jaw was dropped as Apsara's face was contorted into annoyance at Kamaria's impulsiveness.

"Let's go," she said, pushing the stone door open. Through the sliver, she could see her little sister Esi in chains, her black curls matted with blood. It was enough for Kamaria to see red as she entered the chamber. She wouldn't show *any* of them mercy.

———

Finding his mother didn't take Khai much effort at all, unlike what he thought. Like how there was something pulling him to the Mortiferis, there was something pulling him to his mother, Queen Aoife. As though she were calling for him.

He snuck through the halls of the Aureum palace, keeping close to the walls. He didn't want to run into Prince Ardryll again. He knew if he did, it would end in a slaughter. Either his or Ardryll's.

It was late in the night, though, and Khai didn't think anyone else would be wandering the halls. The pull grew stronger as he started to pass a white, stone door. However, it wasn't guarded.

Khai looked down both sides of the hall before crossing

towards the door. He turned the knob in his hand, easily, as he pushed it open. It wasn't locked either.

No guards, an unlocked door—it was as if his mother wasn't a prisoner at all. As if she was willingly staying there.

"Mom?" Khai whispered as he entered the room. His mother was standing at the window of her ornately decorated chamber. No doubt his mother annoyed everyone in the palace until she got exactly what she wanted. Queen Aoife would rather be dead than stay in a prison cell.

She turned towards him. Her light brown hair, the same as Khai's, was down, along her back. She was wearing a white nightgown as her brown eyes met his.

"My son," she said, almost breathing out a sigh of relief. She walked over to where Khai was, and he braced for the slap that was bound to hit the side of his face. Instead, she wrapped her arms around him.

"I was worried about you," she said. Khai froze. His mother didn't show affection often—hardly ever. But, it was all he ever wanted from her. He slowly put his arms around her body, hugging her back. She pulled away, a smile on her face.

"Did you do it?" she asked. The warmth Khai had felt from her slowly melted away as his arms fell.

"Uh, Mom, I'm here to get you out of the Aureum palace," he muttered. Aoife's smile disappeared as she took a step back, to look at him clearer.

"You didn't do it," she said, her voice like stone.

"Mother—"

"I've given you everything you've ever wanted, have I not? And you couldn't do this one thing for me? This one thing for *yourself?*" Aoife hissed, her brown eyes like blades.

"The opportunity didn't present itself," Khai mumbled.

"Didn't present itself?" Aoife scoffed. "You were in Caedoxia. How did it not *present* itself?" He looked away from his mother, his hand on his pocket, feeling the outline of the Mortiferis tooth. He received it at Poseidon's request. But, Poseidon didn't say he couldn't use it before giving it over.

"I didn't want to kill hi—" Aoife stiffened, causing Khai to stop talking. She narrowed her eyes as she took another step towards him.

"Turn around," she ordered.

"What?"

"Turn. Around." Khai slowly obeyed her as he turned to face the still slightly ajar stone door. He felt Aoife lift up his shirt and heard the disgusted sigh that followed afterwards. The shirt slowly met his skin once more as he turned to look back at his mother. She had turned to face the window.

"You have the Death mark on you." Khai blinked. He wasn't sure if she was upset about the fact that Death was coming for him or if she was upset that he failed.

"Khalon has it," he answered. "He... gave it to me."

"You failed," she hissed. "You tried to kill him, and you *failed*." Khai wasn't surprised at Aoife's response, but his chest still ached.

"He's a Champion, Mom. You raised him to be—" She whirled around.

"*Raised* him? Don't blame this on me. You're *weak*. You've *always* been so weak. The spirit of the dragon couldn't have chosen you. Not when you have no resolve. No honor." It felt like the breath was knocked out of Khai's chest.

"Chosen?" he whispered. He didn't realize that the spirit of the dragon truly made a choice to attach itself onto someone. And that the spirit didn't choose him. Purposefully didn't choose him.

"Do you know what's happening right now, Khai?" she asked, her eyes like moonstone as she met his gaze. "Khalon is going to try to take the throne."

"You don't know—"

"I know *everything*," she said through gritted teeth. "The curse of my bloodline. I know too much." She looked back out the window, silence stretching between Khai and her. Khai made a step towards her, and she shook her head as she looked at him once more. He could see her back's reflection against the mirror behind her next to the window. The part of her back that was showing flexed.

"You'll try again," she said, nodding to herself as she grabbed a bottle from her dresser. Khai backed away from her.

"I'm not going to kill him, Mom. I can't—"

"You *will*," she said, grabbing his head. She gripped his jaw hard as she forced his mouth open. Khai struggled against her, but the smell of metal showed him that he wouldn't be able to move much. She uncorked the bottle with her mouth and started to pour the liquid down Khai's throat. As his mind was screaming for her to stop, he could feel his body become stronger. The thirst for more burning his throat.

"Mom," he gurgled. "*Please.*" Her eyes were almost crazed, continuing to pour. Pain erupted around his jaw as he reached for the Mortiferis tooth. He pulled it out of his pocket and his mother's eyes flickered towards the movement. She stopped pouring as her eyebrows pulled together. She looked back at Khai, laughter escaping her lips as she let go of his jaw.

"You're going to try to get rid of me?" she said, her voice low. Khai rubbed his jaw as he took a hesitant step forward.

"You need to stop, Mom, or I'll—"

"Kill me?" she said, her voice eerily calm. She met his gaze as the metallic smell filled the room. Wind started to whip around them, and Khai felt the familiar feeling of fear settle into the pit of his stomach.

"You forget what I am, dear son," she whispered, her eyes starting to have a silvery glint to them. Khai felt something invisible wrap around his neck as he was pulled upwards into the air. The Mortiferis tooth clattered to the ground as he clawed at his neck, gasping for breath.

"You make me so *sad*, Khai," she murmured. "I wanted *so* much for you."

"You'd. Kill. Me. For. Khalon?" he managed to get out in between gasps.

"I'll kill you to get you out of my way," her voice was flat. Khai could feel his body automatically turning into his dragon form in a biological attempt to protect himself. But, dragon or not, his mother's magic still held him suspended in the air, choking on an invisible rope.

"You could've been such a great ruler, Khai. You could've given so much respect to me. Respect I *deserve*. Instead, you chose him over me? You chose that bastard of Dal's over *me*?" Aoife's voice grew shrill at the thought of Khalon's deceased mother.

"You chose *her* over me? Over your own mother?" Khai's

vision started to grow blurry as he felt his life begin to slip away from him.

Suddenly, his mother's head whipped to the side to look towards someone next to him. He could see in the mirror's reflection Kamaria's round, black eyes. Her red veins were glowing throughout her body faster, showing that her heart was pounding quickly. Her face was splattered in blue blood as she glowered at Aoife.

Khai watched as Kamaria threw an obsidian blade at his mother's chest. He felt his soul scramble back into his body, something in him trying to stop Kamaria. His body fell to the ground, the invisible rope gone from his throat as Aoife used magic to redirect the obsidian blade, having it hit the wall instead.

"The Queen of Ustrina. Trying to save my son? How cute," Aoife said, her face turning into ice. Khai couldn't escape the smell and taste of metal as he coughed, reaching towards Kamaria.

"Go," he whispered. "Run." Aoife's hair seemed to float above her head as magic filled her, filling her brown eyes with silver.

"Listen to the boy, if you know what's best for you," Aoife hissed. "This is a family matter." Kamaria shrugged.

"I can't hear," she responded, pointing to her ears. "So looks like I won't be listening to anyone." She rushed towards Aoife, another blade in her hands. Aoife's eyes widened as she pushed Kamaria back with her magic, but it was as if she was protected from it. It did nothing but blow her braids back. She pressed the obsidian blade against Aoife's neck, crimson blood starting to show against it. Aoife blinked as she glowered at Kamaria.

"Someone's put a protection spell on you," she guessed. Kamaria just smiled, her pointed teeth on full display, as she pressed the blade harder. Aoife flicked her wrist, causing Khai to be pulled back into the air, that invisible rope around his neck once more. He watched as Kamaria's ebony eyes softened, her grip faltering. Aoife took a step back as a smile slithered over her face.

"You try to kill me again, I'll snap his neck." Kamaria's eyelids fluttered as she closed her eyes.

"I hope you die a horrible death in Terra," she barely uttered. Aoife frowned, looking at her.

"What?" she said as Kamaria placed her hands on Aoife's shoulders, pushing her backwards. Aoife lost her balance, the reflection behind her rippling. Her eyes—the eyes that Khai shared—widened as she looked desperately at him. As her magic stopped, Khai fell to the ground, reaching towards his mother. The mirror engulfed Aoife and by the time he reached it, it was smooth glass once more.

He placed his forehead against the reflective glass, closing his eyes. They burned as he felt his body return back into its human form. All he could think about was his mother's arms around him from earlier. The only warmth he ever felt from her since he was a child. And now, the last. Kamaria put a hand on his shoulder. He turned slightly to look at her.

We need to go, she signed. She twisted her face as she paused for a moment before glaring at the mirror. *I'm sorry.* Khai simply looked back at the mirror as he closed his eyes once again. His mother wasn't dead at least, he could feel it.

"It's okay," he mouthed, hoping Kamaria could read his

lips. He pulled away from the mirror as he looked into her round eyes.

It's fine, he signed. *I'm fine.* Her eyes widened before looking away, darting towards his neck where the invisible rope had been. He could see the tears starting to pool in her eyes, but she blinked them into oblivion.

It's okay if you're not fine, Khai, she signed, her eyebrows pulled upwards. Her eyes steeled as she met his gaze once more. *And you can be mad at me for as long as you need to. But you'll never get me to regret saving your life.*

Khai stared deeply into Kamaria's ebony eyes as he took her in. She was covered in blue blood. Her pupils were large and wide from adrenaline. He took her hands into his own, stained with the crimson blood of a dragon.

He would never admit it to her. He couldn't. But, he never felt more safe than when Kamaria was like this. He never felt more at peace than when Kamaria was beside him, covered in blood.

She pressed her stained fingers against Khai's throat, her eyes still meeting his.

"Thank you for always protecting me, Kamaria," he whispered. She closed her own eyes as she felt the vibrations of his voice. Kamaria pulled her hands away as she opened them once more.

Always, she signed.

34

Khalon listened as Aponi told them what happened. She had an old blanket around her that Luke had managed to find, and a drink in her hands. They were sitting around the fire as a sprinkling of snow from earlier in the day covered the ground.

"She wants to use you to jump through time?" Khalon asked, leaning forward. Aponi's face had an orange glow to it as she warmed her hands in front of the fire.

"She said she wants to use me as a conductor," she answered, her upper lip curled in disgust.

"She's with Elion?" Poseidon questioned. Aponi nodded.

"I saw her with him earlier."

"If it's to protect the Saviors, maybe you should let her use you as a conductor, Aponi," Khalon suggested. Her head whipped towards him. He had never seen such visceral hate in her dark eyes before.

"I would rather slit my throat than let another witch use me," she hissed.

"A *tad* dramatic, wouldn't you say?" Poseidon quipped. She directed her glare towards the Sea God. Poseidon held up his hands in defense.

"Hey, it's *your* world at stake."

"Isn't it your world, as well?" Jabulani asked him. Poseidon shrugged as he stared into the yellow-orange flames.

"It's a world that I helped create. All the worlds were ones I created alongside An. Alongside Death. But, I won't be here to see them all destroyed. Thank An," Poseidon said, softly. He clenched his jaw as Valerian put a comforting hand on his thigh.

"You're trying to manipulate me by saying if I don't do this then everything and everyone on Asynithis will die," Aponi said through gritted teeth. Poseidon popped up his head as he looked at her, his eyes hopeful.

"Is it working?" he asked.

"Nope."

"Aponi—" Khalon started. She glowered at him as she stood up from the log she was sitting on.

"Find a different lightning bird to do your bidding, *King* Khalon," she hissed. "Because I'm *not* doing it." She pivoted harshly on one foot, stalking into the tent behind her. He almost winced at the soft sound of the front of the tent closing.

"Rhea said we need to protect the Saviors. This might be the way we're supposed to do it," Khalon muttered, staring at the fire. Poseidon leaned back on his arms as he looked up at the stars.

"She must've went through something traumatic with a witch if she's willing to give up her entire world for it."

He then looked back at Khalon, cocking his head to the side.

"Aren't you cold?" he asked, gesturing towards his body. Khalon looked down at himself. He was wearing pants and a sleeveless vest made of dragon skin. He shook his head.

"Draconians run pretty hot, normally. But, I run hotter than most," he murmured. Poseidon nodded his head along with Khalon's words.

"You have more fire within you, being from two dragons and all," he said.

"There must be some way to convince Aponi to let the witch use her," Khalon mused, looking over at Jabulani. Jabulani's eyes widened as they made eye contact before slowly shaking his head.

"I don't know if Aponi *can* be convinced," he said, slowly. He sighed and leaned forward, resting his head into his hands. "Kamaria found her in a dark place."

"What happened to her?" Khalon asked, his voice low. Jabulani's lips thinned as he looked back at the tent that Aponi had disappeared into.

"All I know is that her witch was really abusive towards her," he said, lowering his voice. "She wanted to amplify her powers and continuously used Aponi to do so. A witch using a lightning bird isn't a pleasant experience. It can be painful. And for Aponi, it was torture."

"It must've been a lot of pain for a lightning bird to kill their witch," Valerian spoke. "It's not easy to get to that place. That headspace." Khalon remained quiet. He knew what it took in order to take another's life. Though, he had only done it in life and death situations. He never experienced killing someone he despised.

"So, she'd be in pain if the witch from Earth used her," Khalon concluded.

"It's not always that they're in pain, but if used unwillingly and if a lot of magic is coursing through them, they can be." Khalon's eyes settled onto the tent Aponi had gone into. He wasn't going to make her do anything she didn't want to. But, he hoped she would change her mind. His eyes wandered back over to Jabulani. His face twisted as he caught Khalon's gaze.

"I'll try to talk to her tomorrow," he muttered. "She... She knows what's at stake Khalon. Just let her process it. A witch just invaded her mind without her permission. You would feel violated as well." Khalon nodded his head. He didn't know if he would feel the same as Aponi, but he never experienced what she went through. If Aoife suddenly appeared in his head, he would—probably—be freaked out, too.

"On that note..." Poseidon turned towards Valerian, patting the dryad's hand that was on his thigh. "Didn't you say you would show me your tree?" A smirk played on Valerian's lips.

"Of course, your holiness," he whispered. Poseidon and Valerian stood up and started to walk towards the trees in the distance. Poseidon looked over his shoulder at Khalon and winked before disappearing into the darkness. Khalon imagined the reaction Rhea would have on her face right now if she were there with them. She'd probably have a bored look on as she would turn towards him, saying, *"Poseidon sleeps with anything that moves."* Khalon hid his smile as his eyes softened.

"I'll probably turn in for the night as well," Jabulani whispered. He moved to get up, but then paused, his eyes not meeting Khalon's. "Do you think they got Esi out safely?" His voice was almost carried away by the soft, winter breeze.

"Kamaria wouldn't let anything happen to her," Khalon promised. "You know how she is with Esi." Jabulani nodded his head, taking in a deep breath before getting up. Khalon watched as his figure disappeared into one of the tents the beastoids had set up for them.

Khalon stared into the flames for a moment longer before kicking some snow into it, distinguishing the fire. He needed to save Rhea, no matter what it took. And if protecting the Saviors in the long run was going to in turn protect her, he would have to convince Aponi.

Without taking a moment to really consider his decision, he turned towards Aponi's tent, stopping in front of it before pulling back the flap.

"I see your shadow there," he heard her say from inside. "Just come inside." Khalon pulled back the fabric and entered her tent. It was smaller than the one he was sharing with Jabulani. But, it had a small fire in the middle, the smoke curling towards the top of the tent.

"What do you want, Khalon?" Aponi asked. Her white hair was pulled up into a bun on the top of her head, but she still hadn't changed for bed. It looked like she had been staring at the flames in the fire this whole time.

"Rhea told me to find the witch, find the portals, and protect the Saviors," Khalon said, sitting down next to her.

"Yeah, so?" Her dark eyes were fixed on the flames.

"So... you found the witch. You have access to the portals. Maybe, you're the one who's supposed to protect them," he muttered. It was a message that Rhea had told him, but maybe it wasn't him who needed to hear it. And Aponi was the first person he told the message to. Maybe, it was always for her to hear. Her gaze hardened.

"I'm not helping a witch."

"Don't think of it as helping her. Don't think of it as a witch using you, Aponi. This is you. This is *your* power. *You're* protecting them. *You're* saving the future of Asynithis," Khalon pressed. Aponi's eyes softened a bit. Enough for Khalon to have permission to continue.

"You're a thunderbird, Aponi. A protector from evil. Without your stolen magic, I can see how powerful you are. And we need that power. Asynithis needs that power." She stayed quiet, shifting her weight as she leaned forward, closer to the fire. Khalon's gaze turned towards it, the flames licking up the cold around them.

"I know what it's like. To take a life. I know what it's like to *want* to take the life of someone you truly despise," he whispered, the memories coming back to him. "I nearly killed someone while thoughts of my father and Queen Aoife plagued me." Liam's face came to the forefront of Khalon's mind. The memory of fighting against him in the Ring of Fire filled Khalon. The *hate* that he felt as he had thought about all the injustices against him.

"But, you *don't* know what it's like," Aponi snapped. "You might know what it feels like to be a prisoner. But, you have *no idea* what I went through." She got up from where she was sitting, her back turned towards him.

"Aponi, please," Khalon said. "You're the only one who can do this."

"You just want to save Rhea," she accused. Khalon stiffened. It was true. He didn't care about anyone other than her. It was clear Aponi was hurting in front of him. Past trauma bubbling up underneath her skin. But, Khalon couldn't care about that. If he did, he would be pushing Rhea aside. And he needed to focus.

"The world needs you, Aponi," Khalon decided to say. "Hell, maybe all the realms need you." He reached a hand out to her, wanting to comfort her in some way. He could almost feel her pain, taste it on his tongue. His arm hung there, in the air, suspended for a moment. But, Khalon's fingers curled into his palm as he pulled his arm back down to his side. Aponi didn't turn around as Khalon exited her tent. And she stood there until she was sure her legs turned to stone.

―――――

"We know where the draconian refugee camp is," Michael said, his bear paw pointing at a spot marked on the map in front of them. "However, I don't know how welcoming your kind will be when they see us."

"I don't think anyone wanted my father's war in the first place," Khalon said, leaning forward to look at the dot. It wasn't too far away from them, on the outskirts of Draconia's border. They were still in No Man's Land. And as long as the Death God lived, Aureum wouldn't dare try to claim this land as their own.

"Let's leave as soon as possible," Khalon said, lifting his head to meet Michael's beady eyes. "We can't delay for much longer." Michael nodded as another beastoid bear rolled up the map. He growled out some orders that Khalon couldn't understand.

"We can leave at noon," he said, turning back towards Khalon, his bear face almost smug. Then, he lowered his gaze as he looked at Khalon more clearly. "There are children and mothers in my camp, however. Not everyone will be able to fight for your cause."

"Don't say it like that," Khalon muttered under his breath. His black eyes met the bear's. "It's for your cause as well."

"I hope you keep your promise, draconian," Michael said, gruffly. The bears left the tent, barking orders at whoever was nearby outside. Khalon's eyes roved over the others left in the tent. Aponi was nowhere to be seen. He raised his eyebrows as he met Jabulani's gaze. Jabulani ran his tongue across his teeth.

"She just wants to be left alone," he said. His eyes steeled as he met Khalon's. "Don't pressure her anymore. She'll do what's best for her."

"What about what's best for Asynithis?" Poseidon said, slowly looking over at Jabulani. Jabulani's nostrils flared as he met the Sea God's challenge.

"If you were thinking about what's best of Asynithis, you would kill yourself. Wouldn't you, God of the Seas?" Jabulani growled. The waves in Poseidon's eyes seemed to be more present as his gaze hardened. Slowly, a small smile spread across his lips.

"That's the plan," he said. "Just can't do it quite yet." Jabulani took a step forward.

"What's stopping you?"

"My soul isn't *that* fragile. Gods forbid, could you imagine if it were?" Poseidon laughed as he turned towards

Valerian. There was something solemn in Valerian's gaze, as if they had already talked about Poseidon's demise.

"How are you going to get your hands on a Mortiferis?" Khalon asked. Poseidon smirked.

"I have my ways." Before Khalon could respond, snarls and growls could be heard outside the tent. He rushed outside, the cold air almost slapping his face as he looked at the scene in front of him. The bear beastoids were poised for attack, growling at the intruders in front of them.

Wolves stood in front of him, a good many of them. They snapped their jaws and snarled at the bears in response. But, as they met Khalon's gaze, they straightened up from their position.

"You're the one who has the spirit of the dragon within you?" the wolf at the front asked, his voice gnarled and twisted due to his voice box. Khalon blinked before nodding in confirmation.

"Yes, that's me." The wolf looked back at the others behind him before turning back towards Khalon.

"We're here to help you. If you promise what you've promised the bears," the wolf said, his teeth bared into a sort of smirk. Khalon looked at the battalion the wolves brought and swallowed the lump in his throat.

"I promise," Khalon vowed.

35

The Aureum palace was in chaos as Khai pulled Kamaria out of the chamber his mother inhabited, making sure to pick up the Mortiferis tooth on his way out. Running down the hall were Maleko and Apsara, Esi in Maleko's arms.

"They know!" Maleko shouted, his voice echoing down the hallways. Khai's eyes were wide as he looked back at them, his grip around Kamaria's wrist tightening. They rushed towards the abandoned greenhouse, pushing the doors open.

Khai quickly grabbed his armor and clothes and ran towards the open window. Kamaria had already jumped through it, her gaze fixed onto the twilight skies. She pointed a finger upwards, a burst of fire pouring out from her. It hit the sky and seemed to burst into fiery glitter.

"What is she doing? She's going to give away our location," Maleko snapped as he pulled himself through the window. Apsara handed Esi, her white eyes glowing while her body was limp, to him before jumping through the window herself.

My Kongamato, Kamaria signed, beaming at Khai. Unfortunately, he remembered her flying beast. On their first meeting, the creature tried to eat him alive as Kamaria laughed.

Great, Khai signed back as he heard the sound of powerful wings above. The Kongamato slowly lowered itself to the ground, its beady eyes focused onto Khai. It snapped its beak-like snout in his direction.

"Yeah, yeah," he muttered at the creature. "I don't really like you either." Kamaria petted the Kongamato's gray scales down as she cooed at it. It stretched out its bat-like wings to its full length before curling them back into itself.

Let's go, she signed. Khai translated for her as he rushed towards the Kongamato. He mounted the beast as she did. Maleko gingerly placed Esi onto the creature, Kamaria holding her in place. Then, he backed away from the Kongamato. Kamaria's eyebrows furrowed as she stared at him.

"You guys aren't hopping on?" Khai asked for her, guessing at her thoughts. Maleko shook his head as he exchanged a look with Apsara.

"I have to save my people," he said, holding his head up high. Apsara cracked her fingers.

"And we have an elf to settle a score with," she hissed. Khai didn't want to be on the other end of *her* fury.

Be careful, Kamaria signed. Khai echoed her sentiment. As the commotion grew louder from the palace, Kamaria made a noise that caused the Kongamato to start to flap its powerful wings. Maleko and Apsara disappeared into the gardens as the elves started to come out of the palace. Arrows filled the air as the Kongamato expertly avoided the pointed projectiles, hurrying out of Regium airspace.

Khai looked over Esi. Her eyes were glowing white, which meant she was having a vision. Her black curls were matted with dried blood and the skin that was visible was covered in bruises.

"She must've not given the right answers to the king," he murmured as he brushed a curl off of her face. He turned towards Kamaria in order to tell her the same thing, but his eyes widened as her face grayed. Her hand was on one side, an arrow sticking out of it.

His heart started to pound in his head as he saw the orange blood, almost like molten lava, pooling into Kamaria's hands. His mouth turned to cotton.

"Kamaria," his voice was hoarse as he pulled himself towards her. She put up a hand, wincing as she pulled the arrow out from beneath her ribs, dropping it over the side of the flying Kongamato. Orange liquid poured out of the wound as she placed her hand on it. She closed her eyes, bringing her hand, covered in her blood, towards her lips. Gingerly, she licked it, cringing as she did. Her face softened as her body seemed to relax.

Are you okay? Khai signed, his face tight. The blood slowed as she nodded her head, a sheen of sweat coating her skin.

It didn't hit anything vital, she signed, breathing heavily. *My blood can heal me.* Khai let out a breath that he didn't know he was holding. Her eyes noted the action, but she didn't mention it, didn't even try to tease him for it.

Are you sure you're okay? he asked. Kamaria grimaced as she tried to sit up more.

I am *a phoenix, Khai,* she smiled. *It takes more to kill me than a single arrow.* Khai's eyes bore holes into her face, memorizing her features. Her eyebrows pulled downwards as she looked away.

Don't look at me like that, she signed.

Like what?

Like you care about me. Her ebony eyes met his. His mouth went dry once more, but for a different reason. He lifted his hands to sign "Of course I do" but then hesitated. She stared at him for a moment longer before thinning her lips.

You can't even admit it, she signed. Her face was contorted into disgust. Or maybe disappointment.

What would it do? Admitting it? he signed back. *What would it change?* Kamaria's gaze softened as her eyebrows pulled together.

Wouldn't it change everything?

They held each other's gaze for what felt like forever. Khai didn't know when he got closer to her, but she was only a hair's distance away from him. Her eyes took up his whole vision. His darted towards her full lips before meeting her round eyes once more.

It would change too much, he signed, slowly. Hurt flickered in her eyes. It was only for a second. But, it was second too much for Khai. And it made every part of him ache.

Of course, she scoffed, pulling back. *You wouldn't dare try to change your status. Even with your mother gone.* Her words didn't register in Khai's brain; it was like he couldn't process it. Only one thought was echoing around in his head. One selfish thought. And a thought that he couldn't contain.

He closed the distance between them, pressing his lips against hers. And it was a different kind of burning that he felt run through his whole body. Different from the thirst of dragon's blood that his body seemed to yearn for. Instead, his body yearned for her, *begged* for her.

He placed his hand on her neck as he kissed her deeper, her hands pulling his head closer as she tangled her fingers in his hair. They kissed like they needed each other to breathe, to live. As if it were inevitable.

"How did I end up here?" Esi's voice broke the spell between them. Khai quickly pulled away, Kamaria's fingers running down the sides of his face as he ripped himself from her. She blinked as he turned towards Esi. Realization started to settle in as she faced her little sister. *Thank Alator*, Khai thought as he remembered Esi was blind. She didn't seem to have heard them kissing, either. Or if she did, she didn't mention it.

"I was having a vision and now I'm in the air?" Esi said, her eyebrows furrowing as her hands felt the scales underneath her. "Am I on a... Kongamato?"

"Kamaria saved you from the elves," Khai said, clearing his throat. Esi blinked her white eyes as she stared in his direction.

"Khalon?" she asked. Her face looked so hopeful that Khai felt bad for telling her the truth. He coughed a little as he exchanged a look with Kamaria.

"No, it's Khai," he said.

"Oh," Esi replied, her eyebrows knitting together once more. "You sounded so solemn just now, like him."

"I guess he and I share at least one trait," Khai muttered. Esi laughed a bit.

"If you're heartbroken, I guess you do," she said. Khai stiffened as Kamaria seemed to tense up before wilting into her seat. She read Esi's lips, which meant she knew what Khai felt. What that kiss meant to him. And what it meant for their future. Her gaze hardened as she turned away, towards the head of the Kongamato. She made a noise, causing the beast to fly faster.

"Yeah, I guess we do," Khai mumbled as he stared at the back of Kamaria's head.

———

"Look at this," Lorena said, her pupils enlarged as she turned on a small black box next to a large, flat black screen. The box whirred to life as she picked up—what Kaydee called—a remote. She pressed a red button and the large glass black screen flashed on.

"What is it?" Elion asked as he leaned in. They had been stuck in Kaydee's apartment for a few days now as they waited for her to make contact with Aponi.

"Kaydee said it's a gaming console. I figured it out while you were sleeping," Lorena said, her smile smug. She picked up some kind of wireless black device, swiveling little knobs around. Lorena pressed a button as Elion's gaze was fixed on the screen. Loud noises came from it and an animated version of what looked like an elf appeared.

"They know about you elves," she said, laughing. Elion's eyebrows furrowed as he took a step closer to the screen.

"They think we look like this?" he asked, looking back at

Lorena. She had a hand over her mouth, hiding her smile. He looked back at the animated elf, his eyes narrowing. "Our ears aren't *that* big." He subconsciously touched the tips of his own elven ears.

Before Lorena could make whatever remark was clearly burning her tongue, the door to Kaydee's apartment opened. She set down the bags that she brought in, closing the door with her foot. It was still unnerving for Elion to see Kaydee. She looked eerily similar to Queen Aoife, just younger.

"Have you convinced her yet?" Elion asked. Lorena was smashing buttons as her gaze looked fiery at the screen. He was sure she was getting all her revenge fantasies out in the game. A shudder ran down his body. Kaydee shook her head, hanging it a little as she didn't meet Elion's eyes.

"When I was at our coven meeting, I tried to make contact with her. But she's... She's angry, understandably. She doesn't want to help at all," she said. She put away the items she got from the market before leaning against her tiny counter.

"We have to figure out some other way," she said.

"So, we have to stay here?" Lorena piped up before smashing buttons again. "Die, you ugly elf!" Elion winced at her words. Kaydee gave him an amused look before turning her gaze towards Lorena.

"I don't know when the elves will come. Sometimes, it's years between the next sighting. Other times, it's a few days. It sounds like you two might be here for a while if Aponi doesn't change her mind," Kaydee said.

"I'm fine with that," Lorena responded, her eyes unmoving from the screen.

"I thought you wanted revenge?" Elion said after a moment of silence. Lorena froze. Her hazel eyes cut across the room until they met Elion's. He swore he felt a cold breeze pass over him.

"Well," Lorena said, her mouth barely moving. "You're here, aren't you?" Elion swallowed. His eyes darted towards the pocket that he knew she was still hiding her dagger in.

"Wouldn't it be better if you killed my brother, Adamar?" Elion suggested. He saw a twinkle pass through her hazel eyes, but she didn't answer. Instead, she opted to go back to her game. She pressed the buttons more aggressively than she did previously.

"Revenge?" Kaydee mouthed.

"Her... whole family was murdered by my brother," Elion said, quietly.

"Because of *him*," Lorena said, ending her game. She got up as she took out her dagger, twirling it around her hand. The pointed end pressed against Elion's chest as she looked up at him. At this angle, Elion had a strong urge to trace over the scar that ran down her face. A reminder of what he did to her.

"Okay," Kaydee said, putting a hand on Lorena's shoulder. She didn't move, her gaze like stone. "Let's just... settle down here." Kaydee shot a glance towards Elion, but his eyes didn't leave Lorena's.

"If we're going to be here for a long time, you can't very well survive here with those ears, can you?" Lorena hissed. Elion stared deep into her swirling hazel eyes, filled with conflicting emotions.

"I mean, I can put a spell on them so that no one notices his ears," Kaydee interrupted. Elion and Lorena ignored her.

"You're right. I can't live long in this realm," he whispered. He moved so that the dagger was pushed more against his chest. "You might as well get rid of me. Avenge Pilar."

"It wasn't just Pilar," Lorena said, her voice low.

"I know." Elion dipped his head slightly, looking at Lorena through his lashes. She stared at him for a moment, before her grip softened.

"Wait, guys—" Kaydee's voice suddenly cut off. Elion looked over at her and her eyes were glazed over, her body frozen stiff.

"Is she…" Lorena lowered the dagger as she took a step closer to Kaydee. "Is she *dead*?" Elion pressed his fingers gingerly onto the witch's neck, her heartbeat hammering like a hummingbird's wings. It thundered against his fingertips.

"No, she's awake. But, whatever she's seeing is making her stressed at the very least. Frightened at the most," he whispered, removing his fingers. Lorena pursed her lips before placing her dagger back into her pocket. She glared at Elion.

"I'll wait until she's done with whatever she's doing," she said, waving her hands around Kaydee. "But, once she's done, you're dead."

"I look forward to it," Elion said, a small smile playing on his lips.

36

Khalon was jolted awake as he held onto the sides of his makeshift bed. Everything in his tent was trembling. An empty bottle fell off of the small table in the corner, shattering into pieces, and Khalon almost fell over as he opened the front of his tent. Jabulani was sound asleep, like the earthquake wasn't disturbing him in the slightest.

Outside, the ground cracked open, showing a set of stairs that descended into darkness. Khalon furrowed his eyebrows as he watched Poseidon look around before going down the steps. *No wonder why Jabulani didn't wake up*, he thought to himself. Not everyone could see the door to the underworld.

Before the ground could close back up, Khalon darted towards it. He ran down a few steps and then dread settled into the pit of his stomach. He was willingly going into the underworld, the land of the undead. What would happen to him if he went down there? Rhea's words echoed in his mind: *"If a living soul goes into the underworld, they won't be able to come back to the surface."* Khalon stopped in his tracks. He looked over his shoulder at the direction he came from. Darkness met him, only the foot in front of him was illuminated by a magical flame on the wall. The ground had closed back up. Khalon closed his eyes, tight. *Shit.*

Well, there's no turning back, he thought as he ran down the seemingly never-ending steps. Besides, if he would die from going into the underworld, why was he able to see it, if he *was* a normal living soul? Or could he see it, and possibly survive the trip, because a dragon's spirit was attached to him? Without knowing exactly why, Khalon felt that he would be okay entering the underworld, a sense of calm washing over him.

After what felt like forever, the narrow stairway opened up into a lobby of sorts. A corpse in a black cloak walked by him, its hollow eye sockets on full display as it turned towards Khalon. He jumped back.

"Oh shit! Fuck!" the curses flew out of his mouth as his stomach turned at seeing the corpse. The corpse continued to walk away, like it had somewhere important to be.

Khalon put a hand over his chest. "I'm so sorry. I didn't mean to..." his voice drifted off as it was clear the corpse wasn't listening to him. While Khalon looked around the lobby, he realized it was full of corpses in different stages of decomposition. The smell was almost unbearable. *Do the reaper's cloak not work while they're in the underworld?* He put a hand over his mouth as he searched the room for Poseidon.

His eyes focused on the back of Poseidon's new body, a woman walking next to him as they were heading in the direction of a room with a large glass window overlooking the lobby area. Khalon recognized the woman as she turned to the side. She was one of the Fates.

He rushed after them, grabbing a cloak from one of the corpses.

"Hey! Excuse me," the corpse said as Khalon threw the cloak onto himself.

"Sorry," he muttered as he hurried away from it. He watched as Poseidon and the Fate disappeared into the room.

Khalon rushed towards the door and opened it only slightly so that he could see inside of it. The other two Fates were standing there, looking at a big red book and cutting red strings. Their hands were in a blur as they cut multiple strings at once.

"What brings you to the underworld, Poseidon?" the first Fate said. Her blonde hair was pulled into a tight bun on the top of her head. Bags of hundreds of sleepless nights hung underneath her blue eyes.

"Yeah, you really shouldn't be here," another Fate said. Her dark hands were a blur as her brown eyes concentrated on the red book.

"Farrah," Poseidon called the blonde.

"Francine," he nodded towards the Fate with the book.

"And darling Felicity," he said, kissing the hand of the Fate with green eyes. Her cheeks turned pink at the action. She was about an inch taller than Poseidon's new body.

"Seriously, Poseidon. What are you doing here?" Farrah said, crossing her arms. He looked around the room, his eyes focusing on an ebony cabinet in the back.

"Does my dear brother come down here often these days?" he asked. Felicity shook her head.

"He hasn't come recently," she said quietly. She and the other Fates exchanged a look with one another.

"What do you know?" he asked, catching their glances. The three of them stayed quiet. Poseidon pursed his lips as he walked around the room, looking at the various pictures on the walls. Khalon ducked behind the door as Poseidon walked by it, but he didn't seem to see him.

"The underworld looks as busy as ever."

"People don't stop dying just because all the other Gods are gone," Farrah snapped. Poseidon's eyebrows raised.

"You're afraid of disappearing, too, aren't you?" Poseidon and Farrah seemed to stare at each other for a long while.

"He's transferring his soul into another body," Felicity finally spoke up. He flashed her a brilliant smile.

"Thank you, my dear," he said. Felicity returned the smile as she ducked her head.

"Felicity!" Francine chastised.

"What? He needs to know. This world is dying," she defended.

"What do you think is going to happen to us once he finds out?" Farrah hissed.

"Osiris will never know," Poseidon said, waving their worries away. "My darling little brother won't be alive for much longer." Francine narrowed her brown eyes as she let go of her scissors. The scissors still moved at lightning speed, cutting the red strings.

"You're going to kill him?" she asked.

"With his *own* creation?" Farrah said, incredulous.

Poseidon shrugged.

"The draconian won't agree to it," Francine pointed out.

"Well, that's why I'm here, actually." He leaned against the wall. "Have you taken a look at Rhea's string lately?"

"We look at it daily," Felicity said, her voice quiet. Poseidon's sepia eyes looked over at her.

"And?"

"And what? If you kill him, you'll kill her. Their souls are intertwined," Farrah snapped. Her jaw clenched as she glared at Poseidon. It was clear on all of their faces that they didn't want to talk about Rhea's possible demise.

"Ah, I know Izanami well. My brother wouldn't let his soul entangle with hers too much. Not since—"

"Don't say her name," Francine warned. Poseidon's eyebrow cocked as he turned his head to the side.

"He's still upset about it?"

"It enrages him," Felicity said, quietly.

"*Still?* It's been hundreds of years."

"It was the only creature he ever cared about, Poseidon. You of all people should understand how lonely he's been throughout the years," Francine pointed out.

"And none of you intervened," Felicity almost accused, her green eyes meeting Poseidon's.

"Is that why..." his words drifted off as he shook his head.

"But, you're right. Rhea's soul isn't as intertwined with his as much as yours and that body's soul is," Farrah said, nodding her head in his direction.

"Would it be possible for her to live?" Poseidon asked, a shadow still cast over his face. Khalon held his breath as the Fates looked at one another.

"Her soul is hanging on by a thread," Francine finally said. "Enough so that the body doesn't die. But, not enough for her to live without the God of Death." She crossed the room and sifted through the many red threads that hung from the ceiling. Her fingers gingerly touched a blackened red string, entwined with a little bit of gold. A single thread was holding the string together. Khalon felt his heart drop.

"Has her death appeared in the book?" Poseidon asked, softly.

"The book only shows the deaths of those who will die on that day, not future deaths. So, we don't know. But, we predict it'll be four days from now," Farrah said, the skin around her eyes tight. "It'll also be when the rest of his soul enters the child's body."

"What child?"

"His child."

"My brother had a *child*?"

"He used King Adamar to do it. The deceased child of Lady Batula and Prince Edwyrd was used as the shell due to Queen Essarae being barren," Farrah explained.

"I'm sorry. Let's just circle back for a second. My brother had a *child*?" Poseidon repeated.

"Yes."

"But, he can't create. They always end up as empty shells. Or monsters... like the Mortiferis," Poseidon said, in disbelief.

"Yes, Than doesn't have a creature's soul within him. Which is why he is moving the rest of his soul into Than's body," Farrah said. "But, he might end up being different than before."

"We really shouldn't be talking about this," Francince muttered under her breath.

"Than? He named his child *Than*?? What? Short for Thanatos? What was he thinking?" Poseidon ran his hands down his face as he looked up towards the ceiling.

"It's the perfect body for him," Felicity shrugged. "No other soul to argue with, fight with." He rubbed his temples as he pushed off of the wall he was leaning against.

"Is there a way Rhea could survive in her body by herself?" Poseidon asked, changing the subject. The Fates exchanged another look with one another.

"We gave the draconian a hint," Francine said, slowly.

"So, dragon's blood?"

"It could strengthen the soul. Heal it," Felicity said, her voice lilting.

"You sound unsure."

"Poseidon, look at her string. I don't even know how it's still being held together," Felicity said, gesturing towards the blackened red string. Tears welled up in her eyes as she looked away.

"We basically raised Rhea. We don't want her to die," Farrah said for Felicity.

"But, the odds are very low," Francine said, barely above a whisper.

"However, look at the dragon slayer's string," Farrah said, sifting through the red threads. She pulled on one. Khalon squinted his eyes as he stared at the red string in her hands. It looked like all the other red strings.

"Now, watch," Farrah said. The scissors, which were cutting other strings, flew to her hands. Khalon watched in horror as the blades tried to cut the red string. But, the thread wouldn't be cut. It couldn't be pierced. Farrah tried slicing it multiple times, but the thread stayed put.

"See? The young king recently drank some dragon's blood. And his string is as good as new and refuses to be cut," she said.

"We think, maybe, it could do the same for Rhea," Felicity said, her eyes hopeful.

"But, to kill my brother..."

"You have to kill her body," Farrah finished for Poseidon. "Yes."

"Which means she won't be able to live," Poseidon put a hand to his chin as he thought.

"But, you could kill Than," Felicity suggested, her eyes steeled.

"Felicity! If he finds out how much we're telling the Sea God..." Francine's voice drifted away as she shuddered at the thought. Poseidon let his head roll side to side as he thought.

"How much of him is in Than already?"

"A quarter," Felicity answered, ignoring Francine's warnings.

"How much in three days' time?"

"...probably more than half."

"Which would make Than aware enough," Poseidon said. He shrugged. "Well, to try is better than to not try."

"We hope the draconian is successful," Felicity said. Poseidon nodded his head.

"We all hope." He hung his head for a moment, lost in thought, before starting towards the door. Khalon scrambled backwards as he ran towards the exit.

He pushed past the rotting corpses, repressing the

disgust at touching bones and rotting flesh beneath dark, reaper cloaks. He rushed up the stairs, eventually hitting his head on the top of the ground. Khalon looked over his shoulder as he tried to process what the Fates and Poseidon had said.

Dragon's blood. Dragon's blood was key. Poseidon had guessed earlier that the dragon underneath Furvus was probably what the Fates were hinting at. But, Khalon didn't know it was dragon's blood that Rhea needed.

A cracking sound was heard throughout the stairwell, and Khalon looked up to see the ground parting slowly. Dirt fell onto his face as he brushed it off, squeezing himself through the growing hole before Poseidon could see him. He ran towards his tent, closing the flap almost all the way. Khalon looked through the sliver as Poseidon walked out of the underworld. His eyes roved over the area, resting on Khalon's tent. He froze.

If the Sea God saw Khalon, he didn't say anything, turning towards his own tent. Khalon let the flap close as he walked back to his bed. He stared up at the top of the tent, watching as the smoke from the fire billowed out of the hole in the top.

Tomorrow morning, they were going to finally end up at the draconian camp. And tomorrow morning, Khalon was going to do whatever it took. He was going to take back Furvus. He would get to the dragon underneath the palace. And he will save Rhea.

No matter how slim of a chance it was.

He will protect her, like how she once did for him. And Khalon would sacrifice anyone to do it.

37

“Can you see where they are?” Khai pressed as Esi’s eyes glowed white. Her eyes moved rapidly while her dark eyebrows furrowed together.

“He’s in some kind of camp,” she muttered, her voice faraway. Kamaria didn’t even look at him. She was staring past the head of her Kongamato, directing the beast to wherever it was they were supposed to go. Khai licked his lips, tasting the memory of her as he stared at the back of her head. They had been flying aimlessly over the ruined Furvus.

“What camp?” Khai asked, his voice laced with irritation.

“A draconian one but... something’s wrong,” she whispered. A chill ran down his spine. The Seer saying something was wrong... meant something was *very* wrong.

“Just spit it out, Esi,” he said, quietly.

“Something’s plaguing this draconian camp. Perhaps,

something that even Khalon won't be able to fix," she said. Her eyes slowly dimmed until they were normal once again. She stared in Khai's direction. She said something, but they fell on deaf ears. Her previous words were echoing around in his head. *"Something that even Khalon won't be able to fix."* Because *Khalon* was able to do it all. *Khalon* was the one everyone looked towards. Not him. *Never* him. Khai squeezed his eyes shut.

"Khai?" Esi's voice broke the sound of his pounding heart. "Did you hear me?"

"Sorry," he mumbled.

"I said the draconian camp is in No Man's Land, near the outskirts of Furvus," she said, softly. She paused for a moment.

"Could you tell Kamaria for me?"

"Of course," he said, swallowing. He took a small deep breath before tapping Kamaria's shoulder. She turned her head only a little, enough that Khai saw one of her dark eyes. He watched as the glowing red veins went throughout her face, like stars twinkling in the night sky. He traced it with his eyes, before meeting hers.

What? She signed.

They're at a camp.

Okay?

In No Man's Land, Khai signed. *Near Furvus.* She nodded her head once, her eyes boring holes into his face. Like she was expecting him to sign something more. He licked his lips again.

Kamaria— he started but she turned around, swiftly. Her braids narrowly missed his face. His lips tightened into a line as he watched her make a clicking noise. The

Kongamato started heading closer to the ground, in the direction of No Man's Land.

"What happened between you two?" Esi asked. Khai blinked.

"How—"

"There's electricity in the air," she said, looking up. The tips of Khai's ears reddened.

"E-Electricity?"

"A storm is brewing," she clarified, her white eyes back on him. "That only happens when Kamaria's angry."

"O-Oh," he relaxed as he looked up at the sky. "Right. That kind of electricity." The clouds were rolling in, and it definitely looked like it was about to rain.

"Her Inkanyamba side," Esi said, shaking her head. "Inkanyambas are known for their terrible temper."

"If that's the case, Ustrina wouldn't be a desert." The Seer smiled.

"Why do you think the Inkanyambas live in only the rain forests of Ustrina?" Esi's smile slowly faded as she glared in Khai's direction.

"So, what did you do?" He shrugged, half-heartedly even though he knew Esi wouldn't be able to see it.

"You know me," he murmured. She leaned back as she clicked her tongue in quick succession.

"You need to stop irritating her. It was fine over a year ago. Funny, even. But, you both are rulers now," Esi pointed out. "You need to work together." He nodded his head as he watched the world go by underneath them.

"Someday, maybe," he muttered. His eyebrows furrowed together as he heard the beating sound of wings in the air. He sat straight up as he searched the clouds around them.

There weren't many wild flying beasts in Asynithis. Not anymore.

"What's wrong?" Esi asked, feeling him stiffen.

"Shh," he whispered. The hair on his body was standing straight up as his eyes rapidly looked around the area. Something was watching them. Hunting them. He could feel it in his bones.

His eyes widened, in horror, as a creature rose from the clouds, red as blood. Eyes fiercely on him.

A dragon.

Not just any dragon, *the* dragon. The last dragon.

The one that was kept underneath the palace of Furvus. Here, in front of him. And it looked positively angry.

"Shit," Khai whispered as he turned towards Kamaria. He made the same clicking noise he heard her make earlier that caused the Kongamato to fly downwards. The Kongamato agreed, only a third of the size of the dragon that was rushing towards them. Kamaria's head whipped around, her eyes quizzical as she met Khai's. But, she caught the sight of the dragon in her peripheral vision, turning right around. She started making other clicking noises, the Kongamato obeying them instantly. It flew sharply to the side, the dragon slower to follow.

Can't you do something? she signed.

What is it that you suggest I do? Khai signed back, in a panic. He could feel it. The dragon's blood coursing through him. The dragon's blood that he stole. And he knew the dragon could sense it in him. He met the dragon's eyes once more and almost shuddered with fear.

Breathe fire at it, Kamaria signed.

Fire? Fire?? What is fire going to do to a dragon? Khai

signed back. *Why don't you use your fire?*

I figured a dragon might be intimidated by another dragon. No dragon would be intimidated by a phoenix. So, you should at least try.

I can't… I can't breathe fire. Kamaria's eyebrows knitted together.

Didn't you drink its blood? Shouldn't you be able to have the powers of a dragon?

It takes years of drinking dragon's blood to be able to breathe fire, probably. Or a great amount of it. She rolled her eyes, dramatically. But, their discussion was interrupted as a series of popping noises were heard. Khai was faced with sharp, ivory teeth, sparks erupting in the back of the dragon's throat.

"Oh dear Alator," he prayed under his breath. Kamaria's gaze steeled as she made more noises. The Kongamato flew straight for the ground, the dragon's fire barely missing them.

"The trees, Kamaria! The trees!" Khai yelled out as he signed desperately at her. She didn't even glance at him as she continued in the direction they were heading towards. The Kongamato hit the treetops. Dead leaves that hadn't fallen yet erupted all around them. The Kongamato let out a heart-shattering screech as it hit the ground, and Khai nearly fell off of the beast, but Kamaria grabbed his arm.

"What the—" She put a finger to her lips as she pointed upwards. The dragon was circling the air above. Khai stayed as quiet as possible as he waited for the longest moment of his life to pass. Eventually, the dragon flew away, letting him breathe normally again.

"That's what's plaguing the draconian camp," Esi said,

after a moment.

"A dragon? A *dragon* is plaguing *draconians*?" Khai said, incredulously.

"It's angry," she mused, signing as she spoke. "It's been eating the other draconians." A dragon eating draconians? It was the most ridiculous statement Khai had ever heard.

Yeah, of course *it's angry,* Kamaria signed, pushing him backwards. *You've been feeding directly off of a living dragon this whole time?*

"Feeding is a strong word," he muttered as he signed. Kamaria just glowered at him. "I mean, how did you *think* I was getting dragon's blood?"

I thought it was like wine, where you just store it for a long period of time.

"You thought it was like wine. So, I don't know why you're getting mad at *me* for being an idiot." Kamaria hit his shoulder, hard.

Ow, he signed, dramatically.

My dear Bongani could've died because of your stupidity.

Is it my *stupidity or was it the sins of my ancestors?* Khai signed.

Is it not *that dragon's blood coursing through your veins? Was it* not *hunting you?*

It's not like I was willingly drinking its blood.

You sure looked like you were enjoying it. Kamaria crossed her arms.

"Are you guys fighting again?" Esi asked, meekly.

"No," Khai said as Kamaria clenched her jaw. She turned towards her Kongamato, making clicking noises. The creature got up from the ground and spread its wings once more.

"I thought your *dear Bongani* was hurt," Khai said as he

signed at her. Kamaria willfully ignored his signs.

"Kamaria has it play dead," Esi responded. Play dead?

"What?"

"It's a strategy of hers. They both play dead and then attack," she said.

"Of course they do," he muttered. Kamaria turned towards them as the Kongamato headed for the skies once more.

We stay low to the trees, she signed. *If you see the dragon again, you tell me immediately. Don't tell Bongani what to do ever again. I'm warning you.* Khai put his hands up, a smile playing on his lips. She jabbed her pointer finger into Khai's chest, moving closer to him.

Stop relying on me to save you, she signed after removing her finger.

I'll protect you next time, Khai signed back. She scoffed.

Yeah, okay.

I promise, Kamaria, he signed. He grabbed her hand before she could turn around.

"I promise," he repeated, his voice so low that he hoped Esi wouldn't hear. Kamaria's gaze softened before she closed her eyes. She slowly removed her hand from his, turning back around.

You better, she signed.

———

The Kongamato landed near the camp, gracefully hitting the ground as powdery snow flew up around them. Khai watched as Khalon walked out of one of the tents. He was wearing draconian armor, all over his body. But, it wasn't that which disturbed Khai. It was the *kind* of armor Khalon was wearing. His armor—made of dragon skin—had the image of a red dragon down the chest of it. Armor that only a king wore.

Khai jumped off of the Kongamato, walking slowly towards Khalon. He glanced at the other draconians nearby. Their faces were full of hate as their eyes followed him. Among them were beastoids. Bears and wolves. And they looked downright murderous.

"What's this?" he asked, gesturing towards the beastoids once he got close enough to Khalon. Khalon's face was like stone.

"They're joining us. To help take back Furvus," he said. Khai nodded, his eyes glancing at Khalon's armor once more.

"Good. We'll need all the help we can get," he said. He snapped his fingers and pointed at a nearby draconian.

"Get some men and take any Chollimas you still might have. There's a dragon that's flying in the air space here that we need to get rid of," Khai ordered. The draconian didn't move. Instead, he turned towards Khalon, as if waiting for permission. Khai's eyes narrowed.

"Did you not hear me? *Go*, right now."

"What do you mean there's a dragon flying around?" Khalon asked, his thick eyebrows furrowing. Khai ignored him.

"Do you not know what your king looks like? Go, or I'll execute you myself," he nearly growled. The draconian finally looked at him, his eyes cold.

"You're not my king," he said, gruffly. Khai stared at him, his brain trying to process the words the draconian said.

"What?" he said, through gritted teeth. "If not me, who is?" Poseidon appeared from behind Khalon.

"Did you get what I asked for?" the Sea God asked. Khai bit his tongue, staring down the draconian, before rummaging through his pocket for the Mortiferis tooth. He threw it in Poseidon's direction. Poseidon caught it easily.

He winked at him. "Thanks."

"Who is your king, draconian? Dragon burnt your tongue?" Khai asked, his voice menacingly low. The draconian raised his chin high.

"The rightful king of Draconia. King Khalon." His stomach fell to his feet as he met his older half-brother's gaze. A flicker of uncertainty passed through Khalon's face, but it was gone as quickly as it came.

"You're king?" But, it came out more like a statement than a question.

"I have the spirit of the dragon within me, Khai," Khalon said, his voice mechanical. "Draconian law clearly states—"

"Can you even *read* Draconian law?" Khai bit. Khalon's gaze hardened.

"You've angered the last dragon," the draconian spoke. Khai's heart was hammering in his chest. His mom was right. His mom had always been right about Khalon.

"You've been feeding off of it, like a filthy vampire. The Fates call you the dragon slayer. We don't want a king that kills our own kind," the draconian spat. "A king that angered the last dragon and let his people face his punishment is not a true king." The other draconians in the camp echoed his sentiment. Khai was going to be sick. But instead of throwing up the acid in his empty stomach, he started laughing.

"You've been following kings who slaughtered dragon after dragon. Who bathed in dragon's blood. But because I fed off of one, I'm suddenly not worthy?" Khai snapped. He turned towards Khalon, ice coursing through his veins.

"I should've killed you when I had the chance," he hissed. A muscle in Khalon's jaw feathered.

"Go ahead and try." Khai was growing taller as the dragon's blood transformed his body. His skin flipped into red scales, and his body became more sturdy, stronger. In response to Khai's transformation, Khalon's body easily turned into his dragon form, growing a foot taller, as his black scales flashed red. He was more magnificent than Khai. Bigger than Khai.

He bared his teeth in anger, and Khai started forward, imagining his own teeth tearing out Khalon's throat, imagining his claws gouging out Khalon's golden dragon eyes.

But, he stopped. Because standing in front of him was Kamaria. Kamaria, her ebony eyes fiery. And Khai could nearly feel his heart shattering.

Move, he haphazardly signed with his dragon hands. She was breathing hard as she looked up at him.

No, she signed back. He growled, low.

You would choose him *over me?* Kamaria paused as she clenched her jaw. Her gaze was like obsidian. Sharp and unyielding.

You sound like your mother, she signed. Khai could feel himself shrink, his body turning back to normal as rage simmered throughout his body.

You choose him because you also think he should be king, don't you? He gets everything, Kamaria. Everything that should have always been mine from the start. He shouldn't have even been born *and... And I'm left with... what? Who am I if I'm not king?* Kamaria's gaze softened.

You're Khai.

Being Khai means being nothing.

Being Khai means being the man I adore. Her eyebrows were pulled upwards as she took a step forward. But, all Khai could see was her look of pity. That disgusting look of pity on her face. He took a step back.

That's not enough for me, he signed. She stopped, mid-step, as hurt flickered across her face.

No, of course not, she signed, her gaze hardening. *Of course it isn't. You were always going to choose to be king. It's the only thing you care about. I was stupid to think otherwise.*

Before Khai could sign anything back to her, she pivoted on her heel, walking by Khalon.

Kill him, she signed as she walked past. Poseidon's eyebrows raised as his eyes met his. Khai's gaze darted away.

"Are you good now?" Khalon asked. Khai just watched Kamaria walk away, his breath becoming shorter and shorter the further she went. Like she was taking his soul away with her.

He took a deep breath, not enough to fill his lungs, but he walked up to Khalon. He leaned forward so that his lips were right next to Khalon's ear, fury boiling his blood.

"I'm going to destroy you." He pulled back, meeting Khalon's dark—almost black—eyes, the same ones as their father's. "One day, you'll feel what I've felt." And it was for a second, for only a split second, that fear seemed to find its home in Khalon's eyes. And it satisfied Khai to no end.

38

Jabulani burst through Aponi's tent, breathing hard as life was breathed back into his dark eyes.

"Kamaria is back," he said. Aponi slowly sat up from her cot. She hadn't been able to have a good night's sleep since the witch had invaded her mind. Aponi had been constantly plagued by scenes of destruction, as if the Fates themselves were implanting images into her head. To convince her otherwise.

"You look like death," Jabulani muttered as he finally got a good look at her.

"Thanks, Jabu," she said, sarcastically, smiling at him as she got up from the cot. "You look great, too. When did you last take a bath?" Jabulani merely smiled, his Inkanyamba pointed teeth on full display.

"What?"

"It seems like you're getting back to your normal self," he said. Aponi merely flashed a disingenuous smile at him.

"Well, the Queen is back, isn't she?" she responded,

straightening her clothes and brushing her fingers through her white hair. "Can't very well be myself around her." His smile faded.

"Kamaria isn't like that."

"I know," she agreed. "I know she doesn't require it. But, I also know my place." He looked around her tent before sitting down on her cot.

"Have you decided yet?" he asked, softly. His long fingers played with her blanket. Aponi sighed.

"Shouldn't you be glued to Kamaria's hip?" she pointed out, changing the subject. A small smile appeared on Jabulani's heart-shaped lips. His dark eyes met hers.

"It looks like her and Khai are in a heated discussion," he murmured. "Didn't want to intrude."

"I knew Khai wouldn't welcome the change in power so easily."

"Well, what can he do? It's Draconian law. And the draconians seem to want Khalon in charge," he said. The draconians were more than okay with Khalon taking the title of king. They cheered when he declared himself as the ruler of Draconia. Aponi had heard some whispers about a curse that Khai had brought about to their people. Something about angering their ancestors.

"They'd follow Khalon anywhere," Aponi said.

"As long as they think he's appeasing the powers that be. If they can't take back Furvus, they'll think the same of him as they think of Khai. That he's not truly the rightful king. Creatures are fickle in mind."

"He'll take back Furvus. And he'll save this world."

"You believe in him a little too much," Jabulani said, his eyes darting away.

"He has the spirit of the dragon within him. He might as well be one of the lesser gods of Asynithis," Aponi said. "Khalon will always do the right thing." Jabulani raised his eyebrows a bit.

"I don't think so," he muttered. "He's not that selfless."

"Wha—"

"So, have you thought about it? About what you should do?" he interrupted. She closed her mouth as she considered him. She opened her mouth once more, but before anything could come out, Kamaria burst through the tent's entrance.

She stopped in her tracks when she saw Jabulani. Kamaria glanced at Aponi and then looked back at Jabulani, her gaze hardening. Aponi's eyebrows knitted together as she saw the expression that was clear in Kamaria's eyes. An expression that she was trying to keep hidden in front of her longtime friend.

"Go," Aponi said, shooing Jabulani away. He frowned as he looked at her.

"Why?"

"Just... go, Jabu," she sighed. His eyebrows raised, but he got up from her cot. As he passed by Kamaria, he gave her a small smile and patted her shoulder. Kamaria's hand patted his before he walked out of the tent, forgiving him for letting her sister be captured.

What happened? Aponi signed. Kamaria studied Aponi for a moment before holding her head high.

I don't know what you mean, she signed back. She walked towards the fire in the center of the tent, sitting down on one of the logs.

You look like you're about to cry, Aponi pointed out.

Kamaria scoffed. *I don't cry.*

You do *cry. I've seen you cry plenty of times. Just... usually after a battle. What's wrong?* After watching Aponi's signing, Kamaria's eyes moved to look at the embers in the fire. Her dark eyes reflected the orange light, and Aponi's eyebrows furrowed together as she took Kamaria in. This wasn't like her. It wasn't like her to push down tears. At least, not in front of Aponi.

Aponi sat down next to her, putting her arms around her queen. Kamaria slowly rested her head on the lightning bird's shoulder and after a few moments, Aponi could feel the small shudders that went through Kamaria's body. Tears fell, soaking her thin shirt.

Aponi continued to pat Kamaria's arm, to comfort her. There was nothing else she could do but be there for her queen, her friend.

They sat there, together, as Kamaria silently cried. And she cried until there was nothing left of her.

———

"Hello Ralnor," Apsara smiled, baring her teeth as she pressed an obsidian blade against the elf's throat. He had just opened the door to his home in Aureum and found the mermaid with vengeance written across her face on his doorstep. She pressed the blade as Ralnor took a couple of steps back, his hands up. The Argentiundan King appeared beside her, larger than Ralnor had last seen him. Though, when he saw him last, Maleko couldn't walk. At his full height, Ralnor had to crane his neck to look him in the eye. He swallowed.

"What can I do for you both?" he asked, keeping his

voice even. Apsara's smile widened, but it didn't reach her eyes.

"Oh, I think you know what we want from you," she said, her voice laced with venom.

"Were you two successful in killing my daughter?" Ralnor dared to ask. Maleko laughed as he clapped a hand over Ralnor's shoulder.

"No, no," he said. "There's a whole plan in process to get rid of Rhea. Don't worry about that. We're here for the merpeople." His expression grew serious suddenly, causing a chill to run down Ralnor's back. They both had always looked dangerous, from the moment Ralnor met them. Like all merpeople, they both had sharp features, like a predator's. But, they looked more desperate then. Worn down. Now... Now, they looked like they were going to tear his heart out and then skin him.

"What do you want to know?" Ralnor asked, backing up against the small table against the wall.

"What do we want to know," Maleko repeated, turning towards Apsara. "I wonder what it is."

"As if it weren't obvious," she drawled.

"You want to know where all the merpeople are, no problem. I can tell you where they are," Ralnor said, as his arm fumbled behind him. He slowly wrapped his hands around the crystal blade resting on the surface of the table.

Apsara's eyes narrowed, and with a speed that Ralnor couldn't track, she brought the blade down on his bicep. Ralnor screamed from pain as he doubled over. Maleko stuffed a cloth into Ralnor's mouth to dull the sound as blue blood splattered over the hardwood floors. His arm clattered to the ground, the knife still in his severed hand.

"Why—" Ralnor's words couldn't form properly around the cloth gag.

"You shouldn't have grabbed a weapon," Apsara chastised.

"You forced our hand. It was self defense," Maleko said. The Argentiundan King flashed the elf a pitying glance as he lowered himself to the ground, where Ralnor had dropped to his knees. The elf looked up at him, but his vision was starting to get blurry as blue blood poured out of him at an alarming speed.

"The merpeople?" Maleko asked. Ralnor continued to try to talk, but couldn't because of the gag. Maleko sighed before pulling the gag out of his mouth.

"Go ahead," he said.

"What are you going to do with them? You have nowhere to go," Ralnor said, his voice growing weaker. Apsara started to search the house, turning his living room upside down.

"We have one place to go to," Maleko said. "The portals are open. Thanks to your daughter."

"You'll go to... Earth?"

"I won't," he said, his gaze like stone. "But, my people will. Those who can."

"Stop chit chatting, Maleko," the mermaid said, her voice cutting through the air. "We don't have much time before he bleeds out."

"Oh right," Maleko said, shaking his head. "Sorry. Where did you say I could find the other merpeople?" Ralnor shivered as death came closer to him. In the corner of his eye, he saw a rotting corpse in a black cloak. Half of its face was falling off, revealing bloodied muscle. The other half didn't have an eye. A corpse was meeting him at his death. Not Ava. He didn't deserve Ava. He bit back the scream that was bubbling up his throat.

"I wrote everything down," he said, his voice trembling. "In my office." He grabbed Maleko's arm with his living hand before he could get up. The merman stared quizzically at him.

"Please," Ralnor croaked. "Please don't let the corpse take me." His eyebrows knitted together.

"Corpse?"

"Please," Ralnor begged, tightening his grip on Maleko. "He's right behind you. Please don't let him take me." He just blinked as Apsara stood next to him.

"What is he talking about?" Maleko asked her.

"Who knows and who cares?" Aspara muttered. "Let's just end it." And with a swift movement, she cut Ralnor's head clean off. His head rolled across the hardwood floor, his body falling to the ground a moment afterwards. And Ralnor watched as the corpse pulled a glowing light out from his dead body. Red. The color of his soul was red. And that was the last image Ralnor ever saw.

———

"I'll do it," Aponi said as she entered Khalon and Jabulani's tent. Khalon was in the process of taking off his armor, a billowing white shirt underneath. Snowflakes twinkled in Aponi's hair as they slowly melted. Khalon and Jabulani wore matching shocked faces as they gawked at her.

"You'll do it?" Khalon finally said.

"Yes," she confirmed, grimacing as she did. "I'll help the

witch protect the Saviors." His expression looked conflicted for a moment before he nodded.

"Okay. I'll jump through the portals with them," he said, determined. Aponi shook her head.

"No, you need to be with the draconians when they take back the capital of Draconia. I'll do it on my own."

"You don't need to do this by yourself, Aponi," he said, concern etching his brow. She shook her head.

"I'm strong enough by myself."

"You are. No one's arguing that," Jabulani spoke up. "But wouldn't it be nice to have someone with you?"

"If not me, then take Jabulani," Khalon insisted. Aponi chewed the inside of her cheek as she studied him.

"Fine," she said. "Fine. He can come with."

"Do you need help getting in touch with the witch?" Khalon asked.

"I can do it now," she said. She paused for a moment before ducking her head. "Will you sit with me as I do? Watch to make sure she doesn't try anything?" Jabulani nodded his head.

"Of course," he said. Aponi took a deep breath as she closed her eyes, wrapping her fingers around Jabulani's hand. She concentrated on the part of her energy that was far away from her. A part that was twisting as she followed the thread of lightning. Lightning skittered down her limbs and she felt herself fall into the familiar pit of darkness in the back of her mind. She opened her eyes once more.

"Thunderbird," the witch said, a smirk on her lips as she shimmered into appearance.

"Witch," Aponi said, her voice like ice. Every part of her

was telling her to run. Warning her of the witch's power. The pain that was to come.

"Have you reconsidered?"

"I wouldn't be here if I didn't," Aponi spat. Kaydee's eyelids fluttered as her face softened.

"You don't have to if you don't want to. I can find another way..."

"There is no other way. This is my fate," Aponi muttered.

"So... you'll help us?" Kaydee asked, her gray eyes pleading. Every cell in Aponi's body was begging her to tell the witch no. But, she gritted her teeth and held her head up high as she met the witch's gaze.

"Yes," Aponi said. "I'll help you protect the Saviors."

"What changed your mind in a few hours?" the witch asked.

"It's been a few days for me here," Aponi said, unfazed by the difference in time. "And it doesn't matter what changed my mind. What matters is that I'll help. I'll let you use me."

It wasn't what she truly wanted. She had vowed to die before letting a witch use her again. But, there was one thing Aponi knew. *She* wasn't going to go down in history as being the one who held Asynithis hostage.

39

Esi caught up to Khalon, a stick in her hands that hit the heel of his shoe. He looked over at her as she stopped, her white eyes searching the space in front of her. Her hand was resting on Luke's bear arm.

"Esi?" he asked. He was dressed in battle armor. His sword at its full length across his back.

"Khalon?" she asked, hesitant. Bruises still peppered her face, but fear didn't linger there. It made him irate at seeing the black and blue marks. What kind of creature could hurt her like this? How could they live with themselves?

Khalon's hand reached up to touch one of them on her cheek, but brought his hand back to himself as he nodded his head.

"Yes, it's me," he said. "Thank you, Luke, for bringing her." Luke nodded his head, taking his leave, as Esi patted his bear paw.

"What's going on, Esi?" he asked.

"Did Aponi agree?" she whispered. Khalon blinked. How did she know about that?

"Uh, yeah. She agreed," he stammered. She let out a sigh of relief.

"I wasn't sure if she would. And she needs to do her part," she muttered, almost under her breath.

"Aponi knows what she needs to do."

"There's one more thing Aponi has to do for Asynithis," she whispered. Her voice was hoarse, like she'd been using it for a long while. Her white eyes met Khalon's. "She needs to close the portals."

"What?"

"After protecting the Saviors from early deaths, she needs to close the portals with the Crispus witch. There's enough power between them. One's magic is on Terra and the other's is here. It'll be enough to close them," Esi explained.

"I... I'll let her know," Khalon said. She put out her dark hands, and Khalon placed his in hers. She held tightly as her eyes moved rapidly.

"She needs to do her part or... you don't understand what is coming in the future," Esi said, her voice trembling. Khalon gripped her hands back, lowering his gaze so that he was eye-to-eye with the Seer. He knew she couldn't see him, but she would be able to hear his voice clearer.

"She'll do her part, Esi. Don't worry. Aponi knows what's at stake," he promised. She paused, her knuckles white as she pulled Khalon closer.

"Do you?" she breathed. He blinked as he pulled his hands away from her.

"Of course I do," he said, quietly.

"If you don't do what the Fates have ordered, what An has put into motion, you will bring the destruction of our world," Esi almost threatened. "You must do what fate has destined for you."

"Esi, what are you trying to—"

"You *must* do your part, Khalon. Everyone has a part. Or... everything will turn to dust. He will be the only being left." She shook her head. "But, maybe you going against fate has always been a part of it." His eyebrows pulled together as he put his hands on Esi's shoulders.

"Don't worry, Esi. Everything will be fine," he said, a slight tone of falsity to his voice. He frowned as he turned her around, beckoning Luke towards them. "Everything will be okay."

"Everything will be destroyed," her voice shook. "It's already begun. It's already veered off fate's thin course."

"I'll fix it, then," Khalon muttered. "I'll fix it. It'll be okay." Esi turned to look at him, a faraway look in her white eyes.

"No one can."

———

"So, how does this work?" Aponi asked the witch. Kaydee's face started to shimmer away as Aponi felt an unimaginable amount of pain run down her spine. She bit back her scream, but Kaydee wasn't quite as stoic. She screamed as she placed her hands on her head.

Back on Earth, she fell to the ground, no longer frozen in place. Elion rushed to her side holding her as Kaydee let out an earth shattering plea.

"What's going on?" Lorena asked, her eyes wide with horror.

"I don't know," Elion whispered. Blood slowly dripped from Kaydee's nose. Her eyes opened, silver, as the air in front of them shimmered, like a reflection in a clear pool of water.

"Go," she croaked out. "It's the portal." Elion grabbed a kitchen knife from Kaydee's counter before helping her to her feet.

"Let's go," he said. He stepped through the shimmering air and found himself in a dark forest in the mountains. Lorena appeared behind him, Kaydee in tow. Across from them, Elion watched as Aponi and a large man walked through a different portal. Aponi's hair was pulled back, and lightning bolts ran down her arms. Her gaze met Elion's and she proceeded to walk over.

"Where is the Savior we're supposed to protect?" she asked, her voice hard. Kaydee wiped the blood from her nose as she looked at the man beside Aponi.

"Who's this?" Kaydee asked. Aponi glanced over at the large man. He was tall, but lanky. His face was expressionless as he took in the trio. It was clear he was Inkanyamba, with his pointed teeth and large, black eyes.

"This is Jabulani," Aponi said, gesturing towards him. She searched the trees. "Are you sure it worked?" Before any of them could answer her, a scream echoed throughout the forest.

"I'm pretty sure it worked," Kaydee said. Elion watched in fascination as Aponi's human form morphed into a large, white bird. She took to the sky, lightning following after her.

"C'mon," the creature called Jabulani said. Then, he stopped as he looked down at what was in Elion's hands.

"You're joking." He gestured towards the kitchen knife. Elion glanced down at it and then back up at Jabulani.

"It's not like I had a bevy of weapons at my disposal," he muttered. Jabulani unsheathed one of the two swords on his belt. He handed the obsidian sword to Elion, which Elion almost immediately dropped. Jabulani's eyebrows furrowed together as he looked him up and down.

"You've never held a sword before?"

"This sword is much heavier than an elven one," Elion retorted. "But, I'll be fine." Jabulani's eyebrows raised as he ran towards the direction Aponi disappeared in.

"Ha! You'll probably fall and die on that sword," Lorena teased as she ran past him.

"I'll be fine!" he repeated after her. Kaydee gave him a pitying look.

"I can bewitch it for you," she said.

"What about 'I'm fine' does nobody seem to understand?" he murmured to himself. He picked up the sword and hurried towards the direction the scream came from, Kaydee at his heels.

Furvus was almost all but abandoned by the Aureum army, it seemed. They didn't even try to rebuild the city that they destroyed. Instead, there was a single tower in the middle of Furvus that looked out for any intruders. Khalon stood in front of the army that gathered for him. Some more draconian warriors had met them there after hearing the rumors that the rightful King of Draconia was going to take back their country from the maddened elves.

Khalon was on top of a Chollima, a winged horse that was able to run faster than any other creature alive. He never thought he would ever be able to ride one, let alone lead an army with one.

"Thank you for joining me here today," Khalon said, raising his voice so the creatures in front of him could hear. "The elves think they can conquer anyone. That they are better than any other creature of Asynithis. They believe themselves to be more civilized and that we deserve to be conquered, that we *need* to be led by them to reach our 'true' potential." His Chollima rode up and down the lengths of the army as he continued.

"They've beat us once because we were divided. Draconians, beastoids, humans... We all have the blood of Asynithis' core within us. Our blood runs red. The color of the strongest creatures to ever walk Asynithis. We will show the elves that no one can conquer a dragon." Khalon stopped, meeting the eyes of everyone within his sight.

"And they'll die trying," he said, holding up his sword. The army cheered as Chollimas took to the sky. The rest of them ran down the length of the hill towards the abandoned city.

Khalon jumped off of his Chollima, more comfortable with fighting on the ground. He ran with the rest of them as arrows rained down upon them. Kamaria, with wings of fire sprouting from her back, rode her Kongamato towards the tower the elves built and brought down a rain of fire. The skies turned gray as storm clouds rolled in.

They entered the abandoned city of Furvus, as rain

started to fall to the ground. Lightning flashed in the sky as the tower came barreling down. And as the tower came apart, elves jumped out of the shadows. An elf grabbed Khalon, holding a knife to his throat. Khalon's body quickly turned into his dragon form, his scales shattering the knife in the elf's hands. Swiftly, Khalon broke the elf's neck, the snapping echoing in the darkest pits of his mind.

In the skies, Khai was riding a Chollima, cutting down the Griffins that came his way. Golden blood splattered over his face while the Griffins screeched as they twisted towards the ground. His eyes searched for Kamaria's Kongamato. She was standing on the back of her Kongamato, fighting against an elf that jumped onto her beast. She cut the elf's head clean off, blue blood spattering onto her face. Khai watched as the elf fell to the ground, Kamaria holding her head up victorious. His eyes widened, a warning in his throat, as an arrow found its place in her Kongamato. The beast yelped as it jolted, causing her to kilter off balance.

It was as if he was watching in slow motion as Kamaria's foot stepped off of the Kongamato, her body flailing through the air. Her wings of fire blew out as she whipped towards the ground at an alarming speed. He pushed his Chollima forwards as he raced against the stormy winds. *Kamaria,* Khai's thoughts screamed. *Kamaria.* Every part of him yelled out her name.

He leaned forward and grabbed her arm as she whipped past him. A snap was heard as she hung in the air, her arm in his grip.

"Kamaria?" he said, his voice small. She didn't move. He quickly pulled her up onto his Chollima. She lay there, limp, as Khai shook her.

"Kamaria!" he shouted, even though he knew she couldn't hear a word that he was saying. He turned her onto her back as his Chollima landed on the ground. Desperately, he brushed her braids off of her dark face.

"Kamaria, please," he muttered as he held her head in his lap. She groaned, trying to get up.

"Kamaria!" he exclaimed, pulling her head to his chest as he hugged her tightly. She pushed him off of her.

What are you doing? She signed slowly. She rolled her shoulders, wincing. She brought a fingertip to her sharp teeth, breaking the skin. A bead of orange blood appeared and she licked it, her face relaxing as the healing blood went through her system. Slowly, her shoulder moved back into place.

I thought you were dead, he signed back, trying to reel in his emotions. Her dark eyes were cold as she regarded him.

Why did you try to save me? Khai tried to lessen the dryness in his mouth. She had every right to hate him. She *should* hate him. He should let her. But, he signed the words anyway.

"I promised to protect you," he said as he signed. Her eyebrows furrowed together as she closed her eyes.

Don't. She jumped off of his Chollima without a second glance back. His eyes followed her figure as she continued to cut down elves with a fury, exchanging signs with a nearby beastoid. But, he knew who her fury was directed at. It wasn't the elves that she hated. It was him. And he knew he deserved every bit of it.

He shut his eyes, trying to drown out the thoughts of her so he could take a breath. He couldn't let his feelings for her distract him. She didn't understand. She would never understand what it felt like to live in the shadow of her sibling. To have a sibling that lived the life that she always wanted.

He kicked the sides of his Chollima, directing the beast back towards the skies. Kamaria and him were too different. And she deserved better than him. She always had deserved better than him.

Khai tasted his lips, the memory playing on repeat in his head since the day he kissed her. And he admitted what he didn't want to confess to himself. For it would reveal how dark his soul truly was. But, he regretted it. He regretted ever deigning to press his lips against hers.

40

Aponi landed, swiftly turning back into her human form. Lightning burst at her feet as she walked up towards the elves who were cornering the Savior. But, she stopped in her tracks as she recognized the girl standing before her.

She had black hair plaited in a single braid down her back. She wore a white, shapeless dress with sleeves like bells. The top of her dress was tied together with a single bow and her unnatural gray eyes seemed to plead with her. She was younger than the one Aponi had seen before, but it was her. The one who fed on another human.

"Jaebal," the girl said in a language Aponi didn't recognize. The young girl got down on her knees, clasping her hands together, as the elves looked at Aponi. Her feet couldn't move, the girl's eyes anchoring her to the ground. She couldn't be more than ten.

"Jaebalyo," the girl pleaded, tears streaking her pale face.

"If you're here to save her, you won't succeed," one elf assassin snapped at Aponi. She ripped her gaze away from the girl to look at the elf who stalked towards her.

"It's my duty," she said through gritted teeth. "So trust me, I will be." She knew this variation of this Savior would turn out to be evil, would kill in her future. But, she also knew what she had to do. Lightning erupted from Aponi, hitting the elf square in the chest.

"You hesitated for way too long," Jabulani whispered into her ear as he rushed past. She rolled her eyes, manipulating her lightning to hit another elf, dropping him to the ground. Jabulani hit swords with another as Elion came out from the woods. He hefted the sword over his head, bringing it down on another elf.

Kaydee held her hands up, her eyes like two silver coins as two elves floated to the air. They exploded, raining down blue blood. Aponi wiped some off of her arm as she shook her hand, splattering blood to the ground.

"Was that really necessary?" she asked over her shoulder.

"We need to hurry," Kaydee said, standing beside Aponi, but not too close to be hit by her lightning. "Don't you feel that?" Aponi cocked her head to the side as she felt this ripping sensation run through her.

"Another portal," she muttered.

"We gotta go," Kaydee said. Jabulani cut the last elf in half, his armor stained blue, but his face somehow clean. Aponi felt the pain start to creep up her spine.

"Let's hurry," she ordered. Kaydee waved her hand in front of the girl who was so stricken by fear that she couldn't make a single sound.

"Sleep," she whispered. The girl immediately closed her eyes and fell to the ground. Kaydee wiped her hands against one another as she walked back towards Aponi.

"Let's hope Aura doesn't have this memory plague her dreams in the future. That happened in one of her lives and she ended up crazy," the witch said, shaking her head. Aura. The Savior's name was Aura.

Aponi gritted her teeth as the waves of pain started to overtake her. Kaydee held her head, unable to keep her pain hidden. Her eyes were like melted silver, glowing in the darkness. Aponi couldn't imagine what she herself might've looked like at that moment, with this much magic coursing through her. As the pain became more unbearable, the air shimmered in front of her.

"Go," she ordered, the word barely comprehensible. Jabulani didn't hesitate, and walked through the portal, Elion and the other girl that Aponi belatedly remembered was named Lorena followed after him. Aponi pulled Kaydee up by her arm as she whimpered.

"You felt this pain with your witch?" Kaydee managed to get out.

"Every day for ten years," Aponi muttered as she pulled her through the portal.

———

Khalon cut through the elves that were in his way, hot blue blood freckling his dragon humanoid face. Another elf tried to stab Khalon with their sword, but it shattered as it hit dragon skin. There was nothing in Asynithis that was stronger than skin of a dragon. Khalon cut him down as though the elf was simply just a weed bothering him.

He stood, surveying the situation as he watched elves swarm the draconians and beastoids. The beastoids were a formidable opponent for the elves, and the draconians were living up to their name of being the best warriors of Asynithis. But, there were too many of them. There were always too many elves.

Something in Khalon's soul was searching, calling out for someone... or something. His chest grew hot as he found himself looking up to the skies. A roar echoed throughout the ruined city of Furvus.

He searched the gray clouds, and his eyes widened as a red dragon flew through them. It seemed like it made eye contact with Khalon as it got lower to the city of Furvus.

"Duck! Hide!" he warned as he realized what the dragon was about to do. The draconians and beastoids who heard Khalon's warning hid as the elves seemed to freeze in place upon seeing the dragon. Arrows hit the side of it, but it couldn't penetrate the skin. The dragon opened its mouth, a popping noise could be heard audibly throughout the city, before flames leaped out of its snout. A streak of fire hit the ground, burning the elves as they screamed while their flesh melted off of their bones. The dragon flew back up to the sky, looking back at Khalon as if telling him that he owed it.

There was silence as the stench of burnt bodies filled the air. The draconians and beastoids came out of their hiding places as Khalon took a couple of steps forward.

"Furvus... it's been won," one of the draconians said, looking at Khalon in awe. Khalon slowly shrunk back down to his normal height as his scales turned back into tan—almost coppery—skin once more.

"He did it," another draconian said. "He's truly the rightful King of Draconia."

"The Dragon King," some started to shout. "Long live the Dragon King." Khalon watched as the draconians touched their heads to the ground. The deepest form of respect in Draconia. His eyes saw past the draconians to see Khai jump off of his Chollima, standing in the back of the group. His arms crossed over his chest as he leaned against a wooden column that used to be part of the entrance of Furvus.

And even in this distance, Khalon could see the hatred in Khai's eyes.

41

Luke met Khalon when he got back to the camp. His black eyes shifted as he wrung his paws together. Kamaria caught up to Khalon's side as she looked the beastoid up and down. Khalon wondered if he also looked how she did. The personification of war. Blood covering her like a second skin.

"What's wrong?" he asked as he ripped his gaze away from the Ustrinian Queen, putting a comforting hand on the bear's shoulder. Luke licked his lips as his eyebrows furrowed.

"It's the Seer, sir," he said, his voice trembling. "She's... something's wrong with her." Khalon looked over at Kamaria who just met his gaze with a quizzical one. She signed something towards Khalon, but he couldn't understand. Kamaria wrinkled her nose when she realized and turned towards the beastoid. She made different signs. Signs that fit the beastoid language. Luke signed back to her.

Kamaria stood frozen for a moment before running at full speed towards the tent where Esi was staying.

"Kamaria!" Khalon called out after her. He raced behind the Ustrinian Queen. And when he got to Esi's tent, he almost trampled over her. Kamaria stood still at the entrance as she watched her sister rocking back and forth on the ground. Her white eyes were glowing while she drew symbols in the dirt over and over again.

"Six eggs that were sent away. She whispered, 'Be loyal and stay true' before she began to decay. One chance to save our world, or our world will forevermore be gray," Esi whispered.

"Forevermore be gray. Forevermore be gray. Forevermore be gray," she almost chanted as she ran her hand through the dirt, destroying the symbols of the Saviors that she drew.

"What's wrong with her?" Khalon breathed.

"I don't know," Luke said, tears welling up in his eyes. "She's been like this for a couple of hours."

"A couple of hours?"

"She keeps repeating that same part of the song. The song about the Saviors," Luke said. "I don't know why."

"Thanks Luke," Khalon said, patting his bear shoulder. "We'll take it from here." Luke bowed his head as he exited the tent. Kamaria swallowed before she went to Esi's side. She held her tight against her chest as her little sister's eyes moved rapidly.

"Esi?" Khalon said her name carefully. Her eyes stopped as she stared in the direction of his voice.

"You'll ruin us," she hissed. "You'll ruin everything." The breath in Khalon's chest stilled.

"What do you mean?" he asked quietly.

"Beware the demon twins," she whispered. "For we'll all be dead unless they're torn. For Darkness on Darkness is the most deadly thing. They'll side with the Mortiferis and become Dark Queen and King."

"You think *I* cause that?" Khalon asked.

"We'll all die. We're all going to die," Esi whispered. "Forevermore be gray. Our world will forevermore be gray." Her eyes went back to searching the air in front of her, rapidly.

"You'll ruin us. The Dragon King... The Dragon King will ruin us..." she whispered, her voice getting weaker. "You said you'll fix it." Her eyes directly met Khalon's for the first time, like she could truly see him. "You don't." Chills crept down his spine as he remembered what the witch in Draconia had once said to him. *"You'll live a long, but miserable, life."*

"Esi?" Khalon whispered, getting down on his knees in front of her. Her glowing eyes dimmed as her breath slowed. Kamaria kept petting the Seer's head until her chest stopped moving. Her hand froze, hovering over Esi's head as she stared at her little sister's face.

Khalon's heart was pounding wildly in his chest as he backed away from Esi's body. Kamaria shook her, looking more closely at her face.

"Esi?" her voice said, thick with tears. "Esi?" She shook her sister once more.

"What happened?" Khai's voice asked, coldly, from the front of the tent.

"Esi is..." Khalon struggled to find the words as he stared at the lifeless body of the Seer. The Seer was dead.

Kamaria hit Esi's chest, leaning down to resuscitate her. Tears flowed freely from her dark eyes as she continued to try to get her sister to breathe life once more.

"Kamaria," Khai breathed, coming to her side. He tried to sign to her but she refused to look at him. She petted her little sister's face as she howled. Her voice broke as she cried louder than Khalon had ever seen anyone cry before. She tried pricking her finger with her teeth, trying to get her sister to drink the orange blood. But, it did nothing for her. She was gone.

"My sister," Kamaria's broken voice howled. "My sister." Khai moved to hold Kamaria, and to his surprise, she let him.

Esi's white eyes were glazed over as she stared up at the ceiling of the tent. Khai's long fingers closed them as Kamaria beat against his chest, screaming. Screaming for Esi back.

Khalon backed out of the tent, his eyes still on the young Seer until the flap of the tent closed. And in the last second before the tent completely closed, he saw her body burst into flames. The death of a phoenix. Her last words echoed around in his head.

"You'll ruin us," she had said, hatred contorting her face as she looked at him. *"The Dragon King... The Dragon King will ruin us."*

The boy with white hair stood in front of a screaming older woman with a bat in his hands. He didn't look to be much older than five years old. But, his gaze seemed older than his body. Aponi watched as the boy swung the bat, hitting one of the elves in the shins as he weaved through them.

"Cyril, right?" Elion asked Kaydee. The witch nodded her head, her lips jutting out as she thought to herself.

"This is his seventh life," Kaydee muttered.

"They try to kill him twice in one life?" Elion asked. Kaydee shrugged as she started muttering chants under her breath. Her gray eyes turned silver once more. Aponi didn't have time to think about what the two of them were talking about as she electrocuted an elf that was about to turn the little boy into a shish kabob.

Aponi dusted her hands off once the last of the elven assassins were nothing but broken corpses on the ground.

"Aponi," she heard a voice say. Her soul was jolted back into her body that was still in Asynithis, still in the tent, Jabulani frozen next to her. Her eyes snapped open to see Khalon standing in front of her.

"You've broken the link," she muttered, stretching her arms upwards as her back cracked.

"Esi told me something before she... before..." Khalon swallowed. Aponi's eyebrows furrowed as she looked at him closer. He was sweating. Profusely.

"What's going on?" she asked. Khalon wiped his forehead as he continued to stammer.

"S-She told me you and the witch need to close the portals, once you're done," he muttered.

"Why are you sweating so much?" she asked. She met Khalon's half-moon shaped eyes. "What happened to Esi?" He shook his head as he squeezed his eyes shut.

"It doesn't matter right now. Just... remember to close the portals. As soon as possible," he said, wiping his forehead once more. Aponi noticed his fists closing and opening, like his hands were clammy as well. Her mouth pulled downwards as she looked away from him.

"Fine, but afterwards, you better tell me what's going on," she said.

"I will," Khalon promised. Aponi gave him a look before closing her dark eyes. She felt the familiar pain crawl its way up her spine as she refrained from screaming.

When her eyes reopened, Kaydee was standing over her body.

"What happened?" she asked, putting a hand on her hip.

"Khalon woke me up," she explained. She sat up from the ground, vaguely recognizing that her bones ached from the fall, and looked Kaydee right in the eyes.

"We need to close the portals," Aponi repeated. Kaydee's eyebrows knitted together.

"How?"

———

As Khalon picked up his sword by the entrance of his tent, he tightened the vest around his chest. He walked out, only to walk into his little brother. Khai looked him up and down and raised his eyebrows.

"You're going after the dragon already?" he asked. Khalon blinked.

"How did... How did you know?"

"Well, I overheard Poseidon and Valerian talking about it after Esi died," Khai said, crossing his arms. "And you look like you're ready for battle. Esi's ashes aren't even in the ground yet—she hasn't been dead for a day—and you're going to slay a dragon?"

"I'm not slaying a dragon, Khai. I'm just getting some of its blood. For—"

"For Rhea. Yeah, we all know," he muttered, waving Khalon's words away.

"What did Poseidon say about it?" Khalon asked, quietly. Esi's corpse flashed through his mind. Kamaria's cries haunting the crevices of his consciousness.

"Poseidon asked Valerian, 'Do you think Khalon will be able to muster the courage to get the dragon's blood?'" Khai imitated Poseidon's voice almost exactly. "And Valerian said, 'Khalon would stop at nothing to save Rhea.' Which... I guess you've proved them right."

"What do you think I should do? I *need* to save Rhea. You heard Esi. I'm going to... ruin... everything," Khalon whispered. Khai rolled his eyes as Khalon wiped his forehead, sweat coating the back of his hand.

"And you think she meant that you chose not to save Rhea? That's what ruins everything? I think you're supposed to let Rhea die and kill the God of Death," Khai pointed out. Khalon shook his head. His heart was pounding in his head as Esi's words echoed over and over.

"No, that can't be right," he said, under his breath. "I need to get the dragon's blood. For Rhea. It'll fix everything. I'll fix everything." Khai's eyebrows furrowed together as he took a closer look at older brother's face.

"Hey, are you okay?" he asked. "Why are you sweating so much?"

"I-It's just hot in here," Khalon said, wiping the back of his neck.

"It's winter."

"I need to go," Khalon said, pushing past him. Khai grabbed his arm, pulling him to a stop.

"You should at least wait until we bury Esi," he said. "Kamaria wants to do a proper burial." Khalon shook his head.

"I… I can't," he whispered. Khai's eyebrows twitched as he studied Khalon for an agonizing second.

"Fine, I'll come with you," he finally said.

"What? No, you need to stay. For…"

"Nothing is keeping me here," he interrupted. An emotion that Khalon couldn't quite place flickered over Khai's face, but it was gone as quick as it had come. He flashed Khalon a smile.

"Besides, you're having a panic attack. Can't really fight a dragon when you're having a panic attack," he said, walking forwards. Khalon caught up to him.

"I'm not going to fight it," he explained. "I'm going to ask the dragon for its blood." Khai barked a dry laugh.

"You're making me more and more grateful that I didn't grow up in the Ring of Fire," he muttered. He glanced over at Khalon. "Because thank Alator I'm not as stupid as you are. You think a *dragon* is going to simply hand over its blood?"

"Did you even *try* asking it for its blood?" Khalon quietly asked. Khai's face tightened as he looked away from him.

"Don't blame me if it eats you," was all Khai said.

42

The man with red hair and copper eyes lifted Aponi up by her neck as he glowered at her. Flames licked at his fingertips as he brought his other hand closer to her face.

"Who are you?" he asked. "What do you want with me?"

"Looks like he could've taken care of himself," the girl named Lorena muttered. "Are you sure I can't slit his throat?"

"He's a Savior," Kaydee hissed. She put her hands up as she approached the man. "Aiden, we're friends. We're not here to hurt you."

"Bullshit." Aponi felt his grip on her neck tighten. She gasped for air as she clawed at his large hand, sending a small jolt of electricity down his arm. His hand immediately opened, as he yelped from pain, dropping Aponi to the ground. She scowled up at him as she rubbed her neck. He stared slack-jawed at her.

"What are you?" he asked.

"None of your concern," Aponi snapped. She stood up as she nodded towards Kaydee. It was time. It was time to close the portals.

"So, the Saviors live normal lives. Have normal human lifespans," Elion said, eyeing the man in front of us. He was a middle-aged man, with gray hair streaking red.

"You're from Asynithis," the man Kaydee called Aiden said. He crossed his arms. "You are, right? Like those vermin."

"They're elves," Kaydee clarified. "You've seen more of them in this lifetime?"

"How do you think I killed *these* ones?" Aiden said. He narrowed his copper eyes as he took a step forward.

"You want me to sacrifice my life to save your world," he said. "I remember."

"What do you mean you remember?" Kaydee said, concern etching her brow.

"Forget about it. Your world is none of my concern. Let it burn," Aiden hissed.

"Why—"

"And I'll melt you to nothing now," Aiden said, raising his hands. Kaydee grabbed Aponi's wrist, pulling her out of the way as a fireball came towards her.

"Let's do this in our current time," the witch said, her eyes starting to glow. "The closing of the portals." Aponi nodded, gritting her teeth as the pain radiated throughout her body. In a second, Kaydee was back in her kitchen. Elion and Lorena next to her.

"Oh thank God," Kaydee murmured, as she held her head.

"Where's Aponi and Jabulani?" Elion asked.

"Probably in their world. What was up with that guy?" Lorena asked, turning towards Kaydee.

"Aiden... Aiden has tough past lives," Kaydee said, almost under her breath. "I just don't know how he remembers anything. Unless, he somehow met Evelyn in a past life."

"Evelyn?" Kaydee waved the question away from her face.

"One of the other Saviors," she answered. She cracked her fingers before cracking her neck as she stared determinedly into the air.

"You two need to get back to Asynithis before the portals close," Kaydee said. Elion's eyebrows jumped.

"Before the portals close? Do you know how to?" Kaydee shrugged, fear flickering in her gray eyes.

"Who knows?" she gave a wry smile. "But, I think it'll take all of my magi—" Her words were cut off as she froze, her gray eyes turning silver.

While her body might've been frozen, her eyes could see Aponi, sitting in a sea of darkness.

"Are you ready?" she asked, her normally dark eyes filled with lightning. Kaydee's heart quickened as she took a step back. The darkness smelled of metal. And it was coming from her.

"Elion and Lorena need to go back to their world," Kaydee whispered. Aponi waved a hand, an archway appearing next to her. When Kaydee peered into the archway, she could see Elion and Lorena. A shimmering appeared in the air in front of them.

"I'm not going," Lorena said as Elion took a step forward. The elf paused before turning to look at her.

"This isn't your world," he said quietly. Lorena looked away.

"What's in Asynithis for me? Humans are looked down upon in every country," she pointed out. "Here... humans rule the world. I belong everywhere." Elion was quiet as he looked through his lashes at Lorena.

"But, you'll never feel at home again," Elion said. "This world isn't your home. And you'll miss the unique smells of Asynithis. The experiences that can only be found in our world. You'll still feel out of place here."

"I—"

"Besides, who's going to kill my brother?" he pointed out, an eyebrow raised. "You really want to stay here knowing he's living perfectly well back on Asynithis?" Lorena's hazel eyes steeled. Her hands gripped her dagger tightly. She let out a dry laugh.

"You won't kill him?" she asked, her voice like ice. Elion shrugged a shoulder.

"I can't kill my brother. He's family." She clenched her jaw as she took a step towards the shimmering air.

"Fine, you've got me. I'll go back to Asynithis. For now. But, when the portals open once more, no matter how old I am, I'm coming back here," Lorena said. She pointed her dagger at Elion. "And I'll be the one to kill your brother. Afterwards, I promise to kill you."

"I expect nothing less, Lorena," Elion said, bowing his head slightly. She scoffed as she walked through the portal. Elion followed after her.

The archway closed as Kaydee was forced to look at Aponi, white lightning crackling in her eye sockets.

"Let's do it, now," she said, her voice dead. Kaydee

nodded her head, putting her hands in Aponi's open palms. Her fingers curled around Kaydee's and the pain was nearly unbearable.

The magic in Kaydee coursed through Aponi, and her magic, amplified, coursed back into her. It split Kaydee's head in half, breaking her bones as the magic ran down her spine. The smell of metal filled her nose as a disembodied scream was heard, from both worlds. Kaydee's body was screaming on Earth while Aponi's voice was from Asynithis. The sound echoed around Kaydee as the magic, intermingled with lightning, filled her. Replaced her bones. Replaced her organs, her cells. Until she was nothing else but pure magic.

She felt her skin burning. Melting away.

"I don't know how much longer I can do this," Kaydee felt herself say through gritted teeth. Aponi held onto her hands harder.

"You must," she ordered. Kaydee closed her eyes as she let the magic pour out of her. To fill the Earth while Aponi's filled Asynithis. One by one, the portals closed. Shutting out the creatures who were trying to go through them. Kaydee winced as she felt multiple creatures be split in half as the portals closed.

Each of them snapped shut. And as they did, Kaydee's own bones snapped. Her throat was hoarse as her voice continued to scratch against it, to alert anyone nearby of the pain that she was experiencing. It felt like she was being burned alive. Burned alive by her own magic.

After what felt like an eternity, Aponi let go of her hands, sweat drenching them. The magic slowly disappeared, leaving Kaydee a panting mess.

"It's done," Aponi said, her eyes back to normal. "I hope to never meet you again, Kaydee."

"The feeling's mutual," she managed to get out as Aponi faded away. Her eyes snapped open, and Kaydee's legs gave out, collapsing onto her kitchen floor. She closed her eyes once more, and let sleep take her. She hoped she'd never wake again.

———

"You think it's on Dragon Mountain?" Khai asked as Khalon stared up at the peak from the base of the mountain.

"I have a feeling," he said.

"What? Like you and the dragon are connected?" Khalon turned towards Khai, eyeing his half brother.

"Why did you come anyways? It's clear you don't want to be here," he pointed out. Khai clenched his jaw as he started walking up the narrow path that encircled Dragon Mountain.

"I'd rather be with you than back there," he said. Khalon's eyebrows jumped.

"What was it that you said to Kamaria, earlier, when you two got to the camp?" Khalon asked, following after Khai. "What did you say that made her so upset?" His brother didn't look back.

"It's nothing that concerns you," he said, his voice monotonous. Khalon's lips thinned.

"Did you mean what you said? To me?"

"What did I say?"

"That you were going to destroy me?" Khai laughed as

he looked over his shoulder, his face looking eerily like Aoife's. Khalon stopped walking as Khai continued.

"Yeah. I'm going to destroy you, someday." He turned around as he met Khalon's gaze, a smirk spreading across his lips. "I'm going to make sure you wish you were never born."

43

Elion looked at where he was. He wrung the bottom of his shirt out as the cold, winter air nearly froze it. Lorena burst out from the lake, gasping for breath as she crawled her way back to solid ground.

"*Why* do the portals *have* to be reflections?" she complained as she stalked out of the water, flinging droplets from her arms. Her teeth chattered as she looked around the area. There was a forest nearby, but that wasn't what concerned Elion. In the distance, smoke was rising towards the darkening sky.

"We need to get out of here," he said, his voice low as he walked towards her. Her hazel eyes widened as her lips parted. But before Elion could turn around, something hit his head, hard. And all he could see was black.

———

"When do you plan on destroying my life, Khai?" Khalon asked as he walked past his little brother. Khai shrugged.

"Could be today, could be tomorrow, could be years from now. But just know, I will destroy you one day," he said.

"I don't doubt it," Khalon replied. He swallowed the fear that started to bubble up in his throat. Khai looked so much like Aoife when he said those words. And, for whatever reason, Khalon was still frightened by her. Like he was still five years old, before she forced his father to throw him into the Ring of Fire.

"So, what's up with this whole king thing?" Khai said, catching up to him. They walked side by side, but Khalon's skin crawled at how close he was to him.

"What about it?"

"I thought you didn't want to be king," Khai pointed out. Khalon shrugged.

"I don't," he said, quietly.

"Then why take it from me?" Khai snapped, turning towards Khalon suddenly. Khalon's foot scuffed the edge of the path, causing him to be off balance. He could feel his body tense as he felt gravity pull him down towards the base of the mountain. Khai grabbed his arm as he almost fell over. His eyes were like stone. So much like Aoife's.

Khalon cleared his throat. "I had to, Khai. I have to save Rhea."

"Rhea, Rhea, Rhea. It's always about Rhea, isn't it?" he said, letting go of his wrist. "Except, I know a part of you wanted to be king. A part of you that thinks you deserve it."

"You can think whatever you want about me, Khai," Khalon muttered. He could see a clearing not far from them, where the God of War's temple used to be. Khalon turned towards him.

"But, I'm king now, Khai. Whether you like it or not. The people chose me." Khai scoffed as he walked towards the clearing.

"The people don't get to choose, Khalon. That's the point of a monarchy."

"You'll understand why I did this when you fall in love someday," Khalon muttered, his voice low. "You'll understand then." His younger brother barked out a laugh.

"Yeah, okay," he said. "I would never choose to save someone the Fates didn't want me to save."

"Even if it was Kamaria?" He froze as Khalon walked around him, entering the clearing.

"I would choose myself over anyone else," Khai said, softly. "If Kamaria dying would save the rest of the world and would allow me to live, then yeah. I wouldn't choose her." Khalon's jaw clenched. He could hear the false tone in Khai's voice.

"Then you don't love her as much as you think you do," Khalon said the words he knew would anger his brother as he walked towards the temple's ruins. The columns were broken down to almost nothing. It didn't look anything like Alator's temple used to look.

Khai spun Khalon around and planted his fist onto the side of his head. Khalon stumbled a little as he looked up at his little brother. Khai's cheeks were flushed as he glowered at Khalon.

"Don't say what I do or don't feel," Khai hissed. Khalon gritted his teeth, straightening up, as he glared down at his little brother.

"Stop acting the way your mother wanted you to," he snapped back.

"She's gone, Khalon. She's not controlling me anymore," Khai whispered. "This is just who I *am*. Sorry I'm a disappointment to you." Before Khalon could say another word, the sound of something large flying above could be heard. He looked up towards the sky. The dragon was circling the space above, and its eyes met Khalon's. Like it was waiting for something.

Khalon felt something tugging at his soul, and he slowly morphed into his dragon form. As if that was what the dragon was waiting for, it flew straight down towards Alator's temple. Its claws landed on the last of the ruins, turning them to pebbles. Snow swirled around the dragon as the cold flakes hit Khalon's face.

The red dragon's scales glistened like rubies in the setting sun. Its red eyes stared curiously at him, regarding him as though he were a long lost family member.

"Well, are you going to ask it for its blood?" Khai said, gesturing towards the mythical creature. The dragon seemed to finally notice Khai, its gaze hardening. Its jaw opened, popping noises coming out from the back of its throat. *It wants to kill him*, the thought quickly ran through Khalon's head, *for taking its blood*. In a protective stance, he stood in front of Khai.

"He's with me," Khalon said, holding up a hand covered in black-red scales. The dragon narrowed its eyes. "He won't hurt you." Those red eyes studied Khalon closely before it slowly closed its mouth. Khai walked around him, going towards the back of the dragon. The dragon's eyes followed his path.

"Where are you going?" Khalon called out. Khai looked up at the dragon in wonder.

"When will I be able to see a whole dragon again? I want to take a good look at it," he responded. The dragon brought its attention back to Khalon.

"Dragon," Khalon said, unsure of what to call it. "I know Khai has stolen your blood. And probably my father did, too. But, will you please let me take some from you? It's to save someone who means a lot to me." The dragon stared Khalon down as it considered his proposal. Khalon took another step forward, close enough to pet the dragon's deep red scales.

"Don't trust, Khai," a voice whispered from next to him. Khalon looked over to see a translucent version of his father.

"Dad?" he asked, his voice barely above a whisper. He took a step towards the image, but his father disappeared as the dragon in front of him roared ferociously. The dragon writhed in pain as Khalon took a couple of startled steps back. His eyes desperately searched around for Khai, only to see a bloody hole in the side of the dragon, the part where the scales had been stripped away.

The dragon's cry rumbled through earth as blood started to sputter out of its mouth. And Khalon could feel its pain as its eyes kept him there. He could feel his insides being hacked apart, blood filling his lungs. The dragon was dead before Khai climbed through its open snout, covered in crimson blood. He spat some out of his mouth, holding a soaked glass bottle filled with the liquid as he dropped the sword on the ground next to him, staining the snow bright red.

Khalon fell to his knees as he looked at his little brother, his black eyes glazed over as the feeling of death radiated through his limbs. Khai just smiled, holding the bottle of blood up.

"I got it," he said.

———

Elion woke up to growls and snarls surrounding him. His eyelids fluttered, looking at Lorena next to him. She was tied up, pushing against her restraints as she glared at whatever it was in front of her. He looked around his surroundings. Beastoids were around the two of them. One of them was a panther, the others were bears. The panther signed something with her humanoid paws at a large black bear. The bear signed back as the others growled at each other, speaking their own language.

"Where are we?" Elion whispered, leaning towards Lorena. She stopped struggling as she let out a sigh of relief.

"Oh Gods, Elion. I thought you were dead," she hissed.

"Thanks for caring," he smiled, wincing as he moved.

"You have a giant gash on your head," she said. "I wouldn't move around too much if I were you." She paused. "And I only care because then it wouldn't have been me to give you the final blow."

"Of course," he said, trying to hide his smile. Lorena bristled.

"The only reason the beastoid didn't kill you is because I told them not to," she hissed.

"More like screamed and tried to kill us if we so much as tried to," the large black bear said. Elion froze as he looked up into the beastoid's face. He had never seen one in person before, and they were every bit as disturbing as the rumors said.

"She told us that you weren't one of the elves after our company," the bear said. "Is that true?" Elion cleared his throat.

"No, I'm not going to hurt any of you. I'm not on the side of Aureum," he managed to get out.

"You're an elf."

"He's one of the better ones," Lorena said, holding her chin up high. Elion's eyes darted towards her, the words warming him. She didn't meet his gaze. The bear put a paw on his own chin as he shrugged.

"We'll wait to see what to do with you two," he grumbled. "The king should be back any moment."

"The king?" Elion asked.

"The King of Dragons," the bear said, its black eyes meeting his. "King Khalon."

44

Khalon emptied his stomach for the thousandth time. Khai patted his back, hard, as he fought the urge to heave once more.

"Really? Just because I killed a dragon?" Khai said. Khalon's head swiveled as he stared at his half-brother in disbelief.

Khai's eyes widened. "What?"

"You just killed our ancestor. What we are. You basically killed another draconian," Khalon seethed. "And you're... covered in its guts." He gagged once again as he doubled over, dry heaving.

"You've killed plenty of draconians in your time," Khai pointed out.

"In the Ring of Fire, Khai. I *had* to or I would die. The dragon wasn't doing anything to you."

"Semantics. The dragon would've killed me eventually," he said, almost under his breath as Khalon straightened back up.

"Dragons aren't just where we come from, Khai. They're also… They're basically lesser gods to the creatures of Draconia and you—you slaughtered it!"

"Oh, get over it, Khalon," Khai droned, walking towards the camp. The blood had crusted and encased him in a dark red shell. He rubbed the dried blood off of his face as the camp loomed before them.

"Are you going to lie to the other draconians? Or are you going to let them maim me to death?" Khai asked, his voice low. Khalon glared at him before walking past. He would leave his brother to question what he would do next. Khalon wished Esi was still alive so that he could ask her about how he saw his father. How he saw *and* heard him.

"Don't trust Khai," he had said. Khalon swallowed the memory down as the draconians and beastoids came towards him. Their eyes filled with horror once they saw the former false king.

"What happened?" Michael asked, looking him up and down.

"The dragon… it attacked. Khai… killed it for me," Khalon said, lying between his teeth. Khai couldn't help the look of surprise that flashed across his face as he took in his older brother like he couldn't believe that Khalon would lie for him. Michael stared at Khalon for a long while before shrugging.

"Well, in your absence, an elf and a human ended up in the river outside of camp," the bear said, walking beside Khalon.

"The Fates were right…" Khalon could hear the whispers as they walked by.

"Khai *is* the dragon slayer."

"What evil."

"What a monster."

"Just like his *mother*."

"Just like King Archion." Khalon shut his eyes for a moment, trying to chase the whispers away. He glanced over at Khai, but his little brother seemed unbothered.

"The girl claims that the elf is good, and the elf claims to know you so we haven't killed them yet. We figured we'd wait until you came back to decide," Michael continued. Khalon nodded, swallowing the unsettling feeling growing in the back of his throat.

"Good call," he managed to utter. They walked past Kamaria, who stared at Khai with a mix of horror and disgust. Khai didn't even look at her. She turned on her heel and walked back into her tent, Aponi peeking her head out. She shrugged out of Kamaria's grips and caught up to Khalon.

"The portals are closed," Aponi said.

"Thank you, Aponi," he said, meeting her gaze.

"When were you going to tell me that Esi was dead?" she snapped. Lightning skittered over her arm. Khalon raised his eyebrows.

"I was going to tell you tonight," he murmured.

"You should've told me when you awoke me," she hissed, giving him a stare that could kill a creature as she stopped walking beside him. He just hung his head in dejection. Esi. He wished he could speak to Esi.

Michael held open the tent's opening, letting Khalon inside. He ducked his head as Khai winked at him, his figure slowly disappearing into the night. Khalon sighed inwardly as he watched Khai walk towards the river.

"Is he someone we need to keep an eye on?" Michael asked, his voice low.

"I don't know anymore," Khalon muttered. Almost under his breath, he said, "I think taking his crown broke him." He turned towards the inside of the tent, his eyes widening as he saw the elf that was tied up in front of him. The elf's light blue eyes widened in response.

"Khalon. I heard you're king now," he said.

"Freya's elf," Khalon breathed.

———

Khai scrubbed the blood from his skin. He didn't know what overcame him when he killed that dragon. He saw the dragon bow its head towards Khalon, and rage filled his body. He didn't even remember slicing through the creature. He only remembered Khalon's horror-stricken face when he exited out of the dragon's mouth, covered in blood.

His breathing quickened as he scrubbed his skin harder, but it was like the blood had stained his skin forever. He killed a dragon. He slaughtered one of the mythical creatures of Asynithis. His ancestors. Where their magic comes from. And he murdered it. In cold blood.

Tears burned his eyes as he kept trying to get rid of the evidence of his sin. A snapping twig made him swallow the burning. He turned around, facing the wrath of Kamaria.

She glowered at him, moonlight washing over her. Her red glowing veins darted through her body. She was beautiful. Impossibly so. Khai rubbed the aching in his chest as he turned away.

She grabbed his arm and spun him around, causing him

to look straight into her eyes. Into the hurt and pain that he wanted to avoid.

What happened? She signed, gesturing to his body. Khai forced a smirk onto his face.

The rumors are true. I've killed a legendary beast. Her upper lip curled in disgust as her dark, round eyes looked him up and down.

What is wrong *with you?* She turned away and Khai didn't know what possessed him, but he grabbed her wrist, still on his knees as he pulled her back. She halfway turned around, her eyebrows pulled together as she stared at him, hate filling her ebony eyes.

I'm sorry, he signed. The burning was coming back. The burning behind his eyes. He rubbed them until he was sure his eyes were going to fall out. Kamaria pulled his hands away from his face, the moonlight reflecting in the dark pools of her eyes.

Why are you doing this? She signed, her lips twisting to the side as she stared at him, expectantly.

I should've stayed here with you. You just lost your sister, the only family you had left, and I left and I'm sorry, he signed back, avoiding her question. She kneeled down, placing her knees into the cold mud next to him.

You're better than this, Khai, she signed. He stared at her for a long while, memorizing every part of her. The lines in her face. The mountains of her lips. The inky ocean of her eyes.

I'm only made from the worst parts of my DNA, Khai signed back. Her lips twisted to the side again. She studied his face before ripping her gaze away to look at the river beside them. She cupped the water in her hands and motioned with her head for Khai to lean forward. He did as he was told.

The freezing water poured from her dark hands, into his hair, down his face, the blood washing away with it. They sat in silence as Kamaria continued to wash the blood out of Khai's hair.

Khai watched her as she rubbed at his hands and arms. He didn't deserve her. He didn't deserve her one bit. He should've never kissed her. If he didn't kiss her, they wouldn't be sitting here like this. Their hearts beating in unison.

Once the blood was washed away, Kamaria got up. She brushed the mud off of her knees as she took one more look at him.

You have a choice. You could be like your ancestors, or you could choose to be better, she signed. *You* can *be better, Khai.*

I don't know if I can... Kamaria shrugged as she looked up at the moon, high in the sky. She said something under her breath as she looked back at him.

You really are trying hard to get me to regret ever saving you that day, aren't you? And Khai... I hope you know that you're succeeding. She pivoted on her heel and walked back to the camp, leaving him kneeling in the mud. He hung his head as the tears that he was keeping back finally were let out. The hot liquid burned his frozen skin.

She deserves better, was all he could think. *This is for the best. She deserves someone better than me.* Because Khai was like his mother, more than he ever let on. He would choose himself over anyone else, would choose revenge over anything, anyone. And he wasn't going to stop now.

45

Poseidon circled the fire pit before taking a seat next to Valerian. Every part of his human body felt like it was electrified being so close to the dryad. That was one thing Poseidon liked about humans. They felt things so deeply. Emotionally. Physically. It was like everything was heightened for them.

"So, Khai got the dragon's blood?" Poseidon asked as Valerian handed him a cup of beer. He gingerly sipped it, unabashedly checking Valerian out. Poseidon swore the dryad blushed under the moonlight. Khalon nodded in response to his question.

"Yeah, he got the dragon's blood," he muttered. "Do you really think it'll work?"

"The Fates seem to think so," Poseidon said. "But, what was it the Seer said?" Khalon's jaw worked as he stared into the flames.

"It'll be fine," he muttered. Poseidon shrugged as he put down his drink. He leaned back onto his arms, staring up at the stars that glittered in the velvet sky.

"This world really is so beautiful," he murmured. "I don't understand why my brother would want to destroy all of this." He rolled his head to look closely at Khalon.

"Don't let him get away once you save Rhea," Poseidon said. "It's important that you kill him."

"I know," Khalon said under his breath. "I know what I have to do."

"Don't screw it up, because I heard the Seer said—"

"I know what she said." Poseidon stilled for a moment before leaning away from Khalon.

"What did Elion say? It was nice to see that kid once again. Glad he's alive, don't you think?" Khalon nodded his head as his eyes glanced upwards in thought.

"Elion seems to think he could get us into the Aureum palace. Without starting a battle," he said.

"What's his solution?"

"The ancient sewers." Poseidon scrunched his nose up in distaste.

"You guys can go on without me," he said, downing the rest of his drink. "I think I'll turn in for the night."

"Are you sure?" Khalon asked, his thick eyebrows scrunching together. "You don't want to come with?"

"I think you guys got it. You don't need an old man like me there," Poseidon teased. He turned towards Valerian, his arm outstretched. "Shall we?" Valerian's golden eyes were fixed onto Khalon. He opened his mouth, but his eyes darted towards Poseidon. His mouth closed.

"Sure," he whispered. Poseidon's dark hands closed around Valerian's as they walked towards his oak tree. Once they were far enough away from the camp, the dryad dropped Poseidon's hand.

"You don't need to do this," he said quietly as Poseidon pulled the Mortiferis tooth out from his pocket. Poseidon's lips thinned as he unwrapped the tooth, the moon glinting off of it.

"I have to, Valerian," he said, relishing the way his name rolled off of his tongue. The dryad's golden eyes seemed to glow in the darkness as he walked up to Poseidon, crushing his lips onto him. Poseidon didn't know when he had started crying, but his tears made their way into their kiss. Destroying it with the taste of the ocean.

"Your brother gets to live," Valerian said, his voice rough as he pulled away.

"My brother isn't going to live. And I can't live here either, not anymore. We're sucking the life out of this world, out of its creatures. Out of you," Poseidon said, biting back the dread that was settling itself into the pit of his stomach.

Valerian scoffed. "You know the draconian won't be successful in killing him. His only chance is to kill the God of Death while he's still in Rhea."

"We don't know—"

"If the Ustrinian Queen is to be believed, Esi's last words were that the Dragon King will ruin everything. *He's* the Dragon King," Valerian pointed out.

"Khai was also a Dragon King. It could be him as well," Poseidon shrugged. "But, what happens doesn't really matter to me." Valerian's features twisted as he took a step away from him.

"You're really going to kill yourself with that thing," he whispered.

"I have to."

"Can't you be selfish? For once?"

"I *was* selfish, Val. I saved myself last time, and I put this world in more danger." Poseidon took a step forward, cupping the dryad's heartbreakingly beautiful face. "I put *you* into more danger."

"I'll never forgive you," he whispered, sorrow contorting that breathtaking face of his. Poseidon just gave him a small smile.

"I hope you despise me forever because of this. At least I'll know I'll still be living then, in your mind," he said as he plunged the Mortiferis tooth into his chest. It was a bad choice. The chest. For only one reason alone: His eyes were the last to go. He watched the horror fill Valerian's golden eyes before he dropped to his knees, unable to look away as Poseidon disintegrated into dust. Poseidon watched despair fill the last creature he'll ever love.

Poseidon's eyes were the last to go. Waves crashing in sepia eyes. Now, dust in the wind.

46

They stood outside of Regium, staring into a round, metal opening that led into the ancient sewers of the city. The sun had set, washing the city into twilight. Aureum never quite got dark enough for it to truly be night. Elves, ironically, didn't like the dark.

"Is this really the best idea?" Khai asked, wrinkling his nose. Khalon turned towards Elion for the answer. Elion shrugged as he took a step in.

"It's the only way to enter the palace undetected," he said.

"How did you even figure that out?" the girl Khalon learned was named Lorena asked. Elion's blue eyes glazed over as a sad smile spread across his lips.

"I used to play in them with..." Lorena held up a hand.

"I don't want to know," she interrupted, her voice hard. She started marching into the tunnel, the darkness enveloping her.

"I like her," Kamaria signed as Aponi translated. She

followed after the human. Khalon checked his pockets to make sure the vial of dragon's blood was still there before following after the others.

"So, where's Poseidon?" Aponi asked, walking slower so that he could catch up to her. He shrugged.

"I didn't see him at all today. Actually, now that you mentioned it, I haven't seen Valerian either."

"He probably passed away," Khai said, piping up from in front of them. He looked over his shoulder at the other two. "I gave him a Mortiferis tooth."

"What?"

"He asked for it," Khai shrugged. "Besides, he said it himself. He can't live without destroying us all. A good reminder for you, by the way." He stared pointedly at Khalon. Khalon bristled as he stood up straighter.

"After we save Rhea, we will kill the God of Death."

Khai's eyebrows raised. "Good. Because if you don't, I will." He pointed a thumb to his back. "I have the mark of Death as well, you know."

"Hopefully, it doesn't come to that," Aponi muttered. The tunnel twisted and turned, but the ancient sewers were, luckily, drier than the deserts of Ustrina. Elion stopped at a dead end, a rusted ladder leaned up against it. Khalon looked up and saw a circular grate with an intricate design.

"Where does this lead?" he asked the elf.

"The servants' quarters," Elion said quietly, glancing over at Lorena as he did. Lorena just grabbed the first rung and pulled herself up. She looked over at the others.

"Well c'mon, then," she said, her voice rough. "We have a God to kill. And I have a king to assassinate."

"I *really* like her," Aponi translated Kamaria's signing,

her face blank. Then, her expression relaxed as she regarded the human. "I like her, too." Lorena made a face as she continued to pull herself up the ladder.

"Thanks, I guess," she muttered. She pushed her palm against the grate, moving it to the side, and then pulled herself out. Khalon followed after her.

He had never been to the Aureum palace before. And everything was so... white. White marble and glittering gold moldings, everywhere. He never felt more out of place. Shaking the unease out of his bones, he turned around and helped Elion out of the hole.

"Do you know where they're keeping her?" he asked. Elion gave him a cautious glance.

"We're not *keeping* her here. Rhea runs the show," he said, softly. "But, she's in Than's quarters. Essarae never leaves Than's side, but I'm guessing she was ordered to keep away so we should be fine."

"Lead the way," Khai said once he pulled himself out. The more of the palace that Khalon saw as he followed Elion, the more unease he felt. It was an ostentatious building and it was so white that the moonlight made the hallways glow instead of keeping them in darkness. He felt so exposed, so vulnerable. Too out in the open.

And it was quiet. Like no one was in the palace.

As if Elion could read Khalon's thoughts, he frowned as he looked around the empty hallways.

"I wonder where everyone is," he said.

"It *is* the winter solstice," Khai pointed out. Elion's frown grew deeper.

"We spend the winter solstice in a smaller castle, in the mountainous region of Aureum. But, to leave the God of

Death here... without any protection?" He shook his head as he continued forward.

"They must think she's protected," Aponi said.

"Or they don't care," Kamaria signed. Elion didn't say any more as they continued down the long hallways of the palace. He stopped in front of a white stone door, unguarded. His eyebrows twitched downwards before opening the door, revealing a large golden bed.

Khalon's heart pounded violently in his chest as he took a step forward into the bedroom. On one side of the bed lay Rhea. Her copper brown hair was splayed out on the pillowcase like she was underwater. The image was too similar to the last time Khalon saw her that his chest felt like his heart was being torn into pieces. *Khalon saw her, her copper hair splayed out around her face. Her eyes that used to hold fire in them were just brown now. They stared up into nothing as Khalon grabbed her head.* He tried to shake the memory from his limbs.

He glanced over at the boy who was on the other side of the bed. He couldn't have been older than eleven or twelve. His hair was down to his shoulders, but the elven ears clearly peeked out from his jet black locks.

Khalon sat down on the side of the bed, his hand trembling as he gently pushed back some of her copper hair. Rhea's eyes flickered open. She stared at Khalon for a long while, like she was trying to figure out if this was a dream or not. And then, her eyebrows knitted together as her gaze fixated on him.

"Khalon?" her voice said. The heaviness that weighed against his chest lifted and left his body with a single breath of relief.

"Rhea," he breathed as he put a hand on the side of her face. He couldn't help himself as he leaned forward, breathing in her sweet scent. He kissed her deeply, and at first, Rhea returned the kiss. But then she pulled away. Confusion filled her entire face.

"What are you doing?" she asked.

"I'm saving you," he whispered. Rhea's eyebrows pulled downwards as she pushed herself up into a sitting position.

"What do you mean you're saving me?" her voice was flat.

"We're going to separate your soul from the God of Death's," Khalon explained. "And you'll be able to live because—"

"No," she said, her voice low. "No, you can't do that."

"Why can't I?"

"Don't you understand, Khalon? I thought you *understood*. You have to kill me while he's still in me," she said, leaning forward. Her copper eyes still had flames flickering behind her irises. But it was more subdued than before.

"I can kill him when he's—"

"If he finishes putting his entire soul into that child's body, we are *doomed*, Khalon. This world, all the other worlds, they'll be *destroyed*."

"I don't care, Rhea. I can't live without you," Khalon whispered. She stared at him in disbelief. Grabbing his hands, she tried to look deeper into his eyes.

"Khalon, I wish I could live a life of happiness with you. Truly I do. That's all that I want. But, I'm a Celestial. I was never supposed to have a happy life... with anybody," she whispered. "You need to kill me. You have the Death mark on you. You can kill *him* by killing me. Now." Khalon stared at Rhea for a long while before letting go of her hands. He slowly pulled out the vial of dragon's blood. His mind was made up a long time ago. Nothing she said was going to convince him otherwise.

"I... I can't, Rhea. I won't."

"Good thing I can," he heard Khai say. With a small dagger, too fast for Khalon to react, he slit Rhea's throat. Her copper brown eyes were wide as silver blood poured from her throat and bubbled out of her mouth. The silver blood of a God's.

I love you, she mouthed.

Waves of anguish were sent down Khalon's body as he roared. He reached towards Rhea, pouring the vial into her mouth as her eyes started to dim. He couldn't lose her again. He couldn't. Not this time.

With his blood pounding in his head, he watched with hopeful eyes as the gash on her throat slowly healed. The light weakly was brought back to her eyes as she took in a clear breath. Relief washed over his tensed body. She was alive. Thank Alator, she was alive.

Rhea stared up at him as realization filled her face. Her hands fluttered around her neck in horror as she looked over at the boy next to her, pushing Khalon away. Rhea grabbed Khai's wrist, still holding the bloody dagger, pulling the blade across her throat over and over again. But, red scales instead covered her neck, protecting her from death. She let out a guttural cry as she continued to drag the knife over her throat, making Khai do the deed over and over again. Even Khai's light brown eyes were filled with horror.

"Rhea..." Khalon whispered, moving closer to her. The hatred in her eyes froze him in place. Then, she closed them.

Her hand released Khai's as she slumped against the pillows behind her, defeated. She slowly looked over at Than whose black eyes were opened.

Khai was quicker in reacting than Khalon. He jumped towards the boy, but the boy, with a small smile on his lips, disappeared into the shadows. The palace rumbled as Rhea's dead eyes met Khalon's.

"What have you done?"

-To be continued-

THE SAVIORS POEM

White, Gold, Red, Gray, Green, Blue.
    Six eggs that were sent away.
    She whispered, "Be loyal and stay true"
    Before she began to decay.
    They were all sent to a different world that had mortals who didn't believe.
    The Mortiferis caused havoc and burned,
    But don't worry, the Saviors didn't forever leave.
    Seven lives they will live before they come back.
    In return for our suffering they'll give their lives when the demons attack.

Six eggs were sent away
    But six will come to stay
    For when the heir arrives, all will bow
    For no one can resist
    The Gods' ancient vow.
    Everchanging eyes, who see all

Only he can stop the Mortiferis
And reverse death's fall.

The one who can pierce through
With the rays of the sun.
She can breathe life into
Mortiferis' and Death's one.
But beware the holy burning of this child.
She might be God's gift
But her mind dares to become wild.

The King of the Seas,
The uniter of ocean floors,
He will cure the disease
That plagues creatures beyond shores.
He will lead the creatures of water
Back to the seas of Asynithis
And help stop the slaughter
Of creature blood since.

Asynithis will awaken
Once the Mother takes a step.
The world will be retaken
Once the Mother has wept.
For she has all life
Coursing through her veins.
And the world will grow despite
The ash that remains.

Born of wind and born of fire,
Ice in her veins and darkness in his

Apart, they bring strength and can inspire.
But beware the demon twins,
For we'll all be dead
Unless they're torn.
For Darkness on Darkness
Is the most deadly thing.
They'll side with the Mortiferis
And become Dark Queen and King.

White, Gold, Red, Gray, Green, Blue.
Six eggs that were sent away.
She whispered, "Be loyal and stay true"
Before she began to decay.
One chance to save our world
Or our world will forevermore be gray.

EXPLANATIONS

CHAPTER 8

1. Kamaria's signing is usually in quotes in Khalon's perspective because Khalon is hearing a translation being voiced out loud by someone else.
2. In other perspectives, if the character knows sign language, then the dialogue will be italicized because nothing is being spoken out loud.

ALSO BY BIANCA K. GRAY

Shadowverse Series

Fine